A VOYAGE ROUND THE WORLD.

IN SEARCH OF

THE CASTAWAYS

JULES VERNE

CONTENTS

CHAPTER I

THE SHARK.

On the 26th of July, 1864, under a strong gale from the northeast, a magnificent yacht was steaming at full speed through the waves of the North Channel. The flag of England fluttered at her yard-arm, while at the top of the mainmast floated a blue pennon, bearing the initials E. G., worked in gold and surmounted by a ducal coronet. The yacht was called the Duncan, and belonged to Lord Glenarvan, one of the sixteen Scottish peers sitting in the House of Lords, and also a most distinguished member of the "Royal Thames Yacht Club," so celebrated throughout the United Kingdom.

Lord Edward Glenarvan was on board with his young wife, Lady Helena, and one of his cousins, Major MacNabb. The Duncan, newly constructed, had just been making a trial voyage several miles beyond the Frith of Clyde, and was now on her return to Glasgow. Already Arran Island was appearing on the horizon, when the look-out signaled an enormous fish that was sporting in the wake of the yacht. The captain, John Mangles, at once informed Lord Glenarvan of the fact, who mounted on deck with Major MacNabb, and asked the captain what he thought of the animal.

"Indeed, your lordship," replied Captain Mangles, "I think it is a shark of large proportions."

"A shark in these regions!" exclaimed Glenarvan.

"Without doubt," replied the captain. "This fish belongs to a species of sharks that are found in all seas and latitudes. It is the 'balance-fish,' and, if I am not greatly mistaken, we shall have an encounter with one of these fellows. If your lordship consents, and it pleases Lady Helena to witness such a novel chase, we will soon see what we have to deal with."

"What do you think, MacNabb?" said Lord Glenarvan to the major; "are you of a mind to try the adventure?"

"I am of whatever opinion pleases you," answered the major, calmly.

"Besides," continued Captain Mangles, "we cannot too soon exterminate these terrible monsters. Let us improve the opportunity, and, if your lordship pleases, it shall be an exciting scene as well as a good action."

"Very well, captain," said Lord Glenarvan. He then summoned Lady Helena, who joined him on deck, tempted by the exciting sport.

The sea was magnificent. You could easily follow along its surface the rapid motions of the fish, as it plunged and rose again with surprising agility. Captain Mangles gave his orders, and the sailors threw over the starboard ratling a stout rope, to which was fastened a hook baited with a thick piece of pork.

THE LAST MOUTHFUL.

The shark, although still at a distance of fifty yards, scented the bait offered to his voracity. He rapidly approached the yacht. You could see his fins, gray at their extremity and black at their base, beat the waves with violence, while his "caudal appendage" kept him in a rigorously straight line. As he advanced, his great glaring eyes seemed inflamed with eagerness, and his yawning jaws, when he turned, disclosed a quadruple row of teeth. His head was large, and shaped like a double-headed hammer. Captain Mangles was right. It was a very large specimen of the most rapacious family of sharks,—the "balance fish" of the English and the "jew-fish" of the Provençals.

All on board of the Duncan followed the movements of the shark with lively attention. The animal was soon within reach of the hook; he turned upon his back, in order to seize it better, and the enormous bait disappeared down his vast gullet. At the same time he hooked himself, giving the line a violent shake, whereupon the sailors hoisted the huge creature by means of a pulley at the end of the yard-arm.

The shark struggled violently at feeling himself drawn from his natural element, but his struggles were of no avail. A rope with a slip-noose confined his tail and paralyzed his movements. A few moments afterward he was hauled over the ratlings, and precipitated upon the deck of the yacht. One of the sailors at once approached him, not without caution, and with a vigorous blow of the hatchet cut off the formidable tail of the animal.

The chase was ended, and there was nothing more to fear from the monster. The vengeance of the sailors was satisfied, but not their curiosity. Indeed, it is customary on board of every vessel to carefully examine the stomachs of sharks. The men, knowing the inordinate voracity of the creature, wait with some anxiety, and their expectation is not always in vain.

Lady Glenarvan, not wishing to witness this strange "exploration," retired to the cabin. The shark was still panting. He was ten feet long, and weighed more than six hundred pounds. These dimensions are nothing extraordinary; for if the balance-fish is not classed among the giants of this species, at least he belongs to the most formidable of their family.

The enormous fish was soon cut open by a blow of the hatchet, without further ceremony. The hook had penetrated to the stomach, which was absolutely empty. Evidently the animal had fasted a long time, and the disappointed seamen were about to cast the remains into the sea, when the attention of the mate was attracted by a bulky object firmly imbedded in the viscera.

"Ha! what is this?" he exclaimed.

"That," replied one of the sailors, "is a piece of rock that the creature has taken in for ballast."

"Good," said Glenarvan; "wash the dirty thing, and bring it into the cabin."

"Good!" said another; "it is probably a bullet that this fellow has received in the stomach, and could not digest."

"Be still, all of you!" cried Tom Austin, the mate; "do you not see that the animal was a great drunkard? and to lose nothing, has drank not only the wine, but the bottle too!"

"What!" exclaimed Lord Glenarvan, "is it a bottle that this shark has in his stomach?"

"A real bottle!" replied the mate, "but you can easily see that it does not come from the wine-cellar."

"Well, Tom," said Glenarvan, "draw it out carefully. Bottles found in the sea frequently contain precious documents."

"Do you think so?" said Major MacNabb.

"I do; at least, that it may happen so."

"Oh! I do not contradict you," replied the major. "Perhaps there may be a secret in this."

"We shall see," said Glenarvan. "Well, Tom?"

"Here it is," said the mate, displaying the shapeless object that he had just drawn with difficulty from the interior of the shark.

"Good," said Glenarvan; "wash the dirty thing, and bring it into the cabin."

Tom obeyed; and the bottle found under such singular circumstances was placed on the cabin-table, around which Lord Glenarvan, Major MacNabb, and Captain John Mangles took their seats, together with Lady Helena; for a woman, they say, is always a little inquisitive.

Everything causes excitement at sea. For a moment there was silence. Each gazed wonderingly at this strange waif. Did it contain the secret of a disaster, or only an insignificant message confided to the mercy of the waves by some idle navigator?

"OLD IN BOTTLE."

However, they must know what it was, and Glenarvan, without waiting longer, proceeded to examine the bottle. He took, moreover, all necessary precautions. You would have thought a coroner was pointing out the particulars of a suspicious quest. And Glenarvan was right, for the most insignificant mark in appearance may often lead to an important discovery.

Before examining it internally, the bottle was inspected externally. It had a slender neck, the mouth of which was protected by an iron wire considerably rusted. Its sides were very thick, and capable of supporting a pressure of several atmospheres, betraying evidently previous connection with champagne. With these bottles the wine-dressers of Aï and Epernay block carriage-wheels without their showing the slightest fracture. This one could, therefore, easily bear the hardships of a long voyage.

"A bottle of the Maison Cliquot," said the major quietly; and, as if he ought to know, his affirmation was accepted without contradiction.

"My dear major," said Lady Helena, "it matters little what this bottle is, provided we know whence it comes."

"We shall know, my dear," said Lord Edward, "and already we can affirm that it has come from a distance. See the petrified particles that cover it, these substances mineralized, so to speak, under the action of the sea-water. This waif had already taken a long voyage in the ocean, before being engulfed in the stomach of a shark."

"I cannot but be of your opinion," replied the major; "this fragile vase, protected by its strong envelope, must have made a long journey."

"But whence does it come?" inquired Lady Glenarvan.

"Wait, my dear Helena, wait. We must be patient with bottles. If I am not greatly mistaken, this one will itself answer all our questions."

And so saying, Glenarvan began to scrape off the hard particles that protected the neck. Soon the cork appeared, but very much damaged with the salt water.

"This is a pity," said Glenarvan; "for if there is any paper in it, it will be in a bad condition."

"That's what I fear," replied the major.

"I will add," continued Glenarvan, "that this badly-corked bottle would soon have sunk; and it is fortunate that this shark swallowed it, and brought it on board of the Duncan."

"Certainly," interposed Captain Mangles; "it would have been better, however, had it been caught in the open sea on a well-known latitude and longitude. We could then, by studying the atmospheric and marine currents, have discovered the course traversed; but with a guide like one of these sharks, that travel against wind and tide, we cannot know whence it comes."

"We shall soon see," answered Glenarvan. At the same time he drew out the cork with the greatest care, and a strong saline odor permeated the cabin.

"Well?" said Lady Helena, with a truly feminine impatience.

"Yes," said Glenarvan; "I am not mistaken! Here are papers!"

"Documents! documents!" cried Lady Helena.

The fragments soon strewed the table, and several pieces of paper were perceived adhering to each other. Glenarvan drew them out carefully.

"Only," replied Glenarvan, "they appear to be damaged by the water. It is impossible to remove them, for they adhere to the sides of the bottle."

"Let us break it," said MacNabb.

"I would rather keep it whole," replied Glenarvan.

"I should, too," said the major.

"Very true," added Lady Helena; "but the contents are more valuable than that which contains them, and it is better to sacrifice one than the other."

"Let your lordship only break off the neck," said the captain, "and that will enable you to draw them out without injury."

"Yes, yes, my dear Edward!" cried Lady Glenarvan.

It was difficult to proceed in any other way, and, at all hazards, Glenarvan determined to break the neck of the precious bottle. It was necessary to use a hammer, for the stony covering had acquired the hardness of granite. The fragments soon strewed the table, and several pieces of paper were perceived adhering to each other. Glenarvan drew them out carefully, separating and examining them closely, while Lady Helena, the major, and the captain crowded around him.

Chapter II

THE THREE DOCUMENTS.

These pieces of paper, half destroyed by the sea-water, exhibited only a few words, the traces of handwriting almost entirely effaced. For several minutes Lord Glenarvan examined them attentively, turned them about in every way, and exposed them to the light of day, observing the least traces of writing spared by the sea. Then he looked at his friends, who were regarding him with anxious eyes.

"There are here," said he, "three distinct documents, probably three copies of the same missive, translated into three different languages: one English, another French, and the third German. The few words that remain leave no doubt on this point."

"But these words have at least a meaning?" said Lady Glenarvan.

"That is difficult to say, my dear Helena. The words traced on these papers are very imperfect."

"Perhaps they will complete each other," said the major.

"That may be," replied Captain Mangles. "It is not probable that the water has obliterated these lines in exactly the same places on each, and by comparing these remains of phrases we shall arrive at some intelligible meaning."

"We will do so," said Lord Glenarvan; "but let us proceed systematically. And, first, here is the English document."

It showed the following arrangement of lines and words:

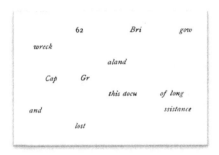

"That does not mean much," said the major, with an air of disappointment.

"Whatever it may mean," replied the captain, "it is good English."

"There is no doubt of that," said his lordship. "The words *wreck, aland, this, and, lost,* are perfect. *Cap* evidently means *captain,* referring to the captain of a shipwrecked vessel."

"Let us add," said the captain, "the portions of the words *docu* and *ssistance,* the meaning of which is plain."

"Well, something is gained already!" added Lady Helena.

"Unfortunately," replied the major, "entire lines are wanting. How can we find the name of the lost vessel, or the place of shipwreck?"

"We shall find them," said Lord Edward.

"Very likely," answered the major, who was invariably of the opinion of every one else; "but how?"

"By comparing one document with another."

"Let us see!" cried Lady Helena.

The second piece of paper, more damaged than the former, exhibited only isolated words, arranged thus:

COMPARATIVE PHILOLOGY.

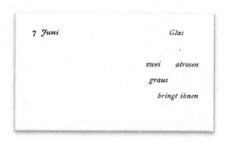

"This is written in German," said Captain Mangles, when he had cast his eyes upon it.

"And do you know that language?" asked Glenarvan.

"Perfectly, your lordship."

"Well, tell us what these few words mean."

The captain examined the document closely, and expressed himself as follows:

"First, the date of the event is determined. *7 Juni* means June 7th, and by comparing this figure with the figures '62,' furnished by the English document, we have the date complete,—June 7th, 1862."

"Very well!" exclaimed Lady Helena. "Go on."

"On the same line," continued the young captain, "I find the word *Glas*, which, united with the word *gow* of the first document, gives *Glasgow*. It is plainly a ship from the port of Glasgow."

"That was my opinion," said the major.

"The second line is missing entirely," continued Captain Mangles; "but on the third I meet with two important words *zwei*, which means *two*, and *atrosen*, or rather *matrosen*, which signifies *sailors* in German."

"There were a captain and two sailors, then?" said Lady Helena.

"Probably," replied her husband.

"I will confess, your lordship," said the captain, "that the next word, *graus*, puzzles me. I do not know how to translate it. Perhaps the third document will enable us to understand it. As to the two last words, they are easily explained. *Bringt ihnen* means *bring to them*, and if we compare these with the English word, which is likewise on the sixth line of the first document (I mean the word *assistance*), we shall have the phrase *bring them assistance*."

"Yes, bring them assistance," said Glenarvan. "But where are the unfortunates? We have not yet a single indication of the place, and the scene of the catastrophe is absolutely unknown."

"Let us hope that the French document will be more explicit," said Lady Helena.

"Let us look at it, then," replied Glenarvan; "and, as we all know this language, our examination will be more easy."

Here is an exact fac-simile of the third document:

"There are figures!" cried Lady Helena. "Look, gentlemen, look!"

troi	*ats*		*tannia*		
	gonie			*austral*	
			abor		
contin	*pr*		*cruel*	*indi*	
	jeté			*ongit*	
et 37° 11′	*lat*				

"Let us proceed in order," said Lord Glenarvan, "and start at the beginning. Permit me to point out one by one these scattered and incomplete words. I see from the first letters *troi ats* (*trois-mats*), that it is a brig, the name of which, thanks to the English and French documents, is entirely preserved: *The Britannia.* Of the two following words, *gonie* and *austral,* only the last has an intelligible meaning."

THE PUZZLE EXPLAINED.

"That is an important point," replied Captain Mangles; "the shipwreck took place in the southern hemisphere."

"That is indefinite," said the major.

"I will continue," resumed Glenarvan. "The word *abor* is the trace of the verb *aborder* (to land). These unfortunates have landed somewhere. But where? *Contin!* Is it on a continent? *Cruel!*"

"'Cruel!'" cried Mangles; "that explains the German word *graus, grausam, cruel.*"

"Go on, go on!" cried Glenarvan, whose interest was greatly excited as the meaning of these incomplete words was elucidated. "*Indi!* Is it India, then, where these sailors have been cast? What is the meaning of the word *ongit?* Ha, longitude! And here is the latitude, 37° 11'. In short, we have a definite indication."

"But the longitude is wanting," said MacNabb.

"We cannot have everything, my dear major," replied Glenarvan; "and an exact degree of latitude is something. This French document is decidedly the most complete of the three. Each of them was evidently a literal translation of the others, for they all convey the same information. We must, therefore, unite and translate them into one language, and seek their most probable meaning, the one that is most logical and explicit."

"Shall we make this translation in French, English, or German?" asked the major.

"In English," answered Glenarvan, "since that is our own language."

"Your lordship is right," said Captain Mangles, "besides, it was also theirs."

"It is agreed, then. I will write this document, uniting these parts of words and fragments of phrases, leaving the gaps that separate them, and filling up those the meaning of which is not ambiguous. Then we will compare them and form an opinion."

Glenarvan at once took a pen, and, in a few moments, presented to his friends a paper on which were written the following lines:

June 7, 1862	brig Britannia	Glasgow
wrecked	gonia	Southern
ashore		two sailors
Captain Gr	rea	
contin pr	cruel	Indi
thrown this document		of longitude
and 37° 11′ of latitude	Bring them assistance	
lost.		

At this moment a sailor informed the captain that the Duncan was entering the Frith of Clyde, and asked his orders.

"What are your lordship's wishes?" said the captain, addressing Lord Glenarvan.

"Reach Dumbarton as quickly as possible, captain. Then, while Lady Helena returns to Malcolm Castle, I will go to London and submit this document to the authorities."

The captain gave his orders in pursuance of this, and the mate executed them.

"Now, my friends," said Glenarvan, "we will continue our investigations. We are on the track of a great catastrophe. The lives of several men depend upon our sagacity. Let us use therefore all our ingenuity to divine the secret of this enigma."

"We are ready, my dear Edward," replied Lady Helena.

"First of all," continued Glenarvan, "we must consider three distinct points in this document. First, what is known; second, what can be conjectured; and third, what is unknown. What do we know? That on the 7th of June, 1862, a brig, the Britannia, of Glasgow, was wrecked; that two sailors and the captain threw this document into the sea in latitude 37° 11', and in it ask for assistance."

"Exactly," replied the major.

"LINE UPON LINE."

"What can we conjecture?" resumed Glenarvan. "First, that the shipwreck took place in the South Seas; and now I call your attention to the word *gonia*. Does it not indicate the name of the country which they reached?"

"Patagonia!" cried Lady Helena.

"Probably."

"But is Patagonia crossed by the thirty-seventh parallel?" asked the major.

"That is easily seen," said the captain, taking out a map of South America. "It is so: Patagonia is bisected by the thirty-seventh parallel, which crosses Araucania, over the Pampas, north of Patagonia, and is lost in the Atlantic."

"Well, let us continue our conjectures. The two sailors and the captain *abor, land*. Where? *Contin,*—the *continent*, you understand; a continent, not an island. What becomes of them? We have fortunately two letters, *pr*, which inform us of their fate. These unfortunates, in short, are *captured* (pris) or *prisoners*. By whom? The *cruel Indians*. Are you convinced? Do not the words fit naturally into the vacant places? Does not the document grow clear to your eyes? Does not light break in upon your mind?"

Glenarvan spoke with conviction. His looks betokened an absolute confidence; and his enthusiasm was communicated to his hearers. Like him they cried, "It is plain! it is plain!"

A moment after Lord Edward resumed, in these terms:

"All these hypotheses, my friends, seem to me extremely plausible. In my opinion, the catastrophe took place on the shores of Patagonia. However, I will inquire at Glasgow what was the destination of the Britannia, and we shall know whether she could have been led to these regions."

"We do not need to go so far," replied the captain; "I have here the shipping news of the *Mercantile and Shipping Gazette*, which will give us definite information."

"Let us see! let us see!" said Lady Glenarvan.

Captain Mangles took a file of papers of the year 1862, and began to turn over the leaves rapidly. His search was soon ended; as he said, in a tone of satisfaction,—

"May 30, 1862, Callao, Peru, *Britannia*, Captain Grant, bound for Glasgow."

"Grant!" exclaimed Lord Glenarvan; "that hardy Scotchman who wished to found a new Scotland in the waters of the Pacific?"

"Yes," answered the captain, "the very same, who, in 1861, embarked in the Britannia at Glasgow, and of whom nothing has since been heard."

"Exactly! exactly!" said Glenarvan; "it is indeed he. The Britannia left Callao the 30th of May, and on the 7th of June, eight days after her departure, she was lost on the shores of Patagonia. This is the whole story elucidated from the remains of these words that seemed undecipherable. You see, my friends, that what we can conjecture is very important. As to what we do not know, this is reduced to one item, the missing degree of longitude."

"It is of no account," added Captain Mangles, "since the country is known; and with the latitude alone, I will undertake to go straight to the scene of the shipwreck."

"We know all, then?" said Lady Glenarvan.

"All, my dear Helena: and these blanks that the sea has made between the words of the document, I can as easily fill out as though I were writing at the dictation of Captain Grant."

Accordingly Lord Glenarvan took the pen again, and wrote, without hesitation, the following note:

"June 7, 1862.—The brig Britannia of Glasgow was wrecked on the shores of Patagonia, in the Southern Hemisphere. Directing their course to land, two sailors and Captain Grant attempted to reach the continent, where they will be prisoners of the cruel Indians. They have thrown this document into the sea, at longitude ———, latitude 37° 11'. Bring them assistance or they are lost."

A NOBLE RESOLVE.

"Good! good! my dear Edward!" said Lady Glenarvan; "and if these unfortunates see their native country again, they will owe this happiness to you."

"And they shall see it again," replied Glenarvan. "This document is too explicit, too clear, too certain, for Englishmen to hesitate. What has been done for Sir John Franklin, and so many others, will also be done for the shipwrecked of the Britannia."

"But these unfortunates," answered Lady Helena, "have, without doubt, a family that mourns their loss. Perhaps this poor Captain Grant has a wife, children———"

"You are right, my dear lady; and I charge myself with informing them that all hope is not yet lost. And now, my friends, let us go on deck, for we must be approaching the harbor."

Indeed, the Duncan had forced on steam, and was now skirting the shores of Bute Island. Rothesay, with its charming little village nestling in its fertile valley, was left on the starboard, and the vessel entered the narrow inlets of the frith, passed Greenock, and, at six in the evening, was anchored at the foot of the basaltic rocks of Dumbarton, crowned by the celebrated castle.

Here a coach was waiting to take Lady Helena and Major MacNabb back to Malcolm Castle. Lord Glenarvan, after embracing his young wife, hurried to take the express train for Glasgow. But before going, he confided an important message to a more rapid agent, and a few moments after the electric telegraph conveyed to the *Times* and *Morning Chronicle* an advertisement in the following terms:

"For any information concerning the brig Britannia of Glasgow, Captain Grant, address Lord Glenarvan, Malcolm Castle, Luss, County of Dumbarton, Scotland."

Dumbarton Castle.

CHAPTER III

THE CAPTAIN'S CHILDREN.

THE GLENARVAN ANCESTRY.

The castle of Malcolm, one of the most romantic in Scotland, is situated near the village of Luss, whose pretty valley it crowns. The limpid waters of Loch Lomond bathe the granite of its walls. From time immemorial it has belonged to the Glenarvan family, who have preserved in the country of Rob Roy and Fergus MacGregor the hospitable customs of the ancient heroes of Walter Scott. At the epoch of the social revolution in Scotland, a great number of vassals were expelled, because they could not pay the great rents to the ancient chiefs of the clans. Some died of hunger, others became fishermen, others emigrated. There was general despair.

Among all these the Glenarvans alone believed that fidelity bound the high as well as the low, and they remained faithful to their tenants. Not one left the roof under which he was born; not one abandoned the soil where his ancestors reposed; all continued in the clan of their ancient lords. Thus at this epoch, in this age of disaffection and disunion, the Glenarvan family considered the Scots at Malcolm Castle as their own people. All were descended from the vassals of their kinsmen; were children of the counties of Stirling and Dumbarton, and honestly devoted, body and estate, to their master.

Lord Glenarvan possessed an immense fortune, which he employed in doing much good. His kindness exceeded even his generosity, for one was boundless, while the other was necessarily limited. The lord of Luss, the "laird" of Malcolm, represented his fellows in the House of Lords; but with true Scottish ideas, little pleasing to the southrons, he was disliked by many of them especially because he adhered to the traditions of his ancestors, and energetically opposed some dicta of modern political economy.

He was not, however, a backward man, either in wit or shrewdness; but while ready to enter every door of progress, he remained Scotch at heart, and it was for the glory of his native land that he contended with his racing yachts in the matches of the Royal Thames Yacht Club.

Lord Edward Glenarvan was thirty-two years old. His form was erect and his features sharp, but his look was mild, and his character thoroughly imbued with the poetry of the Highlands. He was known to be brave to excess, enterprising, chivalrous, a Fergus of the nineteenth century; but good above all, better than Saint Martin himself, for he would have given his very cloak to the poor people of the Highlands.

He had been married scarcely three months, having espoused Miss Helena Tuffnel, daughter of the great traveler, William Tuffnel, one of the numerous victims to the great passion for geographical discoveries.

Miss Helena did not belong to a noble family, but she was Scotch, which equaled all nobilities in the eyes of Lord Glenarvan. This charming young creature, high-minded and devoted, the lord of Luss had made the companion of his life. He found her one day living alone, an orphan, almost without fortune, in the house of her father at Kilpatrick. He saw that the poor girl would make a noble wife, and he married her.

Miss Tuffnel was twenty-two, a youthful blonde, with eyes as blue as the waters of the Scotch lakes on a beautiful morning in spring. Her love for her husband exceeded even her gratitude. She loved him as if she had been the rich heiress, and he the friendless orphan. As to their tenants and servants, they were ready to lay down their lives for her whom they called "our good lady of Luss."

LIFE IN THE SCOTTISH HOME.

Lord and Lady Glenarvan lived happily at Malcolm Castle, in the midst of the grand and wild scenery of the Highlands, rambling in the shady alleys of horse-chestnuts and sycamores, along the shores of the lake, where still resounded the war cries of ancient times, or in the depths of those uncultivated gorges in which the history of Scotland lies written in ruins from age to age. One day they would wander in the forests of beeches and larches, and in the midst of the masses of heather; another, they would scale the precipitous summits of Ben Lomond, or traverse on horseback the solitary glens, studying, comprehending, and admiring this poetic country, still called "the land of Rob Roy," and all those celebrated sites so grandly sung by Walter Scott.

In the sweet, still evening, when the "lantern of Mac Farlane" illumined the horizon, they would stroll along the "bartizans," an old circular balcony that formed a chain of battlements to Malcolm Castle, and there, pensive, oblivious, and as if alone in the world, seated on some detached rock, under the pale rays of the moon, while night gradually enveloped the rugged summits of the mountains, they would continue wrapt in that pure ecstasy and inward delight known only to loving hearts.

Thus passed the first months of their married life. But Lord Glenarvan did not forget that his wife was the daughter of a great traveler. He thought that Lady Helena must have in her heart all the aspirations of her father, and he was not mistaken. The Duncan was constructed, and was designed to convey Lord and Lady Glenarvan to the most beautiful countries of the world, along the waves of the Mediterranean, and to the isles of the Archipelago. Imagine the joy of Lady Helena when her husband placed the Duncan at her disposal! Indeed, can there be a greater happiness than to lead your love towards those charming "isles where Sappho sung," and behold the enchanting scenes of the Orient, with all their spirit-stirring memories?

Meantime Lord Glenarvan had started for London. The safety of the unfortunate shipwrecked men was at stake. Thus, in his temporary absence, Lady Helena showed herself more anxious than sad. The next day a dispatch from her husband made her hope for a speedy return; in the evening a letter hinted at its postponement. His proposal had to encounter some difficulties, and the following day a second letter came, in which Lord Glenarvan did not conceal his indignation against the authorities.

"Please, madam, speak! I am strong against grief, and can hear all."

On that day Lady Helena began to be uneasy. At evening she was alone in her chamber, when the steward of the castle, Mr. Halbert, came to ask if she would see a young girl and boy who desired to speak with Lord Glenarvan.

"People of the country?" asked Lady Helena.

"No, madam," replied the steward, "for I do not know them. They have just arrived by the Balloch railway, and from Balloch to Luss they tell me they have made the journey on foot."

"Bid them come up, steward," said Lady Glenarvan.

The steward withdrew. Some moments afterward the young girl and boy were ushered into Lady Helena's chamber. They were brother and sister; you could not doubt it by their resemblance.

The sister was sixteen. Her pretty face showed weariness, her eyes must have shed many tears; her resigned, but courageous, countenance, and her humble, but neat, attire, all prepossessed one in her favor. She held by the hand a boy of twelve years, of determined look, who seemed to take his sister under his protection. Indeed, whoever had insulted the young girl would have had to settle with this little gentleman.

The sister stopped, a little surprised at seeing herself before Lady Helena; but the latter hastened to open the conversation.

"You wish to speak with me?" said she, with an encouraging look at the young girl.

"ONE TOUCH OF NATURE."

"No," answered the boy, in a decided tone; "not with you, but with Lord Glenarvan himself."

"Excuse him, madam," said the sister, looking at her brother.

"Lord Glenarvan is not at the castle," replied Lady Helena; "but I am his wife, and if I can supply his place with you———"

"You are Lady Glenarvan?" said the young girl.

"Yes, miss."

"The wife of Lord Glenarvan, of Malcolm Castle, who published an advertisement in the *Times* in regard to the shipwreck of the Britannia?"

"Yes, yes!" answered Lady Helena, with alacrity. "And you?"

"I am Miss Grant, and this is my brother."

"Miss Grant! Miss Grant!" cried Lady Helena, drawing the young girl towards her, and taking her hands, while she also drew the boy towards her.

"Madam," replied the young girl, "what do you know of the shipwreck of my father? Is he living? Shall we ever see him again? Speak! oh, please tell me!"

"My dear child," said Lady Helena, "God forbid that I should answer you lightly on such a subject; I would not give you a vain hope——"

"Please, madam, speak! I am strong against grief, and can hear all."

"My dear child," answered Lady Helena, "the hope is very slight, but with the help of God who can do everything, it is possible that you will one day see your father again."

"Alas, alas!" exclaimed Miss Grant, who could not restrain her tears, while Robert covered the hands of Lady Glenarvan with kisses.

When the first paroxysm of this mournful joy was past, the young girl began to ask innumerable questions. Lady Helena related the story of the document, how that the Britannia had been lost on the shores of Patagonia; in what way, after the shipwreck, the captain and two sailors, the only survivors, must have reached the continent; and, at last, how they implored the assistance of the whole world in this document, written in three languages, and abandoned to the caprices of the ocean.

During this recital Robert Grant devoured Lady Helena with his eyes; his life seemed to hang on her lips. In his childish imagination he reviewed the terrible scenes of which his father must have been the victim. He saw him on the deck of the Britannia; he followed him to the bosom of the waves; he clung with him to the rocks of the shore; he dragged himself panting along the beach, out of reach of the waves.

Often during the course of this narration words escaped his lips.

"Oh, papa! my poor papa!" he cried, pressing close to his sister.

As for Miss Grant, she listened with clasped hands, and did not utter a word until the story was ended, when she said,—

"Oh, madam, the document! the document!"

"I no longer have it, my dear child," replied Lady Helena.

"You no longer have it?"

"No; for the very sake of your father, Lord Glenarvan had to take it to London; but I have told you all it contained, word for word, and how we succeeded in discovering the exact meaning. Among these remains of the almost effaced words the water had spared some characters. Unfortunately the record of the longitude had altogether been destroyed, but that was the only missing point. Thus you see, Miss Grant, the minutest details of this document are known to you as well as me."

"Yes, madam," replied the young girl; "but I would like to have seen my father's writing."

WAITING FOR THE VERDICT.

"Well, to-morrow, perhaps, Lord Glenarvan will return. My husband desired to submit this indisputable document to the authorities in London, to induce them to send a vessel immediately in search of Captain Grant."

"Is it possible, madam!" cried the young girl. "Did you do this for us?"

"Yes, my dear miss, and I expect Lord Glenarvan every moment."

"Madam," said the young girl, in a deep tone of gratitude, and with fervency, "may Heaven bless Lord Glenarvan and you!"

"Dear child," answered Lady Helena, "we deserve no thanks. Any other person in our place would have done the same. May the hopes that are kindled be realized! Till Lord Glenarvan's return you will remain at the castle."

"Madam," said the young girl, "I would not presume on the sympathy you show to us strangers——"

"Strangers! Dear child, neither your brother nor you are strangers in this house; and I desire that Lord Glenarvan on his arrival should inform the children of Captain Grant of what is to be attempted to save their father."

It was not possible to refuse an invitation made with so much cordiality. It was, therefore, decided that Miss Grant and her brother should await at Malcolm Castle the return of Lord Glenarvan.

CHAPTER IV

LADY GLENARVAN'S PROPOSAL.

During this conversation, Lady Helena had not spoken of the fears expressed in her husband's letters concerning the reception of his petition by the London officials; nor was a word said in regard to the probable captivity of Captain Grant among the Indians of South America. Why afflict these poor children with their father's situation, and check the hopes they had just conceived? It would not change matters. Lady Helena was, therefore, silent on this point, and, after satisfying all Miss Grant's inquiries, she questioned her concerning her life, and situation in the world in which she seemed to be the sole protectress of her brother. It was a simple and touching story, which still more increased Lady Glenarvan's sympathy for the young girl.

Mary and Robert Grant were the only children of Captain Harry Grant, whose wife had died at the birth of Robert, and during his long voyages his children were left to the care of his good old cousin. Captain Grant was a hardy sailor, a man well acquainted with his profession, and a good negotiator, combining thus a twofold aptitude for his calling commercially. His home was at Dundee, in the county of Forfar, and he was moreover, by birth, a child of that "bonnie" place. His father, a minister of Saint Catherine's Church, had given him a thorough education, knowing that it would be sure to help all, even a sea-captain.

IDEAS AND REALITIES.

During his early voyages, first as mate, and afterwards in the capacity of skipper, Harry Grant prospered, and some years after the birth of his son Robert, he found himself the possessor of a considerable fortune.

Then a great idea entered his mind which made his name popular throughout Scotland. Like the Glenarvans and several other great families of the Highlands, he was opposed in heart, if not in deed, to the advance and prevalence of English thought and feeling. The interests of his country could not be in his eyes the same as those of the Anglo-Saxons, and, in order to give the former a peculiar and national development, he resolved to found a Scottish colony in some part of the Southern World. Did he dream of that independence in the future of which the United States had set the example, and which the Indies and Australia cannot fail one day to acquire? Very likely; but he allowed his secret hopes to be divined. It was, therefore, known that the Government refused to lend their aid in his project of colonization; nay, they even raised obstacles which in any other country would have overcome the project.

But Harry Grant would not be discouraged. He appealed to the patriotism of his countrymen, gave his fortune to serve the cause, built a vessel and furnished it with a fine crew, confided his children to the care of his old cousin, and set sail to explore the great islands of the Pacific.

It was the year 1861. Until May, 1862, they had received news of him, but since his departure from Callao, in the month of June, no one had heard anything of the Britannia, and the marine intelligencers became silent concerning the fate of the captain.

At this juncture of affairs the old cousin of Harry Grant died, and the two children were left alone in the world. Mary Grant was then fourteen. Her courageous soul did not flinch at the situation that was presented, but she devoted herself entirely to her brother, who was still a child. She must bring him up and instruct him. By dint of economy, prudence, and sagacity, laboring night and day, sacrificing all for him, denying herself everything, the sister succeeded in educating her brother and bravely fulfilled her sisterly duties.

The two children lived thus at Dundee, and valiantly overcame their sorrowful and lonely circumstances. Mary thought only of her brother, and dreamed of a happy future for him. As for herself, alas! the Britannia was lost forever, and her father dead! We must not, therefore, attempt to depict her emotion when the advertisement in the *Times* accidentally met her eye, and suddenly raised her from her despair.

It was no time to hesitate. Her resolution was immediately taken. Even if she should learn that her father's dead body had been found on a desert coast, or in the hull of a shipwrecked vessel, it was better than this continual doubt, this eternal torment of uncertainty. She told her brother all; and the same day the two children took the Perth Railroad, and at evening arrived at Malcolm Castle, where Mary, after so many harassing thoughts, began to hope.

Such was the sorrowful story that the young girl related to Lady Glenarvan, in an artless manner, without thinking that through all those long years of trial she had behaved herself like an heroic daughter. But Lady Helena thought of this, and several times, without hiding her tears, she clasped in her arms the two children of Captain Grant.

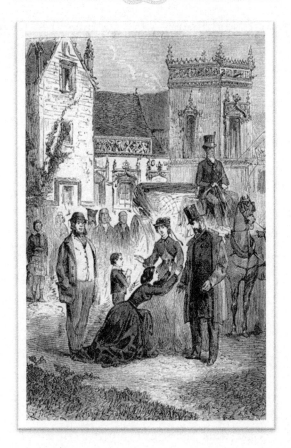

"My father, my poor father!" cried Mary Grant, throwing herself at the feet of Lord Glenarvan.

As for Robert, it seemed as if he heard this story for the first time: for he opened his eyes in astonishment, as he listened to his sister; comprehended what she had done, what she had suffered; and at last, encircling her with his arms, he exclaimed, unable longer to restrain the cry that came from the very depths of his heart,—

"Oh, mamma! my dear mamma!"

Night had now fully set in; and Lady Helena, remembering the fatigue of the two children, would not longer continue the conversation. Mary and Robert were conducted to their chambers, and fell asleep dreaming of a brighter future.

After they had retired, Lady Helena saw the major, and told him all the events of the day.

"That Mary Grant is a brave girl," said MacNabb, when he had heard his cousin's story.

"May Heaven grant my husband success in his enterprise!" replied Lady Helena; "for the situation of the two children would be terrible!"

"He will succeed," answered MacNabb, "or the hearts of the authorities must be harder than the stone of Portland."

In spite of the major's assurance, Lady Helena passed the night in the greatest anxiety, and could scarce gain an hour's repose.

"BROKEN CISTERNS."

The next morning Mary and her brother rose at daybreak, and were walking in the galleries and water terraces of the castle, when the sound of a coach was heard in the great court-yard. It was Lord Glenarvan returning to Malcolm Castle at the full speed of his horses. Almost immediately Lady Helena, accompanied by the major, appeared in the court-yard, and flew to meet her husband. But he seemed sad, disappointed, and angry. He clasped his wife in his arms, and was silent.

"Well, Edward!" she exclaimed.

"Well, my dear Helena," he replied, "those people have no hearts!"

"They refused?"

"Yes, they refused me a vessel: they spoke of the millions vainly spent in searching for Franklin; they declared the document was vague and unintelligible; they said that the shipwreck of these unfortunates had happened two years ago, and that there was little chance of finding them. They maintained too, that, if prisoners of the Indians, they must have been carried into the interior of the country; that they could not ransack all Patagonia to find three men,—three Scotchmen; the search would be vain and perilous, and would cost the lives of more men than it would save. In short, they gave all the absurd reasons of people who mean to refuse. They remembered the captain's projects, and I fear that the unfortunate man is forever lost!"

"My father, my poor father!" cried Mary Grant, throwing herself at the feet of Lord Glenarvan.

"Your father! What, Miss——?" said he, surprised at seeing a young girl at his feet.

"Yes, Edward, Miss Grant and her brother," replied Lady Helena; "the two children of Captain Grant, who have thus been condemned to remain orphans."

"Ah, miss!" answered Lord Glenarvan, "if I had known of your presence——"

He said no more. A painful silence, interrupted only by sobs, reigned in the court-yard. No one raised his voice, neither Lord Glenarvan, Lady Helena, the major, nor the servants of the castle, who were standing about even at this early hour. But by their attitude they all protested against the conduct of the officials.

After several moments the major resumed the conversation, and, addressing Lord Glenarvan, said,—

"Then you have no more hope?"

"None."

"Well," cried young Robert, "I will go to these people, and—we shall see——"

He did not finish his threat, for his sister stopped him; but his clinched hands indicated his intentions.

"No, Robert," said she, "no; let us thank these kind people for what they have done for us. Let us always keep them in remembrance; but now we must take our departure."

"Mary!" cried Lady Helena.

"Miss, where would you go?" said Lord Glenarvan.

"I am going to throw myself at the feet of the Queen," replied the young girl, "and we shall see if she will be deaf to the prayers of two children imploring help for their father."

Lord Glenarvan shook his head; not that he doubted the clemency of Her Gracious Majesty, but he doubted whether Mary Grant would gain access to her; for but few suppliants reach the steps of a throne.

Lady Helena understood her husband's thoughts. She knew that the young girl might make a fruitless journey, and she pictured to herself these two children leading henceforth a cheerless existence. Then it was that she conceived a grand and noble idea.

"Mary Grant," she exclaimed, "wait, my child; listen to what I am about to say."

The young girl held her brother by the hand, and was preparing to go. She stopped.

Then Lady Helena, with tearful eye, but firm voice and animated features, advanced towards her husband.

"NOBLY PLANNED."

"Edward," said she, "when Captain Grant wrote that letter, and cast it into the sea, he confided it to the care of God himself, who has brought it to us. Without doubt He designed to charge us with the safety of these unfortunates."

"What do you mean, Helena?" inquired Lord Glenarvan, whilst all waited in silence.

"I mean," replied Lady Helena, "that we ought to consider ourselves happy in beginning our married life with a good action. You, my dear Edward, to please me, have planned a pleasure voyage. But what pleasure can be more genuine or more beneficent than to save these unfortunates whom hope has almost abandoned?"

"Helena!" cried Lord Glenarvan.

"Yes, you understand me, Edward. The Duncan is a good, staunch vessel. It can brave the Southern seas; it can make the tour of the world,—and it will, if necessary! Let us start, Edward,—let us go in search of Captain Grant!"

At these courageous words Lord Glenarvan had extended his arms to his wife. He smiled. He pressed her to his heart, while Mary and Robert kissed her hands.

And during this touching scene the servants of the castle, affected and enthusiastic, uttered from their hearts this cry of gratitude,—

"Hurrah for the lady of Luss! Hurrah! three times hurrah, for Lord and Lady Glenarvan!"

CHAPTER V

THE DEPARTURE OF THE DUNCAN.

It has been already said that Lady Helena had a brave and generous soul. What she had just done was an undeniable proof of it, and Lord Glenarvan had good reason to trust in this noble woman, who was capable of comprehending and following him. The idea of sailing to the rescue of Captain Grant had already taken possession of him when he saw his petition rejected at London; but he could not have thought of separating from her. Yet, since she desired to go herself, all hesitation was at an end. The servants of the castle had received her proposal with cries of joy; the safety of their brother Scots was at stake, and Lord Glenarvan joined heartily in the hurrahs that greeted the lady of Luss.

The scheme once resolved upon, there was not an hour to lose. That very day Lord Glenarvan sent to Captain Mangles orders to bring the Duncan to Glasgow, and make every preparation for a voyage to the South Seas, which might become one of circumnavigation. Moreover, in her plans Lady Helena had not overestimated the qualities of the Duncan: of first-class construction with regard to strength and swiftness, she could without injury sustain a long voyage.

FITTING FOR SEA.

The Duncan was a steam yacht of one hundred and ten tons burden. She had two masts,—a foremast with fore-sail, main-sail, foretop and foretop-gallant sails; and a mainmast, carrying a main-sail and fore-staff. Her rigging was, therefore, sufficient, and she could profit by the wind like a simple clipper; but she relied especially upon her mechanical power. Her engine was of an effective force of one hundred and sixty horse power, and was constructed on a new plan. It possessed apparatus for overheating, which gave its steam a very great tension. It was a high-pressure engine, and produced motion by a double screw. The Duncan under full steam could acquire a speed equal to any vessel of that day. Indeed, during her trial trip in the Frith of Clyde, she had made, according to the log, seventeen knots an hour. She was, therefore, fully capable of circumnavigating the world; and her captain had only to occupy himself with the internal arrangement.

His first care was to increase his store-room, and take in the greatest possible quantity of coal, for it would be difficult to renew their supplies on the voyage. The same precaution was taken with the steward's room, and provisions for two years were stowed away. Money, of course, was not wanting, and a pivot-gun was furnished, which was fixed at the forecastle. You do not know what may happen, and it is always best to have the means of defense in your reach.

Captain Mangles, we must say, understood his business. Although he commanded only a pleasure yacht, he was ranked among the ablest of the Glasgow captains. He was thirty years of age, with rather rough features, indicating courage and kindness. When a child, the Glenarvan family had taken him under their care, and made him an excellent seaman. He had often given proofs of skill, energy, and coolness during his long voyages, and when Lord Glenarvan offered him the command of the Duncan, he accepted it with pride and pleasure, for he loved the lord of Malcolm Castle as a brother, and until then had vainly sought an opportunity to devote himself to his service.

The mate, Tom Austin, was an old sailor worthy of all confidence; and the crew of the Duncan was composed of twenty-five men, including the captain and mate. They all belonged to the county of Dumbarton, were all tried seamen, sons of the tenants of the family, and formed on shipboard a genuine clan of honest people, who of course were not without the national bagpipe. Lord Glenarvan had, in them, a band of faithful subjects, happy in their avocation, devoted, courageous, and skillful in the use of arms, as well as in the management of a ship, while they were ready to follow him on the most perilous expeditions. When they learned where they were going, they could not restrain their joyous emotion, and the echoes of the rocks of Dumbarton awoke to their cries of enthusiasm.

Captain Mangles, while occupied in lading and provisioning his craft, did not forget to prepare Lord and Lady Glenarvan's apartments for a long voyage. He likewise provided cabins for Captain Grant's children, for Lady Helena could not refuse Mary permission to accompany her on the expedition.

As for young Robert, he would have hidden in the hold sooner than not go; even if he had been compelled to serve as cabin-boy, like Lord Nelson and Sir John Franklin, he would have embarked on board the Duncan. To think of opposing such a little gentleman! It was not attempted. They were even obliged to take him other than as passenger, for as cabin-boy or sailor he *would serve*. The captain was accordingly commissioned to teach him the duties of a seaman.

"Good!" said Robert; "and let him not spare a few blows of the rope's end if I do not walk straight."

"Be easy, my boy," replied Glenarvan, without adding that the use of the "cat-o'-nine-tails" was prohibited, and moreover quite needless, on board the Duncan.

GLASGOW GOSSIP.

To complete the roll of the passengers, it will be sufficient to describe Major MacNabb. The major was a man of fifty, of calm, regular features, who did as he was bid; of an excellent and superior character, modest, taciturn, peaceable, and mild; always agreeing with anything or any one, disputing nothing, and neither contradicting himself nor exaggerating. He would mount with measured step the staircase to his bed-chamber, even were a cannon-ball behind him; and probably to his dying day would never find an opportunity to fly into a passion.

This man possessed, in a high degree, not only the common courage of the battle-field (that physical bravery due only to nervous strength), but, better still, moral courage, that is to say, firmness of soul. If he had a fault, it was that of being absolutely Scotch from head to foot, a pure-blooded Caledonian, an infatuated observer of the ancient customs of his country. Through his relationship to the Glenarvans he lived at Malcolm Castle; and as major and military man it was very natural that he should be found on board the Duncan.

Such, then, were the passengers of this yacht, summoned by unforeseen circumstances to accomplish one of the most surprising voyages of modern times. Since her arrival at the wharf at Glasgow, she had monopolized the public attention. A considerable number came every day to visit her. They were interested in her alone, and spoke only of her, to the great umbrage of the other captains of the port, among others Captain Burton, commanding the Scotia, a magnificent steamer, moored beside the Duncan, and bound for Calcutta. The Scotia, from her size, had a right to consider the Duncan as a mere fly-boat. Nevertheless, all the attraction centred in Lord Glenarvan's yacht, and increased from day to day.

The time of departure approached. Captain Mangles had shown himself skillful and expeditious. A month after her trial trip in the Frith of Clyde, the Duncan, laden, provisioned, and equipped, was ready to put to sea. The 25th of August was appointed for the time of departure, which would enable the yacht to reach the southern latitudes by the beginning of spring. Lord Glenarvan, when his plan was matured, did not neglect to make investigations into the hardships and perils of the voyage; yet he did not hesitate on this account, but prepared to leave Malcolm Castle.

On the 24th of August, Lord and Lady Glenarvan, Major MacNabb, Mary and Robert Grant, Mr. Olbinett, the steward of the yacht, and his wife, who was in the service of Lady Glenarvan, left the castle, after taking an affectionate farewell of their family servants. Several hours afterward they found themselves on board. Many of the population of Glasgow welcomed with sympathetic admiration the young and courageous lady who renounced the pleasures of a life of luxury, and sailed to the rescue of the shipwrecked sailors.

The apartments of Lord Glenarvan and his wife occupied the entire stern of the vessel. They consisted of two bed-chambers, a parlor, and two dressing-rooms, adjoining which was an open square inclosed by six cabins, five of which were occupied by Mary and Robert Grant, Mr. and Mrs. Olbinett, and Major MacNabb. As for the cabins of the captain and the mate, they were situated in the forecastle, and opened on the deck. The crew were lodged between-decks very comfortably, for the yacht of course carried nothing but her coal, provisions, and armament.

The Duncan was to start on the night of the 24th, as the tide fell at three o'clock in the morning. But first those who were present were witness to a touching scene. At eight in the evening Lord Glenarvan and his companions, the entire crew, from the firemen to the captain, all who were to take part in this voyage of sacrifice, left the yacht, and betook themselves to Saint Mungo, the ancient cathedral of Glasgow. This antique church, an uninjured relic in the midst of the ruins caused by the Reformation, and so marvelously described by Walter Scott, received beneath its massive arches the owners and sailors of the Duncan.

PRAYER, AND PROGRESS.

A numerous throng accompanied them. There in the spacious aisle, filled with tombs of the great and good, the Rev. Mr. Morton implored the blessing of Heaven, and commended the expedition to the care of Providence. For a moment the voice of Mary Grant arose in the old church. The young girl was praying for her benefactors, and shedding before God the sweet tears of gratitude. The assembly retired under the influence of a deep emotion.

At eleven, every one was on board. The captain and the crew occupied themselves with the final preparations. At midnight the fires were kindled, and soon clouds of black smoke mingled with the vapors of the night; the sails of the Duncan had been carefully reefed in a canvas sheathing, which served to protect them from injury. The wind blew from the southeast, and did not favor the progress of the vessel; but at two o'clock the ship began to heave under the action of her boilers. The manometer indicated a pressure of four atmospheres, and the overheated steam whistled through the escape-valves. The sea was tranquil, and soon daylight enabled them to distinguish the passes of the Clyde between the buoys and beacons, whose lights were gradually extinguished as the morning dawned.

Captain Mangles informed Lord Glenarvan, who at once came on deck. Very soon the ebb-tide was felt. The Duncan gave a few shrill whistles, slackened her cables, and separated from the surrounding vessels. Her screw was set in motion, which propelled her into the channel of the river. The captain had taken no pilot. He was perfectly acquainted with the navigation of the Clyde, and no one could have commanded better. At a sign from him the yacht started. With his right hand he controlled the engine, and with his left the tiller, with silent but unerring skill.

The Rev. Mr. Morton implored the blessing of Heaven, and commended the expedition to the care of Providence.

A CHANGE OF SCENE.

Soon the last workshops on the shore gave place to villas, built here and there upon the hills, and the sounds of the city died away in the distance. An hour afterwards, the Duncan passed the rocks of Dumbarton; two hours later she was in the Frith of Clyde; and at six o'clock in the morning she doubled Cantyre Point, emerged from the North Channel, and gained the open sea.

CHAPTER VI

AN UNEXPECTED PASSENGER.

During the first day's voyage the sea was quite rough, and the wind freshened towards evening. The Duncan rolled considerably, so that the ladies did not appear on deck, but very wisely remained in their cabins. The next day the wind changed a point, and the captain set the main-, fore-, and foretop-sails, thus causing less perception of the rolling and pitching motion.

Lady Helena and Mary Grant were able before daybreak to join Lord Glenarvan, the major, and the captain, on deck. The sunrise was magnificent. The orb of day, like a gilded metal disk, rose from the ocean, as from an immense and silvery basin. The ship glided in the midst of a splendid iridescence, and you would truly have thought that her sails expanded under the influence of the sun's rays, whilst even the crew of the yacht silently admired this reappearance of the orb of day.

"What a magnificent spectacle!" said Lady Helena, at last. "This is the beginning of a beautiful day. May the wind not prove contrary, but favor the progress of the Duncan!"

"No better weather could be desired, my dear Helena," replied Lord Glenarvan; "we have no reason to complain of the commencement of the voyage."

"Will it be a long one, my dear Edward?"

"That is for the captain to answer," said he. "Are we progressing well? Are you satisfied with your vessel, captain?"

"Very well indeed," was the answer. "She is a marvelous craft, and a sailor likes to feel her under his feet. Never were hull and engine more in unison. See how smooth her wake is, and how easily she rides the waves. We are moving at the rate of seventeen knots an hour. If this continues, we shall cross the line in ten days, and in five weeks shall double Cape Horn."

"You hear, Mary," said Lady Helena: "in five weeks!"

"Yes," replied the young girl, "I hear; and my heart beat quickly at the words of the captain."

"And how do you bear this voyage, Miss Mary?" inquired Lord Glenarvan.

"Very well, my lord; I do not experience very many discomforts. Besides, I shall soon be accustomed to it."

"And young Robert?"

COMPLIMENTS AND CONGRATULATIONS.

"Oh, Robert!" replied Captain Mangles: "when he is not engaged with the engine he is perched at mast-head. I tell you he is a boy who mocks sea-sickness. Only look at him!"

At a gesture of the captain, all eyes were turned towards the mainmast, and every one could perceive Robert, suspended by the stays of the foretop-gallant sail, a hundred feet aloft. Mary could not restrain a motion of fear.

"Oh, be easy, miss!" said Captain Mangles. "I will answer for him, and promise you I will present, in a short time, a famous sailor to Captain Grant; for we shall find that worthy captain."

"May Heaven hear you, sir!" replied the young girl.

"My dear child," said Lord Glenarvan, "there is in all this something providential, which ought to give us hope. We are not merely going, we are led; we are not seeking blindly, we are guided. And then see all these brave people enrolled in the service of so good a cause. Not only shall we succeed in our enterprise, but it will be accomplished without difficulty. I have promised Lady Helena a pleasure voyage; and, if I am not mistaken, I shall keep my word."

"Edward," said Lady Glenarvan, "you are the best of men."

"Not so; but I have the best of crews, on the best of ships. Do you not wonder at our Duncan, Miss Mary?"

"On the contrary, my lord," answered the young girl, "I don't so much wonder as admire; for I am well acquainted with ships."

"Ah! indeed!"

"When a mere child, I played on my father's ships. He ought to have made a sailor of me. If it were necessary, perhaps I should not now be embarrassed in taking a reef or twisting a gasket."

"What is that you're saying, miss?" exclaimed the captain.

"If you talk so," continued Lord Glenarvan, "you will make a great friend of Captain John; for he thinks nothing in the world can equal the life of a sailor. He sees no other, even for a woman. Is it not so, John?"

"Undoubtedly, your lordship," replied the young captain; "and yet, I confess, Miss Grant is better in her place on deck, than taking a reef in the top-sail. But still I am very much flattered to hear her speak so."

"And especially when she admires the Duncan!" added Glenarvan.

"Right, my lord; for she deserves it."

"Upon my word," said Lady Helena, "since you are so proud of your yacht, you make me anxious to examine her to the very hold, and see how our brave sailors are quartered between-decks."

"Admirably," replied the captain; "they are quite at home there."

"Indeed they are, my dear Helena," said Lord Glenarvan. "This yacht is a part of our old Caledonia,—a detached portion of the county of Dumbarton, traveling by special favor, so that we have not left our country. The Duncan is Malcolm Castle, and the ocean is Loch Lomond."

"Well, then, my dear Edward, do the honors of the castle," said Lady Helena.

"I am at your disposal, madam," answered her husband; "but first let me inform Olbinett."

The steward of the yacht was an excellent manager, a Scotchman, who deserved to have been a Frenchman from his self-importance, and, moreover, fulfilled his duties with zeal and intelligence. He was at once ready for his master's commands.

"Olbinett, we are going to make a tour of the vessel before breakfast," said Glenarvan, as if a journey to Tarbet or Loch Katrine was in question. "I hope we shall find the table ready on our return."

Olbinett bowed gravely.

"Do you accompany us, major?" asked Lady Helena.

"If you order it," replied MacNabb.

This man, tall, lank, and shriveled, might have been forty years old. He resembled a long, broad-headed nail, for his head was large and thick, his forehead high, his nose prominent, his mouth wide, and his chin blunt.

"Oh!" said Lord Glenarvan, "the major is absorbed in the smoke of his cigar; we must not disturb him, for I assure you he is an inveterate smoker, Miss Mary; he smokes all the time, even in his sleep."

The major made a sign of assent, and the passengers descended between-decks.

MacNabb remained alone, talking to himself, according to his custom, but never contradicting himself. Enveloped in a dense cloud of smoke, he stood motionless, gazing back at the wake of the yacht. After a few moments of contemplation, he turned and found himself face to face with a new character. If *anything* could have surprised him, it must have been this meeting, for the passenger was absolutely unknown to him.

A TELESCOPIC APPARITION.

This man, tall, lank, and shriveled, might have been forty years old. He resembled a long, broad-headed nail, for his head was large and thick, his forehead high, his nose prominent, his mouth wide, and his chin blunt. As for his eyes, they were hidden behind enormous eye-glasses, and his look seemed to have that indecision peculiar to nyctalops. His countenance indicated an intelligent and lively person, while it had not the crabbed air of those stern people who from principle never laugh, and whose stupidity is hidden beneath a serious guise. The nonchalance and amiable freedom of this unknown nonentity clearly proved that he knew how to take men and things at their best advantage. Even without his speaking you felt that he was a talker; but he was abstracted, after the manner of those who do not see what they are looking at or hear what they are listening to. He wore a traveling cap, stout yellow buskins and leather gaiters, pantaloons of maroon velvet, and a jacket of the same material, whose innumerable pockets seemed stuffed with note-books, memoranda, scraps, portfolios, and a thousand articles as inconvenient as they were useless, not to speak of a telescope which he carried in a sling.

The curiosity of this unknown being was a singular contrast to the calmness of the major. He walked around MacNabb, and gazed at him questioningly, whilst the latter did not trouble himself whence the stranger came, whither he was going, or why he was on board the Duncan.

When this enigmatical character saw his approaches mocked by the indifference of the major, he seized his telescope, which at its full length measured four feet; and motionless, with legs straddled, like a sign-post on a highway, he pointed his instrument to the line where sky and water met. After a few moments of examination, he lowered it, and resting it on the deck, leaned upon it as upon a cane. But immediately the joints of the instrument closed, and the newly discovered passenger, whose point of support suddenly failed, was stretched at the foot of the mainmast.

Any one else in the major's place would at least have smiled, but he did not even wink. The unknown then assumed his rôle.

"Steward!" he cried, with an accent that betokened a foreigner.

He waited. No one appeared.

"Steward!" he repeated, in a louder tone.

Mr. Olbinett was passing just then on his way to the kitchen under the forecastle. What was his astonishment to hear himself thus addressed by this tall individual, who was utterly unknown to him!

"Where did this person come from?" said he to himself. "A friend of Lord Glenarvan? It is impossible."

However, he came on deck, and approached the stranger.

"Are you the steward of the vessel?" the latter asked him.

"Yes, sir," replied Olbinett; "but I have not the honor——"

"I am the passenger of cabin number six."

"Number six?" repeated the steward.

"Certainly; and your name is——?"

"Olbinett."

"Well, Olbinett, my friend," answered the stranger of cabin number six, "I must think of dinner, and acutely, too. For thirty-six hours I have eaten nothing, or, rather, have slept, which is pardonable in a man come all the way from Paris to Glasgow. What hour do you dine, if you please?"

"At nine o'clock," answered Olbinett, mechanically.

The stranger attempted to consult his watch; but this took some time, for he did not find it till he came to his ninth pocket.

CONFUSION WORSE CONFOUNDED.

"Well," said he, "it is not yet eight o'clock; therefore, Olbinett, a biscuit and a glass of sherry for the present; for I am fainting with hunger."

Olbinett listened without understanding. Moreover, the unknown kept talking, and passed from one subject to another with extreme volubility.

"Well," said he, "has not the captain risen yet? And the mate? What is he doing? Is he asleep, too? Fortunately, the weather is beautiful, the wind favorable, and the ship goes on quite by herself——"

Just as he said this, Captain Mangles appeared at the companion-way.

"Here is the captain," said Olbinett.

"Ah, I am delighted," cried the stranger, "delighted to make your acquaintance, Captain Burton!"

If any one was ever astounded, John Mangles certainly was, not less at hearing himself called "Captain Burton," than at seeing this stranger on board his vessel.

The latter continued, with more animation:

"Permit me to shake hands with you, and if I did not do so day before yesterday, it was that no one might be embarrassed at the moment of departure. But to-day, captain, I am truly happy to meet you."

Captain Mangles opened his eyes in measureless astonishment, looking first at Olbinett, and then at the new comer.

"Now," continued the latter, "the introduction is over, and we are old friends. Let us have a talk; and tell me, are you satisfied with the Scotia?"

"What do you mean by the Scotia?" asked the captain, at last.

"Why, the Scotia that carries us: a good ship, whose commander, the brave Captain Burton, I have heard praised no less for his physical than his moral qualities. Are you the father of the great African traveler of that name? If so, my compliments!"

"Sir," replied Captain Mangles, "not only am I not the father of the traveler Burton, but I am not even Captain Burton."

"Ah!" said the unknown, "it is the mate of the Scotia then, Mr. Burdness, whom I am addressing at this moment?"

"Mr. Burdness?" replied Captain Mangles, who began to suspect the truth. But was he talking to a fool, or a rogue? This was a question in his mind, and he was about to explain himself intelligibly, when Lord Glenarvan, his wife, and Miss Grant came on deck.

The stranger perceived them, and cried,—

"Ah! passengers! passengers! excellent! I hope, Mr. Burdness, you are going to introduce me——"

And advancing with perfect ease, without waiting for the captain,—

"Madam" said he to Miss Grant, "Miss" to Lady Helena, "Sir" he added, addressing Lord Glenarvan.

"Lord Glenarvan," said Captain Mangles.

"My lord," continued the unknown, "I beg your pardon for introducing myself, but at sea we must relax a little from etiquette. I hope we shall soon be acquainted, and that, in the society of these ladies, the passage of the Scotia will seem as short to us as agreeable."

Lady Helena and Miss Grant could not find a word to answer. They were completely bewildered by the presence of this intruder.

"Sir," said Glenarvan, at length, "whom have I the honor of addressing?"

"Jacques Eliacim François Marie Paganel, secretary of the Geographical Society of Paris; corresponding member of the societies of Berlin, Bombay, Darmstadt, Leipsic, London, St. Petersburg, Vienna, and New York; honorary member of the Royal Geographical and Ethnographical Institute of the East Indies, who, after passing twenty years of his life in studying geography, designs now to enter upon a roving life, and is directing his course to India to continue there the labors of the great travelers."

CHAPTER VII

JACQUES PAGANEL IS UNDECEIVED.

The secretary of the Geographical Society must have been an agreeable person, for all this was said with much modesty. Lord Glenarvan, moreover, knew perfectly whom he had met. The name and merit of Jacques Paganel were well known to him. His geographical labors, his reports on modern discoveries, published in the bulletins of the Society, his correspondence with the entire world, had made him one of the most distinguished scientific men of France. Thus Glenarvan extended his hand very cordially to his unexpected guest.

"And now that our introduction is over," added he, "will you permit me, Monsieur Paganel, to ask you a question?"

"Twenty, my lord," replied Jacques Paganel; "it will always be a pleasure to converse with you."

"You arrived on board this vessel the day before yesterday?"

"Yes, my lord, day before yesterday, at eight o'clock in the evening. I took a cab from the Caledonian Railway to the Scotia, in which I had engaged cabin number six at Paris. The night was dark. I saw no one on board. Feeling fatigued by thirty hours of travel, and knowing that a good way to avoid sea-sickness is to go to bed on embarking, and not stir from your bunk for the first days of the voyage, I retired immediately, and have conscientiously slept thirty-six hours, I assure you."

Jacques Paganel's hearers now knew the reason of his presence on board. The Frenchman, mistaking the vessel, had embarked while the crew of the Duncan were engaged in the ceremony at Saint Mungo. Everything was explained. But what would the geographer say, when he learned the name and destination of the vessel on which he had taken passage?

"So, Monsieur Paganel," said Glenarvan, "you have chosen Calcutta as your centre of action?"

"Yes, my lord. To see India is an idea that I have cherished all my life. It is my brightest dream, which shall be realized at last in the country of the elephants and the Thugs."

"Then you would not care to visit another country?"

"No, my lord; it would be even disagreeable, for I have letters from Lord Somerset to the governor-general of India, and a mission from the Geographical Society which I must fulfil."

"Ah! you have a mission?"

"Yes, a useful and curious voyage to undertake, the programme of which has been arranged by my scientific friend and colleague, M. Vivien de Saint Martin. It is to follow in the steps of the brothers Schlagintweit, and many other celebrated travelers. I hope to succeed where Missionary Krick unfortunately failed in 1846. In a word, I wish to discover the course of the Yaroo-tsang-bo-tsoo, which waters Thibet, and finally to settle whether this river does not join the Brahmapootra in the northeast part of Assam. A gold medal is promised to that traveler who shall succeed in supplying this much-needed information on Indian geography."

Paganel was grandiloquent. He spoke with a lofty animation, and was carried away in the rapid flight of imagination.

Paganel was grandiloquent. He spoke with a lofty animation, and was carried away in the rapid flight of imagination. It would have been as impossible to check him as to stay the Rhine at the Falls of Schaffhausen.

"Monsieur Jacques Paganel," said Lord Glenarvan, after a moment of silence, "that is certainly a fine voyage, and one for which science would be very grateful; but I will not further prolong your ignorance. For the present, you must give up the pleasure of seeing India."

"Give it up! And why?"

"Because you are turning your back upon the Indian peninsula."

"How? Captain Burton——"

"I am not Captain Burton," replied John Mangles.

"But the Scotia?"

"This vessel is not the Scotia."

Paganel's amazement cannot be depicted. He looked first at Lord Glenarvan, always serious; then at Lady Helena and Miss Grant, whose features expressed a sympathetic disappointment; and finally at Captain Mangles, who was smiling, and the imperturbable major. Then, raising his shoulders and drawing down his glasses from his forehead to his eyes, he exclaimed,—

"What a joke!"

But at that his eyes fell upon the steering wheel, on which were inscribed these two words, thus:

"The Duncan! the Duncan!" he cried in a tone of real despair; and, leaping down the companion-way, he rushed to his cabin.

When the unfortunate geographer had disappeared, no one on board, except the major, could retain gravity, and the laugh was communicated even to the sailors. To mistake the railroad was not so bad; to take the train to Dumbarton, instead of Edinburgh, would do. But to mistake the vessel, and be sailing to Chili, when he wished to go to India, was the height of absent-mindedness.

ABSENT-MINDEDNESS.

"On the whole, I am not astonished at this on the part of Jacques Paganel," said Glenarvan; "he is noted for such blunders. He once published a celebrated map of America, in which he located Japan. However, he is a distinguished scholar, and one of the best geographers of France."

"But what are we going to do with the poor gentleman?" asked Lady Helena. "We cannot take him to Patagonia."

"Why not?" replied MacNabb gravely. "We are not responsible for his errors. Suppose he were in a railroad car, would it stop for him?"

"No; but he could get out at the first station," answered Lady Helena.

"Well," said Glenarvan, "he can do so now, if he pleases, at our first landing."

At this moment Paganel, woeful and humble, reappeared on deck, after convincing himself that his baggage was on board. He kept repeating those fatal words: "The Duncan! the Duncan!" He could find no others in his vocabulary. He went to and fro, examining the rigging of the yacht, and questioning the mute horizon of the open sea. At last he returned to Lord Glenarvan.

"And this Duncan is going———?" he asked.

"To America, Monsieur Paganel."

"And where especially?"

"To Concepcion."

"To Chili! to Chili!" cried the unfortunate geographer. "And my mission to India! But what will M. de Quatrefages say, the President of the Central Commission? How shall I represent myself at the sessions of the Society?"

COURTESY AND CONVERSE.

"Come, monsieur," said Glenarvan, "do not despair. Everything can be arranged, and you will only have to submit to a delay of little consequence. The Yaroo-tsang-bo-tsoo will wait for you in the mountains of Thibet. We shall soon reach Madeira, and there you will find a vessel to take you back to Europe."

"I thank you, my lord, and must be resigned. But we can say this is an extraordinary adventure, which would not have happened but for me. And my cabin which is engaged on board the Scotia?"

"Oh, as for the Scotia, I advise you to give her up for the present."

"But," said Paganel after examining the vessel again, "the Duncan is a pleasure yacht."

"Yes, sir," replied Captain Mangles, "and belongs to his lordship, Lord Glenarvan——"

"Who begs you to make free use of his hospitality," said Glenarvan.

"A thousand thanks, my lord," replied Paganel; "I am truly sensible to your courtesy. But permit me to make a simple remark. India is a beautiful country. It offers marvelous surprises to travelers. These ladies have probably never visited it. Well, the man at the helm needs only to give a turn to the wheel, and the Duncan will go as easily to Calcutta as Concepcion. Now, since this is a pleasure voyage——"

The negative reception that met Paganel's proposal did not permit him to develop it. He paused.

"Monsieur Paganel," said Lady Helena at length, "if this were only a pleasure voyage, I would answer: 'Let us all go to India,' and Lord Glenarvan would not disapprove. But the Duncan is going to recover some shipwrecked sailors, abandoned on the coast of Patagonia; and she cannot change so humane a course."

In a few moments the Frenchman was acquainted with the situation of affairs, and learned, not without emotion, the providential discovery of the documents, the story of Captain Grant, and Lady Helena's generous proposal.

"Madam," said he, "permit me to admire your conduct in all this, and to admire it without reserve. May your yacht continue on her course; I would reproach myself for delaying her a single day."

"Will you then join in our search?" asked Lady Helena.

"It is impossible, madam; I must fulfil my mission. I shall disembark at your first landing."

"At Madeira then," said Captain Mangles.

"At Madeira let it be. I shall be only one hundred and eighty leagues from Lisbon, and will wait there for means of further conveyance."

"Well, Monsieur Paganel," said Glenarvan, "it shall be as you desire; and, for my part, I am happy that I can offer you for a few days the hospitalities of my vessel. May you not grow weary of our company."

"Oh, my lord," exclaimed the geographer, "I am still too happy in being so agreeably disappointed. However, it is a very ludicrous situation for a man who takes passage for India, and is sailing to America."

In spite of this mortifying reflection, Paganel made the best use of a delay that he could not avoid. He showed himself amiable, and even gay; he enchanted the ladies with his good humor, and before the end of the day he was the friend of every one. At his request the famous document was shown to him. He studied it carefully, long and minutely. No other interpretation appeared to him possible. Mary Grant and her brother inspired him with the liveliest interest. He gave them good hopes. His way of distinguishing the events, and the undeniable success that he predicted for the Duncan, elicited a smile from the young girl.

THIS, OR THAT, OR NEITHER.

As to Lady Helena, when he learned that she was the daughter of William Tuffnel, there was an outburst of surprise and admiration. He had known her father. What a bold discoverer! How many letters they had exchanged when the latter was corresponding member of the Society! He it was who had introduced him to M. Malte-Brun. What a meeting! and how much pleasure to travel with the daughter of such a man! Finally, he asked Lady Helena's permission to kiss her, to which she consented, although it was perhaps a little "improper."

CHAPTER VIII

THE GEOGRAPHER'S RESOLUTION.

Meanwhile the yacht, favored by the currents, was advancing rapidly towards the equator. In a few days the island of Madeira came in view. Glenarvan, faithful to his promise, offered to land his new guest here.

"My dear lord," replied Paganel, "I will not be formal with you. Before my arrival on board, did you intend to stop at Madeira?"

"No," said Glenarvan.

"Well, permit me to profit by the consequences of my unlucky blunder. Madeira is an island too well known. Everything has been said and written about it; and it is, moreover, rapidly declining in point of civilization. If, then, it is all the same to you, let us land at the Canaries."

"Very well, at the Canaries," replied Glenarvan. "That will not take us out of our way."

"I know it, my dear lord. At the Canaries, you see, there are three groups to study, not to speak of the Peak of Teneriffe, which I have always desired to see. This is a fine opportunity. I will profit by it; and, while waiting for a vessel, will attempt the ascent of this celebrated mountain."

"As you please, my dear Paganel," replied Glenarvan, who could not help smiling, and with good reason.

The Canaries are only a short distance from Madeira, scarcely two hundred and fifty miles, a mere trifle for so good a vessel as the Duncan.

The same day, at two o'clock in the afternoon, Captain Mangles and Paganel were walking on the deck. The Frenchman pressed his companion with lively questions concerning Chili. All at once the captain interrupted him, and pointing towards the southern horizon, said,—

"Mr. Paganel!"

"My dear captain," replied the geographer.

"Please cast your eyes in that direction. Do you see nothing?"

"Nothing."

"You are not looking right. It is not on the horizon, but above, in the clouds."

"In the clouds? I look in vain."

"Stop, now, just on a line with the end of the bowsprit."

"I see nothing."

"You do not wish to see. However that may be, although we are forty miles distant, you understand, the Peak of Teneriffe is visible above the horizon."

Whether Paganel wished to see or not, he had to yield to the evidence some hours afterwards, or, at least, confess himself blind.

"You perceive it now?" said his companion.

"Yes, yes, perfectly!" replied Paganel. "And that," added he in a contemptuous tone, "is what you call the Peak of Teneriffe?"

"The same."

"It appears to be of very moderate height."

"Yet it is eleven thousand feet above the level of the sea."

"Not so high as Mont Blanc."

"Very possibly; but when you come to climb it, you will find it, perhaps, high enough."

"Oh! climb it, my dear captain? What is the use, I ask you, after Humboldt and Bonpland? What can I do after these great men?"

"Indeed," replied Captain Mangles, "there is nothing left but to wander about. It is a pity, for you would be very tired waiting for a vessel at Teneriffe. You cannot look for many distractions there."

"Except my own," said Paganel, laughing. "But, my dear captain, have not the Cape Verd Islands important landings?"

"Certainly. Nothing is easier than to land at Villa-Praïa."

"Not to speak of an advantage that is not to be despised," answered Paganel; "that the Cape Verd Islands are not far from Senegal, where I shall find fellow-countrymen."

"As you please, Mr. Paganel," replied Captain Mangles. "I am certain that geographical science will gain by your sojourn in these islands. We must land there to take in coal; you will, therefore, cause us no delay."

They could scarcely see the city, which was on an elevated plain in the form of a terrace, resting on volcanic rocks three hundred feet in height. The appearance of the island through this rainy curtain was misty.

Peak of Teneriffe.

DECLINED, WITH THANKS.

So saying, the captain gave the order to pass to the southeast of the Canaries. The celebrated peak was soon left on the larboard; and the Duncan, continuing her rapid course, cut the Tropic of Cancer the next morning at five o'clock. The weather there changed. The atmosphere had the moisture and oppressiveness of the rainy season, disagreeable to travelers, but beneficial to the inhabitants of the African islands, who have no trees, and consequently need water. The sea was boisterous, and prevented the passengers from remaining on deck; but the conversation in the cabin was not less animated.

The next day Paganel began to collect his baggage preparatory to his approaching departure. In a short time they entered the bay of Villa-Praïa, and anchored opposite the city in eight fathoms of water. The weather was stormy and the surf high, although the bay was sheltered from the winds. The rain fell in torrents so that they could scarcely see the city, which was on an elevated plain in the form of a terrace, resting on volcanic rocks three hundred feet in height. The appearance of the island through this rainy curtain was misty.

Shipping the coal was not accomplished without great difficulty, and the passengers saw themselves confined to the cabin, while sea and sky mingled their waters in an indescribable tumult. The weather was, therefore, the topic of conversation on board. Each one had his say except the major, who would have witnessed the deluge itself with perfect indifference. Paganel walked to and fro, shaking his head.

"It is an imperative fact," said he.

"It is certain," replied Glenarvan, "that the elements declare themselves against you."

"I will see about that."

"You cannot face such a storm," said Lady Helena.

"I, madam? Certainly. I fear only for my baggage and instruments. They will all be lost."

"Our landing is the only thing doubtful," resumed Glenarvan. "Once at Villa-Praïa, you will not have very uncomfortable quarters; rather uncleanly, to be sure, in the company of monkeys and swine, whose surroundings are not always agreeable; but a traveler does not regard that so critically. Besides, you can hope in seven or eight months to embark for Europe."

"Seven or eight months!" exclaimed Paganel.

"At least that. The Cape Verd Islands are very rarely frequented during the rainy season. But you can employ your time profitably. This archipelago is still little known. There is much to do, even now."

"But," replied Paganel in a pitiful tone, "what could I do after the investigations of the geologist Deville?"

"That is really a pity," said Lady Helena. "What will become of you, Monsieur Paganel?"

Paganel was silent for a few moments.

"You had decidedly better have landed at Madeira," rejoined Glenarvan, "although there is no wine there."

"My dear Glenarvan," continued Paganel at last, "where shall you land next?"

"At Concepcion."

"Alas! but that would bring me directly away from India!"

"No; for when you have passed Cape Horn you approach the Indies."

"I very much doubt it."

"Besides," continued Glenarvan with the greatest gravity, "as long as you are at the Indies, what difference does it make whether they are the East or the West?"

"'What difference does it make'?"

"The inhabitants of the Pampas of Patagonia are Indians as well as the natives of the Punjab."

"Eh! my lord," exclaimed Paganel, "that is a reason I should never have imagined!"

BAIT FOR A TRAVELLER.

"And then, my dear Paganel, you know that you can gain the gold medal in any country whatever. There is something to do, to seek, to discover, everywhere, in the chains of the Cordilleras as well as the mountains of Thibet."

"But the course of the Yaroo-tsang-bo-tsoo?"

"Certainly. You can replace that by the Rio Colorado. This is a river very little known, and one of those which flow on the map too much according to the fancy of the geographer."

"I know it, my dear lord; there are errors of several degrees. I do not doubt that at my request the Society would have sent me to Patagonia as well as to India; but I did not think of it."

"The result of your continual abstraction."

"Well, Monsieur Paganel, shall you accompany us?" asked Lady Helena in her most persuasive tone.

"And my mission, madam?"

"I inform you that we shall pass through the Strait of Magellan," continued Glenarvan.

"My lord, you are a tempter."

"I add that we shall visit Port Famine."

"Port Famine!" cried the Frenchman, assailed on all sides; "that port so celebrated in geographical fasts!"

"Consider also, Monsieur Paganel," continued Lady Helena, "that in this enterprise you will have the right to associate the name of France with that of Scotland."

"Yes; doubtless."

"A geographer may be very serviceable to our expedition; and what is more noble than for science to enlist in the service of humanity?"

"That is well said, madam."

"Believe me, try chance, or rather Providence. Imitate us. It has sent us this document; we have started. It has cast you on board the Duncan; do not leave her."

"And do you, indeed, wish me, my good friends?" replied Paganel. "Well, you desire me to stay very much?"

"And you, Paganel, you are dying to stay," retorted Glenarvan.

"Truly," cried the geographer, "but I fear I am very indiscreet."

Thus far the Duncan had acquitted herself admirably: in every way her powers for steaming or sailing had been sufficiently tested, and her captain and passengers were alike satisfied with her performance and with one another.

CHAPTER IX

THROUGH THE STRAIT OF MAGELLAN.

The joy on board was general, when Paganel's resolution was known. Young Robert threw himself on his neck with very demonstrative delight. The worthy geographer almost fell backwards. "A rough little gentleman," said he; "I will teach him geography." As Captain Mangles had engaged to make him a sailor, Glenarvan a man of honor, the major a boy of coolness, Lady Helena a noble and generous being, and Mary Grant a pupil grateful towards such patrons, Robert was evidently to become one day an accomplished gentleman.

The Duncan soon finished shipping her coal, and then leaving these gloomy regions she gained the current from the southeast coast of Brazil, and, after crossing the equator with a fine breeze from the north, she entered the southern hemisphere. The passage was effected without difficulty, and every one had good hopes. On this voyage in search of Captain Grant, the probabilities increased every day. Their captain was one of the most confident on board; but his confidence proceeded especially from the desire that he cherished so strongly at heart, of seeing Miss Mary happy and consoled. He was particularly interested in this young girl; and this feeling he concealed so well, that, except Miss Grant and himself, no one on board the Duncan had perceived it.

As for the learned geographer, he was probably the happiest man in the southern hemisphere. He passed his time in studying the maps with which he covered the cabin-table; and then followed daily discussions with Mr. Olbinett, so that he could scarcely set the table.

But Paganel had all the passengers on his side except the major, who was very indifferent to geographical questions, especially at dinner-time. Having discovered a whole cargo of odd books in the mate's chests, and among them a number of Cervantes' works, the Frenchman resolved to learn Spanish, which nobody on board knew, and which would facilitate his search on the shores of Chili. Thanks to his love for philology, he did not despair of speaking this new tongue fluently on arriving at Concepcion. He therefore studied assiduously, and was heard incessantly muttering heterogeneous syllables. During his leisure hours he did not fail to give young Robert practical instruction, and taught him the history of the country they were rapidly approaching.

In the meantime the Duncan was proceeding at a remarkable rate. She cut the Tropic of Capricorn, and her prow was headed toward the strait of the celebrated geographer. Now and then the low shores of Patagonia were seen, but like an almost invisible line on the horizon. They sailed along the coast for more than ten miles, but Paganel's famous telescope gave him only a vague idea of these American shores.

The vessel soon found herself at the head of the strait, and entered without hesitation. This way is generally preferred by steam-vessels bound for the Pacific. Its exact length is three hundred and seventy-six miles. Ships of the greatest tonnage can always find deep water, even near its shores, an excellent bottom, and many springs of water. The rivers abound in fish, the forest in game, there are safe and easy landings at twenty places, and, in short, a thousand resources that are wanting in the Strait of Lemaire, and off the terrible rocks of Cape Horn, which are continually visited by storms and tempests.

Sometimes the tips of her yards would graze the branches of the beeches that hung over the waves.

During the first hours of the passage, till you reach Cape Gregory, the shores are low and sandy. The entire passage lasted scarcely thirty-six hours, and this moving panorama of the two shores well rewarded the pains the geographer took to admire it under the radiant beams of the southern sun. No inhabitant appeared on the shores of the continent; and only a few Fuegians wandered along the barren rocks of Terra del Fuego.

At one moment the Duncan rounded the peninsula of Brunswick between two magnificent sights. Just here the strait cuts between stupendous masses of granite. The base of the mountains was hidden in the heart of immense forests, while their summits, whitened with eternal snow, were lost in the clouds. Towards the southeast Mount Taru towered six thousand five hundred feet aloft. Night came, preceded by a long twilight, the light melting away insensibly by gentle degrees, while the sky was studded with brilliant stars.

In the midst of this partial obscurity, the yacht boldly continued on her course, without casting anchor in the safe bays with which the shores abound. Sometimes the tips of her yards would graze the branches of the beeches that hung over the waves. At others her propeller would beat the waters of the great rivers, starting geese, ducks, snipe, teal, and all the feathered tribes of the marshes. Soon deserted ruins appeared, and fallen monuments, to which the night lent a grand aspect; these were the mournful remains of an abandoned colony, whose name will be an eternal contradiction to the fertility of the coasts and the rich game of the forests. It was Port Famine, the place that the Spaniard Sarmiento colonized in 1581 with four hundred emigrants. Here he founded the city of San Felipe. But the extreme severity of the cold weakened the colony; famine devoured those whom the winter had spared, and in 1587 the explorer Cavendish found the last of these four hundred unfortunates dying of hunger amid the ruins of a city only six years in existence.

CHEERLESS MEMORIES.

The vessel coasted along these deserted shores. At daybreak she sailed in the midst of the narrow passes, between beeches, ash-trees, and birches, from the bosom of which emerged ivy-clad domes, cupolas tapestried with the hardy holly, and lofty spires, among which the obelisk of Buckland rose to a great height. Far out in the sea sported droves of seals and whales of great size, judging by their spouting, which could be seen at a distance of four miles. At last they doubled Cape Froward, still bristling with the ices of winter. On the other side of the strait, on Terra del Fuego, rose Mount Sarmiento to the height of six thousand feet, an enormous mass of rock broken by bands of clouds which formed as it were an aerial archipelago in the sky.

Port Famine.

Cape Froward is the real end of the American continent, for Cape Horn is only a lone rock in the sea. Passing this point the strait narrowed between Brunswick Peninsula, and Desolation Island. Then to fertile shores succeeded a line of wild barren coast, cut by a thousand inlets of this tortuous labyrinth.

The Duncan unerringly and unhesitatingly pursued its capricious windings, mingling her columns of smoke with the mists on the rocks. Without lessening her speed, she passed several Spanish factories established on these deserted shores. At Cape Tamar the strait widened. The yacht rounded the Narborough Islands, and approached the southern shores. At last, thirty-six hours after entering the strait, the rocks of Cape Pilares were discerned at the extreme point of Desolation Island. An immense open glittering sea extended before her prow, and Jacques Paganel, hailing it with an enthusiastic gesture, felt moved like Ferdinand Magellan himself, when the sails of the Trinidad swelled before the breezes of the Pacific.

CHAPTER X

THE COURSE DECIDED.

Eight days after doubling Cape Pilares the Duncan entered at full speed the Bay of Talcahuana, a magnificent estuary, twelve miles long and nine broad. The weather was beautiful. Not a cloud is seen in the sky of this country from November to March, and the wind from the south blows continually along these coasts, which are protected by the chain of the Andes.

Captain Mangles, according to Lord Glenarvan's orders, had kept close to the shore of the continent, examining the numerous wrecks that lined it. A waif, a broken spar, a piece of wood fashioned by the hand of man, might guide the Duncan to the scene of the shipwreck. But nothing was seen, and the yacht continued her course and anchored in the harbor of Talcahuana forty-two days after her departure from the waters of the Clyde.

LEARNING SPANISH!

Glenarvan at once lowered the boat, and, followed by Paganel, landed at the foot of the palisade. The learned geographer, profiting by the circumstance, would have made use of the language which he had studied so conscientiously; but, to his great astonishment, he could not make himself understood by the natives.

"The accent is what I need," said he.

"Let us go to the Custom-house," replied Glenarvan.

There they were informed by means of several English words, accompanied by expressive gestures, that the British consul resided at Concepcion. It was only an hour's journey. Glenarvan easily found two good horses, and, a short time after, Paganel and he entered the walls of this great city, which was built by the enterprising genius of Valdivia, the valiant companion of Pizarro.

How greatly it had declined from its ancient splendor! Often pillaged by the natives, burnt in 1819, desolate, ruined, its walls still blackened with the flames of devastation, eclipsed by Talcahuana, it now scarcely numbered eight thousand souls. Under the feet of its idle inhabitants the streets had grown into prairies. There was no commerce, no activity, no business. The mandolin resounded from every balcony, languishing songs issued from the lattices of the windows, and Concepcion, the ancient city of men, had become a village of women and children.

Glenarvan appeared little desirous of seeking the causes of this decline—though Jacques Paganel attacked him on this subject—and, without losing an instant, betook himself to the house of J. R. Bentock, Esq., consul of Her Britannic Majesty. This individual received him very courteously, and when he learned the story of Captain Grant undertook to search along the entire coast.

The question whether the Britannia had been wrecked on the shores of Chili or Araucania was decided in the negative. No report of such an event had come either to the consul, or his colleagues in other parts of the country.

But Glenarvan was not discouraged. He returned to Talcahuana, and, sparing neither fatigue, trouble, or money, he sent men to the coast, but their search was in vain. The most minute inquiries among the people of the vicinity were of no avail. They were forced to conclude that the Britannia had left no trace of her shipwreck.

In Concepcion.

"TRY AGAIN!"

Glenarvan then informed his companions of the failure of his endeavors. Mary Grant and her brother could not restrain their grief. It was now six days since the arrival of the Duncan at Talcahuana. The passengers were together in the cabin. Lady Helena was consoling, not by her words—for what could she say?—but by her caresses, the two children of the captain. Jacques Paganel had taken up the document again, and was regarding it with earnest attention, as if he would have drawn from it new secrets. For an hour he had examined it thus, when Glenarvan, addressing him, said,—

"Paganel, I appeal to your sagacity. Is the interpretation we have made of this document incorrect? Is the sense of these words illogical?"

Paganel did not answer. He was reflecting.

"Are we mistaken as to the supposed scene of the shipwreck?" continued Glenarvan. "Does not the name Patagonia suggest itself at once to the mind?"

Paganel was still silent.

"In short," said Glenarvan, "does not the word *Indian* justify us still more?"

"Perfectly," replied MacNabb.

"And therefore, is it not evident that these shipwrecked men, when they wrote these lines, expected to be prisoners of the Indians?"

"There you are wrong, my dear lord," said Paganel, at last; "and if your other conclusions are just, the last at least does not seem to me rational."

"What do you mean?" asked Lady Helena, while all eyes were turned towards the geographer.

"I mean," answered Paganel, emphasizing his words, "that Captain Grant is *now prisoner of the Indians*: and I will add that the document leaves no doubt on this point."

"Explain yourself, sir," said Miss Grant.

"Nothing is easier, my dear Mary. Instead of reading *they will be prisoners*, read *they are prisoners*, and all will be clear."

"But that is impossible," replied Glenarvan.

"Impossible? And why, my noble friend?" asked Paganel, smiling.

"Because the bottle must have been thrown when the vessel was breaking on the rocks. Hence the degrees of longitude and latitude apply to the very place of shipwreck."

"Nothing proves it," said Paganel, earnestly; "and I do not see why the shipwrecked sailors, after being carried by the Indians into the interior of the country, could not have sought to make known by means of this bottle the place of their captivity."

"Simply, my dear Paganel, because to throw a bottle into the sea it is necessary, at least, that the sea should be before you."

"Or, in the absence of the sea," added Paganel, "the rivers which flow into it."

An astonished silence followed this unexpected, yet reasonable, answer. By the flash that brightened the eyes of his hearers Paganel knew that each of them had conceived a new hope. Lady Helena was the first to resume the conversation.

"What an idea!" she exclaimed.

"What a *good* idea!" added the geographer, simply.

"Your advice then?" asked Glenarvan.

"My advice is to find the thirty-seventh parallel, just where it meets the American coast, and follow it, without deviating half a degree, to the point where it strikes the Atlantic. Perhaps we shall find on its course the survivors of the Britannia."

"A feeble chance," replied the major.

"However feeble it may be," continued Paganel, "we ought not to neglect it. If I am right that this bottle reached the sea by following the current of a river, we cannot fail to come upon the traces of the prisoners. Look, my friends, look at the map of this country, and I will convince you beyond a doubt."

NIL DESPERANDUM!

So saying, Paganel spread out before them upon the table a large map of Chili and the Argentine Provinces. "Look," said he, "and follow me in this passage across the American continent. Let us pass over the narrow strip of Chili and the Cordilleras of the Andes, and descend into the midst of the Pampas. Are rivers, streams, water-courses, wanting in these regions? No. Here are the Rio Negro, the Rio Colorado, and their affluents, cut by the thirty-seventh parallel, all of which might have served to transport the document. There, perhaps, in the midst of a tribe, in the hands of settled Indians, on the shores of these unknown rivers, in the gorges of the sierras, those whom I have the right to call our friends are awaiting an interposition of Providence. Ought we, then, to disappoint their hopes? Do you not think we should follow across these countries an unswerving course? And if, contrary to all expectation, I am still mistaken, is it not our duty to trace this parallel to the very end, and, if necessary, make upon it the tour of the world?"

These words, spoken with a noble enthusiasm, excited a deep emotion among Paganel's hearers. All rose to shake hands with him.

"Yes, my father is there!" cried Robert Grant, devouring the map with his eyes.

"And wherever he is," replied Glenarvan, "we shall find him, my child. Nothing is more consistent than our friend Paganel's interpretation, and we must follow without hesitation the course he has indicated. Either Captain Grant is in the hands of countless Indians, or is prisoner in a feeble tribe. In the latter case, we will rescue him. In the former, after ascertaining his situation, we will join the Duncan on the eastern coast, sail to Buenos Ayres, and with a detachment, organized by the major, can overcome all the Indians of the Argentine Plains."

"Yes, yes, your lordship," answered Captain Mangles; "and I will add that this passage of the continent will be without peril."

"Without peril, or fatigue," continued Paganel. "How many have already accomplished it who had scarcely our means for success, and whose courage was not sustained by the grandeur of the undertaking!"

"Sir, sir," exclaimed Mary Grant, in a voice broken with emotion, "how can I thank a devotion that exposes you to so many dangers?"

"Dangers!" cried Paganel. "Who uttered the word *danger*?"

"Not I!" replied Robert Grant, with flashing eye and determined look.

"Danger!" repeated Paganel; "does such a thing exist? Moreover, what is the question? A journey of scarcely three hundred and fifty leagues, since we shall proceed in a straight line; a journey which will be accomplished in a favorable latitude and climate; in short, a journey whose duration will be only a month at most. It is a mere walk."

"Monsieur Paganel," asked Lady Helena at last, "do you think that, if the shipwrecked sailors have fallen into the power of the Indians, their lives have been spared?"

"Certainly I do, madam. The Indians are not cannibals; far from that, one of my countrymen whom I knew in the Society was three years prisoner among the Indians of the Pampas. He suffered, was ill-treated, but at last gained the victory in this trying ordeal. A European is a useful person in these countries. The Indians know his value, and esteem him very highly."

"Well then, there is no more hesitation," said Glenarvan; "we must start, and that, too, without delay. What course shall we take?"

"An easy and agreeable one," replied Paganel. "A few mountains to begin with; then a gentle descent on the eastern slope of the Andes; and at last a level, grassy, sandy plain, a real garden."

"Let us see the map," said the major.

"Here it is, my dear MacNabb. We shall begin at the end of the thirty-seventh parallel on the coast of Chili. After passing through the capital of Araucania, we shall strike the Cordilleras, and descending their steep declivities across the Rio Colorado, we shall reach the Pampas. Passing the frontiers of Buenos Ayres, we shall continue our search until we reach the shores of the Atlantic."

A STROLL ACROSS THE COUNTRY.

Thus speaking and developing the programme of the expedition, Paganel did not even take the trouble to look at the map spread before him. And he had no need to; educated in the schools of Frézier, Molina, Humboldt, and Miers, his unerring memory could neither be deceived nor baffled. After finishing his plan, he added:

"Therefore, my dear friends, the course is straight. In thirty days we shall accomplish it, and arrive before the Duncan on the eastern shore, since the westerly winds will delay her progress."

"The Duncan then," said Captain Mangles, "will cross the thirty-seventh parallel between Cape Corrientes and Cape St. Antonio?"

"Exactly."

"And whom would you constitute the members of such an expedition?" asked Glenarvan.

"The fewer the better. The only point is to ascertain the situation of Captain Grant, and not to engage in combat with the Indians. I think that Lord Glenarvan, as our chief, the major, who would yield his place to no one, your servant Jacques Paganel——"

"And I!" cried Robert Grant.

"Robert?" said Mary.

"And why not?" answered Paganel. "Travels develop youth. We four, then, and three sailors of the Duncan——"

"What," exclaimed Captain Mangles, "your lordship does not intercede for me?"

"My dear fellow," replied Glenarvan, "we shall leave the ladies on board, the dearest objects we have in the world. Who would watch over them, if not the devoted captain of the Duncan?"

"We cannot accompany you, then," said Lady Helena, whose eyes were dimmed by a mist of sadness.

"My dear wife," replied Glenarvan, "our journey will be performed with unusual rapidity, our separation will be short, and——"

GOOD AFTERNOON!

"Yes, yes; I understand you," answered Lady Helena. "Go, then, and may you succeed in your enterprise."

"Besides, this is not a journey," added Paganel.

"What is it, then?" asked Lady Helena.

"A passage, nothing more. We shall pass, that is all, like honest men, over the country and do all the good possible. '*Transire benefaciendo*' is our motto."

The mate, Tom Austin, Wilson, a powerful fellow, and Mulready, were the fortunate ones.

With these words the discussion ended. The preparations were begun that very day, and it was resolved to keep the expedition secret, in order not to alarm the Indians. The 14th of October was fixed for the day of departure.

When they came to choose the sailors who were to go, they all offered their services, and Glenarvan was forced to make a choice. He preferred to have them draw lots, that he might not mortify such brave men. This was accordingly done; and the mate, Tom

Austin, Wilson, a powerful fellow, and Mulready, were the fortunate ones.

Lord Glenarvan had displayed great energy in his preparations, for he wished to be ready at the day appointed; and he was. Captain Mangles likewise supplied his ship with coal, that he might put to sea at any moment. He wished to gain the Argentine shore before the travelers. Hence there was a real rivalry between Glenarvan and the captain, which was of advantage to both.

At last, on the 14th of October, at the time agreed upon, every one was ready. At the moment of departure the passengers of the yacht assembled in the cabin. The Duncan was on the point of starting, and already her propeller was agitating the quiet waters of Talcahuana Bay. Glenarvan, Paganel, MacNabb, Robert Grant, Tom Austin, Wilson and Mulready, armed with carbines and Colt's revolvers, were preparing to leave the vessel. Guides and mules were waiting for them on shore.

"It is time," said Lord Glenarvan at last.

"Go, then, my husband!" replied Lady Helena, restraining her emotion.

He pressed her to his breast, while Robert threw himself upon the neck of his sister.

"And now, dear companions," said Jacques Paganel, "one last clasp of the hand to last us till we reach the shores of the Atlantic."

It was not asking much, but these were clasps which would strengthen the hopes of the worthy geographer.

They then returned to the deck, and the seven travelers left the vessel. They soon reached the wharf, which the yacht approached within less than half a cable's length.

Lady Helena cried for the last time,—

"My friends, God help you!"

"And he will help us, madam," answered Jacques Paganel; "for, I assure you, we shall help ourselves."

"Forward!" shouted Captain Mangles to his engineer.

"*En route!*" returned Glenarvan; and at the same instant that the travelers, giving reins to their animals, followed the road along the shore, the Duncan started again at full speed on the highway of the ocean.

CHAPTER XI

TRAVELING IN CHILI.

The native troop engaged by Glenarvan consisted of three men and a boy. The leader of the muleteers was an Englishman who had lived in the country for twenty years. His occupation was to let mules to travelers, and guide them across the passes of the Andes. Then he consigned them to the care of a "laqueano" (Argentine guide), who was familiar with the road over the Pampas.

THE PROCESSION FORMED.

This Englishman had not so forgotten his native tongue, in the company of mules and Indians, that he could not converse with the travelers. Hence it was easy for Glenarvan to make known his wishes, and for the muleteer to execute his orders, of which circumstance the former availed himself, since Paganel had not yet succeeded in making himself understood.

This leader, or "catapaz," in the language of Chili, was assisted by two native peons and a boy of twelve. The peons had charge of the mules laden with the baggage of the party, and the boy led the madrina (little mare), which wore small bells, and went in advance of the other ten mules. The travelers were mounted on seven, and the catapaz on one, of these animals, while the two others carried the provisions and a few rolls of cloth designed to insure the good-will of the chiefs of the plains. The peons traveled on foot according to their custom. This journey in South America was, therefore, to be performed under the most favorable conditions of safety and speed.

Crossing the Andes is not an ordinary journey. It cannot be undertaken without employing those hardy mules, of which the most preferable belong to the Argentine Republic. These excellent animals have attained in that country a development superior to their pristine quality and strength. They are not very particular about their food, drink only once a day, and easily make ten leagues in eight hours.

There are no taverns on this route, from one ocean to the other. You eat dried meat, rice seasoned with allspice, and whatever game can be captured on the way. In the mountains the torrents, and in the plains the rivers, furnish water, generally flavored with a few drops of rum, of which each has a supply in an ox-horn called "chiffle." However, care must be taken not to indulge too much in alcoholic drinks, which are specially injurious in a region where the nervous system is peculiarly excited.

As for your bedding, it consists merely of the native saddle called "recado." This saddle is made of sheep-skins tanned on one side and covered with wool on the other, and is supported by broad girths elaborately embroidered. A traveler wrapped in one of these warm coverings can brave with impunity the dampness of the nights, and enjoy the soundest repose.

Glenarvan, who knew how to travel and conform to the customs of different countries, had adopted the Chilian costume for himself and his friends. Paganel and Robert, two children (a large and a small one), felt no pleasure in introducing their heads into the national poncho (a large blanket with a hole in the centre), and their legs into leathern stirrups. They would rather have seen their mules richly caparisoned, with the Arab bit in their mouths, a long bridle of braided leather for a whip, and their heads adorned with metal ornaments and the "alforjas" (double saddle-bags containing the provisions).

LAND AND WATER.

Paganel, always absent-minded, received three or four kicks from his excellent animal just as he was mounting. Once in the saddle, however, with his inseparable telescope in a sling and his feet confined in the stirrups, he confided himself to the sagacity of his beast, and had no reason to repent. As for young Robert, he showed from the first a remarkable capacity for becoming an excellent horseman.

They started. The day was magnificent, the sky was perfectly clear, and the atmosphere sufficiently refreshed by the sea-breezes in spite of the heat of the sun. The little party followed at a rapid pace the winding shores of the bay, and made good progress the first day across the reeds of old dried marshes. Little was said. The parting farewells had left a deep impression upon the minds of all.

They could still see the smoke of the Duncan as she gradually disappeared on the horizon. All were silent, except Paganel; this studious geographer kept asking himself questions, and answering them, in his new language.

The catapaz was, moreover, quite a taciturn man, whose avocation had not made him loquacious. He scarcely spoke to his peons, for they understood their duty very well. Whenever a mule stopped, they urged him with a guttural cry. If this did not suffice, a good pebble thrown with sure aim overcame his obstinacy. If a girth gave way or a bridle was loosened, the peon, taking off his poncho, enveloped the head of the animal, which, when the injury was repaired, resumed its pace.

The custom of the muleteers is to set out at eight o'clock in the morning after breakfast, and travel thus till it is time to rest at four o'clock in the afternoon. Glenarvan, accordingly, conformed to this custom. Precisely when the signal to halt was given by the catapaz, the travelers arrived at the city of Arauco, situated at the southern extremity of the bay, without having left the foam-washed shore of the ocean. They would have had to proceed twenty miles farther to the west to reach the limits of the thirty-seventh parallel; but Glenarvan's agents had already traversed that part of the coast without meeting with any signs of shipwreck. A new exploration became, therefore, useless, and it was decided that the city of Arauco should be chosen as their point of departure. From this their course was to be directed towards the east in a rigorously straight line. The little party entered the city and took up their quarters in the open court of a tavern, whose accommodations were still in a rudimentary state.

While supper was preparing, Glenarvan, Paganel and the catapaz took a walk among the thatch-roofed houses. Except a church and the remains of a convent of Franciscans, Arauco presented nothing interesting. Glenarvan attempted to make some inquiries, but failed, while Paganel was in despair at not being able to make himself understood by the inhabitants. But, since they spoke Araucanian, his Spanish served him as little as Hebrew.

ONWARD, AND ONWARD STILL.

The next day, the madrina at the head, and the peons in the rear, the little troop resumed the line of the thirty-seventh parallel towards the east. They now crossed the fertile territory of Araucania, rich in vineyards and flocks. But gradually solitude ensued. Scarcely, from mile to mile, was there a hut of "rastreadores" (Indian horse-tamers). Now and then they came upon an abandoned relay-station, that only served as a shelter to some wanderer on the plains; and, by means of a ford, they crossed the Rio Tubal, the mountains visible in the distance.

At four o'clock in the afternoon, after a journey of thirty-five miles, they halted in the open country under a group of giant myrtles. The mules were unharnessed, and left to graze at will upon the rich herbage of the prairie. The saddle-bags furnished the usual meat and rice, the pelions spread on the ground served as covering, the saddles as pillows, and each one found on these improvised beds a ready repose, while the peons and the catapaz watched in turn.

As the weather continued pleasant, all the travelers, not excepting Robert, were still in good health; and, since the journey had begun under such favorable auspices, they thought it best to profit by it, and push on. The following day they advanced rapidly, crossed without accident Bell Rapids, and at evening encamped on the banks of the Rio Biobio. There were thirty-five miles more to travel before they were out of Chili.

The country had not changed. It was still rich in amaryllis, violets, date-trees, and golden-flowered cactuses. A few animals, among others the ocelot, inhabited the thickets. A heron, a solitary owl, thrushes and snipes wary of the talons of the hawk, were the only representatives of the feathered tribe.

Of the natives few were seen; only some "guassos" (degenerate children of the Indians and Spanish), galloping on horses which they lacerated with the gigantic spurs that adorned their naked feet, and passing like shadows. They met on the way no one who could inform them, and inquiries were therefore utterly impossible.

AN ASTONISHED CATAPAZ.

Glenarvan thought that Captain Grant, if prisoner of the Indians, must have been carried by them beyond the Andes. Their search could be successful only in the Pampas. They must be patient, and travel on swiftly and continuously.

They advanced in the same order as before, which Robert with difficulty kept, for his eagerness led him to press forward, to the great annoyance of his animal. Nothing but a command from Glenarvan would keep the young boy at his place in the line. The country now became more uneven; and several hillocks indicated that they were approaching the mountains.

Paganel still continued his study of Spanish.

"What a language it is!" exclaimed he; "so full and sonorous!"

"But you are making progress, of course?" replied Glenarvan.

"Certainly, my dear lord. Ah! if there were only no accent! But, alas! there is one!"

In studying this language, Paganel did not, however, neglect his geographical observations. In these, indeed, he was astonishingly clever, and could not have found his superior. When Glenarvan questioned the catapaz about some peculiarity of the country, his learned companion would always anticipate the answer of the guide, who then gazed at him with a look of amazement.

By means of a ford, they crossed the Rio Tubal, the mountains visible in the distance.

That same day they met a road which crossed the line that they had hitherto pursued. Lord Glenarvan naturally asked its name of their guide, and Paganel as naturally answered,—

"The road from Yumbel to Los Angelos."

Glenarvan looked at the catapaz.

"Exactly," replied he.

Then, addressing the geographer, he said,—

"You have traveled in this country?"

"Certainly," replied Paganel gravely.

"On a mule?"

"No; in an arm-chair."

The catapaz did not understand, for he shrugged his shoulders and returned to the head of the troop.

At five o'clock in the afternoon they stopped in a shallow gorge, a few miles above the little town of Loja; and that night the travelers encamped at the foot of the first slopes of the Andes.

CHAPTER XII

ELEVEN THOUSAND FEET ALOFT.

The route through Chili had as yet presented no serious obstacles; but now the dangers that attend a journey across the mountains suddenly increased, the struggle with the natural difficulties was about to begin in earnest.

An important question had to be decided before starting. By what pass could they cross the Andes with the least departure from the prescribed course? The catapaz was questioned on this subject.

"I know," he replied, "of but two passes that are practicable in this part of the Andes."

"Doubtless the pass of Arica," said Paganel, "which was discovered by Valdivia Mendoza."

"Exactly."

"And that of Villarica, situated to the south of Nevado."

"You are right."

"Well, my friend, these two passes have only one difficulty; they will carry us to the south, or the north, farther than we wish."

"Have you another pass to propose?" asked the major.

"Yes," replied Paganel; "the pass of Antuco."

"Well," said Glenarvan; "but do you know this pass, catapaz?"

ATTAINING TO EMINENCE.

"Yes, my lord, I have crossed it, and did not propose it because it is only a cattle-track for the Indian herdsmen of the eastern slopes."

"Never mind, my friend," continued Glenarvan; "where the herds of the Indians pass, we can also; and, since this will keep us in our course, let us start for the pass of Antuco."

The signal for departure was immediately given, and they entered the valley of Los Lejos between great masses of crystalized limestone, and ascended a very gradual slope. Towards noon they had to pass around the shores of a small lake, the picturesque reservoir of all the neighboring streams which flowed into it.

Above the lake extended vast "llanos," lofty plains, covered with grass, where the herds of the Indians grazed. Then they came upon a swamp which extended to the south and north, but which the instinct of the mules enabled them to avoid. Soon Fort Ballenare appeared on a rocky peak which it crowned with its dismantled walls. The ascent had already become abrupt and stony, and the pebbles, loosened by the hoofs of the mules, rolled under their feet in a rattling torrent.

The road now became difficult, and even perilous. The steepness increased, the walls on either side approached each other more and more, while the precipices yawned frightfully. The mules advanced cautiously in single file, with their noses to the ground, scenting the way.

Now and then, at a sudden turn, the madrina disappeared, and the little caravan was then guided by the distant tinkling of her bell. Sometimes, too, the capricious windings of the path would bend the column into two parallel lines, and the catapaz could talk to the peons, while a crevasse, scarcely two fathoms wide, but two hundred deep, formed an impassable abyss between them.

Under these conditions it was difficult to distinguish the course. The almost incessant action of subterranean and volcanic agency changes the road, and the landmarks are never the same. Therefore the catapaz hesitated, stopped, looked about him, examined the form of the rocks, and searched on the crumbling stones for the tracks of Indians.

Glenarvan followed in the steps of his guide. He perceived, he *felt*, his embarrassment, increasing with the difficulties of the way. He did not dare to question him, but thought that it was better to trust to the instinct of the muleteers and mules.

For an hour longer the catapaz wandered at a venture, but always seeking the more elevated parts of the mountain. At last he was forced to stop short. They were at the bottom of a narrow valley,—one of those ravines that the Indians call "quebradas." A perpendicular wall of porphyry barred their exit.

CLIMBING A MOUNTAIN.

The catapaz, after searching vainly for a passage, dismounted, folded his arms, and waited. Glenarvan approached him.

"Have you lost your way?" he asked.

"No, my lord," replied the catapaz.

"But we are not at the pass of Antuco?"

"We are."

"Are you not mistaken?"

"I am not. Here are the remains of a fire made by the Indians, and the tracks left by their horses."

"Well, they passed this way?"

"Yes; but we cannot. The last earthquake has made it impracticable."

"For mules," replied the major; "but not for men."

"That is for you to decide," said the catapaz. "I have done what I could. My mules and I are ready to turn back, if you please, and search for the other passes of the Andes."

"But that will cause a delay."

"Of three days, at least."

Glenarvan listened in silence to the words of the catapaz, who had evidently acted in accordance with his engagement. His mules could go no farther; but when the proposal was made to retrace their steps, Glenarvan turned towards his companions, and said,—

"Do you wish to go on?"

"We will follow you," replied Tom Austin.

"And even precede you," added Paganel. "What is it, after all? To scale a chain of mountains whose opposite slopes afford an unusually easy descent. This accomplished, we can find the Argentine laqueanos, who will guide us across the Pampas, and swift horses accustomed to travel over the plains. Forward, then, without hesitation."

"Forward!" cried his companions.

"You do not accompany us?" said Glenarvan to the catapaz.

"I am the muleteer," he replied.

"As you say."

"Never mind," said Paganel; "on the other side of this wall we shall find the pass of Antuco again, and I will lead you to the foot of the mountain as directly as the best guide of the Andes."

Glenarvan accordingly settled with the catapaz, and dismissed him, his peons, and his mules. The arms, the instruments, and the remaining provisions, were divided among the seven travelers. By common consent it was decided that the ascent should be undertaken immediately, and that, if necessary, they should travel part of the night. Around the precipice to the left wound a steep path that mules could not ascend. The difficulties were great; but, after two hours of fatigue and wandering, Glenarvan and his companions found themselves again in the pass of Antuco.

They were now in that part of the Andes properly so called, not far from the main ridge of the mountains; but of the path traced out, of the pass, nothing could be seen. All this region had just been thrown into confusion by the recent earthquakes.

They ascended all night, climbed almost inaccessible plateaus, and leaped over broad and deep crevasses. Their arms took the place of ropes, and their shoulders served as steps. The strength of Mulready and the skill of Wilson were often called into requisition. Many times, without their devotion and courage, the little party could not have advanced.

Glenarvan never lost sight of young Robert, whose youth and eagerness led him to acts of rashness, while Paganel pressed on with all the ardor of a Frenchman. As for the major, he only moved as much as was necessary, no more, no less, and mounted the path by an almost insensible motion. Did he perceive that he had been ascending for several hours? It is not certain. Perhaps he imagined he was descending.

PRACTICING "EXCELSIOR."

At five o'clock in the morning the travelers had attained a height of seven thousand five hundred feet. They were now on the lower ridges, the last limit of arborescent vegetation. At this hour the aspect of these regions was entirely changed. Great blocks of glittering ice, of a bluish color in certain parts, rose on all sides, and reflected the first rays of the sun.

The ascent now became very perilous. They no longer advanced without carefully examining the ice. Wilson had taken the lead, and with his foot tested the surface of the glaciers. His companions followed exactly in his footsteps, and avoided uttering a word, for the least sound might have caused the fall of the snowy masses suspended eight hundred feet above their heads.

They had reached the region of shrubs, which, four hundred and fifty feet higher, gave place to grass and cactuses. At eleven thousand feet all traces of vegetation disappeared. The travelers had stopped only once to recruit their strength by a hasty repast, and with superhuman courage they resumed the ascent in the face of the ever-increasing dangers.

SOMEWHAT SERIOUS.

The strength of the little troop, however, in spite of their courage, was almost gone. Glenarvan, seeing the exhaustion of his companions, regretted having engaged in the undertaking. Young Robert struggled against fatigue, but could go no farther.

Glenarvan stopped.

"We must take a rest," said he, for he clearly saw that no one else would make this proposal.

"Take a rest?" replied Paganel; "how? where? we have no shelter."

"It is indispensable, if only for Robert."

"No, my lord," replied the courageous child; "I can still walk—do not stop."

"We will carry you, my boy," said Paganel, "but we must, at all hazards, reach the eastern slope. There, perhaps, we shall find some hut in which we can take refuge. I ask for two hours more of travel."

"Do you all agree?" asked Glenarvan.

"Yes," replied his companions.

"I will take charge of the brave boy," added the equally brave Mulready.

Two hours more of terrible exertion followed. They kept ascending, in order to reach the highest summit of this part of the mountain.

They resumed their march towards the east. Two hours more of terrible exertion followed. They kept ascending, in order to reach the highest summit of this part of the mountain.

Whatever were the desires of these courageous men, the moment now came when the most valiant failed, and dizziness, that terrible malady of the mountains, exhausted not only their physical strength but their moral courage. It is impossible to struggle with impunity against fatigues of this kind. Soon falls became frequent, and those who fell could only advance by dragging themselves on their knees.

Exhaustion was about to put an end to this too prolonged ascent; and Glenarvan was considering with terror the extent of the snow, the cold which in this fatal region was so much to be dreaded, the shadows that were deepening on the solitary peaks, and the absence of a shelter for the night, when the major stopped him, and, in a calm tone, said,—

"A hut!"

CHAPTER XIII

A SUDDEN DESCENT.

Any one but MacNabb would have passed by, around, or even over this hut a hundred times without suspecting its existence. A projection on the surface of the snow scarcely distinguished it from the surrounding rocks. It was necessary to uncover it; after half an hour of persistent labor, Wilson and Mulready had cleared away the entrance to the "casucha," and the little party stepped in.

A "RESTAURANT" REOPENED.

This casucha, constructed by the Indians, was made of adobes, a kind of bricks dried in the sun. Ten persons could easily find room inside, and, if its walls had not been sufficiently water-tight in the rainy season, at this time, at least, they were some protection against the severity of the cold. There was, besides, a sort of fireplace with a flue of bricks very poorly laid, which enabled them to kindle a fire, and thus withstand the external temperature.

"Here is a shelter, at least," said Glenarvan, "even if it is not comfortable. Providence has led us hither, and we cannot do better than accept this fortune."

"Why," replied Paganel, "it is a palace. It only wants sentries and courtiers. We shall get along admirably here."

"Especially when a good fire is blazing on the hearth," said Tom Austin; "for, if we are hungry, we are none the less cold it seems to me; and, for my part, a good fagot would delight me more than a slice of venison."

"Well, Tom," said Paganel, "we will try to find something combustible."

"Something combustible on the top of the Andes?" said Mulready, shaking his head doubtfully.

"Since a chimney has been made in this hut," replied the major, "there is probably something here to burn."

"Our friend is right," added Glenarvan. "Prepare everything for supper; and I will play the part of wood-cutter."

"I will accompany you with Wilson," said Paganel.

"If you need me——," said Robert, rising.

"No, rest yourself, my brave boy," replied Glenarvan. "You will be a man when others are only children."

Glenarvan, Paganel, and Wilson went out of the hut. It was six o'clock in the evening. The cold was keen and cutting, in spite of the calmness of the air. The azure of the sky was already fading, and the sun shedding his last rays on the lofty peaks of the mountains.

Reaching a hillock of porphyry, they scanned the horizon in every direction. They had now gained the summit of the Andes, which commanded an extended prospect. To the east the sides of the mountains declined by gentle gradations, down which they could see the peons sliding several hundred feet below. In the distance extended long lines of scattered rocks and stones that had been crowded back by glacial avalanches. The valley of the Colorado was already growing dim in the increasing twilight; the elevations of land, the crags and the peaks, illumined by the rays of the sun, gradually faded, and darkness covered the whole eastern slope of the Andes.

Towards the north undulated a succession of ridges that mingled together insensibly. To the south, however, the view was magnificent; and, as night descended, the grandeur was inimitable. Looking down into the wild valley of Torbido, you saw Mount Antuco, whose yawning crater was two miles distant. The volcano, like some enormous monster, belched forth glowing smoke mingled with torrents of bright flame. The circle of the mountains that inclosed it seemed to be on fire. Showers of incandescent stones, clouds of reddish vapors, and streams of lava, united in glittering columns. A loud rumbling that increased every moment, and was followed by a dazzling flash, filled this vast circuit with its sharp reverberations, while the sun, his light gradually fading, disappeared as a star is extinguished in the shadows of the horizon.

FOOD BROUGHT TO THE DOOR.

Paganel and Glenarvan would have remained a long time to contemplate this magnificent struggle of the fires of earth with those of heaven, and the improvised wood-cutters were becoming admirers of nature; but Wilson, less enthusiastic, reminded them of their situation. Wood was wanting, it is true, but fortunately a scanty and dry moss clothed the rocks. An ample supply was taken, as well as of a plant whose roots were quite combustible. This precious fuel was brought to the hut, and piled in the fire-place; but it was difficult to kindle the fire, and especially to keep it burning.

When the viands were prepared, each one drank several mouthfuls of hot coffee with delight. As for the dried meat, it appeared a little unsatisfactory, which provoked on the part of Paganel a remark as useless as it was true.

"Indeed," said he, "I must confess a llama-steak would not be bad just now."

"What!" cried the major, "are you not content with our supper, Paganel?"

"Enchanted, my good major; but I acknowledge a plate of venison would be welcome."

"You are a sybarite," said MacNabb.

"I accept the title, major; but you yourself, whatever you may say, would not be displeased with a beefsteak."

"Probably not."

"And if you were asked to take your post at the cannon, you would go without a word."

"Certainly: and, although it pleases you———"

His companions had not heard any more, when distant and prolonged howls were heard. They were not the cries of scattered animals, but those of a herd approaching with rapidity. Would Providence, after furnishing them with shelter, give them their supper? Such was the thought of the geographer. But Glenarvan humbled his joy somewhat by observing that the animals of the Andes were never met with in so elevated a region.

"Whence comes the noise, then?" asked Tom Austin. "Hear how it approaches!"

"An avalanche!" said Mulready.

"Impossible! these are real howls!" replied Paganel.

"Let us see," cried Glenarvan.

"Let us see like hunters," answered the major, as he took his rifle.

All rushed out of the hut. Night had come. It was dark, but the sky was studded with stars. The moon had not yet shown her disk. The peaks on the north and east were lost in the darkness, and the eye only perceived the grotesque outlines of a few towering rocks.

The howls—those of terrified animals—were redoubled. They came from the dark side of the mountain. What was going on?

Suddenly there came a furious avalanche, but one of living creatures, mad with terror. The whole plateau seemed to tremble. There were hundreds, perhaps thousands, of these animals. Were they wild beasts of the Pampas, or only llamas? The whole party had only time to throw themselves to the earth, while this living whirlwind passed a few feet above them.

At this moment the report of a fire-arm was heard. The major had shot at a venture. He thought that a large animal fell a few paces from him, while the whole herd, carried along by their resistless motion, disappeared down the slopes illumined by the volcano.

"Ah, I have them!" cried a voice, that of Paganel.

"What have you?" asked Glenarvan.

"My glasses, to be sure!"

"You are not wounded?"

"No, a little kick,—but by what?"

"By this," replied the major, dragging after him the animal he had shot.

Each one hastened to gain the hut; and by the light of the fire MacNabb's prize was examined. It was a pretty animal, resembling a little camel without a hump. It had a small head, flat body, long legs and claws, fine coffee-colored hair, and its breast was spotted with white.

Scarcely had Paganel looked at it when he exclaimed,—

"It is a guanaco!"

"What is that?" asked Glenarvan.

"An animal that eats itself."

"And is it good?"

"A DISH FOR THE GODS."

"Delicious! a dish for the gods! I knew well that you would like fresh meat for supper. And what meat this is! But who will dress the animal?"

"I will," said Wilson.

"Well, I will engage to broil it," replied Paganel.

"You are a cook, then, Monsieur Paganel?" said Robert.

"Certainly, my boy. A Frenchman is always a cook."

In a little while Paganel placed large slices of meat on the coals, and, in a short time, served up to his companions this appetizing viand. No one hesitated, but each attacked it ravenously. To the great amazement of the geographer, a general grimace accompanied by a "pwah!" followed the first mouthful.

"It is horrible!" said one.

"It is not eatable!" replied another.

The poor geographer, whatever was the difficulty, was forced to agree that this steak was not acceptable even to starving men. They therefore began to launch jokes at him, and deride his "dish for the gods," while he himself sought a reason for this unaccountable result.

"I have it!" he cried. "I have it!"

"Is the meat too old?" asked MacNabb, calmly.

"No, my intolerant major; but it has traveled too much. How could I forget that?"

"What do you mean?" asked Tom Austin.

"I mean that the animal is not good unless killed when at rest. I can affirm from the taste that it has come from a distance, and, consequently, the whole herd."

"You are certain of this?" said Glenarvan.

"Absolutely so."

"But what event could have terrified these animals so, and driven them at a time when they ought to be peacefully sleeping in their lairs."

"As to that, my dear Glenarvan," said Paganel, "it is impossible for me to say. If you believe me, let us search no farther. For my part I am dying for want of sleep. Let us retire, major!"

"Very well, Paganel."

Thereupon each wrapped himself in his poncho, the fuel was replenished for the night, and soon all but Glenarvan were buried in profound repose.

He alone did not sleep. A secret uneasiness held him in a state of wakeful fatigue. He could not help thinking of that herd, flying in one common direction, of their inexplicable terror. They could not have been pursued by wild beasts: at that height there were scarcely any, and yet fewer hunters. What fright had driven them over the abysses of Antuco, and what was the cause of it? He thought of their strange situation, and felt a presentiment of coming danger.

However, under the influence of a partial drowsiness, his ideas gradually modified, and fear gave place to hope. He saw himself in anticipation, on the morrow, on the plain at the foot of the Andes. There his actual search was to begin; and success was not, perhaps, far distant. He thought of Captain Grant and his two sailors, delivered from a cruel slavery.

These images passed rapidly before his mind, every instant interrupted by a flash of fire, a spark, a flame, illumining the faces of his sleeping companions, and casting a flickering shadow over the walls of the hut. Then his presentiments returned with more vividness, while he listened vaguely to the external sounds so difficult to explain on these solitary summits.

At one moment he thought he heard distant rumblings, dull and threatening like the rollings of thunder. These sounds could be caused only by a tempest, raging on the sides of the mountain. He wished to convince himself, and left the hut.

The moon had risen, and the sky was clear and calm. Not a cloud was to be seen either above or below, only now and then the moving shadows of the flames of the volcano. At the zenith twinkled thousands of stars, while the rumblings still continued. They seemed to approach, and run along the chain of the mountains.

Glenarvan returned more uneasy than before, seeking to divine what relation there was between these subterranean noises and the flight of the guanacos. He looked at his watch; it was two o'clock.

However, having no certain knowledge of immediate danger, he did not wake his companions, whom fatigue held in a deep repose, but fell himself into a heavy sleep that lasted several hours.

All at once a violent crash startled him to his feet. It was a deafening roar, like the irregular noise of innumerable artillery wagons rolling over a hollow pavement. Glenarvan suddenly felt the earth tremble beneath his feet. He saw the hut sway and start open.

"Look out!" he cried.

The internal rumblings, the din of the avalanche, the crash of the blocks of granite, and the whirlwinds of snow, rendered all communication with each other impossible.

His companions, awakened and thrown into confusion, were hurried down a rapid descent. The day was breaking, and the scene was terrible. The form of the mountains suddenly changed, their tops were truncated, the tottering peaks disappeared, as if a pitfall had opened at their base. A mass, several miles in extent, became detached entire, and slid towards the plain.

"An earthquake!" cried Paganel.

He was not mistaken. It was one of those phenomena frequent on the mountain frontier of Chili. This portion of the globe is disturbed by subterranean fires, and the volcanoes of this chain afford only insufficient outlets for the confined vapors.

In the meantime the plateau, to which seven stunned and terrified men clung by the tufts of moss, glided with the rapidity of an express. Not a cry was possible, not a movement of escape. They could not hear each other. The internal rumblings, the din of the avalanche, the crash of the blocks of granite, and the whirlwinds of snow, rendered all communication with each other impossible.

A STEEP GRADIENT.

At one time the mass would slide without jolts or jars; at another, seized with a pitching and rolling motion like the deck of a vessel shaken by the billows, it would run along the edge of the abysses into which the fragments of the mountain fell, uproot the trees of centuries, and level with the precision of an enormous scythe all the inequalities of the eastern slope.

How long this indescribable scene lasted, no one could tell; in what abyss all were to be engulfed, no one was able to foresee. Whether they were all there alive, or whether one of them was lying at the bottom of a crevasse, no one could say. Stunned by the swiftness of the descent, chilled by the keenness of the cold, blinded by the whirlwinds of snow, they panted, exhausted and almost inanimate, and only clung to the rocks by the supreme instinct of preservation.

All at once a shock of unusual violence arrested their gliding vehicle. They were thrown forward and rolled upon the last declivities of the mountains. The plateau had stopped short.

For a few moments no one stirred. At last one rose, deafened by the shock, but yet firm. It was the major. He shook off the snow that blinded him, and looked around. His companions were not very far from one another. He counted them. All but one lay on the ground. The missing one was Robert Grant.

CHAPTER XIV

PROVIDENTIALLY RESCUED.

The eastern side of the Andes consists of long slopes, declining gradually to the plain upon which a portion of the mass had suddenly stopped. In this new country, garnished with rich pastures and adorned with magnificent vegetation, an incalculable number of apple-trees, planted at the time of the conquest, glowed with their golden fruit and formed true forests. It seemed as if a part of beautiful Normandy had been cast into these monotonous regions, and under any other circumstances the eye of a traveler would have been struck with this sudden transition from desert to oasis, from snowy peak to verdant prairie, from winter to summer.

The earth had regained an absolute immobility, and the earthquake had ceased. But without doubt the subterranean forces were still exerting their devastating action at a distance, for the chain of the Andes is always agitated or trembling in some part. This time, however, the commotion had been of extreme violence. The outline of the mountains was entirely changed; a new view of summits, crests, and peaks was defined against the azure of the sky; and the guide of the Pampas would have sought in vain for his accustomed landmarks.

COMEDY CHANGED TO TRAGEDY.

A wonderfully beautiful day was breaking. The rays of the sun, issuing from their watery bed in the Atlantic, glittered over the Argentine plains and were already silvering the waves of the other ocean. It was eight o'clock in the morning.

Glenarvan and his companions, revived by the aid of the major, gradually recovered consciousness. Indeed, they had only undergone a severe giddiness. The mountain was descended, and they would have applauded a means of locomotion which had been entirely at nature's expense, if one of the feeblest, Robert Grant, had not been missing. Every one loved the courageous boy: Paganel was particularly attached to him; the major, too, in spite of his coldness; but especially Glenarvan.

When the latter learned of Robert's disappearance, he was desperate. He pictured to himself the poor child engulfed in some abyss, and calling vainly for him whom he considered his second father.

"My friends," said he, scarcely restraining his tears, "we must search for him, we must find him! We cannot abandon him thus! Every valley, every precipice, every abyss must be explored to the very bottom! You shall tie a rope around me and let me down! I will do it, you hear me, I will! May Heaven grant that Robert is still living! Without him, how could we dare find his father? What right have we to save Captain Grant, if his rescue costs the life of his child?"

His companions listened without speaking. They felt that he was seeking in their looks some ray of hope, and they lowered their eyes.

"Well," continued Glenarvan, "you understand me; you are silent! You have no more hope!"

A few moments of silence ensued, when MacNabb inquired:

"Who of you, my friends, remembers when Robert disappeared?"

To this question no answer was given.

"At least," continued the major, "you can tell with whom the boy was during the descent."

"With me," replied Wilson.

"Well, at what moment did you last see him with you? Recall the circumstances. Speak."

"This is all that I remember. Robert Grant was at my side, his hand grasping a tuft of moss, less than two minutes before the shock that caused our descent."

"Less than two minutes? Remember, Wilson, the minutes may have seemed long to you. Are you not mistaken?"

"I think not—yes, it is so, less than two minutes."

"Well," said MacNabb; "and was Robert on your right, or on your left?"

"On my left. I remember that his poncho flapped in my face."

"And where were you situated in reference to us?"

"On the left also."

"Then Robert could have disappeared only on this side," said the major, turning towards the mountain, and pointing to the right. "And also considering the time that has elapsed since his disappearance, the child must have fallen at a high part of the mountain. There we must search, and, by taking different ways, we shall find him."

Not a word more was said. The six men, scaling the declivities of the mountain, stationed themselves at different heights along the ridge, and began their search. They kept always to the right of their line of descent, sounding the smallest fissures, descending to the bottom of precipices half filled with fragments of the mass; and more than one came forth with his garments in shreds, his feet and hands lacerated, at the peril of his life.

A SLEEPLESS NIGHT.

All this portion of the Andes, except a few inaccessible plateaus, was carefully explored for many hours without one of these brave men thinking of rest. But it was a vain search. The child had not only found death in the mountains, but also a tomb, the stone of which, made of some enormous rock, was forever closed over him.

Towards noon Glenarvan and his companions, bruised and exhausted, found themselves again in the valley. The former was a prey to the most violent grief. He scarcely spoke, and from his lips issued only these words, broken by sighs,—"I will not go; I will not go!"

Each understood this determination, and respected it.

"We will wait," said Paganel to the major and Tom Austin. "Let us take some rest, and recruit our strength. We shall need it, whether to begin our search or continue our journey."

"Yes," replied MacNabb, "let us remain, since Edward wishes it. He hopes: but what does he hope?"

"God knows!" said Tom Austin.

"Poor Robert!" replied Paganel, wiping his eyes.

Trees thronged the valley in great numbers. The major chose a group of lofty carob-trees, under which was established a temporary encampment. A few blankets, the arms, a little dried meat, and some rice, was all that remained to the travelers. A stream, which flowed not far off, furnished water, still muddy from the effects of the avalanche. Mulready kindled a fire on the grass, and soon presented to his master a warm and comforting repast. But Glenarvan refused it, and remained stretched on his poncho in profound prostration.

Thus the day passed. Night came, clear and calm as the preceding. While his companions lay motionless, although wakeful, Glenarvan reascended the mountain. He listened closely, still hoping that a last cry might reach him. He ventured alone and afar, pressing his ear to the ground, listening, restraining the beatings of his heart, and calling in a voice of despair.

The whole night long he wandered on the mountain. Sometimes Paganel, sometimes the major, followed him, ready to help him on the slippery summits, or on the edge of the chasms, where his rashness led him. But his last efforts were fruitless; and to the cry of "Robert! Robert!" a thousand times repeated, echo alone replied.

Day dawned, and it was necessary to go in search of Glenarvan on the mountain, and bring him in spite of his reluctance back to the encampment. His despair was terrible. Who would now dare to speak to him of departure, and propose leaving this fatal valley? But the provisions were failing. They would soon meet the Argentine guides and horses to take them across the Pampas. To retrace their steps was more difficult than to advance. Besides, the Atlantic was the place appointed to meet the Duncan. All these reasons did not permit a longer delay, and it was for the interest of all that the hour for departure should be no longer deferred.

MacNabb attempted to draw Glenarvan from his grief. For a long time he spoke without his friend appearing to hear him. Glenarvan shook his head. At length, words escaped his lips.

"Go?" said he.

"Yes, go."

"One hour more!"

"Well, one hour more," replied the worthy major.

When it had passed, Glenarvan asked for another. You would have thought a condemned man was praying for his life. Thus it continued till about noon, when MacNabb, by the advice of all, would no longer hesitate, and told Glenarvan that they must go, the lives of his companions depended upon a prompt decision.

"Yes, yes," replied Glenarvan, "we will go, we will go!"

But as he spoke his eyes were turned away from MacNabb. His gaze was fixed upon a black speck in the air. Suddenly his hand rose, and remained immovable, as if petrified.

"There! there!" cried he. "See! see!"

All eyes were raised towards the sky, in the direction so imperatively indicated. At that moment the black speck visibly increased. It was a bird hovering at a measureless height.

"A condor," said Paganel.

"Yes, a condor," replied Glenarvan. "Who knows? He is coming, he is descending! Let us wait."

What did Glenarvan hope? Was his reason wandering? He had said, "Who knows?" Paganel was not mistaken. The condor became more distinct every moment.

This magnificent bird, long revered by the Incas, is the king of the southern Andes. In these regions he attains an extraordinary development. His strength is prodigious; and he often precipitates oxen to the bottom of the abysses. He attacks sheep, goats, and calves wandering on the plain, and carries them in his talons to a great height. Sometimes he hovers at an elevation beyond the limit of human vision, and there this king of the air surveys, with a piercing look, the regions below, and distinguishes the faintest objects with a power of sight that is the astonishment of naturalists.

The bird had raised him by his garments, and was now hovering in mid-air at least one hundred and fifty feet above the encampment. He had perceived the travelers, and was violently striving to escape with his heavy prey.

What had the condor seen? A corpse,—that of Robert Grant? "Who knows?" repeated Glenarvan, without losing sight of him. The enormous bird approached, now hovering, now falling with the swiftness of inert bodies. He soon described circles of larger extent, and could be perfectly distinguished. He measured fifteen feet across his wings, which supported him in the air almost without motion, for it is the peculiarity of these great birds to sail with a majestic calmness unlike all others of the winged tribes.

The major and Wilson had seized their rifles, but Glenarvan stopped them with a gesture. The condor was approaching in the circles of his flight a sort of inaccessible plateau a quarter of a mile distant. He was turning with a vertical rapidity, opening and closing his formidable claws, and shaking his cartilaginous neck.

SOMETHING WORSE.

"There! there!" cried Glenarvan.

Then suddenly a thought flashed through his mind.

"If Robert is still living!" exclaimed he, with a cry of terror, "this bird! Fire, my friends, fire!"

But he was too late. The condor had disappeared behind the lofty boulders. A second passed that seemed an eternity. Then the enormous bird reappeared, heavily laden, and rising slowly.

A cry of horror was uttered. In the claws of the condor an inanimate body was seen suspended and dangling. It was Robert Grant. The bird had raised him by his garments, and was now hovering in mid-air at least one hundred and fifty feet above the encampment. He had perceived the travelers, and was violently striving to escape with his heavy prey.

"May Robert's body be dashed upon these rocks," cried Glenarvan, "rather than serve———"

He did not finish, but, seizing Wilson's rifle, attempted to take aim at the condor. But his arm trembled; he could not sight the piece. His eyes were dimmed.

"Let me try," said the major.

With clear eye, steady hand, and motionless body, he aimed at the bird, that was already three hundred feet above him. But he had not pressed the trigger, when a report resounded in the valley. A light smoke curled up between two rocks, and the condor, shot in the head, fell, slowly turning, sustained by his broad outspread wings. He had not released his prey, and at last reached the ground, ten paces from the banks of the stream.

"Quick! quick!" said Glenarvan; and without seeking whence this providential shot had come, he rushed towards the condor. His companions closely followed him.

"THE LOST IS FOUND."

When they arrived the bird was dead, and the body of Robert was hidden under its great wings. Glenarvan threw himself upon the child, released him from the talons of the condor, stretched him on the grass, and pressed his ear to his breast.

Never did a wilder cry of joy issue from human lips than when Glenarvan rose, exclaiming:

"He lives! he lives!"

In an instant Robert was stripped of his garments, and his face bathed with fresh water. He made a movement, opened his eyes, looked around, and uttered a few words:

"You, my lord—my father!——"

Glenarvan could not speak. Emotion stifled him, and, kneeling, he wept beside this child so miraculously saved.

CHAPTER XV

THALCAVE.

After the great danger that he had just escaped, Robert incurred another, no less great,—that of being overwhelmed with caresses. However feeble he was still, not one of these good people could refrain from pressing him to his heart. But it must be confessed that these well-meant embraces are not fatal, for the boy did not die.

When his rescue was certain, thought reverted to his rescuer, and the major very naturally thought of looking around him. Fifty paces from the stream, a man of lofty stature was standing, motionless, on one of the first ledges of the mountain. A long gun lay at his feet. This individual, who had so suddenly appeared, had broad shoulders, and long hair tied with leathern thongs. His height exceeded six feet, and his bronzed face was red between his eyes and mouth, black below his eyelids, and white on his forehead. After the manner of the Patagonians of the frontiers, the native wore a splendid cloak, decorated with red arabesques, made of the skin of a guanaco, its silky fur turned outward, and sewed with ostrich-tendons. Under his cloak a tippet of fox-skin encircled his neck and terminated in a point in front. At his girdle hung a little bag containing the colors with which he painted his face. His leggings were of ox-hide, and fastened to the ankle with straps regularly crossed.

The figure of this Patagonian was fine, and his face denoted real intelligence in spite of the colors that adorned (!) it. He waited in an attitude full of dignity, and, seeing him so motionless and stern on his pedestal of rocks, you would have taken him for a statue.

The major, as soon as he perceived him, pointed him out to Glenarvan, who hastened towards him. The Patagonian took two steps forward; Glenarvan took his hand, and pressed it. There was in the latter's look, in his physiognomy, such a feeling, such an expression of gratitude, that the native could not mistake it. He inclined his head gently, and uttered a few words that neither the major nor his friend could understand.

The Patagonian, after regarding the strangers attentively, now changed the language; but whatever it was, this new idiom was no better understood than the first. However, certain expressions which he used struck Glenarvan. They seemed to belong to the Spanish language, of which he knew several common words.

"Spanish?" said he.

The Patagonian nodded.

"Well," said the major, "this is our friend Paganel's business. It is fortunate that he thought of learning Spanish."

Paganel was called. He came at once and with all the grace of a Frenchman saluted the Patagonian, to which the latter paid no attention. The geographer was informed of the state of affairs, and was only too glad to use his diligently-acquired knowledge.

SOMETHING WRONG.

"Exactly," said he. And opening his mouth widely in order to articulate better, he said, in his best Spanish,—

"You—are—a—brave—man."

The native listened, but did not answer.

"He does not understand," said the geographer.

"Perhaps you do not pronounce well," replied the major.

"Very true! Curse the pronunciation!"

And again Paganel began, but with no better success.

"I will change the expression," said he. And pronouncing with magisterial slowness, he uttered these words,—

"A—Patagonian,—doubtless?"

The native remained mute as before.

"Answer!" added Paganel.

The Patagonian did not reply.

"Do—you—understand?" cried Paganel, violently enough to damage his organs of speech.

It was evident that the Indian did not understand, for he answered, but in Spanish,—

"I do not understand."

It was Paganel's turn now to be astonished, and he hastily put on his glasses, like one irritated.

"May I be hanged," said he, "if I understand a word of this infernal jargon! It is certainly Araucanian."

"No," replied Glenarvan; "this man answered in Spanish."

And, turning to the Patagonian, he repeated,—

"Spanish?"

A man of lofty stature was standing, motionless, on one of the first ledges of the mountain. This individual had broad shoulders, and long hair tied with leathern thongs.

"Yes," replied the native.

Paganel's surprise became amazement. The major and Glenarvan looked at him quizzingly.

"Ah, my learned friend!" said the major, while a half smile played about his lips, "you have committed one of those blunders peculiar to you."

"What!" cried the geographer, starting.

"Yes, it is plain that this Patagonian speaks Spanish."

"He?"

A PENINSULAR BABEL.

"Yes. By mistake you have learnt another language, while thinking that you studied——"

MacNabb did not finish. A loud "Oh!" from the geographer, accompanied by shrugs of the shoulders, cut him short.

"Major, you are going a little too far," said Paganel in a very dry tone.

"To be sure, since you do not understand."

"I do not understand because this native speaks so badly!" answered the geographer, who began to be impatient.

"That is to say, he speaks badly, because you do not understand," returned the major, calmly.

"MacNabb," said Glenarvan, "that is not a probable supposition. However abstracted our friend Paganel may be, we cannot suppose that his blunder was to learn one language for another."

"Now, my dear Edward, or rather you, my good Paganel, explain to me what the difficulty is."

"I will not explain," replied Paganel, "I insist. Here is the book in which I practice daily the difficulties of the Spanish language! Examine it, major, and you will see whether I impose upon you."

So saying, Paganel groped in his numerous pockets. After searching a few moments, he drew forth a volume in a very bad state, and presented it with an air of assurance. The major took the book, and looked at it.

"Well, what work is this?" he asked.

"The Lusiad," replied Paganel; "an admirable poem which——"

"The Lusiad!" cried Glenarvan.

"Yes, my friend, the Lusiad of the immortal Camoëns, nothing more or less."

"Camoëns!" repeated Glenarvan; "but, unfortunate friend, Camoëns was a Portuguese! It is Portuguese that you have been studying for six weeks."

"Camoëns! Lusiad! Portuguese!"

Paganel could say no more. His eyes wandered, while a peal of Homeric laughter rang in his ears.

The Patagonian did not wink; he waited patiently for the explanation of this event, which was totally incomprehensible to him.

"Insensate! fool!" cried Paganel, at last. "What! is it so? Is it not a mere joke? Have I done this? It is the confusion of languages, as at Babel. My friends! my friends! to start for India and arrive at Chili! to learn Spanish and speak Portuguese! this is too much, and, if it continues, I shall some day throw myself out of the window instead of my cigar."

To hear Paganel take his blunder thus, to see his comical actions, it was impossible to keep serious. Besides, he set the example himself.

"Laugh, my friends," said he, "laugh with a will! you cannot laugh as much as I do at myself."

And he uttered the most formidable peal of laughter that ever issued from the mouth of a geographer.

"But we are none the less without an interpreter," said the major.

"Oh, do not be troubled," replied Paganel. "The Portuguese and Spanish resemble each other so much that I made a mistake. However, this very resemblance will soon enable me to rectify my error, and in a short time I will thank this worthy Patagonian in the language he speaks so well."

Paganel was right, for he could soon exchange a few words with the native. He even learned that his name was Thalcave, a word which signifies in Araucanian "the thunderer." This surname was doubtless given to him for his skill in the use of fire-arms.

BETTER PROSPECTS.

But Glenarvan was particularly rejoiced to discover that the Patagonian was a guide, and, moreover, a guide of the Pampas. There was, therefore, something so providential in this meeting that the success of the enterprise seemed already an accomplished fact, and no one any longer doubted the rescue of Captain Grant.

In the meantime the travelers and the Patagonian had returned to Robert. The latter stretched his arms towards the native, who, without a word, placed his hand upon his head. He examined the child and felt his wounded limbs. Then, smiling, he went and gathered on the banks of the stream a few handfuls of wild celery, with which he rubbed the boy's body. Under this treatment, performed with an extreme gentleness, the child felt his strength revive, and it was plain that a few hours would suffice to restore him.

It was therefore decided that that day and the following night should be passed at the encampment. Besides, two important questions remained to be settled—food, and means of conveyance. Provisions and mules were both wanting.

Fortunately Thalcave solved the difficulty. This guide, who was accustomed to conduct travelers along the Patagonian frontiers, and was one of the most intelligent baqueanos of the country, engaged to furnish Glenarvan all that his little party needed. He offered to take him to a "tolderia" (encampment) of Indians, about four miles distant, where they would find everything necessary for the expedition. This proposal was made partly by gestures, partly by Spanish words which Paganel succeeded in understanding. It was accepted, and Glenarvan and his learned friend, taking leave of their companions, reascended the stream under the guidance of the Patagonian.

They proceeded at a good pace for an hour and a half, taking long strides to keep up to the giant Thalcave. All the region was charming, and of a rich fertility. The grassy pastures succeeded each other, and could easily have fed thousands of cattle. Large ponds, united by a winding chain of streams, gave these plains a verdant moisture. Black-headed swans sported on the mirror-like surface, and disputed the empire of the waters with numberless ostriches that gamboled over the plains, while the brilliant feathered tribes were in wonderful variety.

Jacques Paganel proceeded from admiration to ecstasy. Exclamations of delight continually escaped his lips, to the astonishment of the Patagonian, who thought it very natural that there should be birds in the air, swans on the lakes, and grass on the prairies. The geographer had no reason to regret his walk, or complain of its length. He scarcely believed himself started, or that the encampment would soon come in sight.

This tolderia was at the bottom of a narrow valley among the mountains. Here in huts of branches lived thirty wandering natives, grazing large herds of milch cows, sheep, cattle and horses. Thus they roamed from one pasture to another, always finding a repast ready for their four-footed companions.

GLENARVAN GOING TO MARKET.

Thalcave took upon himself the negotiation, which was not long. In return for seven small Argentine horses, all saddled, a hundred pounds of dried meat, a few measures of rice, and some leathern bottles for water, the Indians received twenty ounces of gold, the value of which they perfectly understood. Glenarvan would have bought another horse for the Patagonian, but he intimated that it was unnecessary.

The bargain concluded, Glenarvan took leave of his new "providers," as Paganel expressed it, and returned to the encampment. His arrival was welcomed by cries of joy at sight of the provisions and horses. Every one ate with avidity. Robert partook of some nourishment; he had almost entirely regained his strength, and the remainder of the day was passed in perfect rest. Various subjects were alluded to: the absent dear ones, the Duncan, Captain Mangles, his brave crew, and Harry Grant who was, perhaps, not far distant.

As for Paganel, he did not leave the Indian. He became Thalcave's shadow, and could not remain quiet in the presence of a real Patagonian, in comparison with whom he would have passed for a dwarf. He overwhelmed the grave Indian with Spanish phrases, to which the latter quietly listened. The geographer studied this time without a book, and was often heard repeating words aloud.

"If I do not get the accent," said he to the major, "you must not be angry with me. Who would have thought that one day a Patagonian would teach me Spanish!"

CHAPTER XVI

NEWS OF THE LOST CAPTAIN.

At eight o'clock the next morning Thalcave gave the signal for departure. The slope was gradual, and the travelers had only to descend a gentle declivity to the sea.

When the Patagonian declined the horse that Glenarvan offered him, the latter thought that he preferred to go on foot, according to the custom of certain guides; and indeed, his long legs ought to have made walking easy. But he was mistaken.

At the moment of departure Thalcave whistled in a peculiar manner. Immediately a magnificent Argentine horse, of superb form, issued from a small wood near by, and approached at the call of his master. The animal was perfectly beautiful. His brown color indicated a sound, spirited and courageous beast. He had a small and elegantly poised head, widely opening nostrils, a fiery eye, large hams, swelling withers, broad breast, long pasterns, in short, all the qualities that constitute strength and suppleness. The major, like a perfect horseman, admired unreservedly this specimen of the horses of the plains. This beautiful creature was called Thaouka, which means "bird" in the Patagonian language, and he justly merited this appellation.

A FRESH START.

When Thalcave was in the saddle, the horse pranced with spirited grace, and the Patagonian, a skillful rider, was magnificent to behold. His outfit comprised two weapons of the chase, the "bolas" and the lasso. The bolas consists of three balls tied together by a leathern string, which are fastened to the front of the saddle. The Indians frequently throw them the distance of a hundred paces at the animal or enemy that they are pursuing, and with such precision that they twist about their legs and bring them to the ground. It is, therefore, in their hands a formidable instrument, and they handle it with surprising dexterity. The lasso, on the contrary, does not leave the hand that wields it. It consists simply of a leathern thong thirty feet in length, terminating in a slip-noose which works upon an iron ring. The right hand throws the slip-noose, while the left hand holds the remainder of the lasso, the end of which is firmly tied to the saddle. A long carbine in a sling completed the Patagonian's armament.

Thalcave, without observing the admiration caused by his natural grace, ease and courage, took the lead, and the party advanced, now at a gallop, and now at a walk, for their horses seemed entirely unaccustomed to trotting. Robert mounted with much boldness, and speedily convinced Glenarvan of his ability to keep his seat.

On issuing from the gorges of the Andes, they encountered a great number of sand-ridges, called "medanos," real waves incessantly agitated by the wind, when the roots of the herbage did not confine them to the earth. This sand is of an extreme fineness; and, at the least breath, they saw it float away in light clouds, or form regular sand-columns which rose to a considerable height.

This spectacle caused pleasure as well as annoyance to the eyes. Pleasure, for nothing was more curious than these columns, wandering over the plain, struggling, mingling, sinking and rising in inexpressible confusion; and annoyance, since an impalpable dust emanated from these innumerable medanos and penetrated the eyelids, however tightly they were closed.

This phenomenon continued during a great part of the day. Nevertheless, they advanced rapidly, and towards six o'clock the Andes, forty miles distant, presented a darkish aspect already fading in the mists of the evening.

The travelers were a little fatigued with their journey, and, therefore, saw with pleasure the approach of the hour for retiring. They encamped on the shores of a turbulent stream, enclosed by lofty red cliffs. Toward noon of the next day, the sun's rays became very oppressive, and at evening a line of clouds on the horizon indicated a change in the weather. The Patagonian could not be deceived, and pointed out to the geographer the western portion of the sky.

"Good, I know," said Paganel, and addressing his companions: "A change in the weather is about to take place. We shall have a 'pampero.'"

TALKING LIKE A BOOK.

He explained that this pampero is frequent on the Argentine Plains. It is a very dry wind from the southwest. Thalcave was not mistaken, and during the night, which was quite uncomfortable for people sheltered with a simple poncho, the wind blew with great violence. The horses lay down on the ground, and the men near them in a close group. Glenarvan feared they would be delayed if the storm continued; but Paganel reassured him after consulting his barometer.

"Ordinarily," said he, "this wind creates tempests, which last for three days; but when the barometer rises as it does now, you are free from these furious hurricanes in a few hours. Be assured, then, my dear friend; at break of day the sky will have resumed its usual clearness."

"You talk like a book, Paganel," replied Glenarvan.

"And I am one," replied Paganel, "which you are free to consult as much as you please."

He was not mistaken. At one o'clock in the morning the wind suddenly subsided, and every one was able to enjoy an invigorating sleep. The next morning they rose bright and fresh, especially Paganel, who displayed great cheerfulness and animation.

During this passage across the continent, Lord Glenarvan watched with scrupulous attention for the approach of the natives. He wished to question them concerning Captain Grant, by the aid of the Patagonian, with whom Paganel had begun to converse considerably. But they followed a path little frequented by the Indians, for the trails over the Pampas, which lead from the Argentine Republic to the Andes, are situated too far to the north. If by chance a wandering horseman appeared in the distance, he fled rapidly away, little caring to come in contact with strangers.

However, although Glenarvan, in the interest of his search, regretted the absence of the Indians, an incident took place which singularly justified the interpretation of the document.

Several times the course pursued by the expedition crossed paths on the Pampas, among others quite an important road—that from Carmen to Mendoza—distinguishable by the bones of such animals as mules, horses, sheep and oxen, whose remains were scattered by the birds of prey, and lay bleaching in the sun. There were thousands of them, and, without doubt, more than one human skeleton had added its bones to those of these humbler animals.

Hitherto Thalcave had made no remark concerning the line so rigorously followed. He understood, however, that if they kept no definite course over the Pampas, they would not come to cities or villages. Every morning they advanced towards the rising sun, without deviating from the straight line, and every evening the setting sun was behind them. In his capacity of guide, Thalcave must, therefore, have been astonished to see that not only he did not guide them, but that they guided him. Nevertheless, if he was astonished, with the reserve natural to the Indians he made no remark. But to-day arriving at the above-mentioned road, he stopped his horse, and turned towards Paganel.

"Road to Carmen," said he.

"Yes, my good Patagonian," replied the geographer, in his purest Spanish; "road to Carmen and Mendoza."

"We do not take it?" resumed Thalcave.

"No," answered Paganel.

"And we are going———?"

"Always to the east."

"That is going nowhere."

"Who knows?"

Thalcave was silent, and gazed at the geographer with profound surprise. He did not admit, however, that Paganel was joking the least in the world. An Indian, with his natural seriousness, never imagines that you are not speaking in earnest.

"You are not going to Carmen then?" he added, after an instant of silence.

A PROFESSORIAL DIFFICULTY.

"No," replied Paganel.

"Nor to Mendoza?"

"No."

At this moment Glenarvan, rejoining Paganel, asked what Thalcave said, and why he had stopped.

When he had told him, Glenarvan said,—

"Could you not explain to him the object of our expedition, and why we must always proceed toward the east?"

"That would be very difficult," answered Paganel, "for an Indian understands nothing of geography."

"But," said the major seriously, "is it the history, or the historian, that he cannot understand?"

"Ah, MacNabb," said Paganel, "you still doubt my Spanish!"

"Try, my worthy friend."

"Very well."

Paganel turned to the Patagonian, and began a discourse, frequently interrupted for want of words and from the difficulty of explaining to a half-ignorant savage details which were rather incomprehensible to him.

The geographer was just then a curious sight. He gesticulated, articulated, and exerted himself in a hundred ways, while great drops of sweat rolled down his face. When his tongue could no longer move, his arm came to his aid. He dismounted, and traced on the sand a geographical map, with lines of latitude and longitude, the two oceans, and the road to Carmen. Never was professor in such embarrassment. Thalcave watched these manœuvres without showing whether he comprehended or not.

The lesson in geography lasted more than half an hour. At last Paganel ceased, wiped his face, which was wet with perspiration, and looked at the Patagonian.

"Did he understand?" inquired Glenarvan.

"We shall see," replied Paganel; "but, if he did not, I give it up."

"PERHAPS!"

Thalcave did not stir. He no longer spoke. His eyes were fixed upon the figures traced on the sand, which the wind was gradually effacing.

"Well?" asked Paganel.

Thalcave did not appear to hear him. Paganel already saw an ironical smile forming upon the lips of the major, and, wishing to save his reputation, had begun with renewed energy his geographical demonstrations, when the Patagonian stopped him with a gesture.

"You are searching for a prisoner?" he said.

An important road—that from Carmen to Mendoza—distinguishable by the bones of such animals as mules, horses, sheep and oxen, whose remains were scattered by the birds of prey, and lay bleaching in the sun.

"Yes," replied Paganel.

"And exactly on the line from the setting to the rising sun?" said Thalcave, indicating by a comparison, in the Indian manner, the course from west to east.

"Yes, yes, that is it!"

"And it is your God," said the Patagonian, "who has confided to the waves of the vast ocean the secrets of the prisoner?"

"God himself."

"May his will be accomplished then!" replied Thalcave, with a certain solemnity. "We will go to the east, and, if necessary, even to the sun."

Paganel, in his exultation over his pupil, immediately translated to his companions the replies of the Indian.

Glenarvan requested Paganel to ask the Patagonian if he had heard of any strangers falling into the hands of the Indians, which was accordingly done.

"Perhaps," replied the Patagonian.

As soon as this word was translated, Thalcave was surrounded by the seven travelers, who gazed at him with questioning looks. Paganel, excited and scarcely finding his words, resumed these interesting interrogatories, while his eyes, fixed upon the grave Indian, strove to anticipate his reply before it issued from his lips. Every word the Patagonian said he repeated in English, so that his companions heard the Indian speak, as it were, in their own language.

"And this prisoner?" inquired Paganel.

"He was a stranger," replied Thalcave slowly; "a European."

"You have seen him?"

"No, but he is mentioned in the accounts of the Indians. He was a brave man."

"You understand, my friends," said Paganel; "a courageous man!"

"My father!" cried Robert Grant.

Then, addressing Paganel:

"How do you say 'It is my father,' in Spanish?" he asked.

"*Es mio padre*," answered the geographer.

Immediately Robert, taking Thalcave's hands, said in a sweet voice,—

"*Es mio padre!*"

"*Suo padre!*" replied the Patagonian, whose look brightened.

He took the boy in his arms, lifted him from his horse, and gazed at him with the most curious sympathy. His intelligent countenance became suffused with a peaceful emotion.

But Paganel had not finished his inquiries. Where was this prisoner? What was he doing? When had Thalcave heard of him? All these questions thronged his mind at once. He did not have to wait long for answers, but learnt that the European was a slave of one of the Indian tribes that scour the plains.

"But where was he last?" asked Paganel.

"With the cazique Calfoucoura," answered Thalcave.

"On the line we have been following?"

"Yes."

"And who is this cazique?"

"The chief of the Poyuches Indians; a man with two tongues and two hearts."

A SCIENTIFIC BATH.

"That is to say, false in word and in deed," said Paganel, after translating to his companions this beautiful metaphor of the Indian language. "And can we rescue our friend?" he added.

"Perhaps so, if your friend is still in the hands of the Indians."

"And when did you hear of him?"

"A long time ago, and, since then, the sun has brought back two summers to the sky."

Glenarvan's joy could not be described. This answer coincided exactly with the date of the document. But one question remained to be asked.

"You speak of a prisoner," said Paganel; "but were there not three?"

"I do not know," replied Thalcave.

"And you know nothing of their actual situation?"

"Nothing."

This last word ended the conversation. It was possible that the three prisoners had been separated a long time. But the substance of the Patagonian's information was that the Indians spoke of a European who had fallen into their power. The date of his captivity, the place where he must have been, everything, even to the Patagonian phrase used to express his courage, related evidently to Captain Harry Grant.

Their progress was now somewhat slow and difficult; their next object being to reach and cross the river Colorado, to which at length their horses brought them. Here Paganel's first care was to bathe "geographically" in its waters, which are colored by a reddish clay. He was surprised to find the depth so great as it really was, this being the result of the snow having melted rapidly under the first heat of summer. The width likewise of this stream was so considerable that it was almost impossible for their horses to swim across; but they happily discovered a sort of weir-bridge, of wattles looped and fastened together, which the Indians were in the habit of using; and by its aid the little troop was enabled to pass over to the left bank, where they rested for the night.

Chapter XVII

A SERIOUS NECESSITY.

They set out at daybreak. The horses advanced at a brisk pace among the tufts of "paja-brava," a kind of grass that serves the Indians as a shelter during the storms. At certain distances, but less and less frequent, pools of shallow water contributed to the growth of willows and a certain plant which is found in the neighborhood of fresh water. Here the horses drank their fill, to fortify themselves for the journey. Thalcave, who rode in advance, beat the bushes, and thus frightened away the "cholinas" (vipers), while the agile Thaouka bounded over all obstacles, and aided his master in clearing a passage for the horses that followed.

Early in the afternoon, the first traces of animals were encountered—the bones of an innumerable drove of cattle, in whitened heaps. These fragments did not extend in a winding line, such as animals exhausted and falling one by one would leave behind them. Thus no one, not even Paganel, knew how to explain this chain of skeletons in a space comparatively circumscribed. He therefore questioned Thalcave, who was not at a loss for a reply.

"What is this?" they asked, after Paganel had inquired of the Indian.

"The fire of heaven," replied the geographer.

"What! the lightning could not have produced such a disaster," said Tom Austin, "and stretched five hundred head of cattle on the earth!"

But Thalcave reaffirmed it, and he was not mistaken; for the storms of the Pampas are noted for their violence.

At evening they stopped at an abandoned rancho, made of interlaced branches plastered with mud and covered with thatch. This structure stood within an inclosure of half-rotten stakes which, however, sufficed to protect the horses during the night against the attacks of the foxes. Not that they had anything to fear personally from these animals, but the malicious beasts gnawed the halters, so that the horses could escape.

A few paces from the rancho, a hole was dug which served as a kitchen and contained half-cooled embers. Within, there was a bench, a bed of ox-hide, a saucepan, a spit, and a pot for boiling maté. The maté is a drink very much in use in South America. It is the Indian's tea, consisting of a decoction of leaves dried in the fire, and is imbibed through a straw. At Paganel's request, Thalcave prepared several cups of this beverage, which very agreeably accompanied the ordinary eatables, and was declared excellent.

They set out at daybreak. The horses advanced at a brisk pace among the tufts of "paja-brava," a kind of grass that serves the Indians as a shelter during the storms.

A CHANGE FOR THE WORSE.

The next day they resumed their journey towards the east. About noon a change took place in the appearance of the Pampas, which could not escape eyes wearied with its monotony. The grass became more and more scanty, and gave place to sickly burdocks and gigantic thistles; while stunted nettles and other thorny shrubs grew here and there. Heretofore, a certain moisture, preserved by the clay of the prairie, freshened the meadows; the vegetation was thick and luxuriant. But now a patchy growth, bare in many places, exposed the earth, and indicated the poverty of the soil. These signs of increasing dryness could not be mistaken, and Thalcave called attention to them.

"I am not sorry at this change," said Tom Austin; "to see always grass, nothing but grass, becomes tiresome before long."

"But where there is grass there is water," replied the major.

"Oh, we are not in want," said Wilson, "and shall find some river on our course."

However, when Wilson said that the supply of water would not fail he had not calculated for the unquenchable thirst that consumed his companions all that day; and, when he added that they would meet with some stream in their journey he had anticipated too much. Indeed, not only were rivers wanting, but even the artificial wells dug by the Indians were empty. On seeing these indications of dryness increase from mile to mile, Paganel asked Thalcave where he expected to find water.

"At Lake Salinas," replied the Indian.

"And when shall we arrive there?"

"To-morrow evening."

The natives ordinarily, when they travel on the Pampas, dig wells, and find water a few feet below the surface; but the travelers, destitute of the necessary implements, could not employ this expedient. It was therefore necessary to obtain a supply in some other way, for, if they did not absolutely suffer from the tormenting desire for drink, no one could entirely allay his thirst.

At evening they halted, after a journey of thirty miles. Every one relied upon a good night to recruit himself after the fatigues of the day; but they were greatly annoyed by a very persistent swarm of mosquitoes, which disappeared, however, after the wind changed.

If the major preserved his calmness in the midst of the petty annoyances of life, Paganel, on the contrary, could not treat the matter so indifferently. He fought the mosquitoes, and sadly regretted the absence of his acid-water, which would have soothed the pain of their bites. Although the major endeavored to console him, he awoke in a very bad humor.

However, he was very easily persuaded to set out at daybreak, for it was important to arrive at Lake Salinas the same day. The horses were very much exhausted: they were dying of thirst; and, although their riders had denied themselves on their account, still their share of water had been very limited. The dryness was to-day even greater, and the heat no less intolerable, with the dusty wind, the simoom of the Pampas.

INDIANS AHEAD!

During the day the monotony of the journey was interrupted. Mulready, who rode in advance, turned back, signaling the approach of a party of Indians. This meeting elicited different opinions. Glenarvan thought of the information that these natives might furnish concerning the shipwrecked seamen of the Britannia. Thalcave, for his part, scarcely enjoyed meeting in his journey the wandering Indians of the plains. He considered them plunderers and robbers, and only sought to avoid them. According to his orders, the little party collected together, and made ready their fire-arms. It was necessary to be prepared for any emergency.

The Indian detachment was soon perceived. It consisted of only ten men, which fact reassured the Patagonian. They approached within a hundred paces, so that they could be easily distinguished. Their high foreheads, prominent rather than receding, their tall forms, and their olive color, showed them to be magnificent types of the Indian race. They were clad in the skins of guanacos, and carried various weapons of war and the chase, while their dexterity in horsemanship was remarkable.

Having halted, they appeared to hold a conference, crying and gesticulating. Glenarvan advanced toward them; but he had not proceeded two yards, when the detachment wheeled about and disappeared with incredible swiftness. The tired horses of the travelers could never have overtaken them.

"The cowards!" cried Paganel.

"They fly too fast for honest men," said MacNabb.

"What are these Indians?" inquired Paganel of Thalcave.

"Gauchos!" replied the Patagonian.

"Gauchos!" repeated Paganel, turning toward his companions, "Gauchos! We had no need, then, to take such precautions. There was nothing to fear!"

"Why?" asked the major.

"Because the Gauchos are inoffensive peasants."

"Do you think so, Paganel?"

"Certainly. They took us for robbers, and fled."

Glenarvan was quite disappointed in not speaking with them, as he expected to obtain additional tidings of the lost sailors; but it was necessary to push on, if they would reach their destination that evening.

At eight o'clock Thalcave, who had gone a little in advance, announced that the lake so long desired was in sight. A quarter of an hour afterward the little party descended the high banks. But here a serious disappointment awaited them,—the lake was dry!

CHAPTER XVIII

IN SEARCH OF WATER.

Lake Salinas terminates the cluster of lagoons that adjoin the Ventana and Guamini mountains. Numerous expeditions are made to this place to obtain supplies of salt, with which these waters are strongly impregnated. But now the water had evaporated under the heat of the sun, and the lake was only a vast glittering basin.

When Thalcave announced the presence of a drinkable liquid at Lake Salinas, he meant the streams of fresh water that flow from it in many places. But at this time its affluents were as dry as itself. The burning sun had absorbed everything. Hence, the consternation was general when the thirsty party arrived at the parched shores of Lake Salinas.

It was necessary to take counsel. The little water in the leathern bottles was half spoiled, and could not quench their thirst, which began to make itself acutely felt. Hunger and fatigue gave place to this imperative want. A "roukah," a kind of upright tent, of leather, which stood in a hollow, and had been abandoned by the natives, served as a refuge for the travelers, while their horses, stretched on the muddy shores of the lake, ate the saline plants and dry reeds, although reluctantly.

When each had sat down in the roukah, Paganel asked Thalcave's advice as to what was best to be done. A rapid conversation, of which Glenarvan caught a few words, ensued between the geographer and the Indian. Thalcave spoke calmly, while Paganel gesticulated for both. This consultation lasted a few minutes, and then the Patagonian folded his arms.

"What did he say?" inquired Glenarvan. "I thought I understood him to advise us to separate."

"Yes, into two parties," replied Paganel. "Those of us whose horses are so overcome with fatigue and thirst that they can scarcely move will continue the journey as well as possible. Those who are better mounted, on the contrary, will ride in advance, and reconnoitre the Guamini River, which empties into Lake San Lucas. If there is sufficient water there, they will wait for their companions on the banks of the stream; if not, they will return to save the rest a useless journey."

"And then?" asked Tom Austin.

"Then we must go southward to the first branches of the Ventana mountains, where the rivers are numerous."

"The plan is good," replied Glenarvan, "and we will follow it without delay. My horse has not suffered so much yet from want of water, and I offer to accompany Thalcave."

"Oh, my lord, take me!" cried Robert, as if a pleasure excursion were in question.

"But can you keep up with us, my child?"

"Yes, I have a good beast that asks nothing better than to go in advance. Will you, my lord? I beseech you!"

"Come then, my boy," said Glenarvan, delighted not to be separated from Robert. "And we three," he added, "will be very stupid if we do not discover some clear and fresh stream."

"And I?" said Paganel.

"Oh, you, my dear Paganel!" replied the major, "you will remain with the reserve detachment. You know the course, the Guamini River, and the Pampas, too well to abandon us. Neither Wilson, Mulready, nor myself are capable of rejoining Thalcave at his rendezvous, unless we advance confidently under the guidance of the brave Jacques Paganel."

"I resign," said the geographer, very much flattered to obtain a higher command.

"But no distractions!" added the major. "Do not lead us where we have nothing to do, and bring us back to the shores of the Pacific!"

"You would deserve it, my intolerable major," said Paganel, smiling. "But tell me, my dear Glenarvan, how will you understand Thalcave's language?"

"I suppose," answered Glenarvan, "that the Patagonian and I will not need to talk. Besides, with the few Spanish words that I know, I shall succeed well enough on an emergency in giving him my opinion and understanding his."

"Go then, my worthy friend," replied Paganel.

"Let us eat first," said Glenarvan, "and sleep till the hour of departure."

They ate supper without drink, which was rather unrefreshing, and then fell asleep. Paganel dreamed of torrents, cascades, streams, rivers, ponds, brooks, nay even full bottles, in short, of everything which generally contains water. It was a real nightmare.

The next morning at six o'clock the horses were saddled. They gave them the last drink of water left, which they took with more dislike than pleasure, for it was very nauseating. The three horsemen then mounted.

"*Au revoir!*" said the major, Austin, Wilson, and Mulready.

Soon the Patagonian, Glenarvan, and Robert (not without a certain throbbing of the heart) lost sight of the detachment confided to the sagacity of the geographer.

"Poor father!" exclaimed Robert; "how he will thank you when you have found him!" And, so saying, he took his lordship's hand and pressed it to his lips.

THE YOUNG SAILOR ON HORSEBACK.

Thalcave was right in first proceeding towards the Guamini, since this stream lay on the prescribed course, and was the nearest. The three horses galloped briskly forward. These excellent beasts perceived, doubtless, by instinct, whither their masters were guiding them. Thaouka, especially, showed a spirit that neither fatigue nor thirst could overcome. The other horses followed, at a slower pace, but incited by his example.

The Patagonian frequently turned his head to look at Robert Grant, and, seeing the young boy firm and erect, in an easy and graceful position, testified his satisfaction by a word of encouragement.

"Bravo, Robert!" said Glenarvan. "Thalcave seems to congratulate you. He praises you, my boy!"

"And why, my lord?"

"Because of the way you ride."

"Oh, I merely keep firm; that is all," replied Robert, who blushed with pleasure at hearing himself complimented.

"That is the main point, Robert," said Glenarvan; "but you are too modest, and I am sure you cannot fail to become an accomplished equestrian."

"Well," said Robert, "but what will papa say, who wishes to make a sailor of me?"

"The one does not interfere with the other. If all horsemen do not make good sailors, all sailors may certainly make good horsemen. To ride on the yards, you must learn to keep yourself firm. As for knowing how to manage your horse, that comes more easily."

"Poor father!" exclaimed Robert; "how he will thank you when you have found him!" And, so saying, he took his lordship's hand and pressed it to his lips.

"You love him well, Robert?"

"Yes, my lord; he was so kind to sister and me. He thought only of us, and every voyage brought us a memento of the countries he visited, and, what was better, tender caresses and kind words, on his return. Ah! you will love him too, when you know him! Mary resembles him. He has a sweet voice like her. It is singular for a sailor, is it not?"

"Yes, very singular, Robert," said Glenarvan.

"I see him still," replied the boy, as if speaking to himself. "Good and brave papa! He rocked me to sleep on his knees, when I was little, and kept humming an old Scottish song which is sung around the lakes of our country. I sometimes recall the air, but indistinctly. How we loved him, my lord! Well, I think one must be very young to love his father well."

"And old to reverence him, my child," replied Glenarvan, quite moved by the words that came from this young heart.

During this conversation, their horses had relaxed their pace and fallen behind the other; but Thalcave called them, and they resumed their former gait. It was soon evident, however, that, with the exception of Thaouka, the horses could not long maintain this speed. At noon it was necessary to give them an hour's rest.

Glenarvan grew uneasy. The signs of dryness did not diminish, and the want of water might result in disastrous consequences. Thalcave said nothing, but probably thought that if the Guamini was dry it would then be time to despair, if indeed an Indian's heart has ever experienced such an emotion.

They therefore kept on, and by use of whip and spur the horses were induced to continue their journey, but they could not quicken their pace. Thalcave might easily have gone ahead, for in a few hours Thaouka could have carried him to the banks of the stream. He doubtless thought of it, but probably did not like to leave his two companions alone in the midst of this desert, and, that he might not outstrip them, he forced Thaouka to lessen his speed. It was not, however, without much resistance, prancing and neighing, that Thalcave's horse consented to keep pace with the others. It was not so much the strength as the voice of his master which restrained him; the Indian actually talked to his horse; and the animal, if he did not answer, at least comprehended him. The Patagonian must have used excellent arguments, for, after "discussing" some time, Thaouka yielded, and obeyed his master's commands.

GAINED AT LAST.

But, if Thaouka understood Thalcave, Thalcave had none the less understood Thaouka. The intelligent animal, through his superior instincts, had perceived a moisture in the air. He inhaled it eagerly, and kept moving his tongue, as if it were steeped in a grateful liquid. The Patagonian could not be deceived; water was not far distant.

He therefore encouraged his companions by explaining the impatience of his horse, which the others were not long in understanding. They made a final effort, and galloped after the Indian.

About three o'clock a bright line appeared in a hollow of the plain. It trembled under the rays of the sun.

"Water!" cried Glenarvan.

"Water, yes, water!" cried Robert.

They had no more need to urge their horses. The poor beasts, feeling their strength renewed, rushed forward with an irresistible eagerness. In a few moments they had reached the Guamini River, and, saddled as they were, plunged to their breasts into the cooling stream. Their masters imitated their example, without reluctance, and took an afternoon bath which was as healthful as it was pleasant.

"Ah, how good it is!" said Robert, as he quenched his thirst in the middle of the river.

"Be moderate, my boy," said Glenarvan, who did not set a good example.

Nothing was heard but the sound of rapid drinking. As for Thalcave, he drank quietly, without hurrying, long and deeply, till they might perhaps fear that the stream would be drained.

"Well," said Glenarvan, "our friends will not be disappointed in their expectations. They are sure, on arriving at the Guamini, to find an abundance of clear water, if Thalcave leaves any!"

"But could we not go to meet them?" asked Robert. "We could spare them several hours of anxiety."

"Doubtless, my boy; but how carry the water? Wilson has charge of the water-bottles. No, it is better to wait, as we agreed.

Calculating the necessary time, and the slow pace of the horses, our friends will be here at night. Let us, then, prepare them a safe shelter and a good repast."

Thalcave had not waited for Glenarvan's orders to search for a place to encamp. He had very fortunately found on the banks of the river a "ramada," a kind of inclosure designed for a cattle-fold and shut in on three sides. The situation was excellent for the purpose, so long as one did not fear to sleep in the open air; and that was the least anxiety of Thalcave's companions. Thus they did not seek a better retreat, but stretched themselves on the ground in the sun to dry their water-soaked garments.

"Well, since here is shelter," said Glenarvan, "let us think of supper. Our friends must be satisfied with the couriers whom they have sent forward; and, if I am not greatly mistaken, they will have no reason to complain. I think an hour's hunting will not be time lost. Are you ready, Robert?"

"Yes, my lord," replied he, with gun in hand.

AN EVENING'S SPORT.

Glenarvan had conceived this idea because the banks of the Guamini seemed to be the haunt of the game of the surrounding plains. "Tinamous," a kind of partridge, plovers called "teru-teru," yellow rails, and water-fowl of magnificent green were seen rising in flocks. As for quadrupeds, they did not make their appearance; but Thalcave, pointing to the tall grass and thick coppice, explained that they were hidden there. The hunters had only to take a few steps to find themselves in one of the best game-coverts in the world.

They began to hunt, therefore, and, disdaining the feathered tribe, their first attempts were made upon the large game of the Pampas. Soon hares and guanacos, like those that had attacked them so violently on the Andes, started up before them by hundreds; but these very timid animals fled with such swiftness that it was impossible to come within gun-shot. The hunters, therefore, attacked other game that was less fleet. A dozen partridges and rails were brought down, and Glenarvan shot a peccary, which was very good eating.

In less than half an hour they had obtained without difficulty all the game they needed. Robert captured a curious animal called an armadillo, which was covered with a sort of helmet of movable bony pieces and measured a foot and a half in length. It was very fat, and would be an excellent dish, as the Patagonian said; while Robert was proud of his success.

As for Thalcave, he showed his companions a "nandou" hunt. This bird, peculiar to the Pampas, is a kind of ostrich, whose swiftness is marvelous.

The Indian did not try to decoy so nimble an animal, but urged his horse to a gallop, straight towards the bird, so as to overtake it at once, for, if the first attack should fail, the nandou would soon fatigue both horse and rider with its giddy backward and forward movements.

Thalcave, arriving at a proper distance, launched his "bolas" with a strong hand, and so skillfully that they twisted about the legs of the ostrich and paralyzed its efforts. In a few moments it lay on the ground. The Indian soon captured his prize and contributed it to the common repast. The string of partridges, Thalcave's ostrich, Glenarvan's peccary, and Robert's armadillo were brought back to camp. The ostrich and the peccary were immediately stripped of their skin and cut into small slices. As for the armadillo, it is a dainty animal which carries its roasting dish with it, and it was, accordingly, placed in its own bony covering on the glowing embers.

The three hunters were satisfied with the partridges for supper, and kept the rounds of beef for their friends. This repast was washed down with clear water, which was then considered superior to all the wines in the world.

The horses were not forgotten. A great quantity of dry fodder, piled in the ramada, served them for food and bedding.

DESERT SILENCE.

When everything was ready, Glenarvan, Robert, and the Indian wrapped themselves in their ponchos, and stretched their limbs on a bundle of alfafares, the usual bed of the hunters of the Pampas.

CHAPTER XIX

THE RED WOLVES.

Night came,—the night of the new moon, only the uncertain light of the stars illumined the plain. On the horizon the zodiacal light faded away in a dark mist. The waters of the Guamini flowed without a murmur, while birds, quadrupeds, and reptiles reposed after the fatigues of the day. The silence of the desert reigned on the vast expanse of the Pampas.

Glenarvan, Robert, and Thalcave had yielded to the common law, and, stretched on their thick beds of grass, they enjoyed a refreshing sleep. The horses, overcome with fatigue, had lain down on the ground: Thaouka alone, like a true blooded horse, slept standing, spirited in repose as in action, and ready to start at the least sign from his master. Perfect tranquillity reigned within the inclosure, and the embers of the night-fire, as they gradually died out, cast their last rays over the silent obscurity.

About ten o'clock, after a short sleep, the Indian awoke. His eyes became fixed beneath his lowered eyebrows, and his head was turned in a listening attitude towards the plain. He seemed endeavoring to detect some scarcely perceptible sound. A vague uneasiness was soon expressed on his face, usually so calm. Had he perceived the approach of prowling Indians, or the coming of jaguars, water-tigers, and other formidable beasts which are numerous in the neighborhood of rivers? This last possibility doubtless appeared plausible to him, for he cast a rapid glance over the combustible materials piled in the inclosure, and his anxiety increased. In fact, all this dry bedding would quickly be consumed, and could not long intimidate the audacious animals.

According to this conjecture, Thalcave had only to await the progress of events, which he did, half reclining, his head resting on his hands, his elbows on his knees, his eyes motionless, in the attitude of a man whom a sudden anxiety has awakened from sleep.

An hour passed. Any other person but Thalcave, reassured by the outward silence, would have lain down again. But where a stranger would have suspected nothing, the highly-trained senses and natural instinct of the Indian foresaw the coming danger.

While he was listening and watching, Thaouka gave a low neigh. His nose was stretched towards the entrance to the ramada. The Patagonian suddenly started.

"Thaouka has scented some enemy," said he.

He arose and scanned the plain attentively. Silence still reigned, but not tranquillity. Thalcave discerned shadows moving noiselessly among the tufts of grass. Here and there glittered luminous points, which spread on all sides, now fading away, and now gleaming forth again. You would have thought fantastic elves were dancing on the surface of an immense lagoon. A stranger would doubtless have taken these flitting sparks for glow-worms, which shine, when night comes, in many parts of the Pampas. But Thalcave was not deceived; he knew with what enemies he had to deal. He loaded his carbine, and took a position near the first stakes of the inclosure.

He did not wait long. A strange cry, a mingling of barks and howls, resounded over the plain. The report of the carbine answered it, and was followed by a hundred frightful yelps. Glenarvan and Robert suddenly awoke.

FEARFUL ODDS.

"What is the matter?" asked Robert.

"Indians?" said Glenarvan.

"No," replied Thalcave, "aguaras."

Robert looked at Glenarvan.

"Aguaras?" said he.

"Yes," replied Glenarvan, "the red wolves of the Pampas."

Both seized their weapons, and joined the Indian. The latter pointed to the plain, from which arose a series of formidable howls. Robert involuntarily took a step backward.

"You are not afraid of the wolves, my boy?" said Glenarvan.

"No, my lord," replied Robert, in a firm tone. "With you I fear nothing."

"So much the better. These aguaras are not very formidable beasts; and were it not for their numbers I should not even think of them."

"What does it matter?" replied Robert. "We are well armed. Let them come."

"And they shall be well received."

Speaking thus, Glenarvan endeavored to reassure the lad; but he did not think without a secret terror of that dense horde of exasperated beasts. Perhaps there were hundreds of them; and these three, however well armed, could not advantageously contend against so many and such antagonists.

By the howls that resounded over the Pampas, and by the multitude of shadows that flitted about the plain, Glenarvan could not be mistaken as to the number. These animals had scented a sure prey, horse-flesh or human flesh, and not one among them would return to his lair without having his portion. The situation was, therefore, very alarming.

Meanwhile the circle of wolves grew gradually narrower. The horses, awakened, gave signs of the liveliest terror. Thaouka alone pawed the ground, seeking to break his halter, and ready to rush out. His master succeeded in calming him only by whistling continually.

Glenarvan and Robert had stationed themselves so as to defend the entrance of the ramada, and with their loaded rifles were about to fire at the first ranks of wolves, when Thalcave turned aside their weapons already poised for a shot.

"What does Thalcave wish?" asked Robert.

"He prohibits us from firing," answered Glenarvan.

"Why?"

"Perhaps he does not consider it the proper time."

This was not, however, the motive which actuated the Indian, but a graver reason, which Glenarvan understood when Thalcave, raising his powder-flask and inverting it, showed that it was almost empty.

"Well?" said Robert.

"We must economize our ammunition. Our hunt to-day has cost us dear, and we are deficient in powder and shot. We have not twenty charges left."

The boy answered nothing.

"You are not afraid, Robert?"

"No, my lord."

"Very well, my boy."

At this moment another report resounded. Thalcave had brought down a too bold enemy. The wolves that were advancing in close ranks recoiled, and gathered together again a hundred paces from the inclosure.

THE LAST HOUR.

Glenarvan, at a sign from the Indian, took his place at once, while the latter, collecting the bedding, grass, and all combustible materials, piled them at the entrance of the ramada and threw on a burning ember. Soon a curtain of flame was defined against the dark background of the sky, and through the openings the plain appeared illumined by great moving reflections. Glenarvan could therefore judge of the great number of animals against which they had to defend themselves. Never had so many wolves been seen together before, nor so excited by rapacity. The fiery barrier that Thalcave had just opposed to them had redoubled their fury. Some, however, advanced to the very fire, crowded by the rear ranks, and burned their paws. From time to time a shot was necessary to check the howling horde, and at the end of an hour fifteen bodies lay on the prairie.

The besieged were now in a situation relatively less dangerous. So long as their supplies lasted, so long as the barrier of fire stood at the entrance to the ramada, invasion was not to be feared. But what was to be done if all these methods of repelling the wolves should fail at the same time?

Glenarvan gazed at Robert, and felt his heart beat quick with excitement. He forgot himself, and thought only of this poor child, who displayed a courage beyond his years. Robert was pale, but his hand did not leave his weapon, and he awaited with firm bearing the assault of the enraged wolves.

Meantime, Glenarvan, after coolly considering the situation, resolved to do something decisive.

"In one hour," said he, "we shall have no more powder, shot, or fire. We must not wait till then to make a sally."

He turned towards Thalcave, and, recalling a few words of Spanish, began a conversation with the Indian, frequently interrupted by the cracks of the rifle.

It was not without difficulty that these two men succeeded in understanding each other. Glenarvan, fortunately, knew the habits of the red wolf. Without this knowledge he could not have interpreted the words and gestures of the Patagonian.

Nevertheless, a quarter of an hour passed before he could give to Robert the meaning of Thalcave's answer. He had questioned the Indian concerning their situation.

"And what did he answer?" inquired Robert.

"He said that, cost what it may, we must hold out till daybreak. The aguara goes out only at night, and when morning comes he returns to his lair. He is the wolf of darkness, a cowardly beast that fears the daylight."

"Well, let us defend ourselves till day."

"Yes, my boy, and with our knives if we can no longer use our guns."

Already Thalcave had set the example, and when a wolf approached the fire, the long knife of the Patagonian was thrust through the flames and drawn back again red with blood.

However, the means of defense were failing. About two o'clock in the morning, Thalcave threw into the fire the last armful of fuel, and the besieged had only five charges left.

Glenarvan cast about him a sorrowful glance. He thought of the child who was there, of his companions, of all whom he loved. Robert said nothing; perhaps the danger did not appear imminent to his hopeful spirit. But Glenarvan pictured to himself that terrible event, now apparently inevitable, the being devoured alive! He was not master of his emotion; he drew the child to his breast, he clasped him to his heart, he pressed his lips to his forehead, while tears flowed from his eyes.

Robert gazed at him with a smile. "I am not afraid," said he.

"No, my boy, no," replied Glenarvan; "and you are right. In two hours, day will appear, and we shall be saved! Well done, Thalcave, my brave Patagonian!" cried he, as the Indian killed with the butt of his gun two enormous beasts that were attempting to cross the glowing barrier.

A DYING HOPE.

But at this moment the dying light of the fire showed him the aguaras advancing in a dense body to assail the ramada. The dénouement of the bloody drama was approaching. The fire gradually subsided, for want of fuel; the flames sank; the plain, before illumined, now relapsed into shadow, and in the shadow reappeared the terrible eyes of the red wolves. A few moments more, and the whole drove would rush into the inclosure.

Thalcave discharged his carbine for the last time, stretched out one more of their enemies, and, as his ammunition was exhausted, folded his arms. His head sank upon his breast; he appeared to be questioning himself. Was he searching for some bold, novel, or rash scheme for repelling this furious herd? Glenarvan did not venture to ask him.

At this moment a change took place in the action of the wolves. They seemed to be retreating, and their howls, so deafening before, suddenly ceased. An ominous silence reigned over the plain.

"They are going," said Robert.

"Perhaps," replied Glenarvan, who was listening with intentness.

But Thalcave shook his head. He knew well that the animals would not abandon a certain prey until at daybreak they returned to their holes and dens.

However, the tactics of their enemies had evidently changed, they no longer endeavored to force the entrance of the ramada; but their new manœuvres were already causing a still more imminent danger.

The wolves, abandoning their design of penetrating the inclosure by this entrance, which was defended by weapon and fire, went to the back of the ramada and sought to assail it in the rear. Their claws were soon heard rattling against the half-decayed wood.

Already their powerful paws and bloody mouths had forced their way between the shattered stakes. The horses, bewildered and panic-stricken, broke their halters and dashed into the inclosure. Glenarvan seized Robert in his arms, to defend him to the last extremity; and he would have attempted a rash flight, and rushed out of the ramada, had not his eyes fallen upon the Indian.

Thalcave, turning like a deer, had suddenly approached his horse, which was neighing with impatience, and was beginning to saddle him carefully, forgetting neither strap nor buckle. He seemed no longer to care for the howls, that were now redoubled. Glenarvan gazed at him with a dark foreboding.

"He is leaving us!" cried he, seeing Thalcave gather up his reins as though he were about to mount.

"He? never!" said Robert.

In truth the Indian was about to make a venture, not to leave his friends, but to save them by sacrificing himself. Thaouka was ready. He champed his bit; he pranced; his eyes, full of a fiery spirit, shot forth lightning flashes; he understood his master.

Just as the Indian was seizing the mane of his horse, Glenarvan caught him by the arm with a convulsive grasp.

"You are going?" said he, pointing to the plain, which was now deserted.

"Yes," replied the Indian, who comprehended the gesture of his companion; and, with vehement gesticulations which were however perfectly intelligible, he added a few words in Spanish, which signified: "Thaouka—good horse—swift—will draw the wolves after him."

"Ha! Thalcave!" cried Glenarvan.

"Quick, quick!" continued the Indian; while Glenarvan said to Robert, in a voice broken by emotion,—

Frightful howls resounded. The wolves, starting on the track of the horse, fled into the darkness with a terrible speed.

"Robert, my lad, you hear! He will sacrifice himself for us; he will rush out over the plain, and turn aside the fury of the wolves upon himself."

"Friend Thalcave," replied Robert, looking imploringly at the Patagonian, "friend Thalcave, do not leave us!"

"No," said Glenarvan, "he will not leave us."

And, turning to the Indian, he added, pointing to the terrified horses crowding against the stakes,—

"Let us go together."

"No," said the Indian, who was not mistaken as to the meaning of these words. "Bad beasts—frightened—Thaouka—good horse."

"Very well," said Glenarvan. "Thalcave shall not leave, Robert. He shows me what I have to do. It is my duty to go, and his to remain with you."

Then, seizing Thaouka's bridle, he added,—

"I will go."

"No," replied the Patagonian, calmly.

"I tell you," cried Glenarvan, taking the bridle from the hands of the Indian, "I will go. Save this boy! I trust him to you, Thalcave!"

Glenarvan, in his excitement, mingled English and Spanish together. But what matters the language? In such a terrible situation, signs tell all, and men quickly understand each other.

SAFETY FOR TWO.

However, Thalcave resisted, and the discussion was prolonged. The danger was increasing every moment. Already the broken stakes were yielding to the teeth and claws of the wolves. But neither Glenarvan nor Thalcave appeared willing to yield. The Indian had drawn Glenarvan towards the entrance of the inclosure. He pointed to the plain, now free from wolves. In his animated language, he explained that not a moment was to be lost; that the danger, if this plan failed, would be greater for those who remained; in short, that he alone knew Thaouka well enough to employ his marvelous agility and speed for the common safety. Glenarvan blindly persisted in his resolve to sacrifice himself, when suddenly he was pushed violently back. Thaouka pranced, reared on his hind legs, and all at once, with a spring, cleared the barrier of fire and the rampart of bodies, while a boyish voice cried,—

"God save you, my lord!"

Glenarvan and Thalcave had scarcely time to perceive Robert, who, clinging to the horse's mane, disappeared in the darkness.

"Robert, unfortunate!" cried Glenarvan.

But these words the Indian himself could not hear. Frightful howls resounded. The wolves, starting on the track of the horse, fled into the darkness with a terrible speed.

Thalcave and Glenarvan rushed out of the ramada. Already the plain had resumed its tranquillity, and they could scarcely distinguish a moving line which undulated afar in the shadows of the night.

Glenarvan sank upon the ground, overcome, in despair, clasping his hands. He gazed at Thalcave, who smiled with his accustomed calmness.

"Thaouka—good horse—brave child—he will be saved!" he repeated, nodding his head.

"But if he falls?" said Glenarvan.

"He will not fall!"

In spite of Thalcave's confidence, his companion passed the night in terrible anguish. He was no longer even mindful of the danger still to be feared from the wolves. He would have gone in search of Robert, but the Indian restrained him, and explained that their horses could not overtake the boy, that Thaouka must have distanced his enemies, and could not be found in the darkness. They must wait for day to start in search of Robert.

At four o'clock in the morning day began to break. The mists of the horizon were soon tinged with pale rays. A sparkling dew covered the plain, and the tall grass began to wave under the first breezes of the dawn.

The moment of departure had arrived.

"Forward!" said the Indian.

Glenarvan did not reply, but sprang upon Robert's horse, and the two were soon galloping towards the west in the direction from which their companions were to come.

For an hour they traveled thus with great speed, gazing around for Robert, and dreading at each step to behold his mangled body. Glenarvan tortured the flanks of his horse with his spurs. Suddenly shots were heard, and reports at regular intervals, like signals for recognition.

"It is they!" cried Glenarvan.

Thalcave and he urged their horses to a more rapid pace, and a few moments afterwards they joined the party led by Paganel.

LIVELY GRATITUDE.

To Glenarvan's joy, Robert was there, alive, borne by the noble Thaouka, who neighed with pleasure at seeing his master.

"Ah, my boy! my boy!" cried Glenarvan, with unspeakable tenderness; and Robert and he, dismounting, rushed into each other's arms.

Then it was the Indian's turn to clasp to his breast the courageous son of Captain Grant.

"He lives! he lives!" exclaimed Glenarvan.

"Yes," replied Robert, "thanks to Thaouka."

The Indian had not waited for these words of gratitude to embrace his horse, but at that very moment he spoke to him and embraced him, as if human blood flowed in the veins of the noble animal. Then, turning towards Paganel, he pointed to young Robert.

"A brave boy!" said he.

Glenarvan, however, asked, even while he admired the lad,—

"Why, my son, did you not let Thalcave or me try this last chance of saving you?"

"My lord," replied he, in accents of the liveliest gratitude, "was it not my duty to sacrifice myself, when Thalcave has saved my life, and you are going to save my father?"

CHAPTER XX

STRANGE SIGNS.

After their first outbursts of joy at meeting were over, Paganel, Austin, Wilson, and Mulready—all who had remained behind, except the major—were conscious of one thing, namely, that they were suffering from thirst. Fortunately, the Guamini flowed at no great distance. They accordingly continued their journey, and at seven o'clock in the morning the little party arrived at the ramada. On seeing its entrance strewn with the bodies of the wolves, it was easy to understand the violence of the attack and the vigor of the defense. The travelers, after fully quenching their thirst, devoted their attention to breakfast in the inclosure. The ostrich-steaks were declared excellent, and the armadillo, roasted in its own covering, was a delicious dish.

"To eat reasonably of this," said Paganel, "would be ingratitude towards Providence. We really must eat immoderately."

And he did so accordingly,—but was not sick, thanks to the clear water of the Guamini, which appeared to possess superior digestive properties.

AEROSTATIC EXPERIMENTS.

At ten o'clock Glenarvan gave the signal for departure. The water-bottles were filled, and they set out. The horses, being greatly revived, evinced much spirit, and maintained an easy and almost continuous canter. The next morning they crossed the boundary which separates the Argentine Plains from the Pampas. Here Thalcave hoped to meet the chiefs in whose hands he doubted not that he should find Harry Grant and rescue him and his two companions from slavery.

Since they had left the Guamini, the travelers noticed, with great satisfaction, a considerable change in the temperature, thanks to the cold winds of Patagonia, which cause continual currents of air. Neither man nor beast had any reason to complain, after suffering so much from dryness and heat. They therefore pushed on with courage and confidence. But, whatever might have been said, the country seemed to be entirely uninhabited, or, to use a more exact word, "disinhabited."

Frequently they skirted the shores of fresh-water lagoons, on whose banks, in the shelter of the bushes, tiny wrens skipped and melodious larks warbled, in company with the brilliant-plumaged tanagers. These pretty birds gayly fluttered about, heedless of the haughty starlings that strutted on the banks like soldiers with their epaulettes and red breasts. In the thorny coppices the nests of the annubis swung like hammocks, and on the shores of the lagoons magnificent flamingoes, marching in regular file, spread their fiery-colored wings to the wind. Their nests were seen, by thousands together, like a small village, in the shape of truncated cones a foot high. The birds were not startled at the approach of the travelers, which was contrary to Paganel's calculations.

"I have been curious for a long time," said he to the major, "to see a flamingo fly."

"Well," said MacNabb.

"Now, since I have an opportunity, I shall profit by it."

"Do so, Paganel."

"Come with me, major, and you too, Robert; I need witnesses."

And Paganel, leaving his companions to go on, proceeded towards the flock of flamingoes, followed by Robert and the major. Arriving within range, Paganel fired a blank charge (for he would not needlessly destroy even a bird), and all the flamingoes flew away, while the geographer gazed at them attentively through his glasses.

"Well," said he to the major, when the flock had disappeared, "did you see them fly?"

"Certainly," replied MacNabb; "you could not do otherwise, unless you were blind. But let us hasten on, for we have fallen a mile behind."

When he had joined his companions, Paganel found Glenarvan in excited conversation with the Indian, whom he did not appear to understand. Thalcave had frequently stopped to examine the horizon, and each time his countenance expressed a lively astonishment. Glenarvan, not seeing his ordinary interpreter present, had attempted, but in vain, to question the Patagonian. So, as soon as he perceived the geographer at a distance, he cried,—

"Come, friend Paganel, Thalcave and I can scarcely succeed in understanding each other."

Paganel conversed a few moments with the Indian, and, turning to Glenarvan, said,—

"Thalcave is astonished at a circumstance that is really strange."

"What?"

"At meeting neither Indians, nor any traces of them, on these plains, which are usually furrowed with their trails, whether they are driving home the cattle stolen from the ranchos, or going to the Andes to sell their zorillo carpets and whips of braided leather."

"And to what does Thalcave attribute this abandonment?"

"He cannot tell; he is astonished. That is all."

"But what Indians did he expect to find in this part of the Pampas?"

"The very ones who have had foreign prisoners; those natives who are commanded by the caziques Calfoucoura, Catriel, and Yanchetruz."

"Who are these caziques?"

"Chiefs of tribes that were very powerful thirty years ago, before they were driven beyond the sierras. Since that time they have been subdued as much as an Indian can be, and now scour the Pampas as well as the province of Buenos Ayres. I am therefore astonished, like Thalcave, at not encountering traces of them in a country where they generally pursue the calling of plunderers."

"Well, then," inquired Glenarvan, "what course ought we to take?"

"I will see," replied Paganel.

After a few moments' conversation with Thalcave, he said,—

"This is his advice, which seems to me very wise. We must continue our journey to the east as far as Fort Independence; and there, if we have no news of Captain Grant, we shall at least know what has become of the Indians of the plain."

"Is Fort Independence far?"

"No; it is situated at Tandil, sixty miles distant."

"And when shall we arrive there?"

"On the evening of the day after to-morrow."

Arriving within range, Paganel fired a blank charge (for he would not needlessly destroy even a bird), and all the flamingoes flew away, while the geographer gazed at them attentively through his glasses.

Glenarvan was quite disconcerted at finding no Indians on the Pampas, a circumstance which was little expected. There are ordinarily too many of them. Some special cause must therefore have removed them. But a serious question was to be considered. If Captain Grant was a prisoner of one of these tribes, had he been carried to the north or to the south? This problem harassed Glenarvan. It was advisable at all hazards to keep track of the captain. In short, it was better to follow Thalcave's advice and reach the village of Tandil, where at least they could obtain information.

About four o'clock in the afternoon they approached a hill that might have passed for a mountain in so level a country. It was Tapalquem Sierra, and at its foot the travelers encamped for the night.

GALLOPING GAUCHOS.

The passage of this mountain was accomplished the next day with the greatest ease. They followed the sandy undulations of a gradually sloping terrace, which certainly did not present difficulties to people who had scaled the Andes, and the horses scarcely relaxed their rapid pace. At noon they reached the abandoned Fort Tapalquem, the first of the chain of forts built on the southern frontier against the plundering natives. But not a shadow of an Indian did they encounter, to the increasing surprise of Thalcave; although, towards the middle of the day, three rovers of the plain, well armed and mounted, gazed for a moment at the little party, but prevented their approach, galloping away with incredible rapidity. Glenarvan was furious.

"Gauchos," said the Patagonian.

"Ah! Gauchos," replied MacNabb. "Well, Paganel, what do you think of these creatures?"

"I think they look like famous bandits," answered Paganel.

"And hence of course are, my dear geographer?"

"Of course, my dear major."

Paganel's avowal was followed by a general laugh, which did not disconcert him at all.

According to Thalcave's orders, they advanced in close ranks, and at evening encamped in a spacious abandoned rancho, where the chief Catriel generally assembled his bands of natives. From an examination of the ground and the absence of fresh tracks, the Patagonian knew that it had not been occupied for a long time.

The next morning Glenarvan and his companions found themselves again on the plain. The first estancias (vast establishments for raising cattle), which border upon the Tandil, were descried; but Thalcave resolved not to stop, but to keep straight on to Fort Independence, where he wished to obtain information, especially concerning the singular condition of this abandoned country.

The trees, so rare since leaving the Andes, now reappeared. The greater part of these have been planted since the arrival of the Europeans on the American continent. They generally surround "corrals," vast cattle-inclosures protected with stakes. Here thousands of cattle, sheep, cows, and horses, branded with the mark of the owner, graze and fatten, while large numbers of huge dogs keep watch. The soil is admirably adapted to raising cattle, and yields an excellent fodder.

The people lead the life of the shepherds of the Bible. Their flocks are perhaps even more numerous than those which fed on the plains of Mesopotamia; but the family element is wanting, and the owners of the great folds of the Pampas have little to recommend themselves or their manner of life.

Paganel explained all these particulars to his companions, and even succeeded in interesting the major.

Thalcave, meanwhile, hastened their progress, as he wished to arrive that evening at Fort Independence. The horses, urged on by their masters, and following the example of Thaouka, dashed through the tall grass. They passed several farms, fortified and defended by deep ditches. The principal house was provided with an elevated terrace, from which the inmates could fire upon the plunderers of the plain. Glenarvan might perhaps have obtained here the information that he sought; but it was wisest to go to the village of Tandil. They did not stop, therefore, and soon the feet of the horses struck the grassy sward of the first mountain slopes. An hour afterward the village appeared at the bottom of a narrow gorge crowned by the embattled walls of Fort Independence.

In fact, they were a dozen young children and boys who were drilling very nicely. Their uniform consisted of a striped shirt confined at the waist by a leathern girdle.

CHAPTER XXI

A FALSE TRAIL.

Paganel, after giving his companions a brief account of the village of Tandil, added that they could not fail to obtain information there; moreover, the fort was always garrisoned by a detachment of national troops. Glenarvan, accordingly, put the horses into the stable of a "fonda;" and Paganel, the major, Robert, and he, under the guidance of Thalcave, proceeded towards Fort Independence.

After ascending the ridges of the mountains for a short time, they arrived at the postern, rather carelessly guarded by a native sentinel. They passed without difficulty, and inferred either great negligence or extreme security. A few soldiers were exercising on the parade-ground of the fort, the oldest of whom was not more than twenty and the youngest scarcely ten. In fact, they were a dozen young children and boys who were drilling very nicely. Their uniform consisted of a striped shirt confined at the waist by a leathern girdle. The mildness of the climate justified this light costume. Each of these young soldiers carried a gun and a sword, which were too long and heavy for the little fellows. All had a certain family resemblance, and the corporal who commanded resembled them too: they were twelve brothers, who were parading under the orders of the thirteenth.

AN ARGENTINE COMMANDANT.

Paganel was not astonished. He remembered his Argentine statistics, and knew that in this country the average number of children in a family exceeds nine. But what surprised him exceedingly was to see these little soldiers practicing the French tactics, and to hear the orders of the corporal given in his own native language.

"This is singular," said he.

But Glenarvan had not come to see boys drill, still less to occupy himself with their nationality or relationship. He did not, therefore, give Paganel time to express further astonishment, but besought him to ask for the commander of the fortress. Paganel did so, and one of the soldiers proceeded towards a small building which served as the barracks.

A few moments after, the commander appeared in person. He was a man of fifty, robust, with a military air, thick whiskers, prominent cheek-bones, gray hair, and commanding look, so far as one could judge through the clouds of smoke that issued from his short pipe.

Thalcave, addressing him, introduced Lord Glenarvan and his companions. While he spoke, the commander kept scrutinizing Paganel with quite embarrassing persistence. The geographer did not know what the trooper meant, and was about to ask him, when the latter unceremoniously seized his hand, and said, in a joyous tone, in his own language,—

"A Frenchman?"

"Yes, a Frenchman," replied Paganel.

"Ah, I am delighted! Welcome, welcome! I am almost a Frenchman," cried the commander, shaking the geographer's arm with rather painful violence.

"One of your friends?" asked the major of Paganel.

"Yes," replied he, with national pride; "we have friends in all parts of the world!"

"Ah, I am delighted! Welcome, welcome! I am almost a Frenchman," cried the commander, shaking the geographer's arm with rather painful violence.

RAISING A REGIMENT.

He then entered into conversation with the commander. Glenarvan would gladly have put in a word in regard to his affairs, but the soldier was telling his story, and was not in the mood to be interrupted. This honest man had left France a long time before; and the native language was no longer perfectly familiar to him: he had forgotten, if not words, at least the manner of combining them. As his visitors soon learned, he had been a sergeant in the French army. Since the foundation of the fort he had not left it, and commanded it by appointment from the Argentine government. He was by parentage a Basque, and his name was Manuel Ipharaguerre. A year after his arrival in the country, Sergeant Manuel was naturalized, joined the Argentine army, and married an honest Indian woman, who had twins,—boys, to be sure, for the sergeant's worthy consort would never present him with daughters. Manuel did not think of any other calling than that of the soldier, and hoped, in time, with the help of God, to offer to the republic a whole battalion of young soldiers.

"You have seen them?" said he. "Charming fellows! Good soldiers! José! Juan! Miguel! Pepe! Pepe is only seven years old, and is already biting his cartridge!"

Pepe, hearing himself complimented, joined his two little feet, and presented arms with perfect precision.

"He will do!" added the sergeant. "He will be a major—or brigadier-general one day!"

This story lasted a quarter of an hour, to Thalcave's great astonishment. The Indian could not understand how so many words could come from a single throat. No one interrupted the commander; and even a French sergeant had to conclude at last, though not without forcing his guests to accompany him to his dwelling. Here they were introduced to Madame Ipharaguerre, who appeared to be "a good-looking person," if this expression may be employed in regard to an Indian.

When he had exhausted himself, the sergeant asked his guests to what he owed the honor of their visit. And now it was their turn to explain.

Paganel, opening the conversation in French, told him of their journey across the Pampas, and ended by asking why the Indians had abandoned the country.

"War!" replied the sergeant.

"War?"

"Yes, civil war."

"Civil war?" rejoined Paganel.

"Yes, war between Paraguay and Buenos Ayres," answered the sergeant.

"Well?"

"Why, all the Indians of the north are in the rear of General Flores, and those of the plains are plundering."

"But the caziques?"

"The caziques with them."

This answer was reported to Thalcave, who shook his head. Indeed, he either did not know, or had forgotten, that a civil war, which was afterwards to involve Brazil, was decimating two-thirds of the republic. The Indians had everything to gain in these internal struggles, and could not neglect such fine opportunities for plunder. The sergeant, therefore, was not mistaken in attributing this desertion of the Pampas to the civil war that was being waged in the northern part of the Argentine Provinces.

But this event disconcerted Glenarvan's hopes. If Captain Grant was a prisoner of the caziques, he must have been carried by them to the northern frontiers. Yet how and where to find him? Must they attempt a perilous and almost useless search to the northern limits of the Pampas? It was a serious matter, which was to be earnestly considered.

However, one important question was still to be asked of the sergeant, and the major thought of this, while his companions were looking at each other in silence.

"Have you heard of any Europeans being retained as prisoners by the caziques of the Pampas?"

Manuel reflected for a few moments, like a man who recalls events to recollection.

"Yes," said he, at length.

"Ah!" cried Glenarvan, conceiving a new hope.

REVELATIONS.

Paganel, MacNabb, Robert, and he now surrounded the sergeant.

"Speak, speak!" cried they, gazing at him with eagerness even in their looks.

"Several years ago," replied Manuel, "yes,—that is it,—European prisoners—but have never seen them."

"Several years ago?" said Glenarvan. "You are mistaken. The date of the shipwreck is definite. The Britannia was lost in June, 1862, less than two years ago."

"Oh, more than that, my lord!"

"Impossible!" cried Paganel.

"Not at all. It was when Pepe was born. There were two men."

"No, three!" said Glenarvan.

"Two," replied the sergeant, in a positive tone.

"Two?" exclaimed Glenarvan, very much chagrined. "Two Englishmen?"

"No," continued the sergeant. "Who speaks of Englishmen? It was a Frenchman and an Italian."

"An Italian who was massacred by the Indians?" cried Paganel.

"Yes, and I learned afterwards—Frenchman saved."

"Saved!" exclaimed Robert, whose very life seemed to hang on the sergeant's lips.

"Yes, saved from the hands of the Indians," replied Manuel.

Each looked to the geographer, who beat his brow in despair.

"Ah! I understand," said he, at last. "All is clear, all is explained."

"But what is to be done?" asked Glenarvan, with as much anxiety as impatience.

"My friends," answered Paganel, taking Robert's hands, "we must submit to a severe misfortune. We have followed a false trail! The captive in question is not the captain, but one of my countrymen (whose companion, Marco Vazello, was actually assassinated by the Indians), a Frenchman who often accompanied these cruel savages to the banks of the Colorado, and who, after fortunately escaping from their hands, returned to France. While thinking that we were on the track of Captain Grant, we have fallen upon that of young Guinnard."

A profound silence followed this declaration. The mistake was palpable. The sergeant's story, the nationality of the prisoner, the murder of his companion, and his escape from the hands of the Indians, all accorded with the evident facts. Glenarvan gazed at Thalcave with a bewildered air. The Indian then resumed the conversation.

"Have you never heard of three English captives?" he asked the sergeant.

"Never," replied Manuel. "It would have been known at Tandil. I should have heard of it. No, it cannot be."

Glenarvan, after this formal response, had nothing more to do at Fort Independence. He and his friends, therefore, departed, not without thanking the sergeant and shaking hands with him.

Glenarvan was in despair at this complete overthrow of his hopes. Robert walked beside him in silence, with tearful eyes, while his protector could not find a single word to console him. Paganel gesticulated and talked to himself. The major did not open his lips. As for Thalcave, his Indian pride seemed humbled at having gone astray on a false trail. No one, however, thought of reproaching him for so excusable an error.

They returned to the encampment, saddened indeed. Still, not one of the courageous and devoted men regretted so many hardships uselessly endured, so many dangers vainly incurred. But each saw all hope of success annihilated in an instant. Could they find Captain Grant between Tandil and the sea? No. If any prisoner had fallen into the hands of the Indians on the Atlantic coast, Sergeant Manuel would certainly have been informed.

An event of such a nature could not have escaped the natives who trade from Tandil to Carmen. Among the traders of the Argentine Plains everything is known and reported. There was therefore but one course now to take,—to join, without delay, the Duncan at Cape Medano, the appointed rendezvous.

In the meantime, Paganel had asked Glenarvan for the document, by relying on which their search had resulted so unfortunately. He read it again with unconcealed vexation, seeking to discover a new interpretation.

"This document is, at all events, clear," said Glenarvan. "It explains in the most definite manner the shipwreck of the captain and the place of his captivity."

"No," replied the geographer, stamping with his foot, "a hundred times no! Since Captain Grant is not on the Pampas, he is not in

America. This document ought to tell where he is; and it shall, my friends, or I am no longer Jacques Paganel."

More than once during the journey, the attention and interest of all, but especially of Paganel, were arrested by the curious illusion of the mirage.

CHAPTER XXII

THE FLOOD.

OMENS AND MIRAGES.

Fort Independence is one hundred and fifty miles from the shores of the Atlantic. But for unforeseen and unexpected delays, Glenarvan could have rejoined the Duncan in four days. He could not, however, reconcile himself to the idea of returning on board without Captain Grant, and failing so completely in his search; and did not therefore, as usual, give the orders for departure. But the major assumed the task of saddling the horses, renewing the provisions, and making his arrangements for the journey. Thanks to his activity, the little party, at eight o'clock in the morning, was on its way down the grassy slopes of the Tandil Sierra.

Glenarvan, with Robert at his side, galloped on in silence. His lordship's bold and resolute character did not permit him to accept this disappointment calmly. His heart beat violently, and his brain was on fire. Paganel, tormented by the mystery of the document, arranged the words in every way, as if to draw from them a new meaning. Thalcave silently resigned himself to Thaouka's sagacity. The major, always confident, performed his duties like a man upon whom discouragement can have no effect. Tom Austin and his two sailors shared their master's annoyance. Once, when a timid hare crossed the path in front of them, the superstitious Scotchmen gazed at one another.

"A bad omen," said Wilson.

"Yes, in the Highlands," replied Mulready.

"What is bad in the Highlands is no better here," added Wilson, sententiously.

About noon the travelers had descended the mountains and gained the undulating plains that extend to the sea; the boundless prairie spread its broad carpet of verdure before them.

More than once during the journey the attention and interest of all, but especially of Paganel, were arrested by the curious illusion of the mirage, by which was presented in the sky, at the limits of the horizon, a semblance of the estancias, the poplars and willows near them, and other objects; the images being so much like the reality that it required a strong effort to realize their deceptive character.

The weather hitherto had been fine, but now the sky assumed a less pleasing aspect. Masses of vapor, generated by the high temperature of the preceding days, condensed into thick clouds and threatened to dissolve in showers of rain. Moreover, the proximity of the Atlantic, and the west wind, which here reigns supreme, rendered the climate of this region peculiarly moist. However, for that day at least the heavy clouds did not break; and at evening the horses, after traveling forty miles, halted on the edge of a deep "cañada," an immense natural ditch filled with water. A shelter was wanting, but the ponchos served for tents as well as clothing, and peaceful slumbers enwrapped all.

The next day, as they progressed farther, the presence of subterranean streams betrayed itself more noticeably, and moisture was seen in every depression of the ground. Soon they came to large ponds, some already deep and others just forming. So long as there were only lagoons, the horses could easily extricate themselves; but with these treacherous swamps it was more difficult. Tall grass obstructed them, and it was necessary to incur the danger before it could be understood. These quagmires had been already fatal to more than one human being.

Robert, who had ridden half a mile in advance, returned at a gallop, crying,—

"Monsieur Paganel! Monsieur Paganel! A forest of horns!"

"What!" replied the geographer, "have you found a forest of horns?"

"Yes, yes; or at least a field."

"A field! you are dreaming, my boy," said Paganel, shrugging his shoulders.

"I am not dreaming," retorted Robert; "you shall see for yourself. This is a strange country! People sow horns, and they spring up like corn! I should like very well to have some of the seed."

"But he speaks seriously," said the major.

"Yes, major, you shall see."

Robert was not mistaken, and soon they found themselves before a vast field of horns, regularly planted.

"Well?" said Robert.

"This is something singular," replied Paganel, turning towards the Indian with a questioning look.

AN ANXIOUS INDIAN.

"The horns come from the ground," explained Thalcave; "and the cattle are under it."

"What!" cried Paganel, "is there a whole drove in this mire?"

"Yes," answered the Patagonian.

In fact, a vast herd had perished in this bog, which had given way beneath them. Hundreds of cattle had thus met their death, side by side, by suffocation in this vast quagmire. This circumstance, which sometimes takes place on the plains, could not be ignored by the Indian, and it was a warning which it was proper to heed. They passed around this immense hecatomb, which would have satisfied the most exacting gods of antiquity; and an hour after the field of horns was far behind.

Thalcave now began to observe with an anxious air the state of things around him. He frequently stopped, and rose in his stirrups. His tall form enabled him to survey a wide range; but, perceiving nothing that could enlighten him, he resumed his undeviating course. A mile farther, he stopped again, and, turning from the beaten track, proceeded a short distance, first to the north, then to the south, and then resumed his place at the head of the party, without saying either what he hoped or what he feared.

These manœuvres, many times repeated, puzzled Paganel and annoyed Glenarvan. The geographer was accordingly requested to interrogate the Indian, which he did at once. Thalcave replied that he was astonished to see the plain so soaked with moisture. Never within his recollection, since he had performed the office of guide, had his feet trodden a soil so saturated. Even in the season of the great rains the Argentine plain was always easily passed.

"But to what do you attribute this increasing moisture?" asked Paganel.

"I know not," replied the Indian; "and what if I did?"

"Do the mountain streams, when swollen with the rains, ever overflow their banks?"

"Sometimes."

"And now, perhaps?"

"Perhaps," said Thalcave.

Paganel was forced to be contented with this answer, and communicated to Glenarvan the result of the conversation.

"And what does Thalcave advise?" inquired Glenarvan.

"What is to be done?" asked Paganel of the Patagonian.

"Advance quickly," replied the Indian.

This advice was easier to give than to follow. The horses were quickly fatigued with treading a soil that sank beneath them deeper and deeper as they progressed, so that this part of the plain might have been compared to an immense basin in which the invading waters would rapidly accumulate. It was advisable, therefore, to cross without delay these sloping terraces that an inundation would have instantly transformed into a lake.

They hastened their pace, though there was no great depth to the water which spread out in a sheet beneath the horses' feet. About two o'clock the flood-gates of the heavens opened, and tropical torrents of rain descended. Never was a finer opportunity presented for showing oneself a philosopher. There was no chance of escaping this deluge, and it was better for the travelers to receive it stoically. Their ponchos were soon dripping, and their hats wet them still more, like roofs whose gutters have overflowed. The fringes of the saddle-cloths seemed so many liquid streams; and the horsemen, bespattered by their animals, whose hoofs splashed in the water at every step, rode in a double shower, which came from the ground as well as the sky.

HYDROPATHIC TREATMENT.

It was in this wretchedly cold and exhausted state that they arrived, towards evening, at a very miserable rancho. Only people who were not fastidious could have given it the name of a shelter, only travelers in distress would consent to occupy it. But Glenarvan and his companions had no choice. They therefore cowered down in the abandoned hut which would not have satisfied even a poor Indian of the plains. A sorry fire of grass, which gave out more smoke than heat, was kindled with difficulty. The torrents of rain made havoc without, and large drops oozed through the mouldy thatch. The fire was extinguished twenty times, and twenty times did Wilson and Mulready struggle against the invading water.

The supper was very meagre and comfortless, and every one's appetite failed. The major alone did justice to the water-soaked repast, and did not lose a mouthful: he was superior to misfortune. As for Paganel, like a Frenchman, he tried to joke; but now he failed.

"My jokes are wet," said he: "they miss fire."

However, as it was more agreeable—if possible, under the circumstances—to sleep, each one sought in slumber a temporary forgetfulness of his fatigues.

The night was stormy. The sides of the rancho cracked as if they would break, while the frail structure bent beneath the gusts of wind and threatened to give way at every shock. The unfortunate horses neighed in terror without, exposed to the inclemency of the tempest; and their masters did not suffer less in their miserable shelter. However, sleep drowned all their troubles at last. Robert first closed his eyes, reclining his head on Lord Glenarvan's shoulder; and soon all the inmates of the rancho slept under the protection of God.

They woke the next morning at the call of Thaouka, who, always ready, neighed without, and struck the wall of the hut vigorously with his hoof, as though to give the signal for departure. They owed him too much not to obey him, and they accordingly resumed their journey.

The rain had ceased, but the hard earth held what had fallen. On the impenetrable clay, pools, marshes, and ponds overflowed and formed immense "bañados" of treacherous depth. Paganel, on consulting his map, judged rightly that the Grande and Nivarota Rivers, into which the waters of the plain usually flow, must have mingled together in one broad stream.

An extremely rapid advance, therefore, became necessary. The common safety was at stake. If the inundation increased, where could they find a refuge? The vast circle of the horizon did not offer a single point, and on this level plain the progress of the water must be rapid. The horses were urged to their utmost speed. Thaouka took the lead, and might have borne the name of sea-horse, for he pranced as if he had been in his native element.

Suddenly, about six o'clock in the evening, he manifested signs of extreme agitation. He turned frequently towards the vast expanse to the south; his neighs were prolonged, his nostrils keenly snuffed the air, and he reared violently. Thalcave, whom his antics could not unseat, managed his steed without difficulty. The froth from the horse's mouth was mingled with blood under the action of the firmly-closed bit, and yet the spirited animal could not be calm. If free, his master felt but too well that he would have fled away at full speed towards the north.

"What is the matter with Thaouka?" asked Paganel. "Has he been bitten by those voracious blood-suckers of the Argentine waters?"

"No," replied the Indian.

"Is he terrified, then, at some danger?"

"Yes, he has scented danger."

"What?"

"I do not know."

Although the eye did not yet reveal the peril that Thaouka divined, the ear could already detect it. A low murmur, like the sound of a rising tide, was heard as from the limit of the horizon. The wind blew in damp gusts laden with spray; the birds, as if fleeing from some unknown phenomenon, shot swiftly through the air; and the horses, wading to their knees, felt the first impulse of the current. Soon a mingled roar, like bellowing, neighing, and bleating, resounded half a mile to the south, and immense herds appeared, tumbling, rising, and rushing, a confused mass of terrified beasts, and fled by with frightful rapidity. It was scarcely possible to distinguish them in the midst of the clouds of spray dashed up by their flight.

"The flood! the flood!" replied Thalcave, spurring his horse towards the north.

"Quick! quick!" cried Thalcave, in a piercing voice.

"What is it?" said Paganel.

"The flood! the flood!" replied Thalcave, spurring his horse towards the north.

"The inundation!" cried Paganel; and his companions, with him at their head, fled away in the track of Thaouka.

It was time. Five miles to the south a high and broad wall of water was rushing over the plain, which was fast becoming an ocean. The tall grass disappeared as before the scythe, and the tufts of mimosas, torn up by the current, separated and formed floating islands. The mass of waters spread itself in broad waves of irresistible power. The dikes of the great rivers had evidently given way, and perhaps the waters of the Colorado and Rio Negro were now mingling in a common stream.

The wall of water descried by Thalcave advanced with the speed of a race-horse. The travelers fled before it like a cloud driven by the storm. Their eyes sought in vain a place of refuge. Sky and water mingled together on the horizon. The horses, excited by the danger, dashed along in a mad gallop, so that their riders could scarcely keep their seats. Glenarvan frequently glanced behind him.

"The water is overtaking us," he thought.

"Quick! quick!" cried Thalcave.

THE ARK.

The unfortunate beasts were urged to a swifter pace. From their flanks, lacerated with the spur, flowed bright red streams, which marked their course on the water by long, crimson lines. They stumbled in the hollows of the ground; they were entangled in the hidden grass; they fell and rose again continually. The depth of the water sensibly increased. Long surges announced the on-rush of the mass of water that tossed its foaming crests less than two miles distant.

For a quarter of an hour this final struggle against the most terrible of elements was prolonged. The fugitives could keep no account of the distance they had traversed; but, judging by the rapidity of their flight, it must have been considerable.

Meantime the horses, immersed to their breasts, could no longer advance without extreme difficulty. Glenarvan, Paganel, Austin, all believed themselves lost, victims of the horrible death of unfortunates abandoned at sea. Their animals began to lose their footing; six feet of water was sufficient to drown them.

We must forbear to picture the acute anguish of these eight men overtaken by a rising inundation. They felt their powerlessness to struggle against these convulsions of nature, superior to human strength. Their safety was no longer in their own hands.

Five minutes after, the horses were swimming, while the current alone carried them along with irresistible force and furious swiftness. All safety seemed impossible, when the voice of the major was heard.

"A tree!" said he.

"A tree!" cried Glenarvan.

"Yes, yonder!" replied Thalcave, and he pointed northward to a kind of gigantic walnut-tree, which rose solitary from the midst of the waters.

His companions had no need to be urged. This tree that was opportunely presented to them they must reach at all hazards. The horses probably could not accomplish the distance; but the men, at least, could be saved,—the current would carry them.

At that moment Tom Austin's horse gave a stifled neigh and disappeared. His rider, extricating himself from the stirrups, began to swim vigorously.

"Cling to my saddle!" cried Glenarvan to him.

"Thanks, my lord," replied he, "my arms are strong."

"Your horse, Robert?" continued Glenarvan, turning towards the boy.

"All right, my lord, all right! He swims like a fish."

"Attention!" cried the major, in a loud voice.

This word was scarcely pronounced, when the enormous wall of water reached them. A huge wave, forty feet high, overwhelmed the fugitives with a terrible roar. Men and beasts, everything, disappeared in a whirlpool of foam. A ponderous liquid mass engulfed them in its furious tide. When the deluge had passed, the men regained the surface, and rapidly counted their numbers; but the horses, except Thaouka, had disappeared forever.

"Courage! courage!" cried Glenarvan, who supported Paganel with one arm and swam with the other.

"All right! all right!" replied the worthy geographer; "indeed I am not sorry——"

What was he not sorry for? No one ever knew; for the poor man was forced to swallow the end of his sentence in half a pint of muddy water.

The major calmly advanced, taking a regular stroke of which the most skillful swimmer would not have been ashamed. The sailors worked their way along like porpoises in their native element. As for Robert, he clung to Thaouka's mane, and was thus drawn along. The horse proudly cut the waters, and kept himself instinctively on a line with the tree, towards which the current bore him, and which was now not far distant.

In a few moments the entire party reached it. It was fortunate; for, if this refuge had failed, all chance of safety would have vanished, and they must have perished in the waves. The water was up to the top of the trunk where the main branches grew, so that it was easy to grasp them.

Thalcave, leaving his horse, and lifting Robert, seized the first limb, and soon his powerful arms had lodged the exhausted swimmers in a place of safety. But Thaouka, carried away by the current, was rapidly disappearing. He turned his intelligent head towards his master, and, shaking his long mane, neighed for him beseechingly.

A huge wave, forty feet high, overwhelmed the fugitives with a terrible roar.
Men and beasts, everything, disappeared in a whirlpool of foam. A ponderous
liquid mass engulfed them in its furious tide.

"Do you abandon him?" said Paganel.

"I?" cried the Indian, and, plunging into the tempestuous waters, he reappeared some distance from the tree. A few moments after, his arm rested upon the neck of Thaouka, and horse and horseman swam away together towards the misty horizon of the north.

CHAPTER XXIII

A SINGULAR ABODE.

The tree upon which Glenarvan and his companions had just found refuge resembled a walnut-tree. It had the same shining foliage and rounded form. It was the "ombu," which is met with only on the Argentine Plains. It had an enormous, twisted trunk, and was confined to the earth not only by its great roots, but also by strong shoots which held it most tenaciously. It had thus resisted the force of the inundation.

AN ORNITHOLOGICAL OMNIUM-GATHERUM.

This ombu measured one hundred feet in height, and might have covered with its shade a circumference of three hundred and sixty feet. All the upper part rested on three great branches, which forked from the top of the trunk, that was six feet in diameter. Two of these branches were nearly perpendicular, and supported the immense canopy of foliage, whose crossed, twisted, and interlaced limbs, as if woven by the hand of a basket-maker, formed an impenetrable shelter. The third branch, on the contrary, extended almost horizontally over the roaring waters; its leaves were bathed in them, while it seemed a promontory to this island of verdure surrounded by an ocean. There was abundant space, also, in the interior of this gigantic tree. The foliage, which was not very dense at its outer circumference, left large openings like sky-lights, and made it well ventilated and cool. At sight of these branches rising in innumerable ramifications towards the clouds, while the parasitic convolvuli bound them to each other, and the rays of the sun shone through the interstices of the leaves, you would really have thought that the trunk of this ombu bore upon itself alone an entire forest.

On the arrival of the fugitives, a feathered population flew away to the top branches, protesting by their cries against so flagrant a usurpation of their dwelling. These birds, that had themselves sought refuge upon this solitary ombu, were seen by hundreds,— blackbirds, starlings, and many other richly-feathered varieties; and when they flew away it seemed as if a gust of wind had stripped the tree of its leaves.

Such was the asylum offered to Glenarvan's little party. Robert and the nimble Wilson were scarcely perched in the tree, before they hastened to climb to the topmost branches. Their heads protruded above the dome of verdure. From this lofty position the view embraced a wide range. The ocean created by the inundation surrounded them on all sides, and their eyes could discern no limit. No other tree emerged from the watery surface; the ombu, alone in the midst of the unconfined waters, groaned at every shock. At a distance, borne along by the impetuous current, floated uprooted trunks, twisted branches, thatch torn from some demolished rancho, beams swept by the waters from the roofs of cattle-folds, bodies of drowned animals, bloody skins, and, on a swaying tree, a whole family of growling jaguars that clung with their claws to this fragile raft. Still farther off, a black speck almost invisible attracted Wilson's attention. It was Thalcave and his faithful Thaouka, disappearing in the distance.

He turned his intelligent head towards his master, and, shaking his long mane, neighed for him beseechingly.

A COMMITTEE OF SUPPLY.

"Thalcave, friend Thalcave!" cried Robert, stretching out his hands towards the courageous Patagonian.

"He will be saved, Mr. Robert," said Wilson; "but let us join Lord Glenarvan."

A moment after, Robert and the sailor descended the three stories of branches and found themselves among their companions. Glenarvan, Paganel, the major, Austin, and Mulready were seated astraddle, or dangling in the branches, according to their own inclinations. Wilson gave an account of their visit to the top of the tree. All shared his opinion in regard to Thalcave. The only question was, whether Thalcave would save Thaouka, or Thaouka Thalcave.

The present situation of these refugees was undeniably insecure. The tree would not probably give way to the force of the current, but the rising waters might reach the top branches, for the depression of the soil made this part of the plain a deep reservoir. Glenarvan's first care, therefore, was to establish, by means of notches, points of comparison which enabled him to note the different heights of the water. The flood was now stationary, and it appeared to have reached its greatest elevation. This was encouraging.

"And now what shall we do?" asked Glenarvan.

"Build our nest, of course," replied Paganel.

"Build our nest!" cried Robert.

"Certainly, my boy, and live the life of birds, since we cannot live the life of fishes."

"Very well," said Glenarvan; "but who will give us our beakful?"

"I," replied the major.

All eyes were turned towards MacNabb, who was comfortably seated in a natural arm-chair formed of two pliant branches, and with one hand was holding out the wet though well-filled saddle-bags.

"Ah, MacNabb," cried Glenarvan, "this is just like you! You think of everything, even under circumstances where it is allowable to forget."

"As soon as it was decided not to be drowned, I concluded not to die of hunger."

"I should not have thought of this," said Paganel, innocently; "but I am so absent-minded!"

"And what do the saddle-bags contain?" inquired Tom Austin.

"Provisions for seven men for two days," replied MacNabb.

"Well," said Glenarvan, "I hope that the inundation will be considerably lower twenty-four hours hence."

"Or that we shall find some means of gaining *terra firma*," added Paganel.

"Our first business, then, is to breakfast," said Glenarvan.

"After drying ourselves," observed the major.

"And fire?" said Wilson.

"Why, we must make one," replied Paganel.

"Where?"

"At the top of the trunk, of course."

"With what?"

"With dead wood that we shall cut in the tree."

"But how kindle it?" said Glenarvan. "Our tinder is like a wet sponge."

"We will manage that," answered Paganel; "a little dry moss, a ray of sunlight, the lens of my telescope, and you will see by what a fire I will dry myself. Who will go for wood in the forest?"

"I!" cried Robert, and, followed by his friend Wilson, he disappeared like a cat in the depths of the foliage.

GOING BIRD'S-NESTING.

During their absence Paganel found dry moss in sufficient quantity; he availed himself of a ray of sunlight, which was easy, for the orb of day now shone with a vivid brightness, and then, with the aid of his lens, he kindled without difficulty the combustible materials which were laid on a bed of leaves in the fork of the branches. It was a natural fireplace, with no danger of conflagration.

Wilson and Robert soon returned with an armful of dead wood, which was cast on the fire. Paganel, to cause a draught, placed himself above the fireplace, his long legs crossed in the Arab fashion; then, moving his body rapidly up and down, he produced, by means of his poncho, a strong current of air. The wood kindled, and a bright, roaring flame soon rose from this improvised oven. Each dried himself in his own way, while the ponchos, hung on the branches, swung to and fro in the breeze.

They now breakfasted, sparingly however, for they had to allow for the following day. The immense basin might not perhaps be empty so soon as Glenarvan hoped, and, moreover, the provisions were limited. The tree bore no fruit; but fortunately it afforded a remarkable supply of fresh eggs, thanks to the numerous nests that loaded the branches, not to speak of their feathered occupants. These resources were by no means to be despised. The question now was, therefore, in case of a prolonged stay, how to secure comfortable quarters.

"Since the kitchen and dining-room are on the ground floor," said Paganel, "we will sleep in the first story. The house is large, the rent reasonable, and we must take our ease. I perceive that above there are natural cradles, in which, when we have once laid ourselves, we shall sleep as well as in the best beds in the world. We have nothing to fear; moreover, we will keep watch, and there are enough of us to repulse all the wild animals."

"Only we have no arms," said Tom Austin.

"I have my revolvers," said Glenarvan.

"And I mine," replied Robert.

"What use," continued Tom Austin, "if Mr. Paganel does not find the means of manufacturing powder?"

"It is not necessary," replied MacNabb, showing a full flask.

"Where did you get that, major?" inquired Paganel.

"Of Thalcave. He thought it might be useful to us, and gave it to me before going back to Thaouka."

"Brave and generous Indian!" cried Glenarvan.

"Yes," added Tom Austin, "if all the Patagonians are fashioned after this model, I pay my respects to Patagonia."

"I desire that the horse be not forgotten," said Paganel. "He forms part of the Patagonian, and, if I am not greatly mistaken, we shall see them again."

"How far are we from the Atlantic?" inquired the major.

"Not more than forty miles," answered Paganel. "And now, my friends, since each is free to act, I ask permission to leave you. I am going to choose an observatory above, and, with the aid of my telescope, will keep you acquainted with what goes on here."

The geographer was allowed to go. He very adroitly swung himself from branch to branch, and disappeared behind the thick curtain of foliage. His companions at once occupied themselves with making the sleeping-room and preparing their beds, which was neither a difficult nor a lengthy task. As there were no bedclothes to fix nor furniture to arrange, each soon resumed his place by the fire.

They then conversed, but not about their present condition, which they must patiently endure. They returned to the inexhaustible subject of Captain Grant's recovery. If the waters subsided, in three days the travelers would be again on board the Duncan. But the captain and his two sailors, those unfortunate castaways, would not be with them; and it even seemed after this failure, after this vain search in South America, as if all hope of finding them were irrevocably lost. Whither direct a new search? What, too, would be the grief of Lady Helena and Mary Grant on learning that the future had no hope in store for them!

"Poor sister!" exclaimed Robert; "all is over for us!"

Glenarvan, for the first time, had no consoling answer to make. What hope could he give the child? Had he not followed with rigorous exactitude the directions of the document?

"At all events," said he, "this thirty-seventh degree of latitude is no vain indication. Have we not supposed, interpreted, and ascertained that it relates to the shipwreck or the captivity of Captain Grant? Have we not read it with our own eyes?"

"All that is true, my lord," replied Tom Austin; "nevertheless our search has not succeeded."

"It is discouraging as well as annoying," said Glenarvan.

"Annoying if you will," replied MacNabb, in a calm tone, "but not discouraging. Precisely because we thus have a definite item, we must thoroughly exhaust all its instructions."

"What do you mean?" inquired Glenarvan. "What do you think ought to be done?"

"A very simple and reasonable thing, my dear Edward. Let us turn our faces towards the east, when we are on board the Duncan, and follow the thirty-seventh parallel even around to our starting-point, if necessary."

"Do you think, my dear major, that I have not thought of this?" replied Glenarvan. "Indeed I have, a hundred times. But what chance have we of succeeding? Is not leaving the American continent departing from the place indicated by Captain Grant himself, from Patagonia, so clearly named in the document?"

"Do you wish to begin your search in the Pampas again," replied the major, "when you are sure that the shipwreck of the Britannia did not take place on the Pacific or Atlantic coast?"

Glenarvan did not answer.

"And however feeble the chance of finding Captain Grant by following this latitude may be, still ought we not to attempt it?"

"I do not deny it," replied Glenarvan.

APPLIED GEOGRAPHY.

"And you, my friends," added the major, addressing the sailors, "are you not of my opinion?"

"Entirely," answered Tom Austin, while Wilson and Mulready nodded assent.

"Listen to me, my friends," continued Glenarvan, after a few moments of reflection, "and you too, Robert, for this is a serious question. I shall do everything possible to find Captain Grant, as I have undertaken to do, and shall devote my entire life, if necessary, to this object. All Scotland would join me to save this noble man who sacrificed himself for her. I too think, however slight may be the chance, that we ought to make the tour of the world on the thirty-seventh parallel; and I shall do so. But this is not the point to be settled: there is a much more important one, and it is this: Ought we once and for all to abandon our search on the American continent?"

Glenarvan, Paganel, the major, Austin, and Mulready were seated astraddle, or dangling in the branches, according to their own inclinations.

This question, so directly asked, was unanswered. No one dared to declare his opinion.

"Well?" resumed Glenarvan, addressing the major more especially.

"My dear Edward," replied MacNabb, "it would involve too great a responsibility to answer you now. The case requires consideration.

But first of all I desire to know what countries the thirty-seventh parallel crosses."

"That is Paganel's business," replied Glenarvan.

"Let us ask him, then," said the major.

The geographer was no longer to be seen, as he was hidden by the thick foliage. It was necessary to call him.

"Paganel! Paganel!" cried Glenarvan.

"Present!" answered a voice which seemed to come to them from the sky.

"Where are you?"

"In my tower."

"What are you doing?"

"Surveying the wide horizon."

"Can you come down a moment?"

"Do you need me?"

"Yes."

"What for?"

"To know what countries the thirty-seventh parallel crosses."

"Nothing easier," replied Paganel; "I need not even disturb myself to tell you."

"Very well, then."

"Leaving America, the thirty-seventh parallel crosses the Atlantic."

"Good."

"It strikes Tristan d'Acunha Island."

"Well?"

"It passes two degrees to the south of the Cape of Good Hope."

"And then?"

"It runs across the Indian Ocean."

"And then?"

"It grazes St. Paul's Island of the Amsterdam group."

"Go on."

"It cuts Australia across the province of Victoria."

"Proceed."

"Leaving Australia——"

This last sentence was not finished. Did the geographer hesitate? Did he know no more? No; but a startling cry was heard in the top of the tree. Glenarvan and his friends grew pale as they gazed at each other. Had a new calamity happened? Had the unfortunate Paganel fallen? Already Wilson and Mulready were hastening to his assistance, when a long body appeared. Paganel dangled from branch to branch. His hands could grasp nothing. Was he alive, or dead? They did not know; but he was about to fall into the roaring waters, when the major, with a strong hand, arrested his progress.

"Very much obliged, MacNabb!" cried Paganel.

"Why, what is the matter with you?" said the major.

> A long body appeared. Paganel dangled from branch to branch. His hands could grasp nothing. Was he alive, or dead?

"What has got into you? Is this another of your eternal distractions?"

"Yes, yes," replied Paganel, in a voice choked with emotion (and leaves). "Yes, a distraction,—phenomenal this time."

"What is it?"

"We have been mistaken! We are still mistaken!"

"Explain yourself."

"Glenarvan, major, Robert, my friends," cried Paganel, "all you who hear me, we are seeking Captain Grant where he is not."

"What do you say?" cried Glenarvan.

"Not only where he is not," added Paganel, "but even where he has never been."

CHAPTER XXIV

PAGANEL'S DISCLOSURE.

A profound astonishment greeted these unexpected words. What did the geographer mean? Had he lost his senses? He spoke, however, with such conviction that all eyes were turned towards Glenarvan. This declaration of Paganel was a direct answer to the question the former had asked. But Glenarvan confined himself to a negative gesture, indicating disbelief in the geographer, who, as soon as he was master of his emotion, resumed.

"Yes," said he, in a tone of conviction, "yes, we have gone astray in our search, and have read in the document what is not written there."

"Explain yourself, Paganel," said the major; "and more calmly."

A NEW IDEA.

"That is very simple, major. Like you, I was in error; like you, I struck upon a false interpretation. When, but a moment ago, at the top of this tree, in answer to the question, at the word 'Australia' an idea flashed through my mind, and all was clear."

"What!" cried Glenarvan, "do you pretend that Captain Grant——"

"I pretend," replied Paganel, "that the word *Austral* in the document is not complete, as we have hitherto supposed, but the root of the word *Australia*."

"This is something singular," said the major.

"Singular!" replied Glenarvan, shrugging his shoulders; "it is simply impossible!"

"Impossible," continued Paganel, "is a word that we do not allow in France."

"What!" added Glenarvan, in a tone of the greatest incredulity, "do you pretend, with that document in your possession, that the shipwreck of the Britannia took place on the shores of Australia?"

"I am sure of it!" replied Paganel.

"By my faith, Paganel," said Glenarvan, "this is a pretension that astonishes me greatly, coming from the secretary of a geographical society."

"Why?" inquired Paganel, touched in his sensitive point.

"Because, if you admit the word Australia, you admit at the same time that there are Indians in that country, a fact which has not yet been proved."

Paganel was by no means surprised at this argument. He seemingly expected it, and began to smile.

"My dear Glenarvan," said he, "do not be too hasty in your triumph. I am going to defeat you completely, as no Englishman has ever been defeated."

"I ask nothing better. Defeat me, Paganel."

"Listen, then. You say that the Indians mentioned in the document belong exclusively to Patagonia. The incomplete word *indi* does not mean Indians, but natives (*indigènes*). Now do you admit that there are natives in Australia?"

It must be confessed that Glenarvan now gazed fixedly at Paganel.

"Bravo, Paganel!" said the major.

"Do you admit my interpretation, my dear lord?"

"Yes," replied Glenarvan, "if you can prove to me that the imperfect word *gonie* does not relate to the country of the Patagonians."

"No," cried Paganel, "it certainly does not mean Patagonia. Read anything you will but that."

"But what?"

"*Cosmogonie! théogonie! agonie!*"

"*Agonie!*" cried the major.

"That is indifferent to me," replied Paganel; "the word has no importance. I shall not even search for what it may signify. The principal point is that *Austral* means Australia, and we must have been blindly following a false trail, not to have discovered before so evident a meaning. If I had found the document, if my judgment had not been set aside by your interpretation, I should never have understood it otherwise."

This time cheers, congratulations, and compliments greeted Paganel's words. Austin, the sailors, the major, and Robert especially, were delighted to revive their hopes, and applauded the worthy geographer. Glenarvan, who had gradually been undeceived, was, as he said, almost ready to surrender.

"One last remark, my dear Paganel, and I have only to bow before your sagacity."

"Speak!"

"How do you arrange these newly-interpreted words, and in what way do you read the document?"

The hunt promised well, and gave hopes of culinary wonders.

"Nothing is easier. Here is the document," said Paganel, producing the precious paper that he had studied so conscientiously for several days. A profound silence ensued, while the geographer, collecting his thoughts, took his time to answer. His finger followed the incomplete lines on the document, while, in a confident tone, he expressed himself in the following terms:

"'June 7th, 1862, the brig Britannia, of Glasgow, foundered after'—let us put, if you wish, 'two days, three days,' or, 'a long struggle,'—it matters little, it is quite unimportant,—'on the coast of Australia. Directing their course to shore, two sailors and Captain Grant endeavored to land,' or 'did land on the continent, where they will be,' or 'are prisoners of cruel natives. They cast this document,' and so forth. Is it clear?"

"It is clear," replied Glenarvan, "if the word _continent_ can be applied to Australia, which is only an island."

"Be assured, my dear Glenarvan, the best geographers are agreed in naming this island the Australian continent."

"Then I have but one thing to say, my friends," cried Glenarvan. "To Australia, and may Heaven assist us!"

"To Australia!" repeated his companions, with one accord.

"Do you know, Paganel," added Glenarvan, "that your presence on board the Duncan is a providential circumstance?"

"Well," replied Paganel, "let us suppose that I am an envoy of Providence, and say no more about it."

A FESTIVE BANQUET.

Thus ended this conversation, that in the future led to such great results. It completely changed the moral condition of the travelers. They had caught again the thread of the labyrinth in which they had thought themselves forever lost. A new hope arose on the ruins of their fallen projects. They could fearlessly leave behind them this American continent, and already all their thoughts flew away to the Australian land. On reaching the Duncan, they would not bring despair on board, and Lady Helena and Mary Grant would not have to lament the irrevocable loss of the captain. Thus they forgot the dangers of their situation in their new-found joy, and their only regret was that they could not start at once.

It was now four o'clock in the afternoon, and they resolved to take supper at six. Paganel wished to celebrate this joyful day by a splendid banquet. As the bill of fare was very limited, he proposed to Robert that they should go hunting "in the neighboring forest," at which idea the boy clapped his hands. They took Thalcave's powder-flask, cleaned the revolvers, loaded them with fine shot, and started.

"Do not go far," said the major, gravely, to the two huntsmen.

After their departure Glenarvan and MacNabb went to consult the notches on the tree, while Wilson and Mulready revived the smouldering embers.

Arriving at the surface of this immense lake, they saw no sign of abatement. The waters seemed to have attained their highest elevation; but the violence with which they rolled from south to north proved that the equilibrium of the Argentine rivers was not yet established. Before the liquid mass could lower, it must first become calm, like the sea when flood-tide ends and ebb begins. They could not, therefore, expect a subsidence of the waters so long as they flowed towards the north with such swiftness.

While Glenarvan and the major were making these observations, reports resounded in the tree, accompanied by cries of joy almost as noisy. The clear treble of Robert contrasted sharply with the deep bass of Paganel, and the strife was which should be the most boyish. The hunt promised well, and gave hopes of culinary wonders.

When the major and Glenarvan returned to the fire, they had to congratulate Wilson upon an excellent idea. The honest sailor had devoted himself to fishing with wonderful success, with the aid of a pin and a piece of string. Several dozen of little fish, delicate as smelts, called "mojarras," wriggled in a fold of his poncho, and seemed likely to make an exquisite dish.

At this moment the hunters descended from the top of the tree. Paganel carefully carried some black swallows' eggs and a string of sparrows, which he meant afterwards to serve up as larks. Robert had adroitly brought down several pairs of "hilgueros,"—little green-and-yellow birds, which are excellent eating, and very much in demand in the Montevideo market. The geographer, who knew many ways of preparing eggs, had to confine himself this time to cooking them in the hot ashes. However, the repast was as varied as it was delicate. The dried meat, the hard eggs, the broiled mojarras, and the roast sparrows and hilgueros, formed a repast which was long remembered.

The conversation was very animated. Paganel was greatly complimented in his twofold capacity of hunter and cook, and accepted these encomiums with the modesty that belongs to true merit. Then he gave himself up to singular observations on the magnificent tree that sheltered them with its foliage, and whose extent, as he declared, was immense.

"Robert and I," said he jokingly, "imagined ourselves in the open forest during the hunt. One moment I thought we should be lost. I could not find my way. The sun was declining towards the horizon. I sought in vain to retrace my steps. Hunger made itself felt acutely. Already the gloomy coppices were resounding with the growls of ferocious beasts,—but no, there are no ferocious beasts, and I am sorry."

"What!" cried Glenarvan, "you are sorry there are no ferocious beasts?"

"Certainly."

"But, when you have everything to fear from their ferocity———"

"Ferocity does not exist,—scientifically speaking," replied the geographer.

"Ha! this time, Paganel," said the major, "you will not make me admit the utility of ferocious beasts. What are they good for?"

"Major," cried Paganel, "they are good to form classifications, orders, families, genera, sub-genera, species———"

"Very fine!" said MacNabb. "I should not have thought of that! If I had been one of Noah's companions at the time of the deluge, I should certainly have prevented that imprudent patriarch from putting into the ark pairs of tigers, lions, bears, panthers, and other animals as destructive as they were useless."

"Should you have done so?" inquired Paganel.

"I should."

"Well, you would have been wrong in a zoological point of view."

"But not in a human one."

"This is shocking," continued Paganel; "for my part, I should have preserved all the animals before the deluge of which we are so unfortunately deprived."

"I tell you," replied MacNabb, "that Noah was right in abandoning them to their fate, admitting that they lived in his time."

"I tell you that Noah was wrong," retorted Paganel, "and deserves the malediction of scholars to the end of time."

The listeners to this argument could not help laughing at seeing the two friends dispute about what Noah ought to have done or left undone. The major, who had never argued with any one in his life, contrary to all his principles, was every day at war with Paganel, who must have particularly excited him.

Glenarvan, according to his custom, interrupted the debate, and said,—

However, the repast was as varied as it was delicate. The dried meat, the hard eggs, the broiled mojarras, and the roast sparrows and hilgueros, formed a repast which was long remembered.

WANTED, A JAGUAR!

"However much it is to be regretted, in a scientific or human point of view, that we are deprived of ferocious animals, we must be resigned to-day to their absence. Paganel could not hope to encounter any in this aerial forest."

"No," replied the geographer, "although we beat the bush. It is a pity, for it would have been a glorious hunt. A ferocious man-eater like the jaguar! With one blow of his paw he can twist the neck of a horse. When he has tasted human flesh, however, he returns to it ravenously. What he likes best is the Indian, then the negro, then the mulatto, and then the white man."

"However that may be, my good Paganel," said Glenarvan, "so long as there are no Indians, mulattoes, or negroes among us, I rejoice in the absence of your dear jaguars. Our situation is not, of course, so agreeable——"

"What!" cried Paganel, "you complain of your lot?"

"Certainly," replied Glenarvan. "Are you at your ease in these uncomfortable and uncushioned branches?"

"I have never been more so, even in my own study. We lead the life of birds; we sing and flutter about. I almost think that men were destined to live in the trees."

"They only want wings," said the major.

"They will make them some day."

"In the meantime," replied Glenarvan, "permit me, my dear friend, to prefer the sand of a park, the floor of a house, or the deck of a vessel to this aerial abode."

"Glenarvan," said Paganel, "we must take things as they come. If favorable, so much the better; if unfavorable, we must not mind it. I see you long for the comforts of Malcolm Castle."

"No, but——"

"I am certain that Robert is perfectly happy," interrupted Paganel, to secure one advocate, at least, of his theories.

"Yes, Monsieur Paganel!" cried the boy, in a joyful tone.

"It is natural at his age," replied Glenarvan.

"And at mine," added the geographer. "The less ease we have, the fewer wants; the fewer wants, the happier we are."

"Well," said the major, "here is Paganel going to make an attack upon riches and gilded splendor."

"No, my dear major," continued Paganel; "but, if you wish, I will tell you, in this connection, a little Arab story that occurs to me."

"Yes, yes, Monsieur Paganel," cried Robert.

"And what will your story prove?" asked the major.

"What all stories prove, my brave companion."

"Not much, then," replied MacNabb. "But go on, Scheherezade, and tell one of those stories that you relate so well."

"There was once upon a time," said Paganel, "a son of the great Haroun-al-Raschid who was not happy. He accordingly consulted an old dervish, who told him that happiness was a very difficult thing to find in this world. 'However,' added he, 'I know an infallible way to procure you happiness.' 'What is it?' inquired the young prince. 'It is,' replied the dervish, 'to put on the shirt of a happy man.' Thereupon the prince embraced the old man, and set out in search of his talisman. He visited all the capitals of the earth; he tried the shirts of kings, emperors, princes, and nobles; but it was a useless task, he was no happier. Then he put on the shirts of artists, warriors, and merchants, but with no more success. He had thus traveled far, without finding happiness. At last, desperate from having tried so many shirts, he was returning very sadly one beautiful day to the palace of his father, when he spied in the field an honest laborer, who was joyously singi

ng as he ploughed. 'Here is, at all events, a man who possesses happiness,' said he to himself, 'or happiness does not exist on earth.' He approached him. 'Good man,' said he, 'are you happy?' 'Yes,' replied the other. 'You wish for nothing?' 'No.' 'You would not change your lot for that of a king?' 'Never!' 'Well, sell me your shirt!' 'My shirt! I have none!'"

They were agreed on this point, that it was necessary to have courage for every fortune, and be contented with a tree when one has neither palace nor cottage.

CHAPTER XXV

BETWEEN FIRE AND WATER.

Jacques Paganel's story had a very great success. He was greatly applauded, but each retained his own opinion, and the geographer obtained the result common to most discussions,—of convincing nobody. However, they were agreed on this point, that it was necessary to have courage for every fortune, and be contented with a tree when one has neither palace nor cottage.

During the course of this confabulation evening had come on. Only a good sleep could thoroughly refresh, after this eventful day. The inmates of the tree felt themselves not only fatigued by the sudden changes of the inundation, but especially overcome by the heat, which had been excessive. Their feathered companions had already set the example; the hilgueros, those nightingales of the Pampas, had ceased their melodious warblings, and all the birds had disappeared in the recesses of the foliage. The best plan was to imitate them.

But before "retiring to their nest," as Paganel said, Glenarvan, Robert, and he climbed to the observatory, to examine for the last time the watery expanse. It was about nine o'clock. The sun had just set in the sparkling mists of the horizon, and all the western part of the firmament was bathed in a warm vapor. The constellations, usually so dazzling, seemed veiled in a soft haze. Still they could be distinguished, and Paganel pointed out to Robert, for Glenarvan's benefit, that zone where the stars are most brilliant.

PHILOSOPHY AND PONCHOS.

While the geographer was discoursing thus, the whole eastern horizon assumed a stormy aspect. A dense and dark band, clearly defined, gradually rose, dimming the light of the stars. This cloud of threatening appearance soon invaded almost the entire vault of the sky. Its motive power must have been inherent in itself, for there was not a breath of wind. Not a leaf stirred on the tree, not a ripple curled the surface of the waters. Even the air seemed to fail, as if some huge pneumatic machine had rarefied it. A strong electric current was perceptible in the atmosphere, and every creature felt it course along the nerves. Glenarvan, Paganel, and Robert were sensibly affected by these electric currents.

"We shall have a storm," said Paganel.

"You are not afraid of thunder?" asked Glenarvan of the boy.

"Oh, no, my lord," replied Robert.

"Well, so much the better; for the storm is now not far distant."

"And it will be violent," continued Paganel, "so far as I can judge from the state of the sky."

"It is not the storm that troubles me," said Glenarvan, "but the torrents of rain with which it will be accompanied. We shall be drenched to the skin again. Whatever you may say, Paganel, a nest cannot suffice a man, as you will soon learn to your cost."

"Oh, yes, it can, with philosophy," briskly replied the geographer.

"Philosophy does not prevent you from getting wet."

"No, but it warms you."

"Well, then," said Glenarvan, "let us join our friends and persuade them to envelop us with their philosophy and their ponchos as closely as possible, and especially to lay in a stock of patience, for we shall need it."

So saying, he gave another look at the threatening sky. The mass of clouds now covered it entirely. A faint line of light towards the horizon was scarcely discernible in the dimness. The sombre appearance of the water had increased, and between the dark mass below and the clouds above there was scarcely a separation. At the same time all perception seemed dulled; and a leaden torpor rested upon both eyes and ears, while the silence was profound.

"Let us go down," said Glenarvan; "the lightning will soon be here."

His two companions and himself slid down the smooth branches, and were somewhat surprised to find themselves in a remarkable kind of twilight, which was produced by myriads of luminous objects that crossed each other and buzzed on the surface of the water.

"Phosphorescences?" said Glenarvan.

"No," replied Paganel, "but phosphorescent insects, real glow-worms,—living diamonds, and not expensive, of which the ladies of Buenos Ayres make magnificent ornaments for themselves."

"What!" cried Robert, "are these things, that fly like sparks, insects?"

"Yes, my boy."

Robert caught one of the brilliant creatures. Paganel was right. It was a kind of large beetle, an inch in length, to which the Indians give the name of "tuco-tuco." This curious insect threw out flashes at two points situated in front of its sheath, and its light would have enabled one to read in the darkness. Paganel, on bringing it close to his watch, saw that it was ten o'clock.

Glenarvan now joined the major and the three sailors, and gave them instructions for the night. A terrible storm was to be expected. After the first rollings of the thunder, the wind would doubtless break forth and the tree be violently shaken. It was, therefore, advisable for every one to tie himself firmly to the bed of branches that had been appropriated to him. If they could not avoid the torrents of the sky, they must at least guard against those of the earth, and not fall into the rapid current that broke against the trunk of the tree. They wished each other good night without much hope of passing one, and then each, getting into his aerial resting-place, wrapped himself in his poncho and waited for sleep.

But the approach of a mighty tempest brings to the hearts of most sentient beings a vague anxiety of which the bravest cannot divest themselves. The occupants of the tree, agitated and fearful, could not close their eyes, and the first thunder-clap found them all awake. It took place about eleven o'clock, resembling a distant rumbling. Glenarvan climbed to the end of the branch, and peered out from the foliage. The dark firmament was fitfully illumined by vivid and brilliant flashes, which the waters brightly reflected, and which disclosed great rifts in the clouds. Glenarvan, after surveying the zenith and the horizon, returned to his couch.

"What do you think, Glenarvan?" asked Paganel.

"I think that the storm is beginning, and, if it continues, it will be terrible."

The incessant flashes assumed various forms. Some, darting perpendicularly towards the earth, were repeated five or six times in the same place; others spread in zigzag lines, and produced on the dark vault of the heavens astonishing jets of arborescent flame.

"So much the better," replied the enthusiastic Paganel. "I like a fine spectacle, especially when I cannot avoid it. Only one thing would make me anxious, if anxiety served to avert danger," added he, "and that is, that the culminating point of this plain is the ombu upon which we are perched. A lightning-conductor would be very useful here, for this very tree among all those of the Pampas is the one that particularly attracts the lightning. And then, as you are aware, my friends, meteorologists advise us not to take refuge under trees during a storm."

"Well," said the major, "that is timely advice."

"It must be confessed, Paganel," replied Glenarvan, "that you choose a good time to tell us these encouraging things!"

"Bah!" replied Paganel; "all times are good to receive information. Ah, it is beginning!"

AN EXTRAORDINARY STORM.

Violent thunder-claps interrupted this conversation, and their intensity increased till they reached the most deafening peals. They soon became sonorous, and made the atmosphere vibrate in rapid oscillations. The firmament was on fire, and during this commotion it was impossible to distinguish from what electric spark emanated the indefinitely-prolonged rumblings that reverberated throughout the abysses of the sky.

The incessant flashes assumed various forms. Some, darting perpendicularly towards the earth, were repeated five or six times in the same place; others, separating into a thousand different branches, spread in zigzag lines and produced on the dark vault of the heavens astonishing jets of arborescent flame. Soon the sky, from east to north, was crossed by a phosphorescent band of intense brilliancy. This illumination gradually overspread the entire horizon, lighting up the clouds like a bonfire, and was reflected in the mirror-like waters, forming what seemed to be an immense circle of fire, of which the tree occupied the centre.

Glenarvan and his companions watched this terrific spectacle in silence. Sheets of dazzling light glided towards them, and blinding flashes followed in rapid succession, now showing the calm countenance of the major, then the speculative face of Paganel or the energetic features of Glenarvan, and again the frightened look of Robert or the unconcerned expression of the sailors. The rain, however, did not fall as yet, nor had the wind risen. But soon the flood-gates of the heavens opened, and the rain came down in torrents, the drops, as they struck the surface of the water, rebounding in thousands of sparks illuminated by the incessant lightning.

Did this rain predict the end of the storm? Were Glenarvan and his companions to be released with a few thorough drenchings? At the height of this struggle of the elements, suddenly there appeared at the end of the branch which extended horizontally, a flaming globe, of the size of a fist, and surrounded by a black smoke. This ball, after revolving a few moments, burst like a bombshell, and with a noise that was distinguishable in the midst of the general tumult. A sulphurous vapor filled the atmosphere. There was a moment of silence, and then Tom Austin was heard crying,—

"The tree is on fire!"

He was right. In a moment the flame, as if it had been communicated to an immense piece of fireworks, spread along the west side of the tree. The dead limbs, the nests of dry grass, and finally the live wood itself, furnished material for the devouring element.

The wind now rose and fanned the flames into fury. Glenarvan and his friends, speechless with terror, and venturing upon limbs that bent beneath their weight, hastily took refuge in the other, the eastern part of the tree.

Meantime the boughs shriveled, crackled, and twisted in the fire like burning serpents. The glowing fragments fell into the rushing waters and floated away in the current, sending forth flashes of ruddy light. The flames at one moment would rise to a fearful height, to be lost in the aerial conflagration, and the next, beaten back by the furious hurricane, would envelop the tree like a robe of molten gold.

Glenarvan, Robert, the major, Paganel, and the sailors, were terrified. A thick smoke was stifling them; an intolerable heat was scorching them. The fire was extending to the lower part of the tree on their side; nothing could stop or extinguish it; and they felt themselves irrevocably doomed to the torture of those victims who are confined within the burning sides of a sacrificial fire-basket.

At last their situation was no longer tenable, and of two deaths they were forced to choose the least cruel.

"To the water!" cried Glenarvan.

Wilson, whom the flames had reached, had already plunged into the current, when they heard him cry, in tones of the greatest terror,—

"Help! help!"

Austin rushed towards him and assisted him to regain the trunk.

"What is the matter?"

"Caymans! caymans!" replied Wilson. And, in truth, the foot of the tree was seen to be surrounded by the most formidable monsters. Their scales glittered in broad plates of light, sharply defined by the conflagration. Their flat tails, their pointed heads, their protruding eyes, their jaws, extending back of their ears, all these characteristic signs were unmistakable. Paganel recognized the voracious alligators peculiar to America, and called caymans in Spanish countries. There were a dozen of them, beating the water with their powerful tails, and attacking the tree with their terrible teeth.

At this sight the unfortunate travelers felt themselves lost indeed. A horrible death was in store for them,—to perish either by the flames or by the teeth of the alligators. There are circumstances in which man is powerless to struggle, and where a raging element can only be repulsed by another equally strong. Glenarvan, with a wild look, gazed at the fire and water leagued against him, not knowing what aid to implore of Heaven.

The storm had now begun to abate; but it had developed in the air a great quantity of vapor, which the electric phenomena were about to set in violent commotion. To the south an enormous water-spout was gradually forming,—an inverted cone of mist, uniting the raging waters below to the stormy clouds above. It advanced revolving with frightful rapidity, collected at its centre a liquid column, and by a powerful attraction, caused by its gyratory motion, drew towards it all the surrounding currents of air.

In a few moments the gigantic water-spout struck the ombu, and enveloped it in its watery folds.

A STRANGE BARK.

In a few moments the gigantic water-spout struck the ombu and enveloped it in its watery folds. The tree was shaken to its very base, so that Glenarvan might have thought that the alligators had attacked it with their powerful jaws and were uprooting it from the ground. His companions and he, clinging to one another, felt the mighty tree give way and fall, and saw its flaming branches plunge into the tumultuous waters with a frightful hiss. It was the work of a second. The water-spout had passed, to exert elsewhere its destructive violence, and pumping the waters of the plain as if it would exhaust them.

The tree now, loosened from its moorings, floated onward under the combined impulses of wind and current. The alligators had fled, except one which crawled along the upturned roots and advanced with open jaws; but Mulready, seizing a large brand, struck the creature so powerful a blow that he broke its back. The vanquished animal sank in the eddies of the torrent, still lashing his formidable tail with terrible violence.

Glenarvan and his companions, delivered from these voracious creatures, took refuge on the branches to leeward of the fire, while the tree, wrapped by the blast of the hurricane in glowing sheets of flame, floated on like a burning ship in the darkness of the night.

CHAPTER XXVI

THE RETURN ON BOARD.

For two hours the tree floated on the immense lake without reaching *terra firma*. The flames had gradually died out, and thus the principal danger of this terrible voyage had vanished. The current, still keeping its original direction, flowed from southwest to northeast; the darkness, though illumined now and then by flashes, had become profound, and Paganel sought in vain for his bearings. But the storm was abating, the large drops of rain gave place to light spray that was scattered by the wind, while the huge distended clouds were crossed by light bands.

The tree advanced rapidly on the impetuous torrent, gliding with surprising swiftness, as if some powerful propelling means were inclosed within its trunk. There was as yet no certainty that they would not float on thus for many days. About three o'clock in the morning, however, the major observed that the roots now and then struck the bottom. Tom Austin, by means of a long branch, carefully sounded, and declared that the water was growing shallow. Twenty minutes later, a shock was felt, and the progress of the tree was checked.

"Land! land!" cried Paganel, in ringing tones.

The ends of the charred branches had struck against a hillock on the ground, and never were navigators more delighted to land. Already Robert and Wilson, having reached a firm plateau, were uttering shouts of joy, when a well-known whistle was heard. The sound of a horse's hoofs was heard upon the plain, and the tall form of the Indian emerged from the darkness.

The sound of a horse's hoofs was heard upon the plain, and the tall form of the Indian emerged from the darkness.

"Thalcave!" cried Robert.

"Thalcave!" repeated his companions, as with one voice.

"Friends!" said the Patagonian, who had waited for them there, knowing that the current would carry them as it had carried him.

At the same moment he raised Robert in his arms and clasped him to his breast. Glenarvan, the major, and the sailors, delighted to see their faithful guide again, shook his hands with the most earnest cordiality. The Patagonian then conducted them to an abandoned estancia. Here a good fire was burning, which revived them, and on the coals were roasting succulent slices of venison, to which they did ample justice. And when their refreshed minds began to reflect, they could scarcely believe that they had escaped so many perils,—the fire, the water, and the formidable alligators.

Thalcave, in a few words, told his story to Paganel, and ascribed to his intrepid horse all the honor of having saved him. Paganel then endeavored to explain to him the new interpretation of the document, and the hopes it led them to entertain. Did the Indian understand the geographer's ingenious suppositions? It was very doubtful; but he saw his friends happy and very confident, and he desired nothing more.

It may be easily believed that these courageous travelers, after their day of rest on the tree, needed no urging to resume their journey. At eight o'clock in the morning they were ready to start. They were too far south to procure means of transport, and were therefore obliged to travel on foot. The distance, however, was only forty miles, and Thaouka would not refuse to carry from time to time a tired pedestrian. In thirty-six hours they would reach the shores of the Atlantic.

IN THE DARK.

As soon as refreshed the guide and his companions left behind them the immense basin, still covered with the waters, and proceeded across elevated plains, on which, here and there, were seen groves planted by Europeans, meadows, and occasionally native trees. Thus the day passed.

The next morning, fifteen miles before reaching the ocean, its proximity was perceptible. They hastened on in order to reach Lake Salado, on the shores of the Atlantic, the same day. They were beginning to feel fatigued, when they perceived sand-hills that hid the foaming waves, and soon the prolonged murmur of the rising tide struck upon their ears.

"The ocean!" cried Paganel.

"Yes, the ocean!" replied Thalcave.

And these wanderers, whose strength had seemed almost about to fail, climbed the mounds with wonderful agility. But the darkness was profound, and their eyes wandered in vain over the gloomy expanse. They looked for the Duncan, but could not discern her.

"She is there, at all events," said Glenarvan, "waiting for us."

"We shall see her to-morrow," replied MacNabb.

Tom Austin shouted seaward, but received no answer. The wind was very strong, and the sea tempestuous. The clouds were driving from the west, and the foaming crests of the waves broke over the beach in masses of spray. If the Duncan was at the appointed rendezvous, the lookout man could neither hear nor be heard. The coast afforded no shelter. There was no bay, no harbor, no cove; not even a creek. The beach consisted of long sand-banks that were lost in the sea, and the vicinity of which is more dangerous than that of the rocks in the face of wind and tide. These banks, in fact, increase the waves; the sea is peculiarly boisterous around them, and ships are sure to be lost if they strike on these bars in heavy storms.

It was therefore very natural that the Duncan, considering this coast dangerous, and knowing it to be without a port of shelter, kept at a distance. Captain Mangles must have kept to the windward as far as possible. This was Tom Austin's opinion, and he declared that the Duncan was not less than five miles at sea.

The major, accordingly, persuaded his impatient relative to be resigned, as there was no way of dissipating the thick darkness. And why weary their eyes in scanning the gloomy horizon? He established a kind of encampment in the shelter of the sand-hills; the remains of the provisions furnished them a final repast; and then each, following the major's example, hollowed out a comfortable bed in the sand, and, covering himself up to his chin, was soon wrapped in profound repose.

Glenarvan watched alone. The wind continued strong, and the ocean still showed the effects of the recent storm. The tumultuous waves broke at the foot of the sand-banks with the noise of thunder. Glenarvan could not convince himself that the Duncan was so near him; but as for supposing that she had not arrived at her appointed rendezvous, it was impossible, for such a ship there were no delays. The storm had certainly been violent and its fury terrible on the vast expanse of the ocean, but the yacht was a good vessel and her captain an able seaman; she must, therefore, be at her destination.

These reflections, however, did not pacify Glenarvan. When heart and reason are at variance, the latter is the weaker power. The lord of Malcolm Castle seemed to see in the darkness all those whom he loved, his dear Helena, Mary Grant, and the crew of the Duncan. He wandered along the barren coast which the waves covered with phosphorescent bubbles. He looked, he listened, and even thought that he saw a fitful light on the sea.

"I am not mistaken," he soliloquized; "I saw a ship's light, the Duncan's. Ah! why cannot my eyes pierce the darkness?"

Then an idea occurred to him. Paganel called himself a nyctalops; he could see in the night.

The geographer was sleeping like a mole in his bed, when a strong hand dragged him from his sandy couch.

"Who is that?" cried he.

"I."

"Who?"

"Glenarvan. Come, I need your eyes."

"My eyes?" replied Paganel, rubbing them vigorously.

"Yes, your eyes, to distinguish the Duncan in this darkness. Come."

"And why my eyes?" said Paganel to himself, delighted, nevertheless, to be of service to Glenarvan.

He rose, shaking his torpid limbs in the manner of one awakened from sleep, and followed his friend along the shore. Glenarvan requested him to survey the dark horizon to seaward. For several moments Paganel conscientiously devoted himself to this task.

"Well, do you perceive nothing?" asked Glenarvan.

"Nothing. Not even a cat could see two paces before her."

"Look for a red or a green light, on the starboard or the larboard side."

"I see neither a red nor a green light. All is darkness," replied Paganel, whose eyes were thereupon involuntarily closed.

For half an hour he mechanically followed his impatient friend in absolute silence, with his head bowed upon his breast, sometimes raising it suddenly. He tottered along with uncertain steps, like those of a drunken man. At last Glenarvan, seeing that the geographer was in a state of somnambulism, took him by the arm, and, without waking him, led him back to his sand-hole, and comfortably deposited him therein.

At break of day they were all started to their feet by the cry,—

IMPATIENCE.

"The Duncan! the Duncan!"

"Hurrah! hurrah!" replied Glenarvan's companions, rushing to the shore.

The Duncan was indeed in sight. Five miles distant, the yacht was sailing under low pressure, her main-sails carefully reefed, while her smoke mingled with the mists of the morning. The sea was high, and a vessel of her tonnage could not approach the shore without danger.

Glenarvan, provided with Paganel's telescope, watched the movements of the Duncan. Captain Mangles could not have perceived them, for he did not approach, but continued to coast along with only a reefed top-sail.

At this moment Thalcave, having loaded his carbine heavily, fired it in the direction of the yacht. They gazed and listened. Three times the Indian's gun resounded, waking the echoes of the shore.

At last a white smoke issued from the side of the yacht.

"They see us!" cried Glenarvan. "It is the Duncan's cannon."

A few moments after, a heavy report rang out on the air, and the Duncan, shifting her sail and putting on steam, was seen to be approaching the shore. By the aid of the glass they saw a boat leave the ship's side.

"Lady Helena cannot come," said Tom Austin: "the sea is too rough."

"Nor Captain Mangles," replied MacNabb: "he cannot leave his vessel."

Glenarvan watched alone. He could not convince himself that the Duncan was so near him; but as for supposing that she had not arrived at her appointed rendezvous, it was impossible, for such a ship there were no delays.

"My sister! my sister!" cried Robert, stretching his arms towards the yacht, which rolled heavily.

"I hope I shall soon get on board!" exclaimed Glenarvan.

"Patience, Edward! You will be there in two hours," replied MacNabb.

Glenarvan now joined Thalcave, who, standing with folded arms alongside of Thaouka, was calmly gazing at the waves.

They pushed off, and the boat was rapidly borne from the shore by the ebbing tide. For a long time the motionless outline of the Indian was seen through the foam of the waves.

Glenarvan took his hand, and, pointing to the yacht, said,—

"Come!"

The Indian shook his head.

"Come, my friend!" continued Glenarvan.

"No," replied Thalcave, gently. "Here is Thaouka, and there are the Pampas!" he added, indicating with a sweep of his hand the vast expanse of the plains.

It was clear that the Indian would never leave the prairies, where the bones of his fathers whitened. Glenarvan knew the strong attachment of these children of the desert to their native country. He therefore shook Thalcave's hand, and did not insist; not even when the Indian, smiling in his peculiar way, refused the price of his services, saying,—

"It was done out of friendship."

His lordship, however, desired to give the brave Indian something which might at least serve as a souvenir of his European friends. But what had he left? His arms, his horses, everything had been lost in the inundation. His friends were no richer than himself. For some moments he was at a loss how to repay the disinterested generosity of the brave guide; but at last a happy idea occurred to him. He drew from his pocket-book a costly medallion inclosing an admirable portrait, one of Lawrence's master-pieces, and presented it to Thalcave.

"My wife," said Glenarvan.

Thalcave gazed with wonder at the portrait, and pronounced these simple words,—

"Good and beautiful!"

Then Robert, Paganel, the major, Tom Austin, and the two sailors bade an affectionate adieu to the noble Patagonian, who clasped each one in succession to his broad breast. All were sincerely sorry at parting with so courageous and devoted a friend. Paganel forced him to accept a map of South America and the two oceans, which the Indian had frequently examined with interest. It was the geographer's most precious possession. As for Robert, he had nothing to give but caresses, which he freely lavished upon his deliverer and upon Thaouka.

At that instant the Duncan's boat approached, and, gliding into the narrow channel between the sand-banks, grounded on the beach.

"My wife?" asked Glenarvan.

"My sister?" cried Robert.

"Lady Helena and Miss Grant await you on board," replied the cockswain. "But we have not a moment to lose, my lord, for the tide is beginning to ebb."

The last acknowledgments were given, and Thalcave accompanied his friends to the boat. Just as Robert was about to embark, the Indian took him in his arms and gazed at him tenderly.

"Now go," said he; "you are a man!"

"Adieu, my friend, adieu!" cried Glenarvan.

"Shall we ever see each other again?" asked Paganel.

"Who knows?" replied Thalcave, raising his arms towards heaven.

They pushed off, and the boat was rapidly borne from the shore by the ebbing tide. For a long time the motionless outline of the Indian was seen through the foam of the waves. Then his tall form grew indistinct, and soon became invisible. An hour afterwards they reached the Duncan. Robert was the first to spring upon the deck, where he threw himself upon his sister's neck, while the crew of the yacht filled the air with their joyous shouts.

Thus had our travelers accomplished the journey across South America on a rigorously straight line. Neither mountains nor rivers had turned them aside from their course; and, although they were not forced to struggle against the evil designs of men, the relentless fury of the elements had often tested their generous intrepidity to its utmost powers of endurance.

Chapter XXVII

A NEW DESTINATION.

The first moments were consecrated to the happiness of meeting. Lord Glenarvan did not wish the joy in the hearts of his friends to be chilled by tidings of their want of success. His first words, therefore, were,—

"Courage, my friends, courage! Captain Grant is not with us, but we are sure to find him."

It needed only such an assurance to restor

e hope to the passengers of the Duncan. Lady Helena and Mary Grant, while the boat was approaching the ship, had experienced all the anguish of suspense. From the deck they endeavored to count those who were returning. At one time the young girl would despair; at another she would think she saw her father. Her heart beat quickly; she could not speak; she could scarcely stand. Lady

Helena supported her, while Captain Mangles stood beside her in silence. His keen eyes, accustomed to distinguish distant objects, could not discern the captain.

"He is there! he is coming! my father!" murmured the young girl.

But as the boat gradually drew near, the illusion vanished. Not only Lady Helena and the captain, but Mary Grant, had now lost all hope. It was, therefore, time for Glenarvan to utter his assuring words.

"BREAKFAST!"

After the first embraces, all were informed of the principal incidents of the journey; and, first of all, Glenarvan made known the new interpretation of the document, due to the sagacity of Jacques Paganel. He also praised Robert, of whom his sister had a right to be proud. His courage, his devotion, and the dangers that he had overcome, were conspicuously set forth by his noble friend, so that the boy would not have known where to hide himself, if his sister's arms had not afforded him a sure refuge.

"You need not blush, Robert," said Captain Mangles; "you have behaved like the worthy son of Captain Grant."

He stretched out his arms towards Mary's brother, and pressed his lips to the boy's cheeks, which were still wet with tears.

They then spoke of the generous Thalcave. Lady Helena regretted that she could not have shaken hands with the brave Indian. MacNabb, after the first outbursts of enthusiasm, repaired to his cabin to shave himself. As for Paganel, he flitted hither and thither, like a bee, extracting the honey of compliments and smiles. He wished to embrace all on board the Duncan, and, beginning with Lady Helena and Mary Grant, ended with Mr. Olbinett, the steward, who could not better recognize such politeness than by announcing breakfast.

Lady Helena and Mary Grant, while the boat was approaching the ship, had experienced all the anguish of suspense. From the deck they endeavored to count those who were returning.

"Breakfast!" cried Paganel.

"Yes, Mr. Paganel," replied Olbinett.

"A real breakfast, on a real table, with table-cloth and napkins?"

"Certainly."

"And shall we not eat hard eggs, or ostrich steaks?"

"Oh, Mr. Paganel!" replied the worthy steward, greatly embarrassed.

"I did not mean to offend you, my friend," said the geographer; "but for a month our food has been of that sort, and we have dined, not at a table, but stretched on the ground, except when we were astride of the trees. This breakfast that you have just announced seemed to me, therefore, like a dream, a fiction, a chimera."

"Well, we will test its reality, Monsieur Paganel," replied Lady Helena, who could not help laughing.

"Accept my arm," said the gallant geographer.

"Has your lordship any orders to give?" inquired Captain Mangles.

"After breakfast, my dear fellow," replied Glenarvan, "we will discuss in council the programme of the new expedition."

The passengers and the young captain then descended to the cabin. Orders were given to the engineer to keep up steam, that they might start at the first signal. The major and the travelers, after a rapid toilette, seated themselves at the table. Ample justice was done to Mr. Olbinett's repast, which was declared excellent and even superior to the splendid banquets of the Pampas. Paganel called twice for every dish, "through absent-mindedness," as he said. This unfortunate word led Lady Helena to inquire if the amiable Frenchman had occasionally shown his habitual failing. The major and Lord Glenarvan looked at each other with a smile. As for Paganel, he laughed heartily, and promised "upon his honor" not to commit a single blunder during the entire voyage. He then in a very comical way told the story of his mistake in the study of Spanish.

"After all," he added, in conclusion, "misfortunes are sometimes beneficial, and I do not regret my error."

"And why, my worthy friend?" asked the major.

"Because I not only know Spanish, but Portuguese also. I speak two languages instead of one."

"By my faith, I should not have thought of that," replied MacNabb. "My compliments, Paganel, my sincere compliments!"

TABLE-TALK IN THE SOUTH ATLANTIC.

Paganel was applauded, but did not lose a single mouthful. He did not, however, notice one peculiarity observed by Glenarvan, and that was the young captain's attentions to his neighbor, Mary Grant. A slight sign from Lady Helena to her husband told him how matters stood. He gazed at the two young people with affectionate sympathy, and finally addressed the captain, but upon a different subject.

"How did you succeed with your voyage, captain?" he inquired.

"Excellently," replied the captain; "only I must inform your lordship that we did not return by way of the Strait of Magellan."

"What!" cried Paganel, "you doubled Cape Horn, and I was not there!"

"Hang yourself!" said the major.

"Selfish fellow! you give me this advice in order that you may share my rope!" retorted the geographer.

"Well, my dear Paganel," added Glenarvan, "unless we are endowed with ubiquity, we cannot be everywhere. Since you crossed the Pampas, you could not at the same time double Cape Horn."

"Nevertheless, I am sorry," replied the geographer.

Captain Mangles now told the story of his voyage, and was congratulated by Glenarvan, who, addressing Mary Grant, said,—

"My dear young lady, I see that Captain John pays his homage to your noble qualities, and I am happy to find that you are not displeased with his ship."

"Oh, how could I be?" replied Mary, gazing at Lady Helena, and perhaps also at the young captain.

"My sister loves you, Mr. Captain," cried Robert, "and I do too."

"And I return your love, my dear boy," replied Captain Mangles, a little confused by Robert's words, which also brought a slight blush to the face of the young girl.

Then, changing the conversation to a less embarrassing subject, the captain added,—

"Since I have related the Duncan's voyage, will not your lordship give us a few particulars of your travels, and the exploits of our young hero?"

No recital could have been more agreeable to Lady Helena and Miss Grant, and Glenarvan hastened to satisfy their curiosity. He told, word for word, all about their journey from ocean to ocean. The passage of the Andes, the earthquake, Robert's disappearance, his capture by the condor, Thalcave's fortunate shot, the adventure with the wolves, the boy's devotion, the meeting with Sergeant Manuel, the inundation, their refuge in the tree, the lightning, the fire, the alligators, the water-spout, the night on the shores of the Atlantic, all these incidents, cheerful or serious, excited alternately the joy and terror of his hearers. Many a circumstance was related that brought Robert the caresses of his sister and Lady Helena. Never was boy more highly praised, or by more enthusiastic friends.

"Now, my friends," remarked Lord Glenarvan, when he had finished his recital, "let us think of the present. Let us return to the subject of Captain Grant."

When breakfast was over, the party repaired to Lady Helena's state-room, and, taking seats around a table loaded with maps and charts, resumed the conversation. Glenarvan explained that the shipwreck had not taken place on the shores either of the Pacific or the Atlantic, and that, consequently, the document had been wrongly interpreted so far as Patagonia was concerned; that Paganel, by a sudden inspiration, had discovered the mistake and proved that they had been following a false trail. The geographer was accordingly asked to explain the French document, which he did to the satisfaction of every one. When he had finished his demonstration, Glenarvan announced that the Duncan would immediately set sail for Australia.

The major, however, before the order was given, asked permission to make a single remark.

"Speak, major," said Glenarvan.

"My object," said MacNabb, "is not to invalidate the arguments of my friend Paganel, still less to refute them. I consider them rational, sagacious, and worthy of our whole attention. But I desire to submit them to a final examination, that their validity may be incontestable."

No one knew what the prudent MacNabb meant, and his hearers listened with some anxiety.

"Go on, major," said Paganel: "I am ready to answer all your questions."

"Nothing can be simpler," said the major. "Five months ago, in the Frith of Clyde, when we studied the three documents, their interpretation seemed clear to us. No place but the western coast of Patagonia could, we thought, have been the scene of the shipwreck. We had not even the shadow of a doubt on the subject."

"Very true," added Glenarvan.

"My object," said MacNabb, "is not to invalidate the arguments of my friend Paganel, still less to refute them."

"Afterwards," resumed the major, "when Paganel, in a moment of providential absent-mindedness, embarked on board our vessel, the documents were submitted to him, and he unhesitatingly sanctioned our search upon the American coast."

"You are right," observed the geographer.

"And, nevertheless, we are mistaken," said the major.

"Yes, we are mistaken," repeated Paganel; "but to be mistaken is only to be human, while it is the part of a madman to persist in his error."

"Wait, Paganel," continued the major; "do not get excited. I do not mean that our search ought to be prolonged in America."

"What do you ask, then?" inquired Glenarvan.

"Simply the acknowledgment that Australia now seems to be the scene of the Britannia's shipwreck as much as South America did before."

"Granted," replied Paganel.

"Who knows, then," resumed the major, "whether, after Australia, another country may not offer us the same probabilities, and whether, when this new search proves vain, it may not seem evident that we ought to have searched elsewhere?"

FRIENDS IN COUNCIL.

Glenarvan and Paganel glanced at each other. The major's remarks were strictly correct.

"I desire, therefore," added MacNabb, "that a final test be made before we start for Australia. Here are the documents and maps. Let us examine successively all points that the thirty-seventh parallel crosses, and see if there is not some other country to which the document has as precise a reference."

"Nothing is easier," replied Paganel.

The map was placed before Lady Helena, and all showed themselves ready to follow Paganel's demonstration. After carefully examining the documents, it was unanimously agreed that Paganel's interpretation was the correct one.

At sunrise they saw the conical peak of Tristan, seemingly separated from all the rest of the rocky group.

"I leave you, therefore, my friends," said he, in conclusion, "to decide whether all the probabilities are not in favor of the Australian continent."

"Evidently," replied the passengers and the captain with unanimity.

"Captain," said Glenarvan, "have you sufficient provisions and coal?"

"Yes, my lord, I procured ample supplies at Talcahuana, and, besides, we can lay in a fresh stock of fuel at Cape Town."

"One more remark," said the major.

"A thousand, if you please!"

"Whatever may be the guarantees for success in Australia, will it not be well to call for a day or two, in passing, at the islets of Tristan d'Acunha and Amsterdam? They are situated so near our strict line of search, that it is worth our while to ascertain if there be on them any trace of the shipwreck of the Britannia."

"The unbeliever!" said Paganel.

"I do not want to have to return to them, monsieur, if Australia does not after all realize our newly-conceived expectations."

"The precaution is not a bad one," said Glenarvan.

A few hours of their united toil resulted in the death of a large number of seals who were "caught napping."

"And I do not wish to dissuade you; quite the contrary," replied the geographer.

"Well, then, we will adopt it, and start forthwith," said Lord Glenarvan.

"Immediately, my lord," replied the captain, as he went on deck, while Robert and Mary Grant uttered the liveliest expressions of gratitude; and the Duncan, leaving the American coast and heading to the east, was soon swiftly ploughing the waves of the Atlantic.

CHAPTER XXVIII

TRISTAN D'ACUNHA AND THE ISLE OF AMSTERDAM.

LOOKING ALOFT.

The Duncan now had before her a broad stretch of ocean but little traversed by navigators. Between the shores of South America and the little speck in the ocean known by the name of Tristan d'Acunha, there was no probability of her meeting with any strange sail; and under some circumstances, or in some company, the days might have been monotonous and the hours might have hung wearily. But so ardent was the desire for success, and so accomplished, yet varied, were the characters of those who composed the little assembly, that the voyage on the South Atlantic, though devoid of striking incident, was by no means wanting in interest. Much of the time was spent on deck, where the ladies' cabins were now located, Mary Grant especially training her hand, head, and heart in feeling, thought, and action. The geographer set to work on a composition entitled "Travels of a Geographer on the Argentine Pampas;" but many a blank page did he leave. Tho Scottish peer (when tired of examining for the thousandth time all that belonged to his yacht) could look at the books and documents which he had brought with him, intending to peruse them carefully. And as to the major he was never in company and never out of company; his cigar insured, nothing else was wanted.

Ever and anon many miles of the ocean would be covered by masses of sea-weed; these different species of algæ would afford subject for research; specimens must be preserved, authorities must be consulted, and as one result at least all would become wiser. Then a discussion would ensue on some geographical problem, and maps that were not attainable were of course appealed to by each disputant, though the subject in question was often of very trivial moment. It was in the midst of a debate of this kind, during the evening, that a sailor cried out,—

"Land ahead!"

"In what direction?" asked Paganel.

"To windward," replied the sailor.

The landsmen's eyes were strained, but to no purpose. The geographer's telescope was brought into requisition, but with no avail. "I do not see the land," said its owner.

"Look into the clouds," said the captain.

"Ah!" replied Paganel, struck with the idea, and shortly with the reality also; for there was the barren mountain-top of Tristan d'Acunha.

"Then," said he, "if I remember aright, we are eighty miles from it. Is not that the distance from which this mountain is visible?"

"Exactly so," replied the captain.

Our friends found a few voluntary exiles on the former island, who, by means of seal-fishing, eke out a scanty existence in this out-of-the-way spot.

A few hours brought them much nearer to the group of high and steep rocks, and at sunrise they saw the conical peak of Tristan, seemingly separated from all the rest of the rocky group, and reflecting the glory of the blue heavens and of the rising orb on the placid sea at its base.

Inasmuch as this was sufficient to cook fish, Paganel decided that it was not necessary for him to bathe here "geographically."

There are three islets in this group,—Tristan d'Acunha, Inaccessible, and Rossignol; but it was only at the first of these that the Duncan called. Inquiry was made of the authorities (for these islets are governed by a British official from the Cape of Good Hope) if there were any tidings of the Britannia. But nothing was known of such a ship; they were told of the shipwrecks which had occurred, but there was nothing that afforded a clue to that which they sought. They spent some hours in examination of the fauna and flora, which were not very extensive. They saw and were seen by the sparse population that subsist here, and in the afternoon of the same day the yacht left the islands and islanders so rarely visited.

Whilst the passengers had been thus engaged, Lord Glenarvan had allowed his crew to employ their time advantageously to themselves in capturing some of the seals which are so plentiful in these latitudes. A few hours of their united toil resulted in the death of a large number of seals who were "caught napping," and in the stowing away, for the profit of the crew when they should reach the Australian market, several barrels of the oil obtained from their carcases.

Still onward on the same parallel lay the course of the Duncan, towards the Isles of Amsterdam and St. Paul; and the same subjects of conversation, study, and speculation engaged them all, until, one morning, they espied the first mentioned island, far ahead; and as they drew nearer, a peak rose clearly before their vision which strongly reminded them of the Peak of Teneriffe they had beheld a few months before.

WARM SPRINGS AND WARM TALK.

The Isle of Amsterdam or St. Peter, and the Isle of St. Paul, have been visited by very few, and but little is known of them. The latter is uninhabited; but our friends found a few voluntary exiles on the former island, who, by means of seal-fishing, eke out a scanty existence in this out-of-the-way spot. Here again inquiry was made, but in vain, for any information of the Britannia, her voyage, or her shipwreck. Neither on the Isle of Amsterdam nor on that of St. Paul, which the whalers and seal-fishers sometimes visit, had there been any trace of the catastrophe.

Desolate as these lonely islands appeared to our travelers, they still were not devoid of objects of interest. They were meagre enough in vegetation and in animal life; but there were warm springs which well repaid a visit. Captain Mangles found the temperature of their waters to be 166° Fahrenheit; and, inasmuch as this was sufficient to cook fish, Paganel decided that it was not necessary for him to bathe here "geographically."

When they resumed their course, though many miles were before them, there was a growing sense of anticipation; they were not to pause again until the "Australian continent" was reached; and more and more did the conversation and discussions tend towards this continent as their subject. On one occasion so certain was Paganel as to the ease with which they would be able to pursue their search, when they arrived, that he asserted that more than fifty geographers had already made the course clear for them.

"What! fifty, do you say?" asked the major, with an air of doubt.

"Yes, MacNabb, decidedly," said the geographer, piqued at the hesitancy to believe him.

"Impossible!" replied the major.

"Not at all; and if you doubt my veracity, I will cite their names."

"Ah!" said the major, quietly, "you clever people stick at nothing."

"Major," said Paganel, "will you wager your rifle against my telescope that I cannot name at least fifty Australian explorers?"

"Of course, Paganel, if you like," replied MacNabb, seeing that he could not now recede from his position without incurring the ridicule of the company.

"Well, then," said Paganel to Lady Helena and Miss Grant, "come and be umpires, and Master Robert shall count for us." And forthwith the learned geographer opened his budget, and poured forth the history of the discovery of Australia, with the names of its discoverers and the dates of their explorations, as fluently as though his sole calling in life was to be professor of Australian history. Rapidly he mentioned the first twenty who found or traversed the Austral shores; as rapidly did the names of the second score flow from his lips; and after the prescribed fifty had been enumerated, he kept on as though his list were inexhaustible.

"Enough, enough, Monsieur Paganel!" said Lady Helena. "You have shown that there is nothing, great or small, about Australia, of which you are ignorant."

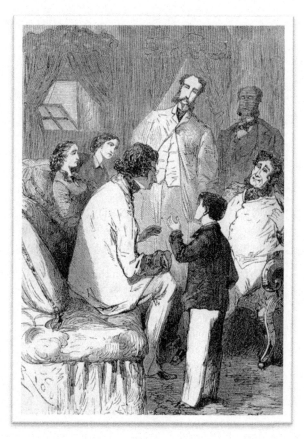

"Master Robert shall count for us." And forthwith the learned geographer opened his budget, and poured forth the history of the discovery of Australia.

"Nay, madam," said the geographer, with a bow.

Then, with a peculiar expression, he smiled as he said to the major, "We will talk about the rifle at another time."

"Major," said Paganel, "will you wager your rifle against my telescope that I cannot name at least fifty Australian explorers?"

CHAPTER XXIX

THE STORM ON THE INDIAN OCEAN.

Two days after this conversation, Captain Mangles took an observation, and the passengers saw, to their great satisfaction, upon consulting the map, that they were in the vicinity of Cape Bernouilli, which they might expect to reach in four days. The west wind had hitherto favored the progress of the yacht, but for several days it had shown a tendency to fail, and now there was a perfect calm. The sails flapped idly against the masts, and had it not been for her powerful screw, the Duncan would have been becalmed on the ocean.

FOREBODINGS OF DISASTER.

This state of things might be prolonged indefinitely. At evening Glenarvan consulted the captain on the subject. The latter, whose supply of coal was rapidly diminishing, appeared much disturbed at the subsidence of the wind. He had covered his ship with canvas, and set his studding- and main-sails, that he might take advantage of the least breeze; but, in nautical language, there was not enough wind "to fill a hat."

"At all events," said Glenarvan, "we need not complain. It is better to be without wind than to have a contrary one."

"Your lordship is right," replied Captain Mangles; "but I dread some sudden change in the weather. We are now in the neighborhood of the trade-winds, which, from October to April, blow from the northeast, and our progress will, therefore, be very much retarded."

"But what can we do, captain? If this misfortune occurs, we must submit to it. It will only be a delay, after all."

"Probably, if a storm does not come upon us too."

"Do you fear bad weather?" asked Glenarvan, looking at the sky, which, however, was cloudless.

"Yes," replied the captain. "I tell your lordship, but would conceal my apprehensions from Lady Helena and Miss Grant."

"You act wisely. What do you apprehend?"

"There are signs of a great storm. Do not trust the appearance of the sky, my lord; nothing is more deceptive. For two days the barometer has fallen to an alarming degree. This is a warning that I cannot disregard. I particularly fear the storms of the South Seas, for I have been already exposed to them."

"John," replied Glenarvan, "the Duncan is a stout vessel, and her captain a skillful seaman. Let the storm come; we will take care of ourselves."

Captain Mangles, while giving expression to his fears, was by no means forgetful of his duty as a sailor. The steady fall of the barometer caused him to take every measure of precaution. The sky, as yet, gave no indication of the approaching tempest; but the warnings of his infallible instrument were not to be disregarded.

The young captain accordingly remained on deck all night. About eleven o'clock the sky grew threatening towards the south. All hands were immediately called on deck, to take in the sails. At midnight the wind freshened. The creaking of the masts, the rattling of the rigging, and the groaning of bulkheads informed the passengers of the state of affairs. Paganel, Glenarvan, the major, and Robert came on deck to render assistance if it should be needed. Over the sky, that they had left clear and studded with stars, now rolled thick clouds broken by light bands and spotted like the skin of a leopard.

"Has the storm broken upon us?" asked Glenarvan.

"Not yet, but it will presently," replied the captain.

At that moment he gave the order to reef the top-sail. The sailors sprang into the windward rattlings, and with difficulty accomplished their task. Captain Mangles wished to keep on as much sail as possible, to support the yacht and moderate her rolling. After these precautions had been taken, he told the mate and the boatswain to prepare for the assault of the tempest, which could not be long in breaking forth. Still, like an officer at the storming of a breach, he did not leave the point of observation, but from the upper deck endeavored to draw from the stormy sky its secrets.

AN ADDED CALAMITY.

It was now one o'clock in the morning. Lady Helena and Miss Grant, aroused by the unusual bustle, ventured to come on deck. The wind was sharply whistling through the cordage, which, like the strings of a musical instrument, resounded as if some mighty bow had caused their rapid vibrations; the pulleys clashed against each other; the ropes creaked with a sharp sound in their rough sockets; the sails cracked like cannon, and vast waves rolled up to assail the yacht, as it lightly danced on their foaming crests.

When the captain perceived the ladies, he approached and besought them to return to the cabin. Several waves had already been shipped, and the deck might be swept at any moment. The din of the elements was now so piercing that Lady Helena could scarcely hear the young captain.

"Is there any danger?" she managed to ask him during a momentary lull in the storm.

"No, madam," replied he; "but neither you nor Miss Mary can remain on deck."

The ladies did not oppose an order that seemed more like an entreaty, and returned to the cabin just as a wave, rolling over the stern, shook the compass-lights in their sockets. The violence of the wind redoubled; the masts bent under the pressure of sail, and the yacht seemed to rise on the billows.

"Brail up the main-sail!" cried the captain; "haul in the top-sails and jibs!"

The sailors sprang to their places; the halyards were loosened, the brails drawn down, the jibs taken in with a noise that rose above the storm, and the Duncan, whose smoke-stack belched forth torrents of black smoke, rolled heavily in the sea.

Glenarvan, the major, Paganel, and Robert gazed with admiration and terror at this struggle with the waves. They clung tightly to the rigging, unable to exchange a word, and watched the flocks of stormy petrels, those melancholy birds of the storm, as they sported in the raging winds.

At that moment a piercing sound was heard above the roar of the hurricane. The steam was rapidly escaping, not through the escape-valve, but through the pipes of the boiler. The alarm-whistle sounded with unusual shrillness; the yacht gave a terrible lurch, and Wilson, who was at the helm, was overthrown by an unexpected blow of the wheel. The vessel was in the trough of the sea, and no longer manageable.

"What is the matter?" cried Captain Mangles, rushing to the stern.

"The ship is careening!" replied Austin.

"Is the rudder unhinged?"

"To the engine! to the engine!" cried the engineer.

The captain rushed down the ladder. A cloud of steam filled the engine-room; the pistons were motionless in their cylinders, and the cranks gave no movement to the shaft. The engineer, seeing that all efforts were useless, and fearing for his boilers, had let out the steam through the escape-valve.

"What has happened?" asked the captain.

"The screw is either bent or entangled," replied the engineer; "it will not work."

"Is it impossible to free it?"

"Impossible, at present."

To attempt to repair the accident at that moment was out of the question. The screw would not move, and the steam, being no longer effective, had escaped through the valves. The captain was, therefore, forced to rely on his sails, and seek the aid of the wind, which had been hitherto his most dangerous enemy.

He came on deck, and, briefly informing Glenarvan of the situation, begged him to return to the cabin with the others; but the latter wished to remain.

"No, my lord," replied Captain Mangles, in a firm tone: "I must be alone here with my crew. Go! The ship may be in danger, and the waves would drench you unmercifully."

"But we may be of use——"

"Go, go, my lord; you must! There are times when I am master on board. Retire, as I wish!"

THE STRUGGLE CONTINUED.

For John Mangles to express himself so authoritatively, the situation must have been critical. Glenarvan understood that it was his duty to obey. He therefore left the deck, followed by his three companions, and joined the ladies in the cabin, who were anxiously awaiting the result of this struggle with the elements.

"My brave John is an energetic man," remarked Glenarvan as he entered.

Meantime Captain Mangles lost no time in extricating the ship from her perilous situation. He resolved to keep towards the Cape, that he might deviate as little as possible from his prescribed course. It was, therefore, necessary to brace the sails obliquely to the wind. The top-sail was reefed, a kind of fore-sail rigged on the main-stay, and the helm crowded hard aport. The yacht, which was a stanch and fleet vessel, started like a spirited horse that feels the spur, and proudly breasted the angry billows.

The rest of the night was passed in this situation. They hoped that the tempest would abate by break of day. Vain hope! At eight o'clock in the morning it was still blowing hard, and the wind soon became a hurricane.

The captain said nothing, but he trembled for his vessel and those whom she carried. The Duncan now and then gave a fearful lurch; her stanchions cracked, and sometimes the yards of the mainmast struck the crests of the waves. At one moment the crew thought the yacht would not rise again. Already the sailors, hatchet in hand, were rushing to cut away the fore-shrouds, when they were violently torn from their fastenings by the blast. The ship righted herself, but, without support on the waves, she was tossed about so terribly that the masts threatened to break at their very foundations. She could not long endure such rolling; she was growing weak, and soon her shattered sides and opening seams must give way for the water.

Then, impelled by the hurricane, the billows outran her; they leaped over the taffrail, and the whole deck was swept with tremendous violence.

NEARING THE END.

Captain Mangles had but one resource,—to rig a storm-jib. He succeeded after several hours' labor, but it was not until three o'clock in the afternoon that the jib was hauled to the main-stay and set to the wind. With this piece of canvas the Duncan flew before the wind with inconceivable rapidity. It was necessary to keep up the greatest possible speed, for upon this alone depended her safety. Sometimes, outstripping the waves, she cut them with her slender prow and plunged beneath them, like an enormous sea-monster, while the water swept her deck from stem to stern. At other times her swiftness barely equaled that of the surges, her rudder lost all power, and she gave terrific lurches that threatened to capsize her. Then, impelled by the hurricane, the billows outran her; they leaped over the taffrail, and the whole deck was swept with tremendous violence.

The situation was indeed alarming. The captain would not leave his post for an instant. He was tortured by fears that his impassive face would not betray, and persistently sought to penetrate with his gaze the gathering gloom. And he had good cause for fear. The Duncan, driven out of her course, was running towards the Australian coast with a swiftness that nothing could arrest. He felt, too, as if by instinct, that a strong current was drawing him along. At every moment he feared the shock of a reef upon which the yacht would be dashed into a thousand pieces, and he calculated that the shore was not more than a dozen miles to leeward.

Finally he went in search of Lord Glenarvan, consulted with him in private, explained their actual situation, viewed it with the coolness of a sailor who is ready for any emergency, and ended by saying that he should be obliged perhaps to run the Duncan ashore.

"To save those she carries, if possible, my lord," he added.

"Very well, captain," replied Glenarvan.

"And Lady Helena and Miss Grant?"

"I will inform them only at the last moment, when all hope is gone of keeping at sea. You will tell me."

"I will, my lord."

Glenarvan returned to the ladies, who, without knowing all the danger, felt it to be imminent. They displayed, however, a noble courage, equal at least to that of their companions. Paganel gave himself up to the most unreasonable theories concerning the direction of atmospheric currents, while the major awaited the end with the indifference of a Mussulman.

About eleven o'clock the hurricane seemed to moderate a little, the heavy mists were gradually dissipated, and through the openings the captain could see a low land at least six miles to leeward. He steered directly for it. Huge waves rolled to a prodigious height, and he knew that they must have a firm point of support to reach such an elevation.

"There are sand-bars here," said he to Tom Austin.

"That is my opinion," replied the mate.

"We are in the hands of God," continued the captain. "If He does not himself guide the Duncan over the bar, we are lost."

"It is high tide now, captain; perhaps we may do it."

"But see the fury of those waves! What ship could resist them? God help us, my friend!"

Meantime the Duncan dashed towards the shore with terrible swiftness. Soon she was only two miles from the sand-bars. The mists still continued to conceal the land. Nevertheless Captain Mangles thought he perceived, beyond this foaming barrier, a tranquil haven, where the Duncan would be in comparative safety. But how to reach it?

He called the passengers on deck, for he did not wish, when the hour of shipwreck had come, that they should be confined in the cabin. Glenarvan and his companions gazed at the awful sea. Mary Grant grew pale.

"John," said Glenarvan in a low tone to the young captain, "I will try to save my wife, or will perish with her. Do you take charge of Miss Grant."

OILY INFLUENCES.

"Yes, your lordship," was the prompt reply.

The Duncan was now only a few cable-lengths from the sand-bars. As it was high tide, there would doubtless have been sufficient water to enable the yacht to cross these dangerous shoals; but the enormous waves upon which she rose and fell would infallibly have wrecked her. Was there then any means of allaying these billows, of calming this tumultuous sea?

A sudden idea occurred to the captain.

"The oil!" cried he; "pour on oil, men, pour on oil!"

These words were quickly understood by all the crew. They were about to employ a method that sometimes succeeds. The fury of the sea can often be appeased by covering it with a sheet of oil, which floats on the surface and destroys the shock of the waters. The effect is instantaneous, but transient. As soon as a ship has crossed this treacherous sea, it redoubles its fury; and woe to those who would venture to follow.

The barrels containing the supply of seal-oil were hoisted into the forecastle by the crew, to whom the danger gave new strength. Here they were stove in with a blow of the hatchet, and suspended over the starboard rattlings.

"Hold on!" cried the captain, waiting for the favorable moment.

In a few seconds the yacht reached the entrance to the pass, which was barred by a terrible line of foam.

"Let go!" cried the young captain.

The barrels were inverted, and from their sides streamed floods of oil. Immediately the unctuous liquid leveled the foaming surface of the sea, and the Duncan sailed on calm waters, and was soon in a quiet harbor beyond the terrible sand-bars; and then the ocean, released from its fetters, bounded after its escaped prey with indescribable fury.

"Let go!" cried the young captain. The barrels were inverted, and from their sides streamed floods of oil.

CHAPTER XXX

A HOSPITABLE COLONIST.

The captain's first care was to secure anchorage. He moored the vessel in five fathoms of water. The bottom was good, a hard gravel, affording an excellent hold. There was no danger of drifting, or of stranding at low tide. The Duncan, after so many hours of peril, was now in a sort of creek sheltered by a high promontory from the fury of the wind.

Lord Glenarvan shook the hand of the young captain, saying,—

"Thanks, John!"

And Captain Mangles felt himself fully rewarded by these simple words. Glenarvan kept to himself the secret of his anguish, and neither Lady Helena, Mary Grant, nor Robert suspected the magnitude of the perils they had just escaped.

One important point remained to be settled. On what part of the coast had the Duncan been cast by the storm? How could she regain her prescribed course? How far were they from Cape Bernouilli? Such were the first questions addressed to the captain, who at once took his bearings and noted his observations on the map. The Duncan had not deviated very far from her route. She was at Cape Catastrophe, on the southern coast of Australia, not three hundred miles from Cape Bernouilli.

But could the Duncan's injuries be repaired? This was the question to decide. The captain wished to know the extent of the damage. It was discovered, by diving, that a flange of the screw was bent and came in contact with the stern-post. Hence it was impossible for the screw to rotate. This injury was considered serious enough to necessitate going into dry-dock, which of course could not be done in their present locality.

Glenarvan and the captain, after mature reflection, resolved that the Duncan should follow the western shore, seeking traces of the Britannia, should stop at Cape Bernouilli, where further information could be obtained, and then continue southward to Melbourne, where her injuries could be repaired; and, as soon as this was done, that she should cruise along the eastern shores to finish the search.

This arrangement was approved, and Captain Mangles resolved to take advantage of the first favorable wind. He did not have to wait long. Towards evening the hurricane had entirely subsided, and a moderate breeze was blowing from the southwest. Preparations were made for getting under way; new sails were set, and at four o'clock in the morning the sailors heaved at the capstan, the anchor was weighed, and the Duncan, with all sails set, cruised close to windward along the coast.

They arrived at Cape Bernouilli without finding the least trace of the lost vessel. But this failure proved nothing. Indeed, during the two years since the shipwreck, the sea might have scattered or destroyed the fragments of the brig. Besides, the natives, who scent shipwrecks as a vulture does a corpse, might have carried away every vestige of it. Harry Grant and his two companions, therefore, without doubt, had been taken prisoners the moment the waves cast them ashore, and been carried into the interior of the country.

HOPING AGAINST HOPE.

But here one of Paganel's ingenious suppositions failed. So long as they were in the Argentine territory, the geographer could rightly maintain that the latitude of the document referred to the place of captivity,—not to the scene of the shipwreck. Indeed, the great rivers of the Pampas and their numerous affluents could easily bear the document to the sea. In this part of Australia, on the contrary, few streams cross the thirty-seventh parallel, and the principal Australian rivers—the Murray, the Yara, the Torrens, and the Darling—either flow into each other, or empty into the ocean by mouths where navigation is active. What probability was there, then, that a fragile bottle could have descended these continually navigated waters, and reached the Indian Ocean? This consideration could not escape such sagacious minds. Paganel's supposition, plausible in Patagonia, was illogical in Australia. The geographer perceived this in a discussion on the subject with the major. It was clear that the latitude applied only to the place of shipwreck, and that consequently the bottle had been cast into the sea where the Britannia was wrecked,—on the western coast of Australia.

However, as Glenarvan justly observed, this interpretation did not preclude the possibility of Captain Grant's captivity, who, moreover, had intimated as much by the words "where they will be prisoners of the cruel Indians." But there was no more reason for seeking the prisoners on the thirty-seventh parallel than on any other.

This conclusion, after much discussion, was finally accepted, and it was decided that, if no traces of the Britannia were found at Cape

Bernouilli, Lord Glenarvan should return to Europe, relinquishing all hope of finding the object of their search.

This resolution occasioned profound grief to the children of the lost captain. As the boats containing the whole of the party were rowed ashore, they felt that the fate of their father would soon be probably decided; irrevocably, we may say, for Paganel, in a former discussion, had clearly demonstrated that the shipwrecked seamen would have reached their country long ago, if their vessel had stranded on the other, the eastern coast.

A NEW PROSPECT.

"Hope! hope! never cease to hope!" said Lady Helena to the young girl seated beside her, as they approached the shore. "The hand of God will never fail us."

"Yes, Miss Mary," said the captain; "when men have exhausted human resources, then Heaven interposes, and, by some unforeseen event, opens to them new ways."

"God grant it, captain!" replied Mary.

The shore was now only a cable's length distant. The cape terminated in gentle declivities extending far out into the sea. The boat entered a small creek, between banks of coral in process of formation, which in time would form a chain of reefs along the southern coast of the island.

The passengers of the Duncan disembarked on a perfectly barren shore. Steep cliffs formed a lofty sea-wall, and it would have been difficult to scale this natural rampart without ladders or cramping-irons. Fortunately, the captain discovered a breach half a mile southward, caused by a partial crumbling of the cliffs. Probably the sea, during violent equinoctial storms, had beaten against this fragile barrier, and thus caused the fall of the upper portions of the mass.

As the boats containing the whole of the party were rowed ashore, they felt that the fate of their father would soon be probably decided.

Glenarvan and his companions entered this opening, and reached the summit of the cliffs by a very steep ascent. Robert climbed an abrupt declivity with the agility of a cat, and arrived first at the top, to the great chagrin of Paganel, who was quite mortified at seeing himself outstripped by a mere lad of twelve. However, he distanced the peaceable major; but that worthy was utterly indifferent to his defeat.

The little party surveyed the plain that stretched out beneath them. It was a vast, uncultivated tract, covered with bushes and brushwood, and was compared by Glenarvan to the glens of the Scottish lowlands, and by Paganel to the barren lands of Brittany. But though the country along the coast was evidently uninhabited, the presence of man, not the savage, but the civilized worker, was betokened by several substantial structures in the distance.

"A mill!" cried Robert.

True enough, at no great distance apparently, the sails of a mill were seen.

"It is indeed a mill," replied Paganel. "Here is a beacon as modest as it is useful, the sight of which delights my eyes."

"It is almost a belfry," said Lady Helena.

"Yes, madam; and while one makes bread for the body, the other announces bread for the soul. In this respect they resemble each other."

"Let us go to the mill," replied Glenarvan.

They accordingly started. After half an hour's walk the soil assumed a new aspect. The transition from barren plains to cultivated fields was sudden. Instead of brushwood, quick-set hedges surrounded an inclosure freshly ploughed. Some cattle, and half a dozen horses, grazed in pastures encircled by acacias. Then fields of corn were reached, several acres of land bristling with the yellow ears, haycocks like great bee-hives, vineyards with blooming inclosures, a beautiful garden, where the useful and the ornamental mingled; in short, a fair and comfortable locality, which the merry mill crowned with its pointed gable and caressed with the moving shadow of its sails.

At this moment a man of about fifty, of prepossessing countenance, issued from the principal house, at the barking of three great dogs that announced the coming of the strangers. Five stout and handsome boys, his sons, accompanied by their mother, a tall, robust woman, followed him. This man, surrounded by his healthful family, in the midst of these new erections, in this almost virgin country, presented the perfect type of the colonist, who, endeavoring to better his lot, seeks his fortune and happiness beyond the seas.

Glenarvan and his friends had not yet introduced themselves, they had not had time to declare either their names or their rank, when these cordial words saluted them:—

AN AUSTRALIAN HOME.

"Strangers, welcome to the house of Patrick O'Moore."

"You are an Irishman?" said Glenarvan, taking the hand that the colonist offered him.

"I was," replied Mr. O'Moore. "Now I am an Australian. But come in, whoever you are, gentlemen; this house is at your service."

The invitation so hospitably given was accepted without ceremony. Lady Helena and Mary Grant, conducted by Mrs. O'Moore, entered the house, while the colonist's sons relieved the visitors of their fire-arms.

A large, cool, airy room occupied the ground-floor of the house, which was built of stout beams arranged horizontally. Several wooden benches, built into the walls, and painted in gay colors, ten stools, two oaken trunks, in which white china and jugs of polished pewter were arranged, and a long table, at which twenty people could be comfortably seated, constituted the furniture, worthy of the house and its hardy inhabitants.

Dinner was soon served. Dishes of soup smoked between roast beef and legs of mutton, flanked by large plates of olives, grapes, and oranges. The host and hostess had such an engaging air, and the fare was so tempting, so ample, and so abundantly furnished, that it would have been unbecoming not to accept this rural bounty. The domestics of the farm, the equals of their master, had already come to partake of the repast; and the host reserved the place of honor for the strangers.

"I expected you," said he, quietly, to Lord Glenarvan.

"You did?" replied the latter, very much surprised.

"I always expect those who are coming," replied the Irishman.

Then, in a grave voice, while his household stood respectfully, he invoked a Divine blessing. Lady Helena was much affected by his perfect simplicity of manner, and a look from her husband told her that he likewise was touched by it.

A fair and comfortable locality, which the merry mill crowned with its pointed gable and caressed with the moving shadow of its sails.

THE OLD QUESTION.

Ample justice was done to the repast. The conversation was general. The colonist told his story. It was like that of most deserving and voluntary emigrants. Many go far to seek their fortunes, and find only sorrow and disaster; they accuse fate, forgetting to blame their ignorance, laziness, and vices. The man who is sober and persevering, economical and honest, is almost sure to succeed.

This had been the case with Mr. O'Moore. He had left Dundalk, where he was poor, and, emigrating with his family to Australia, had landed at Adelaide. At first he engaged in mining, but soon relinquished this for the less hazardous pursuits of the farmer, in which he had been successful beyond his highest anticipations. His agricultural knowledge was a great aid to him. He economized, and bought new lands with the profits of the first. His family flourished, as well as his farm. The Irish peasant had become a landed proprietor, and, although his establishment was only two years old, he owned at that moment five hundred acres of well-cultivated land and five hundred head of cattle, was his own master, and as independent as one can be even in the freest country in the world.

His guests congratulated him sincerely when his story was finished. He doubtless expected a similar confidence, but did not urge it. Glenarvan had an immediate interest in speaking of the Duncan, of his own presence at Cape Bernouilli, and of the search that they had pursued so perseveringly. But, like a man who considers the main object in view, he first questioned his host concerning the shipwreck of the Britannia.

The Irishman's answer was not cheering. He had never heard of the ship. No vessel had for some time been lost on the coast; and, as the shipwreck had occurred only two years before, he could affirm with absolute certainty that the sailors had not been cast on that part of the western shore.

"And now, my lord," added he, "may I be allowed to ask why you have inquired of me concerning this shipwreck?"

Glenarvan then told the story of the document, the voyage of the Duncan, and the attempts made to find Captain Grant. He confessed that his dearest hopes had been destroyed by Mr. O'Moore's discouraging information, and that he now despaired of ever finding the shipwrecked seamen of the Britannia.

These words produced a gloomy impression upon his hearers. Robert and Mary listened to them with tearful eyes. Paganel could not find a word of consolation or hope. Captain Mangles suffered a grief that he could not subdue. Despair was seizing upon the souls of the noble people whom the Duncan had vainly brought to these distant shores, when all at once a voice was heard:—

"My lord, praise and thank God! If Captain Grant is living, he is in Australia."

Chapter XXXI

THE QUARTERMASTER OF THE BRITANNIA.

The astonishment that these words produced cannot be described. Glenarvan sprang to his feet, and, pushing back his chair, cried,—

"Who says that?"

"I!" replied one of O'Moore's workmen, seated at the end of the table.

"You, Ayrton?" said the colonist, no less astonished than Glenarvan.

"I," repeated Ayrton, in an excited but firm tone; "I, a Scotchman like yourself, my lord, one of the shipwrecked sailors of the Britannia!"

A FRESH FACE.

Mary Grant, half fainting with emotion, and overcome with happiness, sank into the arms of Lady Helena; while Captain Mangles, Robert, and Paganel went towards the man whom their host had called Ayrton.

He was a somewhat rough-looking, broad-shouldered man, of about forty-five, of more than medium height, and with piercing eyes sunk deeply beneath his projecting brows. His strength must have been unusual, even considering his stature, for he was all bone and sinew. His countenance, full of intelligence and energy, although the features were stern, prepossessed one in his favor. The sympathy that he elicited was still more increased by the traces of recent hardships imprinted upon his face. It was evident that he had suffered much, although he seemed a man able to brave, endure, and conquer suffering.

The travelers felt all this at first sight. Ayrton's appearance had interested them; and Glenarvan, acting as spokesman for all, pressed him with inquiries. This strange meeting had evidently produced a bewildering effect, and the first questions were, to some extent, without order.

"You are one of the sailors of the Britannia?" asked Glenarvan.

"Yes, my lord; Captain Grant's quartermaster," replied Ayrton.

"Saved with him from the shipwreck?"

"No, my lord. At that terrible moment I was washed overboard and cast ashore."

"You are not one of the sailors, then, of whom the document makes mention?"

"No; I did not know of the existence of such a document. The captain must have thrown it overboard after I was gone."

"But the captain, the captain?"

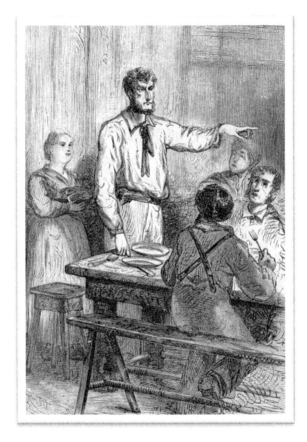

He was a somewhat rough-looking, broad-shouldered man, of about forty-five.

"I suppose he was lost, drowned, with the rest of the crew. I thought I was the sole survivor."

"But you said that Captain Grant was living!"

"No. I said, 'if the captain is living'———"

"'He is in Australia,' you added."

"He can be nowhere else."

"You do not know, then, where he is?"

"When I was washed from the forecastle, as I was hauling down the jib, the Britannia was driving towards the coast of Australia, which was not two cable-lengths distant."

"No, my lord. I repeat that I thought he was buried in the waves or dashed upon the rocks. You say that perhaps he is still living."

"What do you know, then?" asked Glenarvan.

"Simply this, that if Captain Grant is living he is in Australia."

"Where did the shipwreck take place?" inquired the major.

This should have been the first question; but, in the excitement of the moment, Glenarvan, anxious to know where Captain Grant was, had not inquired where the Britannia was lost. From this point the conversation assumed a more definite form, and soon the details of the complicated story appeared clear and exact to the minds of Ayrton's hearers.

To the major's question Ayrton replied,—

"When I was washed from the forecastle, as I was hauling down the jib, the Britannia was driving towards the coast of Australia, which was not two cable-lengths distant. The shipwreck, therefore, took place at that point."

"In latitude thirty-seven?" asked Captain Mangles.

"Thirty-seven," replied Ayrton.

"On the west coast?"

"No. On the east coast."

"And when?"

"On the night of June 27th, 1862."

"The same! the very same!" cried Glenarvan.

"You see, then, my lord," added Ayrton, "that I was right in saying that, if Captain Grant still lives, you must seek him in Australia."

OLD MEMORIES.

"And we will seek, find, and save him, my friend!" cried Paganel. "Ah, precious document!" added he, with perfect simplicity: "it must be confessed that you have fallen into the hands of very sagacious people."

No one noticed these flattering words of Paganel. Glenarvan, Lady Helena, Mary, and Robert had crowded around Ayrton, and eagerly clasped his hands. It seemed as if the presence of this man was a guarantee of the safety of Harry Grant. Since the sailor had escaped the dangers of shipwreck, why should not the captain be safe and sound? Ayrton repeated his declaration that if Captain Grant were living he must be in Australia. He answered with remarkable intelligence and clearness the many questions that were propounded to him. Miss Mary, while he spoke, held one of his hands in her own. This sailor had been a companion of her father, one of the shipwrecked survivors of the Britannia. He had lived with Harry Grant, had sailed the seas with him, had braved the same dangers! She could not withdraw her eyes from that weather-beaten face, and she wept with happiness.

Hitherto no one had thought of doubting the veracity of the quartermaster. Only the major, and perhaps Captain Mangles, questioned whether Ayrton's story merited *entire* confidence. This unexpected meeting might be suspicious. To be sure, Ayrton had mentioned facts and dates that agreed, and striking particulars. But details, however exact they may be, do not constitute a certainty; and generally, as we know, falsehood endeavors to strengthen itself by its preciseness. MacNabb, therefore, reserved his opinion.

As for Captain Mangles, his doubts did not stand long before the assertions of the sailor, and he considered him a real companion of Captain Grant when he heard him speak to the young girl of her father. Ayrton knew Mary and Robert perfectly. He had seen them at Glasgow on the departure of the Britannia. He remembered that they had been present at the farewell dinner given on board to the friends of the captain. Sheriff MacIntyre was one of the guests. Robert—scarcely ten years old—had been confided to the care of Dick Turner, the boatswain, but had escaped from him and climbed to the top-sail yard-arm.

"It is true! it is true!" cried Robert.

The quartermaster remembered, too, a thousand little circumstances to which he did not seem to attach so much importance as did Captain Mangles. When he stopped, Mary said, in her sweet voice,—

When he came to himself, he was in the hands of the natives, who carried him into the interior of the country.

"Mr. Ayrton, please tell us more about our father."

Ayrton acceded to the young girl's request. Glenarvan was reluctant to interrupt him, and yet many more important questions thronged his mind. But Lady Helena, pointing out to him Mary's joyful excitement, checked his inquiries.

At last, exhausted and almost dead, he reached the hospitable dwelling of Mr. O'Moore, where his labor insured him a comfortable livelihood.

TWO YEARS OF SLAVERY.

The quartermaster now told the story of the Britannia and her voyage across the Pacific. During the period of a year Harry Grant landed at the principal ports of Oceanica, opposing unjustifiable captures, and often a victim to the hostility of unjust traders. He found, however, an important point on the western coast of Papua. Here the establishment of a Scottish colony appeared to him feasible, and its prosperity assured. After examining Papua, the

Britannia sailed to Callao for provisions, and left that port on the 30th of May, 1862, to return to Europe by the way of the Indian Ocean and the Cape. Three weeks after her departure, a terrible tempest disabled her. It became necessary to cut away the masts. A leak was discovered in the hold, which they did not succeed in stopping. The crew were soon overtasked and exhausted. The pumps could not be worked. For eight days the vessel was at the mercy of the storm. There were six feet of water in her hold, and she gradually foundered. The boats had been washed overboard, and the crew had given themselves up for lost, when on the night of June 22nd, as Paganel had rightly interpreted, they descried the eastern coast of Australia. The vessel soon stranded. A violent shock was felt. At this moment Ayrton, borne by a wave, was cast into the midst of the breakers, and lost all consciousness. When he came to himself, he was in the hands of the natives, who carried him into the interior of the country. Since then he had heard nothing more of the Britannia, and naturally supposed that she had been wrecked, with all on board, on the dangerous reefs of Twofold Bay.

This was Ayrton's story, which elicited more than once exclamations of sympathy. The major could not justly doubt its correctness; and after this recital the quartermaster's own experiences possessed a more real interest. Indeed, thanks to the document, they no longer doubted that Captain Grant had survived the shipwreck with two of his sailors. From the fate of the one they could fairly conjecture that of the other.

Ayrton was invited to tell of his own adventures, which was soon and simply done. The shipwrecked sailor, prisoner of a native tribe, was carried into the interior regions watered by the Darling. Here he led a very wretched existence, because the tribe itself was miserable; but he was not maltreated. For two long years he endured a painful slavery. However, the hope of regaining his liberty sustained his courage. He watched for the least opportunity of escaping, although his flight would plunge him into the midst of innumerable perils. One night in October he eluded the vigilance of the natives, and took refuge in the depths of extensive forests. For a month, living on roots, edible ferns, and the gum of the mimosa, often overcome by despair, he wandered in those vast solitudes, with the sun as his guide by day and the stars by night. In this way he crossed marshes, rivers, mountains, in short, all that uninhabited portion of country that few travelers have explored. At last, exhausted and almost dead, he reached the hospitable dwelling of Mr. O'Moore, where his labor insured him a comfortable livelihood.

"And if Ayrton is pleased with me," said the Irish colonist, when the story was finished, "I cannot but be pleased with him. He is an honest and intelligent man, a good worker, and, if he chooses, this house shall long be at his service."

Ayrton thanked Mr. O'Moore, and waited for further questions. He probably thought, however, that the legitimate curiosity of his hearers ought to be satisfied. What could he say that had not been repeated a hundred times already? Glenarvan was, therefore, about to open the conversation on a new topic, to profit by the information received from Ayrton, when the major, addressing him, said:

"You were quartermaster of the Britannia?"

"Yes," replied Ayrton.

But perceiving that a certain feeling of distrust, a doubt, however slight, had suggested this inquiry, he added,—

"I saved my contract from the wreck."

He immediately left the room in search of this authoritative document. During his absence, which lasted but a few moments, Mr. O'Moore said:

"My lord, I will answer for it that Ayrton is an honest man. During the two months that he has been in my employ, I have had no fault to find with him. I knew the story of his shipwreck and captivity. He is a true man, and worthy of your entire confidence."

Glenarvan was about to answer that he had never doubted Ayrton's honesty, when the latter returned and presented his contract. It was a paper signed by the owners of the Britannia and Captain Grant, whose writing Mary recognized immediately. It stated that "Tom Ayrton, able seaman, was engaged as quartermaster on board the brig Britannia of Glasgow." There was, therefore, no possible doubt of Ayrton's identity, for it would have been difficult to suppose that this contract could be in his hands and not belong to him.

ENTANGLEMENTS.

"Now," said Glenarvan, "I appeal to you all for advice as to what is best to be done. Your advice, Ayrton, would be particularly valuable, and I should be much obliged if you would give it to us."

The sailor reflected a few moments, and then replied:

"I thank you, my lord, for the confidence you place in me, and hope to show myself worthy of it. I have some knowledge of the country, and of the customs of the natives; and, if I can be of use to you——"

"Certainly," replied Glenarvan.

"I think, like you," continued Ayrton, "that Captain Grant and his two sailors were saved from the shipwreck; but, since they have not reached the English possessions, since they have not reappeared, I doubt not that their fate was the same as my own, and that they are prisoners of the natives."

"You repeat, Mr. Ayrton, the arguments that I have already substantiated," said Paganel. "The shipwrecked seamen are evidently prisoners of the natives, as they feared. But ought we to suppose that, like you, they have been carried to the north?"

"It is quite likely, sir," replied Ayrton. "The hostile tribes would hardly remain in the neighborhood of the English provinces."

"This fact will complicate our search," said Glenarvan, quite disconcerted. "How shall we find the traces of the prisoners in the interior of so vast a continent?"

A prolonged silence followed this remark. Lady Helena frequently cast a questioning glance at her companions, but without eliciting a responsive sign. Paganel himself was silent, contrary to his custom. His usual ingenuity now failed him. Captain Mangles paced the room with long strides, as if he had been on the deck of his vessel, involved in some difficulty.

"And you, Mr. Ayrton," said Lady Helena, at length, to the quartermaster, "what would you do?"

"Madam," replied he, promptly, "I should re-embark on board the Duncan, and go straight to the place of the shipwreck. There I should act according to circumstances, or indications that chance might furnish."

"Very good," said Glenarvan; "but we must wait till the Duncan is repaired."

"Ah! you have suffered injuries?" inquired Ayrton.

"Yes," replies the captain.

"Serious?"

"No; but they necessitate repairs which cannot be made on board. One of the flanges of the screw is bent, and this work can be done only at Melbourne."

"Can you not sail?" asked the quartermaster.

"Yes; but, if the wind is contrary, it would take considerable time to reach Twofold Bay, and at any rate we should have to return to Melbourne."

"Well, let the yacht go to Melbourne," said Paganel, "and we will go without her to Twofold Bay."

"But how?"

"By crossing Australia, as we crossed South America."

"But the Duncan?" added Ayrton, with singular persistency.

"The Duncan will join us, or we will join her, according to circumstances. If Captain Grant is found during our journey, we will return together to Melbourne. If, on the contrary, we continue our search to the coast, the Duncan shall join us there. Who has any objections to make to this plan? Have you, major?"

"No," replied MacNabb, "if it is practicable."

"So practicable," said Paganel, "that I propose that Lady Helena and Miss Grant accompany us."

"Do you speak seriously, Paganel?" asked Glenarvan.

"Quite seriously, my lord. It is a journey of three hundred and fifty miles. At the rate of twelve miles a day it would last scarcely a month,—long enough to give time for repairing the Duncan."

"But the ferocious animals?" said Glenarvan, wishing to state all possible objections.

OBSTACLES EXPLAINED AWAY.

"There are none in Australia."

"But the savages?"

"There are none in the course we shall take."

"Well, then, the convicts?"

"There are no convicts in the southern provinces of Australia, but only in the eastern colonies."

"Mr. Paganel is perfectly right," said O'Moore; "they have all left the southern provinces. Since I have lived on this farm, I have not heard of one."

"And, for my part, I never met one," added Ayrton.

"You see, my friends," continued Paganel, "that there are few savages, no wild beasts, and no convicts. There are not many countries of Europe of which we could say as much. Well, is it agreed?"

"What do you think, Helena?" asked Glenarvan.

"What we all think," replied she, turning towards her companions. "Forward!"

Chapter XXXII

PREPARATIONS FOR THE JOURNEY.

It was not Glenarvan's habit to lose time in adopting and executing a plan. As soon as Paganel's proposal was accepted, he at once resolved that the preparations for the journey should be completed as soon as possible.

And what was to be the result of this search? The existence of Harry Grant seemed to have become undeniable, which increased the probabilities of success. No one expected to find the captain exactly on the line of the thirty-seventh parallel; but perhaps they would come upon traces of him, and, at all events, their course would bring them straight to the scene of the shipwreck, which was the principal point.

Moreover, if Ayrton would consent to join the travelers, to guide them through the forests, and to the eastern coast, there was another chance of success. Glenarvan felt the importance of this arrangement, and was therefore particularly desirous of obtaining the services of Captain Grant's companion. He inquired of his host whether he was willing for him to propose to Ayrton to accompany them. Mr. O'Moore consented, though not without regret at losing so good an assistant.

"Well, Ayrton, will you aid us in our search for the sailors of the Britannia?"

The quartermaster did not answer immediately; he seemed to hesitate for a few moments, but finally, after reflecting, said:

"Yes, my lord, I will follow you; and, if I do not set you upon the track of Captain Grant, I will at least guide you to the place where his vessel was wrecked."

"Thanks," replied Glenarvan.

"One question, my lord."

"Ask it."

"Where will you join the Duncan?"

"At Melbourne, if we do not cross Australia; on the eastern coast, if our search is continued so far."

"But the captain of the Duncan?"

"He will await my orders at Melbourne."

"Very well, my lord," said Ayrton; "rely on me."

"I will," replied Glenarvan.

The quartermaster was heartily thanked by the travelers. Captain Grant's children lavished upon him their most grateful caresses. All were delighted at his decision, except the colonist, who would lose in him an intelligent and faithful assistant. But he understood the importance that Glenarvan attached to this new addition to his force, and was resigned. He had, moreover, engaged to furnish them with the means of conveyance for the journey, and, this business being settled, the party returned on board.

This business being settled, the party returned on board.

Everything was now changed; all hesitation had vanished. These courageous searchers were no longer to wander on blindly. Harry Grant, they believed, had found a refuge on the continent, and each heart was full of the satisfaction that certainty brings when it takes the place of doubt. In two months, perhaps, the Duncan would land the lost captain on the shores of Scotland.

When Captain Mangles seconded the proposal that they should attempt to cross Australia with the ladies, he supposed that this time he would accompany the expedition. He therefore consulted Glenarvan on the subject, and brought forward various arguments in his own favor, such as his desire to take part in the search for his countryman, and his usefulness in the undertaking.

"One question, John," said Glenarvan. "You have absolute confidence in your mate?"

"Absolute," replied he. "Tom Austin is a good sailor. He will take the Duncan to Melbourne, repair her thoroughly, and bring her back at the appointed time. He is a man devoted to duty and discipline, and will never take the responsibility of changing or delaying the execution of an order. You can rely upon him as fully as on myself."

"Very well, captain," replied Glenarvan; "you shall accompany us; for," added he, smiling, "you certainly ought to be present when we find Mary Grant's father."

"Ah, my lord!" murmured Captain Mangles, with something like a blush upon his swarthy cheeks.

A PALACE-CART.

The next day the captain, accompanied by the carpenter and by the sailors loaded with provisions, returned to the farm of Mr. O'Moore, who was to assist him in the preparations. All the family were waiting for him, ready to work under his orders. Ayrton was there, and freely gave them the benefit of his experience. He and his employer were agreed on this point, that the ladies ought to make the journey in an ox-cart, and the gentlemen on horseback. The colonist could procure them the animals and vehicle.

The vehicle was a cart twenty feet long and covered with an awning, the whole resting upon four wheels, without spokes, felloes, or tires. The front wheels were a long way from the hind ones, and were joined together by a rude contrivance that made it impossible to turn short. To the body of the cart was attached a pole thirty-five feet long, to which three pairs of oxen were coupled. The animals, thus arranged, drew by means of a yoke across their necks, to which the bow was fastened with an iron pin. It required great skill to manage this long, narrow, tottering vehicle, and guide the oxen by means of the whip. But Ayrton had served his apprenticeship at O'Moore's farm, and his employer guaranteed his dexterity. Upon him, therefore, devolved the duty of driving.

The cart, being without springs, was not very easy; but our travelers were obliged to conform to circumstances as much as they could. As no change was possible in its rude construction, Captain Mangles arranged the interior in the most comfortable manner. He divided it into two compartments by a wooden partition. The rear one was designed for the provisions, the baggage, and Mr. Olbinett's portable kitchen, while the forward one was reserved exclusively for the ladies. The carpenter converted it into a convenient chamber, covered it with a thick carpet, and furnished it with a dressing-table and two berths for Lady Helena and Mary Grant. Thick leathern curtains secured privacy, when necessary, and were a protection against the chilliness of the night. In rainy weather the men could find shelter under the awning; but a tent was to serve this purpose at the time of encampment. Captain Mangles succeeded in crowding into this narrow space all that two ladies could need, and Lady Helena and Mary Grant did not greatly miss the comfortable cabins of the Duncan.

A RETURN VISIT.

As for the men, seven strong horses were apportioned to Lord Glenarvan, Paganel, Robert Grant, Major MacNabb, Captain Mangles, and the two sailors, Wilson and Mulready, who accompanied this new expeditionary party. The horses and oxen grazed near at hand, and could be easily collected at the moment of departure.

The vehicle was a cart twenty feet long and covered with an awning, the whole resting upon four wheels, without spokes, felloes, or tires.

Having made his arrangements, and given his orders to the carpenter, Captain Mangles returned on board with the colonist's family, who wished to pay Lord Glenarvan a visit. Ayrton thought proper to join them, and about four o'clock the captain crossed the gangway of the Duncan.

Of course, Glenarvan invited his visitors to dinner, and they willingly accepted his return hospitality. Mr. O'Moore was amazed. The furniture of the cabins, the tapestry, the upholstery, and the fancy-work of maple and ebony excited his admiration. Ayrton, on the contrary, gave only a secondary attention to these costly luxuries. He first examined the yacht from a sailor's point of view. He explored the hold; he went down into the engine-room; he looked at the engine, inquired its effective power and consumption; he visited the coal-house, the pantry, and the powder-magazine, and took particular interest in the gun-room and the mounted cannon in the forecastle. Glenarvan now had to deal with a man who was a critical judge, as he could see by Ayrton's keen inquiries. At last the quartermaster finished his exploration by inspecting the masts and rigging; and, after a few moments of general review, said:

"You have a fine vessel, my lord."

"A good one, too," replied Glenarvan.

"How many tons' burden is she?"

"Two hundred and ten."

"Shall I be greatly mistaken," added Ayrton, "if I say that the Duncan can easily make fifteen knots an hour at full speed?"

"Say seventeen," interposed the captain, "and you will be nearer right."

"Seventeen!" cried the quartermaster: "why, then, no man-of-war, not even the best, could overtake her."

"Not one," said the captain. "The Duncan is a real racing yacht, and is not to be beaten in any way."

"Not even in sailing?" asked Ayrton.

"Not even in sailing."

"Well, my lord, and you, captain, accept the compliments of a sailor who knows what a vessel is worth."

"Thanks, Ayrton," replied Glenarvan; "and now remain on board, and it will be your own fault if the ship is not all you can desire."

"I will think of it, my lord," said the quartermaster, modestly.

Mr. Olbinett now approached, and informed Lord Glenarvan that dinner was ready; and they all adjourned to the saloon.

"That Ayrton is an intelligent man," said Paganel to the major.

"Too intelligent!" growled MacNabb, who, without any apparent reason, disliked the looks and manners of the quartermaster.

During dinner, Ayrton gave some interesting information concerning Australia, with which he was perfectly familiar. He inquired the number of sailors that Glenarvan intended to take with him in his expedition. When he learned that only two, Wilson and Mulready, were to accompany them, he seemed astonished. He advised Glenarvan to form his party of the best seamen of the Duncan. He even insisted upon this point, which must have removed all suspicion from the mind of the major.

"But," said Glenarvan, "is there any danger in our journey across Australia?"

"None," replied Ayrton.

A CHANGE OF RESIDENCE.

"Well, then, let us leave on board as many as possible. There must be men to navigate the Duncan and take charge of her. It is especially important that she should arrive promptly at the place of meeting, which we will appoint hereafter. Let us not, therefore, lessen the crew."

Ayrton seemed to appreciate this reason, and no longer insisted.

At evening the party separated. Ayrton and O'Moore's family returned to their home. The horses and cart were to be ready the next day, and the travelers were to start at eight o'clock in the morning.

Lady Helena and Mary Grant now made their last preparations, which were short and less minute than those of Jacques Paganel. The geographer passed half the night in unscrewing, cleaning, and screwing on again the lenses of his telescope. He was still asleep the next morning, when the major awoke him early with a loud summons.

The baggage had already been conveyed to the farm through the care of Captain Mangles. A boat was waiting for the travelers, and they were not long in embarking. The young captain gave his last orders to Tom Austin, and instructed him above all to await the commands of Lord Glenarvan at Melbourne, and execute them scrupulously whatever they might be. The trusty sailor replied that they might rely on him. In the name of the crew he offered to his lordship their best wishes for the success of the expedition. The boat put off, and a thunder of applause rent the air. In a few moments the party reached the shore, and in no great length of time arrived at O'Moore's farm.

Everything was ready. Lady Helena was delighted with her quarters. The immense cart, with its rude wheels and massive timbers, especially pleased her. The six oxen yoked in pairs seemed to indicate primeval simplicity, and were a novel sight. Ayrton, whip in hand, awaited the orders of his new chief.

"I declare!" said Paganel, "this is an admirable vehicle, worth all the mail-coaches in the world. I know of no better way of traversing the earth than in this style, like mountebanks. A house that moves when you please and stops wherever you please is all you can desire."

"Monsieur Paganel," replied Lady Helena, "I hope to have the pleasure of receiving you in my parlor."

*Ayrton and Olbinett took their places respectively in front and in the rear part
of the cart, while Glenarvan, the major, Paganel, Robert, Captain Mangles,
and the two sailors, mounted their horses.*

"Madam," replied the geographer, "you do me great honor! Have
you chosen a day?"

"I shall be at home every day for my friends," replied Lady Helena,
smiling, "and you are——"

"The most devoted of all," added Paganel, gallantly.

The "Mosquito Plains," whose very name describes them, and serves to tell of the tortures that our friends had to encounter.

This exchange of compliments was interrupted by the arrival of seven horses, all harnessed, driven by one of O'Moore's sons. Lord Glenarvan paid for these new acquisitions, and added many thanks, which the honest colonist seemed to value as highly as the gold and notes which he received.

The signal for departure was now given. Lady Helena and Miss Grant seated themselves in their compartment, Ayrton and Olbinett took their places respectively in front and in the rear part of the cart, while Glenarvan, the major, Paganel, Robert, Captain

Mangles, and the two sailors, all armed with carbines and revolvers, mounted their horses. A "God bless you" was Mr. O'Moore's parting salute, which was echoed in chorus by his family. Ayrton uttered a peculiar cry, and started his long team. The cart moved, the timbers cracked, the axles creaked, and the farm of the honest hospitable Irishman soon disappeared from view at the turn of the road.

CHAPTER XXXIII

AN ACCIDENT.

Our travelers made tolerably good progress by their new mode of conveyance. The heat was great, but endurable, and the road was quite easy for the horses. They were still in the province of South Australia, and in this part at least the scenery was not of the most interesting character. A succession of small hills, with very dusty tracks, small shrubs, and scant herbage, had to be traversed for several miles; and when these had been passed they reached the "Mosquito Plains," whose very name describes them, and serves to tell of the tortures that our friends had to encounter. Both the bipeds and the quadrupeds suffered terribly from the infliction of these flying pests, whom to avoid was impossible; but there was some consolation for the former in the spirits of hartshorn, carried in the medicine-chest, which alleviated the pain caused by the sting of those whom Paganel was continually consigning to a place and person whom they would not visit.

Red-gum Station, the home and settlement of an emigrant engaged in the cattle-breeding which is the source of so much Australian wealth.

But shortly a more pleasant neighborhood was reached. Hedges of acacias, then a newly cut and better made roadway, then European imported trees—oaks, olives, and lemons,—then a well-kept fence,—all these signs told of their approach to Red-gum Station, the home and settlement of an emigrant engaged in the cattle-breeding which is the source of so much Australian wealth. It was in itself an establishment of small importance; but to its owners it was a home, and to its visitors, on this occasion, it was a hotel, as the "station" generally is to the traveler.

Glenarvan's party invariably found beneath the roof of these solitary settlers a well-spread and hospitable table; and in the Australian farmer they always met an obliging host.

After a night spent at this resting-place the party advanced through a grove, and at evening encamped on the shores of a brackish and muddy lake. Mr. Olbinett prepared supper with his usual promptness, and the travelers—some in the cart and others under the tent—were not long in falling asleep, in spite of the dismal howlings of the dingos,—the jackals of Australia.

The next morning Glenarvan and his companions were greeted with a magnificent sight. As far as the eye could reach, the landscape seemed to be one flowery meadow in spring-like luxuriance. The delicate blue of the slender-leaved flax-plant mingled with the flaming scarlet of the acanthus, and the ground was clothed with a rich carpet of green and crimson. After a rapid journey of about ten miles, the cart wound through tall groups of acacias, mimosas, and white gum-trees. The vegetable kingdom on these plains did not show itself ungrateful towards the orb of day, and repaid in perfume and color what it received in sunshine.

As for the animal kingdom, it was no less lavish of its products. Several cassowaries bounded over the plain with unapproachable swiftness. The major was skillful enough to shoot a very rare bird,—a "jabiru," or giant crane. This creature was five feet high; and its broad, black, sharp conical beak measured eighteen inches in length. The violet and purple colors of its head contrasted strongly with the lustrous green of its neck, the dazzling white of its breast, and the vivid red of its long legs.

The major was skillful enough to shoot a very rare bird,—a "jabiru," or giant crane. This creature was five feet high; and its broad, black, sharp conical beak measured eighteen inches in length.

A FOUR-FOOTED ARMY.

This bird was greatly admired, and the major would have won the honors of the day, if young Robert had not encountered a few miles farther on, and bravely vanquished, an unsightly beast, half hedgehog, half ant-eater, a chaotic-looking animal, like those of pre-historic periods. A long, glutinous, extensible tongue hung out of its mouth, and fished up the ants that constituted its principal food. Of course, Paganel wished to carry away the hideous creature, and proposed to put it in the baggage-room; but Mr. Olbinett opposed this with such indignation that the geographer gave up his idea of preserving this curious specimen.

Hitherto few colonists or squatters had been seen. The country seemed deserted. There was not even the trace of a native; for the savage tribes wander farther to the north, over the immense wastes watered by the Darling and the Murray. But now a singular sight was presented to Glenarvan's party. They were fortunate enough to see one of those vast herds of cattle which bold speculators bring from the eastern mountains to the provinces of Victoria and South Australia.

About four o'clock in the afternoon, Captain Mangles descried, three miles in advance, an enormous column of dust that spread along the horizon. What occasioned this? It would have been very difficult to say. Paganel was inclined to regard it as some phenomenon, for which his lively imagination already sought a natural cause. But Ayrton dissipated all his conjectures by declaring that this cloud of dust proceeded from a drove of cattle.

The quartermaster was not mistaken. The thick cloud approached, from the midst of which issued a chorus of bleatings, neighings, and bellowings, while the human voice mingled in cries and whistles with this pastoral symphony. A man emerged from the noisy multitude; it was the commander-in-chief of this four-footed army. Glenarvan advanced to meet him, and friendly relations were established without ceremony. The leader, or, to give him his real title, the "stock-keeper," was proprietor of a part of the herd. His name was Sam Machell, and he was on his way from the eastern provinces to Portland Bay. His cattle comprised one thousand oxen, eleven thousand sheep, and seventy-five horses. All these animals, bought when lean on the plains of the Blue Mountains, were to be fattened in the healthy pastures of South Australia, where they would be sold for a large price.

Sam Machell briefly told his story, while the drove continued its course through the clumps of mimosas. Lady Helena, Mary Grant, and the horsemen dismounted, and, seated in the shade of a huge gum-tree, listened to the stock-keeper's narrative.

He had set out seven months before, and had made about ten miles a day, at which rate his journey would last three months longer. To aid him in this laborious task, he had with him twenty dogs and thirty men. Five of the men were blacks, who are very skillful in recovering stray animals. Six carts followed the drove; and the drivers, provided with stock-whips, the handles of which were eighteen inches and the lashes nine feet in length, moved among the ranks and maintained order, while the canine light dragoons hovered about on the wings.

The travelers were amazed at the discipline of this novel army. The different classes advanced separately, for wild oxen and sheep do not associate well; the first will never graze where the second have passed. Hence it was necessary to place the oxen at the head; and these accordingly, divided into two battalions, took the lead. Five regiments of sheep, commanded by five drivers, followed, and the platoon of horses formed the rear-guard.

The stock-keeper observed to his hearers that the leaders of the army were neither dogs nor men, but oxen, whose superiority was recognized by their mates. They advanced in the front rank with perfect gravity, choosing the best course by instinct, and thoroughly convinced of their right to be treated with consideration.

AN UNFORESEEN HINDRANCE.

Thus the discipline was maintained, for the drove obeyed them without resistance. If it pleased them to stop, the others were obliged to yield, and it was useless to attempt to resume the line of march if the leaders did not give the signal.

Such was Sam Machell's account, during which a great part of the herd had advanced in good order. It was now time for him to join his army, and choose the best pastures. He therefore took leave of Lord Glenarvan, mounted a fine native horse that one of his men was holding for him, and a few moments after had disappeared in a cloud of dust, while the cart, resuming its interrupted journey, stopped at nightfall at the foot of Mount Talbot.

The next day they reached the shores of the Wimerra, which is half a mile wide, and flows in a limpid stream between tall rows of gum-trees and acacias. Magnificent myrtles raised aloft their long, drooping branches, adorned with crimson flowers, while thousands of goldfinches, chaffinches, and golden-winged pigeons, not to speak of chattering parrots, fluttered about in the foliage. Below, on the surface of the stream, sported a pair of black swans, shy and unapproachable.

Meantime the cart had stopped on a carpet of turf whose fringes hung over the swiftly flowing waters. There was neither raft nor bridge, but they must cross at all hazard. Ayrton busied himself in searching for a practicable ford. A quarter of a mile up-stream, the river seemed to him less deep, and from this point he resolved to reach the other bank. Various soundings gave a depth of only three feet. The cart could, therefore, pass over this shallow without running much risk.

"Is there no other way of crossing the river?" asked Glenarvan of the quartermaster.

"No, my lord," replied Ayrton; "but this passage does not seem to me dangerous. We can extricate ourselves from any difficulty."

"Shall Lady Helena and Miss Grant leave the cart?"

"Not at all. My oxen are sure-footed, and I will engage to keep them in the right track."

"Well, Ayrton," said Glenarvan, "I trust to you."

The horsemen surrounded the heavy vehicle, and the party boldly entered the river. Usually, when these fordings are attempted, the carts are encircled by a ring of empty barrels, which support them on the water. But here this buoyant girdle was wanting, and it was, therefore, necessary to confide to the sagacity of the oxen, guided by the cautious Ayrton. The major and the two sailors dashed through the rapid current some distance ahead, while Glenarvan and Captain Mangles, one on each side of the cart, stood ready to assist the ladies, and Paganel and Robert brought up the rear.

Everything went well till they reached the middle of the river, but here the depth increased, and the water rose above the felloes. The oxen, if thrown out of their course, might lose their footing and overturn the unsteady vehicle. Ayrton exerted himself to the utmost. He leaped into the water, and, seizing the oxen by the horns, succeeded in keeping them in the right track.

At this moment an accident, impossible to foresee, took place. A crack was heard; the cart inclined at an alarming angle; the water reached the feet of the ladies, and the whole vehicle threatened to give way. It was an anxious moment.

Fortunately a vigorous blow upon the yoke brought the cart nearer the shore. The river grew shallower, and soon men and beasts were in safety on the opposite bank. Only the front wheels of the cart were damaged, and Glenarvan's horse had lost the shoes of his fore-feet.

This mishap required immediate repair. The travelers gazed at each other in some degree of perplexity, when Ayrton proposed to go to Black Point Station, twenty miles to the north, and bring a farrier.

FOOD, PHYSICAL AND MENTAL.

"Very well, Ayrton," said Glenarvan. "How much time do you need to make the journey and return to the encampment?"

"Fifteen hours," replied Ayrton.

"Go, then; and, while waiting for your return, we will encamp on the banks of the Wimerra."

A few moments after, the quartermaster, mounted on Wilson's horse, disappeared behind the thick curtain of mimosas.

CHAPTER XXXIV

AUSTRALIAN EXPLORERS.

After the departure of Ayrton, and during this compulsory halt, promenades and conversations became the order of the day. There was an abundance of agreeable surroundings to talk about, and nature seemed dressed in one of her most attractive garbs. Birds, novel and varied in their plumage, with flowers such as they had never before gazed on, were the constant theme of the travelers' remark; and when, in addition, they had in Mr. Olbinett one who knew how to spread before them and make the best of all the culinary novelties that were within reach, a very substantial foundation was possible for the "feast of reason and the flow of soul" which followed, and for which, as usual, they were to no small extent indebted to their learned historico-geographical professor, whose stock of information was as varied as it was pleasant.

After dinner the traveling party had, as if in anticipation, seated themselves at the foot of a magnificent banksia; the young moon was rising high into the heavens, lengthening the twilight, and prolonging it into the evening hour; whilst the smoke of the major's cigar was seen curling upwards, losing itself in the foliage of the tree.

"Monsieur Paganel," said Lady Helena, "you have never given us the history that you promised when you supplied us with that long list of names."

The gentleman addressed did not require any lengthened entreaties on this subject, but, with an attentive auditory, and in the grandest of all lecture-rooms, he rehearsed to them the two great dramas of Australian travel, which have made the names of Burke and Stuart immortal in the history of that continent.

He told them that it was on the 20th of August, 1860, that Robert O'Hara Burke set out, under the auspices of the Royal Society of Melbourne, to cross the continent from south to north, and so to reach the Indian Ocean. Eleven others—including a botanist, an astronomer, and an army officer—accompanied him, with horses and other beasts of burden. But the expedition did not long continue so numerous or so well provided; in consequence of misunderstandings, several returned, and Burke pressed on with but few followers and fewer aids. Again, on the 20th of November, he still further diminished his numbers by leaving behind at an encampment several of his companions, that he and three others might press on towards the north with as little incumbrance as possible. After a very painful journey across a stony desert, they arrived at the extreme point reached by Stuart in 1845; and from this point, after determining as accurately as possible their latitude and longitude, they again started northward and seaward.

A crack was heard; the cart inclined at an alarming angle; the water reached the feet of the ladies, and the whole vehicle threatened to give way. It was an anxious moment.

LYING DOWN TO DIE.

By the 7th of January they had gone so far as to reach the southern limit of the tropical heat; and now under a scorching sun, deceived by the mirage, often without water, and then hailing a storm as a source of refreshment, now and then meeting with the aborigines, who could in no wise help them, they had indeed a hard road to travel, though having neither rivers, lakes, nor mountains to bar their path.

At length, however, there were various signs that they were approaching the sea; by-and-by they reached the bank of a river which flows into the Gulf of Carpentaria; and finally Burke and Wills, after terrible hardships, arrived at the point where the sea-water flowed up to and inundated the marshes, though the sea-shore itself they did not reach. With naught but barrenness in sight on either hand, their great desire was to get back and rejoin their companions; but peril after peril awaited them, many of which their note-book has preserved an account of, but many more will be forever unrecorded. The three survivors (for one of the party had succumbed to the hardships) now strained every effort to reach the encampment, where they hoped to find their companions and a store of provisions. On the 21st of April they gained the goal, but the prize was missing; only seven hours before, after five months of waiting in vain, their companions had taken their departure. Of course nothing remained but to follow them with their feeble strength and scanty means of subsistence; but calamities still dogged their footsteps, and at last the leader, Burke, lay down exhausted, saying to his companion, King, "I have not many hours to live; here are my watch and my notes; when I am dead, place a pistol in my right hand, and leave me without burial." His forebodings were realized, and the next morning he died. King, in despair, went in search of some Australian tribe, for now Wills had begun to sink, and he shortly afterwards died also. At length the sole survivor was rescued by an expedition sent out in search of Burke; and thus the sad tale was told of this Australian tragedy.

The narrative concerning Stuart was a less melancholy one, though the trials endured on his expedition were likewise great. Aided by the parliament of South Australia, he likewise proceeded northward, in the year 1862, about seven degrees to the west of the line taken by Burke. He found his route to be a more accessible and easy one than the other, and was rewarded for his toil when, on the 24th of July, he beheld the waters of the Indian Ocean, and proudly unfurled the Australian flag from the topmost branch of the highest tree he could find. His return to the inhabited regions was successfully accomplished, and his entry into Adelaide, on the 17th of December, was an ovation indeed. But his health was shattered, and, after receiving the gold medal of the Royal Geographical Society, and returning to his native Scotland, he died on the 5th of June, 1866.

"When I am dead, place a pistol in my right hand, and leave me without burial." His forebodings were realized, and the next morning he died.

The histories of these Australian travels were lengthy, as told by Paganel. When he had finished, hope and despair seemed to fight for the mastery in the breasts of his listeners; but they did not fight long, for peaceful slumbers soon enwrapped the company, except those whose turn it was to watch over their fellow-travelers.

He beheld the waters of the Indian Ocean, and proudly unfurled the Australian flag from the topmost branch of the highest tree he could find.

After dinner the traveling party had, as if in anticipation, seated themselves at the foot of a magnificent banksia; the young moon was rising high into the heavens, lengthening the twilight, and prolonging it into the evening hour.

CHAPTER XXXV

CRIME OR CALAMITY?

THE MISCHIEF REPAIRED.

It was not without a certain feeling of apprehension that the major had seen Ayrton leave the Wimerra to procure a farrier at Black Point Station. However, he did not breathe a word of his personal suspicions, but contented himself with exploring the surroundings of the river, whose tranquillity was undisturbed. As for Glenarvan, his only fear was to see Ayrton return alone. In the absence of skilled labor, the cart could not resume its journey, which would be interrupted for several days perhaps; and his longings for success and eagerness to attain his end admitted of no delay.

Fortunately, Ayrton had lost neither his time nor his trouble. The next morning he reappeared at break of day. A man accompanied him, by profession a farrier. He was a tall, stout fellow, but of a low and brutish appearance, which did not prepossess one in his favor. However, this was of little importance, if he knew his business. At all events his breath was not wasted in idle words.

"Is he an efficient workman?" inquired Captain Mangles of the quartermaster.

"I know no more than you, captain," replied Ayrton. "We shall see."

The farrier began his work. He was a man who understood his trade, as one could see by the way in which he repaired the wheels of the cart. He labored skillfully and with uncommon energy.

During the operation, the major noticed that the farrier's wrists were considerably eroded, and that they were each encircled by a blackish ring of extravasated blood. These were the marks of recent wounds, which the sleeves of a miserable woolen shirt but partially concealed. MacNabb questioned the man about these erosions, which must have been very painful. He, however, made no reply, but stolidly kept on at his work.

Two hours after, the injuries of the cart were repaired. As for Glenarvan's horse, he was quickly shod. The farrier had taken care to bring shoes all prepared. There was a peculiarity about them, however, which did not escape the major. It was a trefoil rudely carved on the outer rim. He pointed it out to Ayrton.

"It is the Black Point mark," replied the quartermaster, "which enables them to follow the tracks of the horses that stray from the station, and not confound them with others."

The farrier, having done all that was required of him, now claimed his wages, and departed without having spoken four words.

Half an hour later, the travelers were on the move. Beyond the curtain of mimosas extended a broad, uncovered space, which justly deserved its name of "open plain." Fragments of quartz and ferruginous rocks lay among the bushes, tall grass, and hedgerows that protected numerous flocks. Several miles farther on, the wheels of the cart sank deeply in the marshy lowlands, through which ran winding creeks, half hidden beneath a canopy of gigantic rushes. The journey, notwithstanding, was neither difficult nor tedious.

Lady Helena invited the horsemen to call upon her in turn, for her parlor was very small. Each was thus relieved from the fatigue of horseback riding, and enjoyed the society of this amiable lady, who, assisted by Miss Mary, performed with perfect grace the honors of her movable mansion. Captain Mangles was not forgotten in these invitations, and his rather sober conversation was not at all displeasing.

At eleven o'clock they arrived at Carlsbrook, quite an important municipality. Ayrton thought it best to pass by the city without entering. Glenarvan was of the same opinion; but Paganel, always eager for something new, desired to visit the place. Accordingly, the geographer, taking Robert with him as usual, started on his explorations, while the cart slowly continued its journey. Their inspection of the town was very rapid, and shortly afterwards they had joined their companions.

While they were passing through this region, the travelers requested Paganel to give them some account of its progress, and the geographer, in compliance with their wishes, had just begun a lecture upon the civilization of the country, when he was interrupted by a shrill whistle. The party were not a mile from the railroad.

A locomotive, coming from the south, and going slowly, had stopped just where the road they were following crossed the iron track. At this point the railway passes over the Lutton on an iron bridge, and thither Ayrton directed his cart, preceded by the horsemen. The travelers were attracted, moreover, by a lively feeling of curiosity, for a considerable crowd was already rushing towards the bridge. The inhabitants of the neighboring stations, leaving their houses, and the shepherds their flocks, lined the sides of the track. Frequent cries were heard. Some serious event must have taken place to cause such excitement,—a great accident, perhaps.

Glenarvan, followed by his companions, urged on his horse, and in a few moments arrived at Camden Bridge. Here the cause of this agitation was at once manifest. A terrible accident had occurred, not a collision, but a running off the track and a fall into the river, which was filled with the fragments of cars and locomotives. Either the bridge had given way, or the engine had run off the track; for five coaches out of six had been precipitated into the bed of the Lutton. The last car, miraculously preserved by the breaking of its coupling, stood on the very verge of the abyss. Below was to be seen nothing but a terrible heap of blackened and bent axletrees, broken cars, twisted rails, and charred timbers. The boiler, which had burst at the shock, had thrown its iron plates to an enormous distance. From this mass of unsightly objects issued flames and spiral wreaths of steam, mingled with black smoke. Large spots of blood, scattered limbs, and trunks of burnt bodies appeared here and there; and no one dared to estimate the number of victims buried beneath the ruins.

Glenarvan, Paganel, the major, and Captain Mangles mingled with the crowd, and listened to the conjectures that passed from one to another. Each sought to explain the catastrophe, while laboring to save what was left.

"The bridge has broken," said one.

CAUSES AND EFFECTS.

"Broken?" replied others. "That cannot be, for it is still uninjured. They forgot to close it for the passage of the train, that is all."

It was a draw-bridge, which had been constructed for the convenience of the shipping. Had the man on guard, through unpardonable negligence, forgotten to close it, and thus precipitated the train, at full speed, into the bed of the Lutton? This supposition seemed plausible, for one half of the bridge lay beneath the fragments of the cars, while the other still hung intact in its chains. Doubt was no longer possible; surely carelessness must have caused the calamity.

The accident had happened to the night express, which left Melbourne at forty-five minutes past eleven. It must have been a quarter-past three in the morning when the train reached Camden Bridge, where this terrible destruction of life and property took place. The travelers and employés of the last car at once busied themselves in seeking assistance; but the telegraph-wires, whose poles lay on the ground, were no longer available. It took the authorities of Castlemaine three hours to reach the scene of the disaster; and it was, therefore, six o'clock in the morning before a corps of workers was organized under the direction of the surveyor-general of the district, and a detachment of policemen, commanded by an officer. The squatters had come to their aid, and exerted themselves to extinguish the fire, which consumed the heap of ruins with unconquerable fierceness. Several unrecognizable bodies lay on the edge of the embankment, but it was impossible to rescue a living being from this furnace. The fire had rapidly accomplished the work of destruction. Of the travelers in the train, whose number was not known, only ten survived, those in the last car. The railroad company had just sent an extra locomotive to convey them to Castlemaine.

Meantime, Lord Glenarvan, having made the acquaintance of the surveyor-general, was conversing with him and the police-officer. The latter was a tall, thin man, of imperturbable coolness, who, if he had any feeling, betrayed no sign of it on his impassible features. He was like a mathematician engaged upon a problem; he was seeking to elucidate the mystery of the disaster. To Glenarvan's first words, "This is a great calamity!" he replied, calmly, "It is more than that."

A terrible accident had occurred, not a collision, but a running off the track and a fall into the river, which was filled with the fragments of cars and locomotives.

"More than that!" cried Glenarvan; "and what can be more than that?"

"It is a crime!" replied the officer, coolly.

Glenarvan turned to Mr. Mitchell, the surveyor-general, with a questioning look.

"That is correct," said the latter; "our examination has convinced us that the catastrophe is the result of a crime. The last baggage-wagon was robbed. The surviving travelers were attacked by a party of five or six malefactors. The bridge was opened intentionally; and, taking into account this fact with the disappearance of the guard, I cannot but come to the conclusion that the miserable man was the accomplice of the criminals."

The police-officer, at these words, slowly shook his head.

"You are not of my opinion?" inquired Mr. Mitchell.

"Not as regards the complicity of the guard."

"At any rate, this assumed complicity," continued the surveyor-general, "enables us to attribute the crime to the natives who wander about the country. Without the guard's assistance these natives could not have opened the draw-bridge, for they do not understand its working."

"Exactly," replied the officer.

"Now, it is known," added Mr. Mitchell, "from the testimony of a boatman, whose boat passed Camden Bridge at forty minutes past ten in the evening, that the bridge was closed according to regulation, after his passage."

"Quite right."

"Therefore the complicity of the guard seems to me to be proved incontestably."

The officer again made a gesture of dissent.

"Then you do not attribute the crime to the natives?" inquired Glenarvan.

"I do not."

"To whom, then?"

At this moment a loud uproar was heard half a mile up the river. A crowd had formed, which rapidly increased, and was now approaching the station. In the midst of the multitude two men were bearing a corpse. It was that of the guard, already cold. A poniard-thrust had pierced him to the heart. The assassins had dragged the body some distance from Camden Bridge, doubtless intending by this means to mislead the police in their first investigations. This discovery clearly justified the doubts of the officer. The natives had no hand in the crime.

"Those who struck the blow," said he, "are persons already familiar with the use of these little instruments."

As he spoke he displayed a pair of "darbies," a kind of manacles consisting of a double ring of iron, furnished with a padlock.

"Before long," added he, "I shall have the pleasure of presenting them with these bracelets as a new year's gift."

"Then you suspect——?"

"People who have 'traveled free on Her Majesty's vessels.'"

"What! convicts?" cried Paganel, who recognized the phrase employed in the Australian colonies.

"I thought," observed Glenarvan, "that those who have been transported had no right to stay in the province of Victoria."

"Ah, well," replied the officer, "if they have not the right, they take it! Sometimes they escape; and, if I am not greatly mistaken, these fellows have come direct from Perth. Well, they shall return again, you may be sure."

In the midst of the multitude two men were bearing a corpse. It was that of the guard, already cold. A poniard-thrust had pierced him to the heart.

A RAILROAD SLEEPER.

Mr. Mitchell nodded approvingly at the words of the officer. At this moment the cart arrived at the railroad crossing. Glenarvan, wishing to spare the ladies the spectacle at Camden Bridge, took leave of the surveyor-general, and made a sign to his companions to follow him.

"There is no occasion," said he, "for us to interrupt our journey."

On reaching the cart, Glenarvan simply told Lady Helena that a railroad accident had taken place, without mentioning the part that the convicts had played in the catastrophe. He reserved this matter that he might question Ayrton in private. The little party then crossed the track, not far above the bridge, and resumed their route towards the east.

CHAPTER XXXVI

FRESH FACES.

They had not proceeded far before they reached a native cemetery, pleasantly situated and with abundance of shady trees. Here for a time they halted, and, whilst Robert and Paganel were exploring, Lord and Lady Glenarvan almost stumbled over a queer object. It was human, indigenous, and sleeping; but at first this was all that they could decide, until, as the eyes opened and the sleeper roused to active life, they saw before them a boy of eight years, with a notice pinned to the back of his jacket which read as follows: "TOLINÉ, to be conducted to Echuca, care of Jeff Smith, Railway Porter. Prepaid."

Here, it would seem, was another waif that Providence had cast in their path. They questioned him, and his answers were pertinent and clear. He had been educated in the Wesleyan Methodist day-school at Melbourne, and was now going for a time to visit his parents, who were living with the rest of their tribe in Lachlan. He had been in the train to which the accident had happened, and had, with childlike confidence, troubled less about his fate than did those of older years. Going to a little distance, and laying himself on the grass, he had soon fallen into the slumber from which our travelers had aroused him.

Paganel and the others had now gathered round, and Toliné had to answer many a question. He came out of his examination very creditably; the reverence with which he spoke of the Creator and of the Bible produced a very favorable impression on the Scottish heads of the expedition, whilst the fact that he had taken "the first prize in geography" was sufficient introduction to Monsieur Paganel, who forthwith tested his knowledge, greatly to his own satisfaction, and considerably to the credit of his young pupil. The curiosity of his discoverers having been fully satisfied, Toliné was made welcome, and partook with the others of the general repast. Many were the plans and purposes concerning him, and much wonder was expressed as to how they could speed him on his way; but in the morning it was discovered that he had solved the problem for himself, and a bouquet of fresh leaves and flowers, laid by the side of Lady Helena's seat, was the only memento that Toliné had left.

A GOLDEN CITY.

The party were now approaching the district which, in the years 1851 and 1852, was so much talked of throughout the civilized world, and attracted from all parts so many reckless adventurers and fortune-hunters. The line of the thirty-seventh parallel, on which they were traveling, led them through the diggings and municipality of Mount Alexander, which was one of the most successful spots for the digger at the commencement of the gold fever, in consequence of the comparatively level nature of the ground and the general richness of the soil, so different from some other localities where only once in a while was some enormous nugget to be found. As they drew near to the streets of this hastily-built town, Ayrton and Mulready, who were in charge of the cart, were sent forward, whilst the others walked through the place to inspect what there might be of interest, as well as to ascertain what might be learned concerning the object of their expedition.

A boy of eight years, with a notice pinned to the back of his jacket which read as follows: "Toliné, to be conducted to Echuca, care of Jeff Smith, Railway Porter. Prepaid."

Paganel and the others had now gathered round, and Toliné had to answer many a question. He came out of his examination very creditably.

Thus, in this strange gathering of all nationalities and creeds and professions, the regular inhabitants beheld a still more extraordinary sight than that every day afforded them: folks who to the refinement which education and civilization give added both the earnestness of the worker and the freshness and vigor of the pleasure-seeking tourist. In the streets, in connection with the strange sign-boards and announcements, the novel erections and purposes to which some of them were adapted, Paganel had a history and commentary for every one.

In the streets, in connection with the strange sign-boards and announcements, the novel erections and purposes to which some of them were adapted, Paganel had a history and commentary for every one.

Still more did he expatiate upon the thousand-and-one topics of interest when they visited the bank building, which here is the centre of more than one agency connected with this great gold-bearing district. Here was the mineralogical museum, in which might be seen specimens illustrative of all the various ways in which the gold has been found, whether in combination with clay or other minerals, or—as it is sometimes, to the great joy of the finder, discovered—*pur et simple*. Here also were models, diagrams, and even the tools themselves, to illustrate the different methods by which the object of search was dug out, or washed, or crushed, or tested. Here also was an almost unequaled collection of precious stones, gems of all sorts, making the gallery in which they were placed a real Golconda for its wealth and attractions.

Besides all this, here was the centre of the varied agencies by which the reports were brought in from the companies established for mining purposes, and also from each isolated worker, of the space purchased, the number of feet or yards dug, the ore extracted, the comparative richness or poverty of the soil here, there, and elsewhere, which in their summarized and aggregate form have greatly helped to a correct knowledge of the comparative and absolute gold-bearing value of various spots. Then, in addition to the usual operations of a banking establishment, it was here that the ore was stored, from hence that it was sent, under government escort and with government guarantee, subject to a fixed, though moderate, charge, so that the transport to Melbourne, which at first was a dangerous and expensive "middle passage," was now as easily and inexpensively accomplished as is the transmission of freight from London to Paris.

Over the whole of this establishment they were conducted by the most courteous and obliging of officials, and the services thus rendered charmed the Frenchman, who was none the less loquacious, and was in truth able even to enlighten his guides.

PLEASING PROGRESS.

But his joy culminated when, after some time spent in the hotel, the party left the town, and passed through the "diggings," properly so called. It was difficult to persuade Paganel and Robert—who kept together—to come on, in order that they might not leave Ayrton and Mulready too long in suspense. Now the Frenchman would see just the key that he needed to understand a point not before clear to him; anon you might see him as in the illustration, when he had picked up a pebble and was sure that it was in itself so interesting as a mineralogical specimen that he must treasure it up for the Bank of France, so that his own land might have at least one part of Australia. All this was done with such a mingling of childish good-nature and scientific and national pride that it was useless to do anything but laugh, and an irrepressible smile came over even the major's features. At length, however, by drawing him into a lecture, they succeeded in persuading him to follow them; and, as they left the diggings, he told them the history of the prophecies, the discovery, and the spread of knowledge as to the rich auriferous deposits of this part of Australia. He could give them facts and incidents and dates as to the ingress into Melbourne, and the exodus therefrom to the diggings, in the year 1852; he told them how the energy and the love of order which characterize the English-speaking peoples had reduced to system, method, subordination, the chaotic surgings and restlessness which marked the first weeks and months of this new era; and he detailed, as though he had studied the subject to the entire neglect of other matters, the working of the system,—how the land was registered, what was the sum paid in the aggregate, how the taxes were collected, wherein the system had been found faulty. All this occupied much time, and, before he had finished, the cart was in sight, in which Lady Helena and Miss Grant reseated themselves, and for the remainder of the day and the succeeding night their progress was in the accustomed order.

Here was the mineralogical museum, in which might be seen specimens illustrative of all the various ways in which the gold has been found.

CHAPTER XXXVII

A WARNING.

At sunrise the travelers left the gold regions and crossed the frontiers of the county of Talbot. Their line of travel now struck the dusty roads of the county of Dalhousie. Half the journey was accomplished. In fifteen days more of travel equally rapid the little party would reach the shores of Twofold Bay. Moreover, every one was in good health. Paganel's assertions as to the salubrity of this climate were verified. There was little or no moisture, and the heat was quite endurable. Neither men nor animals complained.

A PILLARED GROVE.

Only one change had been made in the line of march since leaving Camden Bridge. The criminal disaster on the railway, when made known to Ayrton, had induced him to take precautions hitherto needless. The horsemen were not to lose sight of the cart. During the hours of encampment one of them was always on guard. Morning and evening the priming of the fire-arms was renewed. It was certain that a band of malefactors were scouring the country; and, although nothing gave cause for immediate suspicion, still it was necessary to be ready for any emergency.

In truth they had reason to act thus. An imprudence, or negligence even, might cost them dear. Glenarvan, moreover, was not alone in giving heed to this state of affairs. In the isolated towns and stations the inhabitants and squatters took precautions against any attack or surprise. The houses were closed at nightfall. The dogs were let loose within the palisades, and barked at the slightest alarm. There was not a shepherd, collecting his numerous flocks on horseback for the evening return, who did not carry a carbine suspended from the pommel of his saddle. The news of the crime committed at Camden Bridge was the reason for this excessive caution, and many a colonist who had formerly slept with open doors and windows now carefully locked his house at twilight.

After awhile, the cart entered a grove of giant trees, the finest they had hitherto seen. There was a cry of admiration at sight of the eucalyptuses, two hundred feet high, whose spongy bark was five inches in thickness. The trunks measured twenty feet in circumference, and were furrowed by streams of odorous sap. Not a branch, not a twig, not a wanton shoot, not even a knot, disfigured their perfect symmetry. They could not have issued smoother from the hand of the turner. They were like so many columns exactly mated, and could be counted by hundreds, spreading at a vast height into capitals of finely-shaped branches adorned with vertical leaves, from which hung solitary flowers, whose calices were like inverted urns.

Under this evergreen canopy the air circulated freely. A continual ventilation absorbed the moisture of the earth, and horses, herds of cattle, and carts could easily pass between these trees, which were widely separated and arranged in straight rows. It was neither a wood with thickets crowded and obstructed by brambles, nor a virgin forest barricaded with fallen trunks and entangled with inextricable parasites, where only axe and fire can clear a way for the pioneers. A carpet of herbage below, and a sheet of verdure above; long vistas of noble pillars; little shade or coolness; a peculiar light, like the rays that sift through a delicate tissue; shadows sharply defined upon the ground: all this constituted a strange sight. The forests of Oceanica are entirely different from those of the New World, and the eucalyptus—the "tara" of the aborigines—is the most perfect tree of the Australian flora.

The shade is not dense, nor the darkness profound, beneath these domes of verdure, owing to a strange peculiarity in the arrangement of the leaves of the eucalyptus. Not one presents its face to the sun, but only its sharp edge. The eye sees nothing but profiles in this singular foliage. Thus the rays of the sun glide to the earth as if they had passed between the slats of a window-blind.

Every one observed this and seemed surprised. Why this particular arrangement? This question was naturally addressed to Paganel, who replied like a man who is never at fault.

"What astonishes me," said he, "is not the freak of nature, for she knows what she does; but botanists do not always know what they say. Nature was not mistaken in giving to these trees this singular foliage; but men are wrong in calling them eucalyptuses."

"What does the word mean?" asked Mary Grant.

"It comes from the Greek words εῡ καλὐπτω;, signifying *I cover well*. But you all see that the eucalyptus covers badly."

A SILENT MARCH.

"Just so, my dear Paganel," replied Glenarvan; "and now tell us why the leaves grow thus."

Anon you might see him as in the illustration, when he had picked up a pebble and was sure that it was in itself so interesting as a mineralogical specimen that he must treasure it up for the Bank of France.

"In this country, where the air is dry," said Paganel, "where rains are rare and the soil is parched, the trees need neither wind nor sun. Hence these narrow leaves seek to defend themselves against the elements and preserve themselves from too great an evaporation. They therefore present their edges, and not their faces, to the action of the solar rays. There is nothing more intelligent than a leaf."

At evening they encamped at the foot of some trees that bore the marks of a recent fire. They formed tall chimneys, as it were, for the flames had hollowed them out internally throughout their entire length.

"Nor more selfish," remarked the major. "They thought only of themselves, and not at all of travelers."

The entire party was inclined to be of MacNabb's opinion, except Paganel, who, as he wiped his face, congratulated himself upon traveling beneath these shadowless trees. However, this arrangement of foliage was to be regretted; for the journey through these forests is frequently very long and painful, since nothing protects the traveler from the heat of the sun.

All day long our travelers pursued their way under these interminable arches. They met neither quadruped nor human being. A few cockatoos inhabited the tops of the trees; but at that height they could scarcely be distinguished, and their chattering was an almost inaudible murmur. Sometimes a flock of parrots would shoot across a distant vista, illumining it with a rapid flash of variegated light. But generally a deep silence reigned in this vast temple of verdure, and the measured tread of the horses, a few words exchanged now and then in desultory conversation, the creaking of the cart-wheels, and from time to time a cry from Ayrton as he urged on his sluggish team, were the only sounds that disturbed this vast solitude.

At evening they encamped at the foot of some trees that bore the marks of a recent fire. They formed tall chimneys, as it were, for the flames had hollowed them out internally throughout their entire length. Having only this shell of bark remaining, they no longer suffered severely from this treatment.

However, this lamentable habit of the squatters and natives will finally destroy these magnificent trees, and they will disappear like the cedars of Lebanon, so many centuries old, consumed by the careless fires of wandering encampments.

Olbinett, according to Paganel's advice, kindled a fire in one of these tubular trunks. He obtained a draught at once, and the smoke soon disappeared in the dark mass of foliage. The necessary precautions were taken for the night, and Ayrton, Mulready, Wilson, and Captain Mangles watched by turns till sunrise.

During all the next day the interminable forest presented its long, monotonous avenues, till it seemed as if it would never end. Towards evening, however, the rows of trees became thinner; and a few miles farther on, upon a small plain, appeared a collection of regularly built houses.

"Seymour!" cried Paganel. "This is the last place we shall meet with before leaving the province of Victoria."

"Is it an important town?" inquired Lady Helena.

"Madam," replied he, "it is a simple parish that would like to become a municipality."

"Shall we find a comfortable hotel?" asked Glenarvan.

"I hope so," answered the geographer.

"Well, then, let us go into the town; for the ladies will not be sorry, I imagine, to rest here one night."

"My dear Edward," replied Lady Helena, "Mary and I accept; but on the condition that it shall cause no trouble or delay."

"None at all," said Lord Glenarvan. "Moreover, our oxen are fatigued. To-morrow we will start at break of day."

A TALK AFTER SUPPER.

It was now nine o'clock. The moon was approaching the horizon, and her rays were dimmed by the gathering mist. The darkness was increasing. The whole party, accordingly, entered the broad street of Seymour under the guidance of Paganel, who always seemed to be perfectly acquainted with what he had never seen. But his instinct directed him, and he went straight to Campbell's North British Hotel. Horses and oxen were taken to the stable, the cart was put under the shed, and the travelers were conducted to quite comfortable apartments.

At ten o'clock the guests took their seats at a table, over which Olbinett had cast his experienced eye. Paganel had just explored the town, in company with Robert, and now related his nocturnal impressions in a very laconic style. He had seen absolutely nothing.

However, a man less absent-minded would have observed a certain excitement in the streets of Seymour. Groups were formed here and there, which gradually increased. People talked at the doors of the houses, and questioned each other with an air of anxiety.

Various daily papers were read aloud, commented upon, and discussed. These signs, one might suppose, could not have escaped the most careless observer; Paganel, however, had suspected nothing.

The major, on the contrary, without even leaving the hotel, had ascertained the fears that were agitating the little community. Ten minutes' conversation with the loquacious landlord had informed him; but he did not utter a word. Not until supper was over, and Lady Helena, Mary, and Robert had retired to their chambers, did the major say to his companions:

"They have traced the authors of the crime committed at Camden Bridge."

"Have they been arrested?" asked Ayrton, quickly.

"No," replied MacNabb, without seeming to notice the eagerness of the quartermaster.

"So much the worse," added Ayrton.

"Well," inquired Glenarvan, "to whom do they attribute the crime?"

"Read," said the major, handing to Glenarvan a copy of the *Australian and New Zealand Gazette*, "and you will see that the police-officer was not mistaken."

Glenarvan read aloud the following passage:

"Sydney, Jan. 2, 1865.—It will be remembered that on the night of December 29 an accident took place at Camden Bridge, five miles from Castlemaine Station, on the Melbourne and Sandhurst Railway, by which the night express was precipitated at full speed into the Lutton River. Numerous thefts committed after the accident, and the corpse of the guard found half a mile above, prove that it was the result of a crime; and, in accordance with the verdict at the inquest, this crime is to be attributed to a band of convicts who escaped, six months ago, from the Perth penitentiary, in Western Australia, as they were about to be transferred to Norfolk Island. These convicts are twenty-nine in number, and are commanded by a certain Ben Joyce, a dangerous criminal, who arrived in Australia several months ago in some way, and upon whom justice has not yet succeeded in laying hands. The inhabitants of the cities, and the colonists and squatters of the stations, are warned to be on their guard, and requested to send to the undersigned any information which may assist his investigations.

"J. P. MITCHELL, Surveyor-General."

When Glenarvan had finished reading this article, MacNabb turned to the geographer and said:

"You see, Paganel, that there may yet be convicts in Australia."

"Runaways there may be, of course," replied Paganel, "but not those who have been transported and regularly received. These people have no right to be here."

"Well, at any rate they are here," continued Glenarvan; "but I do not suppose that their presence need cause us to change our plans or delay our journey. What do you think, captain?"

LOOKING AT BOTH SIDES.

Captain Mangles did not answer immediately. He hesitated between the grief that the abandonment of the search would cause the two children, and the fear of compromising the safety of the party.

"If Lady Glenarvan and Miss Grant were not with us," said he, "I should care very little for this band of wretches."

Glenarvan understood him, and added:

They were like so many columns exactly mated, and could be counted by hundreds.

"Of course it is not advisable to give up our undertaking; but perhaps it would be prudent for the sake of the ladies to join the Duncan at Melbourne, and continue our search for Captain Grant towards the east. What do you think, MacNabb?"

"Before replying," said the major, "I should like to hear Ayrton's opinion."

The quartermaster, thus addressed, looked at Glenarvan.

"I think," said he, "that, as we are two hundred miles from Melbourne, the danger, if there is any, is as great on the southern as on the eastern road. Both are little frequented, and one is as good as the other. Moreover, I do not think that thirty malefactors can intimidate eight well-armed and resolute men. Therefore, in the absence of better advice, I should go on."

"Well said," replied Paganel. "By continuing our course we shall cross Captain Grant's track, while by returning to the south we should go directly away from it. I agree with you, therefore, and shall give myself no uneasiness about the runaway convicts."

Thus the determination to make no change in the programme was unanimously approved of.

"One more remark, my lord," said Ayrton, as they were about to separate.

"Speak."

"Would it not be advisable to send an order to the Duncan to sail to the coast?"

"Why?" asked Captain Mangles. "It will be time enough to send the order when we arrive at Twofold Bay. If any unforeseen event should compel us to return to Melbourne, we might be sorry not to find the Duncan there. Moreover, her injuries cannot yet have been repaired. I think, therefore, that it would be better to wait."

"Well," replied Ayrton, without further remark.

The next day the little party, armed and ready for any emergency, left Seymour, and half an hour after re-entered the forest of eucalyptuses, which appeared again towards the east. Glenarvan would have preferred to travel in the open country, for a plain is less favorable to sudden attacks and ambuscades than a thick wood. But they had no alternative; and the cart kept on all day between the tall, monotonous trees, and at evening encamped on the borders of the district of Murray.

They were now setting foot on one of the least frequented portions of the Australian continent, a vast uninhabited region stretching away to the Australian Alps. At some future day its forests will be leveled, and the home of the colonist will stand where now all is desolation; but at present it is a desert. In this region is situated the so-styled "reserve for the blacks." On these remote plains various spots have been set apart, where the aboriginal race can enjoy to the full the privilege of gradually becoming extinct. Though the white man is at perfect liberty to invade this "reserved" territory, yet the black may call it his own.

Paganel, who was in his element wherever statistics or history was concerned, went into full details respecting the native races. He gave a long account of the cruelties to which these unfortunate beings had been subjected at the hands of the early colonists, and showed how little had been done by the interference of the government. As a striking instance of the manner in which the aborigines melt away before the advance of civilization, he cited the case of Tasmania, which at the beginning of this century had five thousand native inhabitants, but in 1863 had only seven.

STUDIES IN ANTHROPOLOGY.

"Fifty years ago," said he, "we should have met in our course many a tribe of natives; whereas thus far we have not seen even one. A century hence, the black race will have utterly disappeared from this continent."

At that moment Robert, halting in front of a group of eucalyptuses, cried out:

"A monkey! there is a monkey!"

The cart was instantly stopped, and, looking in the direction indicated by the boy, our travellers saw a huge black form moving with astonishing agility from branch to branch, until it was lost from view in the depths of the grove.

Of these miserable beings there were about thirty, men, women, and children, dressed in ragged kangaroo-skins.

"What sort of a monkey is that?" asked MacNabb.

"That monkey," answered Paganel, "is a full-blooded Australian."

Just then were heard sounds of voices at some little distance; the oxen were put in motion, and after proceeding a few hundred paces the party came suddenly upon an encampment of aborigines, consisting of some ten or twelve tents, made of strips of bark arranged in the manner of tiles, and giving shelter to their wretched inhabitants on only one side. Of these miserable beings there were about thirty, men, women, and children, dressed in ragged kangaroo-skins. Their first movement was one of flight; but a few words from Ayrton restored confidence, and they slowly approached the party of Europeans.

The major jocularly insisted that Robert was correct in saying that he had seen a monkey; but Lady Helena declined to accept his views, and, getting out of the cart, made friendly advances to these degraded beings, who seemed to look upon her as a divinity. Reassured by her gentle manner, they surrounded the travelers, and began to cast wishful glances at the provisions which the cart contained. Glenarvan, at the request of his wife, distributed a quantity of food among the hungry group.

After this had been dispatched, our friends were favored by their new acquaintances with a sham fight, which lasted about ten minutes, the women urging on the combatants and pretending to mutilate those who fell in the fray. Suddenly the excited crowd dropped their arms, and a profound silence succeeded to the din of war. A flight of cockatoos had made its appearance in the neighboring trees; and the opportunity to display their proficiency in the use of the boomerang was at once improved by the Australians. The skill manifested in the construction and use of this instrument served Lady Helena as a strong argument against the monkey theory, though the major pretended that he was not yet convinced.

Lord Glenarvan was now about to give the order to advance, when a native came running up with the news that he had discovered half a dozen cassowaries. The chase that followed, with the ingenious disguise assumed by the hunter, and the marvelous fidelity with which he imitated the movements and cries of the bird, was witnessed with interest by the travelers. Lady Helena adduced the skill displayed as a still further argument against the major's theory; but the obstinate MacNabb declined to recede from his position, citing to his antagonist the statement of the negroes concerning the orang-outangs,—that they are negroes like themselves, only that they are too cunning to talk, for fear of being made to work.

A sham fight, which lasted about ten minutes, the women urging on the combatants and pretending to mutilate those who fell in the fray.

CHAPTER XXXVIII

WEALTH IN THE WILDERNESS.

After a peaceful night, the travelers, at seven o'clock in the morning, resumed their journey eastward over the plains. Twice they crossed the tracks of squatters, leading towards the north; and then the different hoof-prints would have been confounded if Glenarvan's horse had not left upon the dust the Black Point mark, distinguishable by its three trefoils.

A PIANO IN THE DESERT.

Sometimes the plain was furrowed with winding creeks, bordered by box-wood, which took their source on the slopes of the Buffalo Range, a chain of mountains whose picturesque outlines stretched along the horizon, and which the party resolved to reach that evening. Ayrton urged on his oxen, and, after a journey of thirty-five miles, they reached the place. The tent was pitched beneath a great tree. Night had come, and supper was quickly dispatched; all thought more of sleeping than of eating, after the fatigues of the day.

Paganel, to whom fell the first watch, did not lie down, but, rifle on shoulder, guarded the encampment, walking to and fro that he might the better resist sleep. In spite of the absence of the moon, the night was almost bright with the splendor of the southern constellations; and the geographer amused himself in reading the great book of the firmament, which is always open. The silence of sleeping nature was broken only by the sound of the horses' chains as they rattled against their feet. Paganel was becoming fully absorbed in his astronomical meditations, and occupying himself more with the things of heaven than those of earth, when a distant sound startled him from his reverie.

He listened attentively, and, to his great astonishment, thought he distinguished the tones of a piano. A few boldly-struck chords wafted to his ears their harmonious vibrations. He could not be mistaken.

"A piano in the desert!" said he to himself. "It cannot be!"

It was indeed very surprising, and Paganel began to think that some strange Australian bird was imitating the sound of the instrument.

But at that moment a voice, harmoniously pitched, was heard. The pianist was accompanied by a vocalist. The geographer listened incredulously, but in a few moments was forced to recognize the sublime air that struck upon his ear. It was "*Il mio tesoro tanto*" from Don Juan.

*Paganel did not lie down, but, rifle on shoulder, guarded the encampment,
walking to and fro that he might the better resist sleep.*

A TWOFOLD SURPRISE.

"Parbleu!" thought the geographer, "however strange the
Australian birds may be, or even though the parrots were the most
musical in the world, they could not sing Mozart."

He listened to the end of this grand inspiration of the master. The
effect of this sweet melody, in the stillness of the starlit night, was

indescribable. He remained a long time under the influences of its enchantment. At last the voice ceased, and all was silent.

When Wilson came to relieve the geographer, he found him wrapt in a profound reverie. Paganel said nothing to the sailor, but, reserving his account of the incident for Glenarvan the next day, he crept into the tent.

In the morning the whole party were awakened by unexpected bayings. Glenarvan at once arose. Two magnificent pointers were gamboling along the edge of a small wood; but at the approach of the travelers they disappeared among the trees, barking loudly.

"There must be a station in this desert," said Glenarvan, "and hunters, since those are hunting-dogs."

Paganel was just about to relate his experiences of the past night, when two men appeared, in hunting costume, mounted on fine horses. They naturally stopped at sight of the little party, encamped in gypsy-like fashion, and seemed to be wondering what the presence of armed men in this place meant, when they perceived the ladies, who were alighting from the cart.

They immediately dismounted, and advanced towards them, hat in hand. Glenarvan went to meet them, and introduced himself and party, giving the name and rank of each member. The young men bowed, and one of them, the elder, said:

"My lord, will your ladies, your companions, and yourself do us the honor to accompany us to our house?"

"May I ask, gentlemen, whom I have the honor of addressing?" inquired Glenarvan.

"Michael and Alexander Patterson, proprietors of Hottam Station. You are already on the grounds of the establishment, and have but a quarter of a mile to go."

"Gentlemen," replied Glenarvan, "I should be unwilling to slight a hospitality so graciously offered——"

"My lord," interrupted Michael Patterson, "by accepting you will confer a favor upon two poor colonists, who will be only too happy to extend to you the honors of the desert."

Glenarvan bowed in token of assent.

"Sir," said Paganel, addressing Michael Patterson, "should I be too inquisitive were I to ask if it was you who sang that divine air of Mozart last night?"

"It was I, sir," replied the gentleman; "and my brother accompanied me."

"Well, sir," continued Paganel, extending his hand, "accept the sincere compliments of a Frenchman, who is an ardent admirer of Mozart's music."

The young man modestly returned the geographer's greeting, and then pointed towards the right to the road they were to take. The horses had been confided to the care of Ayrton and the sailors, and the travelers at once betook themselves on foot to Hottam Station, under the guidance of the two young men.

It was a magnificent establishment, characterized by the perfect order of an English park. Immense meadows, inclosed by fences, extended as far as the eye could reach. Here grazed thousands of oxen and sheep. Numerous shepherds and still more numerous dogs tended this vast herd, while with the bellowing and bleating mingled the baying of mastiffs and the sharp crack of stock-whips.

ARTIFICIAL SELECTION.

To the east the prospect was broken by a border of gum-trees, beyond which rose the imposing peak of Mount Hottam, seven thousand five hundred feet high. Long avenues of tall trees stretched in all directions, while here and there stood dense clumps of grass-trees, shrubby plants about ten feet high, resembling the dwarf palm, with a thick foliage of long narrow leaves. The air was laden with the perfume of laurels, whose clusters of white flowers in full bloom exhaled the most delicate fragrance.

With the charming groups of native trees were mingled those transplanted from European climes. The peach, the pear, the apple, the fig, the orange, and even the oak were hailed with delight by the travelers, who, if they were not astonished at walking in the shade of the trees of their country, wondered, at least, at the sight of the birds that fluttered among the branches, the satin-birds with their silky plumage, and the canaries, clad in golden and black velvet.

Here, for the first time, they saw the menure, or lyre-bird, whose tail has the form of the graceful instrument of Orpheus. As the bird fled away among the arborescent ferns, its tail striking the branches, they almost expected to hear those harmonious chords that helped Amphion to rebuild the walls of Thebes.

Lord Glenarvan was not satisfied with merely admiring the fairy wonders of this oasis of the Australian desert. He listened with profound interest to the young men's story. In England, in the heart of civilization, a new-comer would have first informed his host whence he came and whither he was going; but here, by a nice shade of distinction, Michael and Sandy Patterson thought they should make themselves known to the travelers to whom they offered their hospitalities, and briefly told their story.

NATURE AND ART.

It was like that of all intelligent and active young Englishmen, who do not believe that the possession of riches absolves from the responsibility to labor for the welfare of others. Michael and Alexander Patterson were the sons of a London banker. When they were twenty years old, their father had said: "Here is money, my sons. Go to some distant land, found there a useful establishment, and acquire in labor the knowledge of life. If you succeed, so much the better; if you fail, it matters little. We shall not regret the money that will have enabled you to become men." They obeyed; they chose the province of Victoria as the place to sow the paternal bank-notes, and had no reason to repent. At the end of three years their establishment had attained its present prosperity.

They had just finished the brief account of their career, when the dwelling came in sight at the end of a fine avenue of trees. It was a charming house of wood and brick, surrounded by clusters of plants, and had the elegant form of a Swiss cottage, while a veranda, from which hung Chinese lanterns, encircled it like a Roman impluvium. The windows were shaded by brilliant-colored awnings, which at a distance looked almost like masses of flowers. Nothing could be prettier, cozier, or pleasanter to the sight. On the lawn and among the shrubbery round about stood bronze candelabra, supporting elegant lamps with glass globes, which at nightfall illumined the whole garden with a beauteous light.

No farm-hands, stables, or outhouses were to be seen,—nothing that indicated scenes of toil. The dwellings of the workmen—a regular village, consisting of some twenty cottages—were a quarter of a mile distant, in the heart of a little valley. Telegraph-wires secured immediate communication between the village and the house of the proprietors, which, far from all tumult, was in truth "a thing of beauty."

The avenue was soon passed. A little iron bridge, of great elegance, crossing a murmuring stream, gave access to the private grounds. A courteous attendant advanced to meet the travelers; the doors of the house were opened, and the guests of Hottam Station entered the sumptuous dwelling.

All the luxuries of refined and civilized life seemed to be present. Into the vestibule, which was adorned with decorative subjects, illustrating the turf or the chase, opened a spacious parlor, lighted with five windows. A piano, covered with classic and modern music; easels, upon which were half-finished paintings; marble statues, mounted on tasteful pedestals; on the walls, a few pictures by Flemish masters; rich carpets, soft to the feet as grassy meadows; panels of tapestry, descriptive of pleasing mythological episodes; an antique chandelier, costly chinaware, delicate vases, and a great variety of articles of *virtù*, indicated a high appreciation of beauty and comfort. Everything that could please, everything that could relieve the tedium of a voluntary exile, everything that could remind one of a luxurious European home, was to be found in this fairy abode. It would have been easy to imagine oneself in some princely castle of England, France, or Germany.

The five windows admitted, through delicate curtains, a light tempered and softened by the shadows of the veranda. Lady Helena looked out, and was astonished. The house, upon this side, commanded the view of a broad valley, which extended to the eastern mountains. The alternation of meadow and woodland, broken here and there by vast clearings, the graceful sweep of the hill-sides, and the outlines of the entire landscape, formed a picture beyond the power of description. This vast panorama, intersected by broad bands of light and shade, changed every hour with the progress of the sun.

In the mean time, in accordance with the hosts' orders, breakfast had been prepared by the steward of the station, and in less than a quarter of an hour the travelers were seated at a bountiful table. The quality of the viands and the wines was unexceptionable; but what was especially gratifying, in the midst of these refinements of wealth, was the evident pleasure experienced by the young settlers in dispensing to strangers, beneath their own roof, this magnificent hospitality.

Here, for the first time, they saw the menure, or lyre-bird, whose tail has the form of the graceful instrument of Orpheus.

AUSTRALIANS, NATIVE AND IMPORTED.

The young gentlemen were soon made acquainted with the object of the expedition, and took a lively interest in Glenarvan's search, giving also great encouragement to the captain's children.

"Harry Grant," said Michael, "has evidently fallen into the hands of the natives, since he has not appeared in the settlements on the coast. He knew his position exactly, as the document proves, and, as he has not reached any English colony, he must have been made prisoner by the natives as soon as he landed."

"That is precisely what happened to his quartermaster, Ayrton," replied Captain Mangles.

"But, gentlemen," inquired Lady Helena, "have you never heard of the shipwreck of the Britannia?"

"Never, madam," said Michael.

"And what treatment do you think Captain Grant would experience as a prisoner among the Australians?"

"The Australians are not cruel, madam," replied the young settler: "Miss Grant may reassure herself on this point. There are many instances of their kindness; and some Europeans have lived a long time among them, without having any reason to complain of brutality." These words corroborated the information previously given by Paganel and Ayrton.

When the ladies had left the table, the conversation turned upon convicts. The settlers had heard of the accident at Camden Bridge, but the band of runaways gave no uneasiness, they would not dare to attack a station that was guarded by more than a hundred men. They were confident, too, that they would not venture into the deserted regions of the Murray, nor into the colonies of New South Wales, where the roads are well protected.

Glenarvan could not decline the invitation of his amiable hosts to spend the entire day at Hottam Station. The delay thus occasioned could be turned to good account: the horses and oxen would be greatly benefited by their rest in the comfortable stables of the establishment. It was, therefore, decided to remain, and the two young men submitted to their guests a programme for the day's sports, which was adopted with alacrity.

It was a charming house of wood and brick, surrounded by clusters of plants, and had the elegant form of a Swiss cottage.

A DAY'S SPORT.

At noon, seven fine hunters pawed the ground at the gate of the house. For the ladies was provided an elegant coach, and the long reins enabled their driver to show his skill in manœuvring the "four-in-hand." The horsemen, accompanied by outriders, and well armed, galloped beside the carriage, while the pack of hounds bayed joyously in the coppices.

For four hours the cavalcade traversed the paths and avenues of these spacious grounds. As for game, an army of bushmen could not have started up a greater number of animals. Young Robert, who kept close to the major's side, accomplished wonders. The intrepid boy, in spite of his sister's injunctions, was always ahead, and the first to fire. But Captain Mangles had promised to watch over him, a fact which tended not a little to allay Miss Grant's apprehension for her brother's safety.

Of all the sports of the day the most interesting was unquestionably a kangaroo hunt. About four o'clock the dogs started a troop of these curious animals. The little ones took refuge in their mothers' pouches, and the whole drove rushed away in single file. Nothing can be more astonishing than the enormous bounds of the kangaroo, whose hind legs are twice as long as its fore ones, and bend like a spring. At the head of the drove was a male five feet high,—"an old man," in the language of the bushmen.

For four or five miles the chase was briskly continued. The kangaroos did not slacken their pace; and the dogs, who feared, with good reason, the powerful blows of their formidable paws, did not venture to approach them. But at last the drove stopped in exhaustion, and "the old man" braced himself against the trunk of a tree, ready to fight for his life. One of the pointers, carried on by the impetus of his course, rolled within reach of him. A moment after, the unfortunate dog was tossed into the air, and fell back lifeless. The entire pack, deterred by the fate of their comrade, kept at a respectful distance. It became necessary to dispatch the kangaroo with the rifle, and nothing but bullets could bring down the gigantic quadruped.

At this juncture Robert narrowly escaped being the victim of his rashness. In order to make sure of his aim, he approached so near the kangaroo that the animal made a spring at him. Robert fell. A cry of alarm resounded. Mary Grant, speechless with apprehension, stretched her hands towards her brother. No one dared to fire, for fear of hitting the boy.

Suddenly Captain Mangles, with his hunting-knife open, rushed upon the kangaroo, at the risk of his life, and stabbed it to the heart. The beast fell dead, and Robert rose unharmed. An instant after, he was in the arms of his sister.

"Thanks, Captain Mangles! thanks!" said Mary, extending her hand to the young captain.

"I promised to take care of him," replied the captain, as he took the trembling hand of the young girl.

This adventure ended the hunt. The troop of kangaroos had scattered after the death of their leader, whose carcass was brought to the house.

It was now six o'clock, and dinner was in readiness for the hunters; comprising, among other dishes, a soup of kangaroo's tail, prepared in the native style.

After a dessert of ices and sherbet, the party repaired to the parlor, where the evening was devoted to music. Lady Helena, who was a good pianiste, presided at the instrument, while Michael and Alexander Patterson sang with great taste selections from the latest compositions of the modern musical masters.

A FRESH DEPARTURE.

At eleven o'clock tea was served in true English style. Paganel having desired to taste the Australian tea, a liquid, black as ink, was brought to him. It consisted of a quart of water, in which half a pound of tea had been boiled four hours. Paganel, with a wry face, pronounced it excellent. At midnight the guests were conducted to cool and comfortable chambers, where they renewed in dreams the pleasures of the day.

The next morning, at sunrise, they took leave of the two young settlers, with many thanks, and with warmly-expressed hopes to see them at Malcolm Castle at no very distant day. The cart then started, and in a few minutes, as the road wound around the foot of Mount Hottam, the hospitable habitation disappeared, like a passing vision, from the eyes of the travelers. For five miles farther they traversed the grounds of the station, and not till nine o'clock did the little party pass the last palisade and enter upon the almost unknown districts of the country before them.

CHAPTER XXXIX

SUSPICIOUS OCCURRENCES.

A mighty barrier crossed the road on the southeast. It was the chain of the Australian Alps, which extend in capricious windings fifteen hundred miles, and are capped with clouds four thousand feet aloft.

ASCENDING THE MOUNTAINS.

The sky was dull and lowering, and the rays of the sun struggled through dense masses of mist. The temperature was, therefore, endurable; but the journey was difficult on account of the irregularity of the surface. The unevenness of the plain constantly increased, and here and there rose mounds, covered with young green gum-trees. Farther on, these excrescences formed the first slopes of the great Alps. The ascent was very laborious, as was shown by the efforts of the oxen, whose yokes cracked under the tension of the heavy vehicle. The animals panted heavily, and the muscles of their hams were strained almost to breaking. The axles threatened to give way under the sudden jolts that Ayrton, with all his skill, could not prevent. The ladies, however, lost none of their accustomed cheerfulness.

Captain Mangles and the two sailors rode a few hundred paces in advance, to choose practicable passes. It was a difficult and often a perilous task. Several times Wilson was forced to make a way with his hatchet through the midst of dense thickets. Their course deviated in many windings, which impassable obstacles, lofty blocks of granite, deep ravines, and treacherous swamps compelled them to make. At evening they encamped at the foot of the Alps, on the banks of a small stream that flowed along the edge of a plain covered with tall shrubbery, whose bright-red foliage enlivened the banks.

"We shall have difficulty in passing here," said Glenarvan, as he gazed at the chain of mountains, whose outlines were already growing dim in the twilight. "Alps! that is a name suggestive of arduous climbing."

"You will change your opinion, my dear Glenarvan," replied Paganel. "You must not think you are in Switzerland."

"Then these Australian Alps———?" asked Lady Helena.

"Are miniature mountains," continued Paganel. "You will cross them without noticing it."

The next day, in spite of the assurances of the confident geographer, the little party found great difficulty in crossing the mountains. They were forced to advance at a venture, and descend into deep and narrow gorges that, for aught they knew, might end in a wall of rock. Ayrton would doubtless have been eventually nonplused had they not, after an hour's climbing, caught sight of a tavern on one of the paths of the mountain.

"Well!" said Paganel, as they reached the hostelry, "the proprietor of this inn cannot make a great fortune in such a place. Of what use can he be?"

"To give us the information we need for our journey," replied Glenarvan. "Let us go in."

Glenarvan, followed by Ayrton, entered the tavern. The landlord of "Bush Inn" was a coarse man, of forbidding appearance, who had to consider himself as the principal customer for the gin, brandy, and whisky of his tavern, and scarcely ever saw any one but squatters or herdsmen.

He replied in an ill-humored way to the questions that were addressed him; but his answers sufficed to determine Ayrton upon his course. Glenarvan, however, remunerated the tavern-keeper for the little trouble they had given him, and was about to leave the inn, when a placard, affixed to the wall, attracted his attention. It was a notice of the colonial police, detailing the escape of the convicts from Perth, and setting a price upon the head of Ben Joyce—a hundred pounds sterling to any one who should deliver him up.

"Indeed," said Glenarvan, "that is a rascal worth hanging."

"And especially worth taking," replied Ayrton. "A hundred pounds! What a sum! He is not worth it."

"As for the inn-keeper," added Glenarvan, as he left the room, "I scarcely put faith in him, despite his placard."

"Nor I either," said Ayrton.

Glenarvan and the quartermaster rejoined the party, and they all proceeded to where a narrow pass wound across the chain. Here they began the ascent.

Of all the sports of the day the most interesting was unquestionably a kangaroo hunt.

ANOTHER DEATH.

But it was an arduous task. More than once the ladies and their companions had to dismount, and it was often necessary to push the wheels of the heavy vehicle at some steep ascent, or to hold it back along the edge of some dangerous precipice. The oxen, as they could not work to advantage at sudden turns, had frequently to be unyoked, and the cart blocked to prevent it from sliding back. Ayrton was repeatedly forced to bring the already exhausted horses to his assistance.

Whether this exertion was too prolonged, or whether from some other cause, one of the horses gave out during the ascent. He fell suddenly, without an instant's warning. It was Mulready's horse; and when the sailor attempted to help him up, he found that he was dead. Ayrton examined the animal carefully, but did not seem to understand the cause of this sudden death.

"The beast must have burst a blood-vessel," said Glenarvan.

"Evidently," replied Ayrton.

"Take my horse, Mulready," added Glenarvan; "I will join Lady Helena in the cart."

Mulready obeyed, and the little party continued their fatiguing ascent, abandoning the body to the crows.

The next day they began the descent, which was much more rapid. During its course a violent hail-storm burst on them, and they were forced to seek a shelter beneath the rocks. Not hailstones, but pieces of ice as large as one's hand, were precipitated from the angry clouds. A sling could not have hurled them with greater force, and several sharp blows warned Paganel and Robert to be on their guard. The cart was pierced through in many places: indeed, few roofs could have resisted the fall of these cutting missiles, some of which froze to the trunks of the trees. It was necessary to wait for the end of this avalanche, for fear of being stoned to death, and it was an hour before the party regained the steep path, still slippery with icy incrustations. At evening the cart, considerably shattered, but still firm on its wooden wheels, descended the last slopes of the Alps, between tall solitary pines, and reached the plains of Gippsland.

DIVIDED COUNSELS.

All were impatient to gain their destination, the Pacific Ocean, where the Britannia had been wrecked. There only could traces of the shipwrecked seamen be found, and not in these desert regions. Ayrton urged Lord Glenarvan to send an order to the Duncan to repair to the coast, that he might have at his disposal all the aid possible in his search. In his opinion they ought to take advantage of the Lucknow road, which would lead them to Melbourne.

Afterwards this might be difficult, for highways leading directly to the capital would be absolutely wanting.

This advice of the quartermaster seemed reasonable. Paganel seconded it. He thought, too, that the yacht would be very useful under the present circumstances, and added that they could no longer communicate with Melbourne after passing the Lucknow road.

Glenarvan was undecided, and perhaps would have sent the order that Ayrton so particularly desired, if the major had not opposed this plan with great energy. He explained that Ayrton's presence was necessary to the expedition; that on approaching the coast the country would be unknown; that, if chance set them on the track of Captain Grant, the quartermaster would be more capable than any one else of following it; in short, that he alone could point out the place where the Britannia was lost.

MacNabb, therefore, advocated their continuing on the journey without change. Captain Mangles was of the same opinion. The young captain observed that his lordship's orders could more easily reach the Duncan if sent from Twofold Bay, than by dispatching a messenger two hundred miles over a wild country.

The major carried his point, and it was therefore decided that they should proceed to Twofold Bay. MacNabb noticed that Ayrton seemed quite disappointed, but he said nothing, and, according to his custom, kept his thoughts to himself.

Early in the afternoon they passed through a curious forest of ferns. These arborescent plants, in full bloom, measured thirty feet in height. Horses and horsemen could easily pass beneath their drooping branches, and sometimes the rowel of a spur would ring, as it struck against their solid stalks. The coolness of the grove was very grateful to the wearied travelers. Paganel, always demonstrative, gave vent to exclamations of delight that startled flocks of parrots and cockatoos.

All at once his companions saw the geographer reel in the saddle, and fall to the ground like a log. Was it giddiness, or sunstroke, caused by the heat?

They hastened to him.

"Paganel! Paganel! what is the matter?" cried Lord Glenarvan.

"The matter is, my dear friend," replied Paganel, extricating himself from the stirrups, "that I no longer have a horse."

"What! your horse——?"

"Is dead, stricken like Mulready's."

At once Glenarvan, Captain Mangles, and Wilson examined the animal. Paganel was right. His horse had been suddenly stricken dead.

"This is singular," said the captain.

"Very singular indeed," muttered the major.

Glenarvan could not restrain a feeling of uneasiness at this strange occurrence. It was impossible for them to retrace their steps in this desert; while, if an epidemic were to seize all the horses, it would be very difficult to continue the journey.

Before the end of the day his fears seemed to be justified. A third horse, Wilson's, fell dead, and, what was worse, one of the oxen was also stricken. Their means of conveyance now consisted of only three oxen and four horses.

A FINE FERNERY.

The situation had grown serious. The mounted horsemen could, of course, take turns in traveling on foot. But, if it should be necessary to leave the cart behind, what would become of the ladies? Could they accomplish the one hundred and twenty miles that still separated them from Twofold Bay?

Captain Mangles and Glenarvan anxiously examined the remaining horses: perhaps preventives might be found against new calamities. No sign of disease, however, could be detected. The animals were in perfect health, and bravely endured the hardships of the journey. Glenarvan, therefore, was inclined to think that this mysterious epidemic would have no more victims. This was Ayrton's opinion too, who declared that he could not at all understand the cause of the frightful mortality.

They started again, and the cart served to convey the pedestrians, who rode in it by turns. At evening, after a journey of only ten miles, the signal to halt was given, the encampment arranged, and the night was passed comfortably beneath a large group of arborescent ferns, among whose branches fluttered enormous bats.

The next day they made an excellent beginning, and accomplished fifteen miles. Everything led them to hope that they would encamp that evening on the banks of the Snowy River. Evening came, and a fog, clearly defined against the horizon, marked the course of the long-looked-for stream. A forest of tall trees was seen at a bend in the road, behind a moderate elevation. Ayrton guided his oxen towards the tall trunks dimly discerned in the shadow, and was just passing the boundary of the wood, when the cart sank into the earth to the hubs.

"What is the matter?" asked Glenarvan, when he perceived that the cart had come to a stop.

"We are fast in the mud," replied Ayrton.

Early in the afternoon they passed through a curious forest of ferns. These arborescent plants, in full bloom, measured thirty feet in height.

He urged his oxen with voice and whip, but they were up to their knees in the mire, and could not stir.

"Let us encamp here," said Captain Mangles.

"That is the best plan," answered Ayrton. "To-morrow, at daybreak, we can see to extricate ourselves."

"Very well: be it so," replied Glenarvan.

Night had set in rapidly, after a short twilight, but the heat had not departed with the sun. The air was heavy with stifling mists. Flashes of lightning, the dazzling forerunners of a coming storm, every now and then illumined the horizon.

The beds were prepared, and the sunken cart was made as comfortable as possible. The sombre arch of the great trees sheltered the tent of the travelers. Provided no rain fell, they would have no reason to complain.

Ayrton succeeded with difficulty in extricating his three oxen from the mud, in which they had by this time sunk to their flanks. The quartermaster picketed them with the four horses, and would allow no one to give them their fodder. This service he performed himself with great exactness, and that evening Glenarvan observed that his care was redoubled, for which he thanked him, as the preservation of the team was of paramount importance.

Meantime, the travelers partook of a hasty supper. Fatigue and heat had driven away hunger, and they needed rest more than nourishment. Lady Helena and Miss Grant, wishing their companions good-night, retired to their accustomed bedroom. As for the men, some crawled under the tent, while others stretched themselves on the thick grass at the foot of the trees.

Gradually each sank into a heavy sleep. The darkness increased beneath the curtain of dense clouds that covered the sky. Not a breath of air was felt. The silence of the night was only interrupted by the occasional howlings of wild animals.

About eleven o'clock, after an uneasy slumber, the major awoke. His half-closed eyes were attracted by a dim light that flickered beneath the great trees. One would have thought it was a whitish sheet glittering like the surface of a lake. MacNabb imagined, at first, that the flames of a conflagration were spreading over the ground.

Flashes of lightning, the dazzling forerunners of a coming storm, every now and then illumined the horizon.

STRANGE SIGHTS AND SOUNDS.

He rose and walked towards the wood. His surprise was great when he found himself in the presence of a purely natural phenomenon. Before him extended an immense field of mushrooms, which emitted phosphorescent flashes.

The major, who was not selfish, was about to waken Paganel, that the geographer might witness the spectacle with his own eyes, when an unexpected sight stopped him.

The phosphorescent light illumined the wood for the space of half a mile, and MacNabb thought he saw shadows rapidly moving along the edge of the clearing. Did his eyes deceive him? Was he the sport of an illusion?

He crouched down, and, after a long and attentive observation, distinctly perceived several men, who seemed by their movements to be searching the ground for something. What could these men want? He must know, and, without an instant's hesitation or awakening his companions, he crawled along on all-fours, carefully concealing himself in the tall grass.

Chapter XL

A STARTLING DISCOVERY.

INCREASING PERPLEXITIES.

It was a terrible night. At two o'clock in the morning the rain began to fall in torrents, which continued to pour from the stormy clouds till daylight. The tent was an insufficient shelter. Glenarvan and his companions took refuge in the cart, where they passed the time in conversing upon various subjects. The major, however, whose short absence no one had noticed, contented himself with listening in silence. The fury of the tempest gave them considerable uneasiness, since it might cause an inundation, by which the cart, fast in the mire, would be overwhelmed.

More than once Mulready, Ayrton, and Captain Mangles went to ascertain the height of the rushing waters, and returned drenched from head to foot.

He crouched down, and, after a long and attentive observation, distinctly perceived several men.

At length day appeared. The rain ceased, but the rays of the sun failed to penetrate the thick veil of clouds. Large pools of muddy, yellowish water covered the ground. A warm vapor issued from the water-soaked earth and saturated the atmosphere with a sickly moisture.

Glenarvan, first of all, turned his attention to the cart. In his eyes, this was their main support. It was imbedded fast in the midst of a deep hollow of sticky clay. The fore wheels were almost entirely out of sight, and the hind ones were buried up to the hubs. It would be a very difficult matter to pull out the heavy vehicle, and would undoubtedly require the united strength of men, oxen, and horses.

"We must make haste," said Captain Mangles. "If this clay dries, the work will be more difficult."

Glenarvan, the two sailors, the captain, and Ayrton then entered the wood, where the animals had passed the night.

It was a tall forest of gloomy gum-trees. Nothing met the eye but dead trunks, widely separated, which had been destitute of their bark for centuries. Not a bird built its nest on these lofty skeletons; not a leaf trembled on the dry branches, that rattled together like a bundle of dry bones. Glenarvan, as he walked on, gazed at the leaden sky, against which the branches of the gum-trees were sharply defined. To Ayrton's great astonishment, there was no trace of the horses and oxen in the place where he had left them. The fettered animals, however, could not have gone far.

They searched for them in the wood, but failed to find them. Ayrton then returned to the banks of the river, which was bordered by magnificent mimosas. He uttered a cry well known to his oxen, but there was no answer. The quartermaster seemed very anxious, and his companions glanced at each other in dismay.

An hour passed in a vain search, and Glenarvan was returning to the cart, which was at least a mile off, when a neigh fell upon his ear, followed almost immediately by a bellow.

"Here they are!" cried Captain Mangles, forcing his way between the tall tufts of the gastrolobium, which were high enough to conceal a whole herd.

Glenarvan, Mulready, and Ayrton rushed after him, and soon shared his astonishment. Two oxen and three horses lay upon the ground, stricken like the others. Their bodies were already cold, and a flock of hungry crows, croaking in the mimosas, waited for their unexpected prey.

Glenarvan and his friends gazed at each other, and Wilson did not suppress an oath that rose to his lips.

"What is the matter, Wilson?" said Lord Glenarvan, scarcely able to control himself. "We can do nothing. Ayrton, bring the ox and horse that are left. They must extricate us from the difficulty."

"If the cart were once out of the mud," replied Captain Mangles, "these two animals, by short journeys, could draw it to the coast. We must, therefore, at all events, release the clumsy vehicle."

"We will try, John," said Glenarvan. "Let us return to camp, for there must be anxiety at our long absence."

Ayrton took charge of the ox, and Mulready of the horse, and the party returned along the winding banks of the river. Half an hour after, Paganel, MacNabb, Lady Helena, and Miss Grant were told the state of affairs.

"By my faith," the major could not help exclaiming, "it is a pity, Ayrton, that you did not shoe all our animals on crossing the Wimerra."

"Why so, sir?" asked Ayrton.

"Because of all our horses only the one you put into the hands of the farrier has escaped the common fate."

"That is true," said Captain Mangles; "and it is a singular coincidence!"

MISTAKES AND MISAPPREHENSIONS.

"A coincidence, and nothing more," replied the quartermaster, gazing fixedly at the major.

MacNabb compressed his lips, as if he would repress the words ready to burst from them. Glenarvan, the captain, and Lady Helena seemed to expect that he would finish his sentence; but he remained silent, and walked towards the cart, which Ayrton was now examining.

"What did he mean?" inquired Glenarvan of Captain Mangles.

"I do not know," replied the young captain. "However, the major is not the man to speak without cause."

"No," said Lady Helena; "Major MacNabb must have suspicions of Ayrton."

"What suspicions?" asked Glenarvan. "Does he suppose him capable of killing our horses and oxen? For what purpose, pray? Are not Ayrton's interests identical with ours?"

"You are right, my dear Edward," said Lady Helena. "Besides, the quartermaster has given us, ever since the beginning of the journey, indubitable proofs of his devotion to our comfort."

"True," replied Captain Mangles. "But, then, what does the major's remark mean? I must have an understanding."

"Perhaps he thinks he is in league with these convicts?" remarked Paganel, imprudently.

"What convicts?" inquired Miss Grant.

"Monsieur Paganel is mistaken," said Captain Mangles quickly: "he knows that there are no convicts in the province of Victoria."

"Yes, yes, that is so," eagerly replied Paganel, who would fain have retracted his words. "What could I have been thinking of? Convicts? Who ever heard of convicts in Australia? Moreover, as soon as they land, they make very honest people. The climate, you know, Miss Mary, the moral effect of the climate——"

In his desire to correct his blunder, the poor geographer became hopelessly involved. Lady Helena looked at him, wondering what had deprived him of his usual coolness; but, not wishing to embarrass him further, she retired with Mary to the tent, where Mr. Olbinett was engaged in preparing breakfast.

"I deserve to be transported myself," said Paganel piteously.

"I think so," replied Glenarvan.

Ayrton and the two sailors were still trying to extricate the cart. The ox and the horse, yoked side by side, were pulling with all their strength; the traces were stretched almost to breaking, and the bows threatened to give way to the strain. Wilson and Mulready pushed at the wheels, while the quartermaster, with voice and whip, urged on the ill-matched team. But the heavy vehicle did not stir. The clay, now dry, held it as if it had been cemented.

Captain Mangles wetted the clay to make it yield, but to no purpose: the cart was immovable. Unless the vehicle was taken to pieces, they must give up the idea of getting it out of the quagmire. As tools were wanting, of course they could not undertake such a task. Ayrton, however, who seemed determined to overcome the difficulty at any cost, was about to renew his exertions, when Lord Glenarvan stopped him.

"Enough, Ayrton! enough!" said he. "We must be careful of the ox and horse that remain. If we are to continue our journey on foot, one can carry the two ladies and the other the provisions. They may do us good service yet."

"Very well, my lord," replied the quartermaster, unyoking his exhausted animals.

"Now, my friends," added Glenarvan, "let us return to camp, deliberate, consider our situation, know what our chances are, and come to a resolution."

A few minutes after, the travelers were indemnifying themselves for their sleeplessness the past night by a good breakfast, and the discussion of their affairs began.

The first question was to determine the exact position of the encampment. Paganel was charged with this duty, and fulfilled it with his customary precision.

But the heavy vehicle did not stir. The clay, now dry, held it as if it had been cemented.

"How far are we from Twofold Bay?" asked Glenarvan.

"Seventy-five miles," replied Paganel.

"And Melbourne is——?"

"Two hundred miles distant, at least."

"Very well. Our position being determined," continued Glenarvan, "what is it best to do?"

The answer was unanimous,—make for the coast without delay. Lady Helena and Mary Grant engaged to travel fifteen miles a day. The courageous women did not shrink from traversing the entire distance on foot, if necessary.

"But are we certain to find at the bay the resources that we need?" asked Glenarvan.

"Without doubt," replied Paganel. "Eden is not a new municipality; and its harbor must have frequent communication with Melbourne. I even believe that thirty-five miles from here, at the parish of Delegete, we can obtain provisions and the means of conveyance."

"And the Duncan?" asked Ayrton. "Do you not think it advisable to order her to the bay?"

"What say you, captain?" said Glenarvan.

"I do not think that there is any necessity for such a proceeding," replied the young captain, after reflection. "There will be plenty of time to send your orders to Tom Austin and summon him to the coast."

"That is quite true," added Paganel.

"Besides," continued Captain Mangles, "in four or five days we shall be at Eden."

"Four or five days!" interposed Ayrton, shaking his head; "say fifteen or twenty, captain, if you do not wish to regret your error hereafter."

DIFFICULTIES FORESEEN.

"Fifteen or twenty days to make seventy-five miles!" exclaimed Glenarvan.

"At least, my lord. You will have to cross the most difficult portion of Victoria,—plains covered with underbrush, without any cleared roads, where it has been impossible to establish stations. You will have to travel with the hatchet or the torch in your hand; and, believe me, you will not advance rapidly."

Ayrton's tone was that of a man who is thoroughly acquainted with his subject. Paganel, towards whom questioning glances were turned, nodded approvingly at the words of the quartermaster.

"I acknowledge the difficulties," said Captain Mangles, at length. "Well, in fifteen days, my lord, you can send your orders to the Duncan."

"I may add," resumed Ayrton, "that the principal obstacles do not proceed from the roughness of the journey. We must cross the Snowy, and, very probably, have to wait for the subsidence of the waters."

"Wait!" cried the captain. "Can we not find a ford?"

"I think not," replied Ayrton. "This morning I searched in vain for a practicable one. It is unusual to find a river so much swollen at this season; it is a fatality against which I am powerless."

"This Snowy River is broad, then?" remarked Lady Glenarvan.

"Broad and deep, madam," answered Ayrton; "a mile in breadth, with a strong current. A good swimmer could not cross it without danger."

"Well, then, let us build a boat!" cried Robert, who was never at fault for a plan. "We can cut down a tree, hollow it out, embark, and the thing is done."

"Good for the son of Captain Grant!" replied Paganel.

"The boy is right," continued Captain Mangles. "We shall be forced to this. I therefore think it useless to waste our time in further discussions."

"What do you think, Ayrton?" asked Glenarvan.

"I think, my lord, that if no assistance comes, in a month we shall still be detained on the banks of the Snowy."

"But have you a better plan?" inquired Captain Mangles, somewhat impatiently.

"Yes; let the Duncan leave Melbourne, and sail to the eastern coast."

"How can her presence in the bay assist us to arrive there?"

Ayrton meditated for a few moments, and then said, evasively:

"I do not wish to obtrude my opinion. What I do is for the interest of all, and I am disposed to start as soon as your lordship gives the signal for departure."

Then he folded his arms.

"That is no answer, Ayrton," continued Glenarvan. "Tell us your plan, and we will discuss it. What do you propose?"

In a calm and confident tone the quartermaster thereupon expressed himself as follows:

"I propose that we do not venture beyond the Snowy in our present destitute condition. We must wait for assistance in this very place, and this assistance can come only from the Duncan. Let us encamp here where provisions are not wanting, while one of us carries to Tom Austin the order to repair to Twofold Bay."

This unexpected proposal was received with a murmur of astonishment, and Captain Mangles took no pains to conceal his aversion.

"In the mean time," continued Ayrton, "either the waters of the Snowy will have subsided, which will enable us to find a practicable ford, or we shall have to resort to a boat, and shall have time to construct it. This, my lord, is the plan which I submit to your approval."

"If it please your lordship, I will go."

"Very well, Ayrton," replied Glenarvan; "your idea deserves to be seriously considered. Its greatest objection is the delay it will cause; but it spares us severe hardships, and perhaps real dangers. What do you think, friends?"

"Let us hear your advice, major," said Lady Helena. "During the whole discussion you have contented yourself with listening simply."

"Since you ask my opinion," answered the major, "I will give it to you very frankly. Ayrton seems to me to have spoken like a wise and prudent man, and I advocate his proposition."

This answer was rather unexpected; for hitherto MacNabb had always opposed Ayrton's ideas on this subject. Ayrton, too, was surprised, and cast a quick glance at the major. Paganel, Lady Helena, and the sailors had been favorably disposed to the quartermaster's project, and no longer hesitated after MacNabb's declaration. Glenarvan, therefore, announced that Ayrton's plan was adopted.

"And now, captain," added he, "do you not think that prudence dictates this course, and that we should encamp on the banks of the river while waiting for the means of conveyance?"

"Yes," replied Captain Mangles, "if the messenger succeeds in crossing the Snowy, which we cannot cross ourselves."

All looked at the quartermaster, who smiled with the air of a man who knows perfectly well what he is about to do.

"The messenger will not cross the river," said he.

"Ah!" cried Captain Mangles.

"He will strike the Lucknow road, which will take him direct to Melbourne."

"Two hundred miles on foot!" exclaimed the captain.

"On horseback," continued Ayrton. "There is one good horse left. It will be a journey of but four days. Add two days for the Duncan to reach the bay, twenty-four hours for the return to the encampment, and in a week the messenger will be back again with the crew."

CANDIDATES FOR OFFICE.

The major again nodded approvingly at these words, to the great astonishment of Captain Mangles. But the quartermaster's proposition had gained all the votes, and the only question was how to execute this apparently well-conceived plan.

"Now, my friends," said Glenarvan, "it remains only to choose our messenger. He will have a difficult and dangerous mission; that is certain. Who is willing to devote himself for his companions, and carry our instructions to Melbourne?"

Wilson, Mulready, Captain Mangles, Paganel, and Robert offered themselves immediately. The captain particularly insisted that this mission should be confided to him; but Ayrton, who had not yet finished, resumed the conversation, and said:

"If it please your lordship, I will go. I am acquainted with the country, and have often crossed more difficult regions. I can extricate myself where another would fail. I therefore claim, for the common welfare, the right to go to Melbourne. One word will place me on a good footing with your mate, and in six days I engage to bring the Duncan to Twofold Bay."

"Well said!" replied Glenarvan. "You are a brave and intelligent man, Ayrton, and will succeed."

The quartermaster was evidently more capable than any one else of fulfilling this difficult mission. Captain Mangles raised one final objection, that Ayrton's presence was necessary to enable them to find traces of the Brittania or Captain Grant; but the major observed that they should remain encamped on the banks of the Snowy till the messenger's return, that it was not proposed to resume the search without him, and that consequently his absence could be in no way prejudicial to their interests.

"Well then, Ayrton, start," said Glenarvan. "Make haste, and return to the encampment by way of Eden."

A gleam of satisfaction seemed to light up the eyes of the quartermaster. He turned his head to one side, though not so quickly but that Captain Mangles had intercepted his glance, and instinctively felt his suspicions increased.

The quartermaster made his preparations for departure, aided by the two sailors, one of whom attended to his horse, and the other to his provisions. Meantime Glenarvan wrote the letter designed for Tom Austin.

He ordered the mate of the Duncan to repair without delay to Twofold Bay, and recommended the quartermaster to him as a man in whom he could place entire confidence. As soon as he arrived at the bay, he was to send a detachment of sailors under the command of Ayrton.

He had just reached this part of his letter, when the major, who had been looking over his shoulder, asked him, in a singular tone, how he wrote the word Ayrton.

"As it is pronounced," replied Glenarvan.

"That is a mistake," said the major coolly. "It is pronounced Ayrton, but it is written 'Ben Joyce'!"

CHAPTER XLI

THE PLOT UNVEILED.

The sound of the name of Ben Joyce fell upon the party like a thunderbolt. Ayrton suddenly sprang to his feet. In his hand was a revolver. A report was heard; and Glenarvan fell, struck by a bullet.

Before Captain Mangles and the sailors recovered from the surprise into which this unexpected turn of affairs had thrown them, the audacious convict had escaped, and joined his band, scattered along the edge of the wood of gum-trees.

The tent did not offer a sufficient shelter against the bullets, and it was clearly necessary to beat a retreat. Glenarvan, who was but slightly injured, had risen.

"To the cart! to the cart!" cried Captain Mangles, as he hurried on Lady Helena and Mary Grant, who were soon in safety behind its stout sides.

A report was heard; and Glenarvan fell, struck by a bullet.

The captain, the major, Paganel, and the sailors then seized their rifles, and stood ready to repel the convicts. Glenarvan and Robert had joined the ladies, while Olbinett hastened to the common defence.

These events had transpired with the rapidity of lightning. Captain Mangles attentively watched the edge of the wood; but the reports suddenly ceased on the arrival of Ben Joyce, and a profound silence succeeded the noisy fusillade. A few wreaths of white smoke were still curling up between the branches of the gum-trees, but the tall tufts of gastrolobium were motionless and all signs of attack had disappeared.

The major and Captain Mangles extended their examinations as far as the great trees. The place was abandoned. Numerous footprints were seen, and a few half-burnt cartridges smoked on the ground. The major, like a prudent man, extinguished them, for a spark was enough to kindle a formidable conflagration in this forest of dry trees.

"The convicts have disappeared," said Captain Mangles.

"Yes," replied the major; "and this disappearance alarms me. I should prefer to meet them face to face. It is better to encounter a tiger in the open plain than a serpent in the grass. Let us search these bushes around the cart."

UNRAVELINGS.

The major and captain scoured the surrounding country. But from the edge of the wood to the banks of the Snowy they did not meet with a single convict. Ben Joyce's band seemed to have flown away, like a flock of mischievous birds. This disappearance was too strange to inspire a perfect security. They therefore resolved to keep on the watch. The cart, which was a really immovable fortress, became the centre of the encampment, and two men kept guard, relieving each other every hour.

Lady Helena and Mary Grant's first care had been to dress Glenarvan's wound. At the very moment that her husband fell, from Ben Joyce's bullet, in her terror she had rushed towards him. Then, controlling her emotion, this courageous woman had assisted Glenarvan to the cart. Here the shoulder of the wounded man was laid bare, and the major perceived that the ball had lacerated the flesh, causing no other injury. Neither bones nor large muscles seemed affected. The wound bled considerably, but Glenarvan, by moving the fingers of his hand and fore-arm, encouraged his friends to expect a favorable result. When his wound was dressed, he no longer desired any attention, and explanations followed. The travelers, except Wilson and Mulready, who were keeping guard outside, had taken seats as well as possible in the cart, and the major was requested to speak.

Before beginning his story, he informed Lady Helena of the escape of a band of convicts from Perth, their appearance in the province of Victoria, and their complicity in the railway disaster. He gave her the number of the *Australian and New Zealand Gazette* purchased at Seymour, and added that the police had set a price on the head of Ben Joyce, a formidable bandit, whom eighteen months of crime had given a wide-spread notoriety.

But how had MacNabb recognized this Ben Joyce in the quartermaster Ayrton? Here was the mystery that all wished to solve; and the major explained.

Since the day of his meeting with Ayrton he had suspected him. Two or three almost insignificant circumstances, a glance exchanged between the quartermaster and the farrier at Wimerra River, Ayrton's hesitation to pass through the towns and villages, his strong wish to order the Duncan to the coast, the strange death of the animals confided to his care, and, finally, a want of frankness in his actions,—all these facts, gradually noticed, had roused the major's suspicions.

However, he could form no direct accusation until the events that had transpired the preceding night. Gliding between the tall clumps of shrubbery, as was related in the previous chapter, he approached near the suspicious shadows that had attracted his attention half a mile from the encampment. The phosphorescent plants cast their pale rays through the darkness. Three men were examining some tracks on the ground, and among them he recognized the farrier of Black Point Station.

"Here they are," said one.

"Yes," replied another, "here is the trefoil of the hoofs again."

"It has been like this since leaving the Wimerra."

"All the horses are dead."

"The poison is not far away."

"There is enough here to settle an entire troop of cavalry. This gastrolobium is a useful plant."

"Then they were silent," added MacNabb, "and departed. I wanted to know more: I followed them. The conversation soon began again. 'A cunning man, this Ben Joyce,' said the farrier; 'a famous quartermaster, with his invented shipwreck. If his plan succeeds, it will be a stroke of fortune. Devilish Ayrton! Call him Ben Joyce, for he has well earned his name.' These rascals then left the wood of gum-trees. I knew what I wished, and returned to the encampment with the certainty that all the convicts in Australia are not reformed, in spite of Paganel's arguments."

"Then," said Glenarvan, whose face was pale with anger, "Ayrton has brought us here to rob and assassinate us?"

"Yes," replied the major.

"And, since leaving the Wimerra, his band has followed and watched us, waiting for a favorable opportunity?"

FROM DEPTH TO DEPTH.

"Yes."

"But this wretch is not, then, a sailor of the Britannia? He has stolen his name and contract?"

All eyes were turned towards MacNabb, who must have considered this matter.

"These," replied he, in his calm voice, "are the proofs that can be derived from this obscure state of affairs. In my opinion this man's real name is Ayrton. Ben Joyce is his fighting title. It is certain that he knows Harry Grant, and has been quartermaster on board the Britannia. These facts, proved already by the precise details given by Ayrton, are still further corroborated by the conversation of the convicts that I have related. Let us not, therefore, be led astray by vain conjectures, but only be certain that Ayrton is Ben Joyce, a sailor of the Britannia, now chief of a band of convicts."

The major's explanation was accepted as conclusive.

"Now," replied Glenarvan, "will you tell me how and why Harry Grant's quartermaster is in Australia?"

"How, I do not know," said MacNabb; "and the police declare they know no more than I on the subject. Why, it is also impossible for me to say. Here is a mystery that the future will explain."

"The police do not even know the identity of Ayrton and Ben Joyce," said Captain Mangles.

"You are right, John," replied the major; "and such information would be likely to facilitate their search."

"This unfortunate, then," remarked Lady Helena, "intruded into O'Moore's farm with a criminal intention?"

"There is no doubt of it," continued MacNabb. "He was meditating some hostile attack upon the Irishman, when a better opportunity was offered. Chance threw us in his way. He heard Glenarvan's story of the shipwreck, and, like a bold man, he promptly decided to take part in the expedition. At the Wimerra he communicated with one of his friends, the farrier of Black Point, and thus left distinguishable traces of our course. His band followed us. A poisonous plant enabled him to gradually kill our oxen and horses. Then, at the proper moment, he entangled us in the marshes of the Snowy, and surrendered us to the convicts he commanded."

Everything possible had been said concerning Ben Joyce. His past had just been reviewed by the major, and the wretch appeared as he was,—a bold and formidable criminal. His intentions had been clearly proved, and required, on the part of Glenarvan, extreme vigilance. Fortunately, there was less to fear from the detected bandit than the secret traitor.

But one serious fact appeared from this explanation. No one had yet thought of it; only Mary Grant, disregarding the past, looked forward to the future. Captain Mangles first saw her pale and disconsolate. He understood what was passing in her mind.

"Miss Mary!" cried he, "you are weeping!"

"What is the matter, my child?" asked Lady Helena.

"My father, madam, my father!" replied the young girl.

She could not continue. But a sudden revelation dawned on the mind of each. They comprehended Mary's grief, why the tears flowed from her eyes, why the name of her father rose to her lips.

The discovery of Ayrton's treachery destroyed all hope. The convict, to entice Glenarvan on, had invented a shipwreck. In their conversation, overheard by MacNabb, his accomplices had clearly confessed it. The Britannia had never been wrecked on the reefs of Twofold Bay! Harry Grant had never set foot on the Australian continent!

For the second time an erroneous interpretation of the document had set the searchers of the Britannia on a false trail. All, in the face of this situation and the grief of the two children, preserved a mournful silence. Who then could have found words of hope? Robert wept in his sister's arms. Paganel murmured, in a voice of despair,—

CALM AND CLOUDINESS.

"Ah, unlucky document! You can boast of having sorely puzzled the brains of a dozen brave people!"

And the worthy geographer was fairly furious against himself, and frantically beat his forehead.

In the mean time Glenarvan had joined Mulready and Wilson, who were on guard without. A deep silence reigned on the plain lying between the wood and the river. Heavy clouds covered the vault of the sky. In this deadened and torpid atmosphere the least sound would have been clearly transmitted; but nothing was heard. Ben Joyce and his band must have fled to a considerable distance; for flocks of birds that sported on the low branches of the trees, several kangaroos peacefully browsing on the young shoots, and a pair of cassowaries, whose unsuspecting heads were thrust between the tall bushes, proved that the presence of man did not disturb these peaceful solitudes.

"You have not seen nor heard anything for an hour?" inquired Glenarvan of the two sailors.

"Nothing, my lord," replied Wilson. "The convicts must be several miles away."

"They cannot have been in sufficient force to attack us," added Mulready. "This Ben Joyce probably intended to recruit some bandits, like himself, among the bushrangers that wander at the foot of the Alps."

"Very likely, Mulready," replied Glenarvan. "These rascals are cowards. They know we are well armed, and are perhaps waiting for darkness to commence their attack. We must redouble our vigilance at nightfall. If we could only leave this marshy plain and pursue our journey towards the coast! But the swollen waters of the river bar our progress. I would pay its weight in gold for a raft that would transport us to the other side!"

"Why," said Wilson, "does not your lordship give us the order to construct this raft? There is plenty of wood."

"No, Wilson," answered Glenarvan; "this Snowy is not a river, it is an impassable torrent."

A pair of cassowaries proved that the presence of man did not disturb these peaceful solitudes.

READINESS FOR SERVICE.

At this moment Captain Mangles, the major, and Paganel joined Glenarvan. They had been to examine the Snowy. The waters, swollen by the recent rains, had risen a foot above low-water mark, and formed an impetuous current. It was impossible to venture upon this roaring deluge, these rushing floods, broken into a thousand eddies by the depressions of the river-bed. Captain Mangles declared that the passage was impracticable.

"But," added he, "we ought not to remain here without making any attempt. What we wished to do before Ayrton's treason is still more necessary now."

"What do you say, captain?" asked Glenarvan.

"I say that assistance is needed; and since we cannot go to Twofold Bay, we must go to Melbourne. One horse is left. Let your lordship give him to me, and I will go."

"But it is a perilous venture, John," said Glenarvan. "Aside from the dangers of this journey of two hundred miles across an unknown country, all the roads may be guarded by Ben Joyce's accomplices."

"I know it, my lord; but I know, too, that our situation cannot be prolonged. Ayrton only asked eight days' absence to bring back the crew of the Duncan. But I will return in six days to the banks of the Snowy. What are your lordship's orders?"

"Before Glenarvan speaks," said Paganel, "I must make a remark. It is well that one of us should go to Melbourne, but not that these dangers should be incurred by Captain Mangles. He is the captain of the Duncan, and must not, therefore, expose himself. Allow me to go in his place."

"Well said," replied the major; "but why should it be you, Paganel?"

"Are we not here?" cried Wilson and Mulready.

"And do you believe," continued MacNabb, "that I am afraid to make a journey of two hundred miles on horseback?"

"My friends," said Glenarvan, "if one of us is to go to Melbourne, let fate decide. Paganel, write our names——"

"Not yours at least, my lord," insisted Captain Mangles.

"And why?" asked Glenarvan.

"Separate you from Lady Helena, when your wound is not yet healed?"

"Glenarvan," interposed Paganel, "you cannot leave the encampment."

"No," resumed the major; "your place is here. Edward, you must not go."

"There are dangers to incur," replied Glenarvan; "and I will not leave my part to others. Write, Paganel; let my name be mingled with those of my companions, and Heaven grant that it may be the first drawn."

All yielded to this wish; and Glenarvan's name was added to the others. They then proceeded to draw, and the lot fell upon Mulready. The brave sailor uttered a cry of joy.

"My lord, I am ready to go," said he.

Glenarvan clasped his hand, and then turned towards the cart, leaving the major and Captain Mangles to guard the encampment. Lady Helena was at once informed of the decision taken to send a messenger to Melbourne, and of the result of the drawing by lot. She spoke words to Mulready that went to the heart of that noble sailor. They knew that he was brave, intelligent, hardy, and persevering. The lot could not have fallen better.

It was decided that Mulready should depart at eight o'clock, after the short twilight. Wilson charged himself with getting the horse ready. He took the precaution to change the tell-tale shoe that he wore on his left foot, and to replace it by one belonging to the horses that had died in the night. The convicts could not now track Mulready, or follow him, unless mounted.

ANOTHER DISTRACTION.

While Wilson was occupied with these arrangements, Glenarvan was preparing the letter designed for Tom Austin; but his wounded arm disabled him, and he asked Paganel to write for him. The geographer, who seemed absorbed in one idea, was oblivious to what was passing around him. It must be confessed that Paganel, in all this succession of sad misfortunes, thought only of his false interpretation of the document. He turned the words about in every way to draw from them a new meaning, and remained wrapt in these meditations. Thus he did not hear Glenarvan's request, and the latter was forced to repeat it.

"Very well," replied Paganel; "I am ready."

So saying, he mechanically produced his note-book. He tore out a blank page, and then, with his pencil in his hand, made ready to write. Glenarvan began to dictate the following instructions:

"Order for Tom Austin to put to sea, and bring the Duncan——"

Paganel had just finished this last word when his eyes fell upon the number of the *Australian and New Zealand Gazette* that lay upon the ground. The paper, being folded, only allowed him to see the two last syllables of its title. His pencil stopped, and he seemed to completely forget Glenarvan and his letter.

"Well, Paganel?" said Glenarvan.

"Ah!" continued the geographer, uttering a cry.

"What is the matter?" asked the major.

"Nothing! nothing!" replied Paganel. Then, in a lower tone, he repeated: "Aland! aland! aland!"

He had risen; he had seized the paper. He shook it, seeking to repress words ready to escape his lips. Lady Helena, Mary, Robert, and Glenarvan gazed at him without understanding this inexplicable agitation. Paganel was like a man whom a sudden frenzy has seized. But this state of nervous excitation did not last. He gradually grew calm. The joy that gleamed in his eyes died away, and, resuming his place, he said, in a quiet tone:

"When you wish, my lord, I am at your disposal."

Glenarvan continued the dictation of his letter, which was distinctly worded as follows:

"Order for Tom Austin to put to sea, and bring the Duncan to the eastern coast of Australia."

"Australia?" cried Paganel. "Ah, yes, Australia!"

The letter was now finished, and presented to Glenarvan for his signature, who, although affected by his recent wound, acquitted himself as well as possible of this formality. The note was then folded and sealed, while Paganel, with a hand that still trembled from excitement, wrote the following address:

"Tom Austin,
"Mate of the Yacht Duncan,
"Melbourne."

Thereupon he left the cart, gesticulating, and repeating these incomprehensible words:

"Aland! aland! Zealand!"

CHAPTER XLII

FOUR DAYS OF ANGUISH.

The rest of the day passed without any other incident. Everything was ready for the departure of Mulready, who was happy to give his master this proof of his devotion.

Paganel had regained his coolness and accustomed manners. His look still indicated an uneasy state of mind, but he appeared decided to keep his secret. He had doubtless strong reasons for acting thus, for the major overheard him repeating these words, like a man who is struggling with himself:

"No, no! they would not believe me! And, besides what use is it? It is too late!"

This resolution taken, he occupied himself with giving Mulready the necessary directions for reaching Melbourne, and, with the map before him, marked out his course. All the trails of the prairie converged towards the Lucknow road, which, after extending straight southward to the coast, suddenly turned in the direction towards Melbourne. It was simply necessary to follow this, and not attempt to cross the unknown country. Mulready could not, therefore, go astray. As for dangers, they lay only a few miles beyond the encampment, where Ben Joyce and his band were probably lying in wait. This point once passed, Mulready was sure he could easily distance the convicts and accomplish his important mission.

At six o'clock supper was eaten in common. A heavy rain was falling. The tent no longer afforded sufficient shelter, and each had taken refuge in the cart, which was a safe retreat. The sticky clay held it in its place as firm as a fort on its foundations. The fire-arms consisted of seven rifles and seven revolvers, and thus enabled them to sustain a long siege, for neither ammunition nor provisions were wanting. In six days the Duncan would anchor in Twofold Bay. Twenty-four hours after, her crew would reach the opposite bank of the river; and, if the passage was not then practicable, at least the convicts would be compelled to retreat before superior forces. But, first of all, it was necessary that Mulready should succeed in his enterprise.

At eight o'clock the darkness became intense. It was the time to start. The horse was brought out. His feet had been muffled; as an additional precaution, and made no sound. The animal seemed fatigued, but upon his surefootedness and endurance depended the safety of all. The major advised the sailor to spare his beast as soon as he was out of reach of the convicts. It was better to lose half a day and reach his destination safely. Captain Mangles gave him a revolver, which he had loaded with the greatest care. Mulready mounted.

"Adieu, my lord," said he, in a calm voice, and soon disappeared by a path along the edge of the wood.

A GLOOMY PROSPECT.

"Here is the letter which you are to take to Tom Austin," said Glenarvan. "Let him not lose an hour, but start for Twofold Bay; and, if he does not find us there, if we have not crossed the river, let him come to us without delay. Now go, my brave sailor, and may God guide you!"

Glenarvan, Lady Helena, Mary Grant, all clasped Mulready's hand. This departure on a dark and stormy night, over a road beset with dangers, across the unknown stretches of a desert, would have appalled a heart less courageous than that of the sailor.

"Adieu, my lord," said he, in a calm voice, and soon disappeared by a path along the edge of the wood.

At that moment the tempest redoubled its violence. The lofty branches of the trees shook dismally in the darkness. You could hear the fall of the dry twigs on the drenched earth. More than one giant tree, whose sap was gone, but which had stood till then, fell during this terrible hurricane. The wind roared amid the cracking of the trees and mingled its mournful sounds with the rushing of the river. The heavy clouds that chased across the sky poured forth masses of mist, while a dismal darkness increased still more the horrors of the night.

The travelers, after Mulready's departure, ensconced themselves in the cart. Lady Helena, Mary Grant, Glenarvan, and Paganel occupied the front compartment, which had been made water-tight. In the rear part Olbinett, Wilson, and Robert had found a sufficient shelter, while the major and Captain Mangles were on guard without. This precaution was necessary, for an attack by the convicts was easy and possible.

These two faithful guardians, therefore, took turns and philosophically received the blasts that blew sharply in their faces. They strove to pierce with their eyes the shades so favorable for an ambuscade, for the ear could detect nothing amid the din of the storm, the roaring of the wind, the rattling of the branches, the fall of trees, and the rushing of the impetuous waters.

In the mean time there were several lulls in the fury of the tempest, the wind ceasing as if to take breath. The river only moaned adown the motionless reeds and the black curtain of the gum-trees, and the silence seemed more profound during these momentary rests. The major and Captain Mangles now listened attentively. During one of these intervals a sharp whistle reached their ears.

The captain hastened to the major. "Did you hear anything?" asked he.

"Yes," replied MacNabb. "Was it a man or an animal?"

"A man," said the captain.

They both listened again. The mysterious whistle was suddenly repeated, and something like a report followed it, but almost inaudibly, for the storm just then broke forth with renewed violence. They could not hear themselves talk, and took their stations to leeward of the cart.

At this moment the leathern curtains were raised, and Glenarvan joined his two companions. He likewise had heard the suspicious whistle, and the report.

"From what direction?" he asked.

"Yonder," said the captain, pointing to the dark line, towards which Mulready had gone.

"How far?"

"The wind carried it," was the reply. "It must be three miles distant at least."

"Let us go!" said Glenarvan, throwing his rifle over his shoulder.

"No," interposed the major; "it is a decoy to entice us away from the cart."

"But if Mulready has fallen beneath the shots of these wretches!" continued Glenarvan, seizing MacNabb's hand.

"We shall know to-morrow," replied the latter, firmly determined to prevent Glenarvan from committing a useless imprudence.

A CRY IN THE NIGHT.

"You cannot leave the encampment, my lord," said Captain Mangles; "I will go alone."

"No!" cried MacNabb, with energy. "Will you have us, then, perish singly, diminish our numbers, and be left to the mercy of these criminals? If Mulready has been their victim, it is a calamity that we must not repeat a second time. He has gone according to lot. If the lot had chosen me, I should have gone like him, but should neither have asked nor expected any assistance."

In restraining Glenarvan and Captain Mangles the major was right from every point of view. To attempt to reach the sailor, to go on such a dark night to meet the convicts, ambuscaded in some coppice, was useless madness. Glenarvan's little party did not number enough men to sacrifice any more.

However, Glenarvan seemed unwilling to yield to these reasons. His hand played nervously with his rifle. He walked to and fro around the cart; he listened to the least sound; he strove to pierce the dismal obscurity. The thought that one of his friends was mortally wounded, helplessly abandoned, calling in vain upon those for whose sake he had sacrificed himself, tortured him. MacNabb feared that he should not succeed in restraining him, that Glenarvan, carried away by his feelings, would cast himself into the power of Ben Joyce.

"Edward," said he, "be calm; listen to a friend; think of Lady Helena, Mary Grant, all who remain! Besides, where will you go? Where find Mulready? He was attacked two miles distant at least. On what road? What path take?"

At this very moment, as if in answer to the major, a cry of distress was heard.

"Listen!" said Glenarvan.

The cry came from the very direction whence the report had sounded, but less than a quarter of a mile distant. Glenarvan, pushing back MacNabb, was advancing along the path, when, not far from the cart, these words were uttered:

"Help! help!"

It was a plaintive and despairing voice. Captain Mangles and the major rushed towards it. In a few moments they perceived, on the edge of the coppice, a human form that was dragging itself along and groaning piteously. It was Mulready, wounded and half dead. When his companions raised him, they felt their hands dabbling in blood. The rain now increased, and the wind howled through the branches of the dead trees. In the midst of these terrific gusts, Glenarvan, the major, and the captain bore the body of Mulready.

On arriving at the cart, Paganel, Robert, Wilson, and Olbinett came out, and Lady Helena gave up her room to the poor sailor. The major took off Mulready's vest, wet with blood and rain. He discovered the wound. It was a poniard stab, which the unfortunate had received in his right side.

MacNabb dressed it skillfully. Whether the weapon had reached the vital parts, he could not say. A stream of bright-red blood spurted forth, while the paleness and the swoon of the wounded man proved that he had been seriously injured. The major accordingly placed upon the opening of the wound, after first washing it with fresh water, a thick wad of tinder, and then a few layers of lint, confined by a bandage, and thus succeeded in stopping the hemorrhage. The patient was then laid on his side, his head and breast raised, and Lady Helena gave him a refreshing draught.

At the end of a quarter of an hour, the wounded man, who had been motionless till then, made a movement. His eyes half opened, his lips murmured disconnected words, and the major, putting down his ear, heard him say:

"My lord—the letter—Ben Joyce——"

A DAY OF DOUBT.

The major repeated these words, and glanced at his companions. What did Mulready mean? Ben Joyce had attacked the sailor, but why? Was it not simply for the purpose of preventing him from reaching the Duncan? This letter—Glenarvan examined the sailor's pockets. The letter addressed to Tom Austin was gone.

The night passed in anxiety and anguish. They feared every moment that the wounded man would die. A burning fever consumed him. Lady Helena and Mary Grant, as though his sisters, did not leave him; never was patient better nursed, or by more tender hands.

Day appeared. The rain had ceased. Heavy clouds still rolled along the vault of the sky, and the earth was strewn with the fragments of branches. The clay, soaked by floods of water, had yielded; and the sides of the cart became unsteady, but sank no deeper.

Captain Mangles, Paganel, and Glenarvan took a tour of exploration around the camp. They traversed the path still marked with blood, but found no trace of Ben Joyce or his band. They went to the place where the attack had been made. Here two corpses lay on the ground, shot by Mulready. One was the farrier of Black Point. His face, which had mortified, was a horrible sight.

Glenarvan did not pursue his investigations farther, prudence forbidding. He therefore returned to the cart, much alarmed by the seriousness of the situation.

"We cannot think of sending another messenger to Melbourne," said he.

"But we must," replied Captain Mangles; "and I will make the attempt, since my sailor has failed."

"No, John. You have not even a horse to carry you these two hundred miles."

Indeed, Mulready's horse, the only one that remained, had not reappeared. Had he fallen beneath the shots of the murderers? Was he running wild over the desert? Had the convicts captured him?

In the midst of these terrific gusts, Glenarvan, the major, and the captain bore the body of Mulready.

RESOLUTION, AND RECOVERY.

"Whatever happens," continued Glenarvan, "we will separate no more. Let us wait eight or fifteen days, till the waters of the river resume their natural level. We will then reach Twofold Bay by short journeys, and from there send to the Duncan by a surer way the order to sail for the coast."

"This is the only feasible plan," replied Paganel.

"Well, then, my friends," resumed Glenarvan, "no more separation! A man risks too much to venture alone across this desert, infested with bandits. And now may God save our poor sailor and protect ourselves!"

Glenarvan was right in both resolves, first to forbid any single attempt to cross the plains, and next to wait patiently on the banks of the river for a practicable passage. Scarcely thirty-five miles separated them from Delegete, the first frontier town of New South Wales, where they would find means of reaching Twofold Bay. From this point he could telegraph his orders to the Duncan.

These measures were wise, but they had been adopted rather tardily. If they had not sent Mulready with the letter, what misfortunes would have been avoided, not to speak of the attack upon the sailor!

On arriving at the camp, Glenarvan found his companions less anxious; they seemed to have regained hope.

"He is better!" cried Robert, running to meet him.

"Mulready?"

"Yes, Edward," replied Lady Helena. "A reaction has taken place. The major is more encouraged. Our sailor will live."

"Where is MacNabb?" asked Glenarvan.

"With him. Mulready wished to speak with him. We must not disturb them."

Indeed, within an hour the wounded man had rallied from his swoon, and the fever had diminished. But the sailor's first care, on recovering memory and speech was to ask for Lord Glenarvan, or, in his absence, the major MacNabb, seeing him so feeble, would have forbidden all conversation; but Mulready insisted with such energy that he was forced to yield. The interview had already lasted some time, and they were only waiting for the major's report.

Soon the curtains of the cart moved, and he appeared. He joined his friends at the foot of a gum-tree. His face, usually so calm, betokened a serious anxiety. When his eyes encountered Lady Helena and the young girl, they expressed a deep sadness. Glenarvan questioned him, and learned what the sailor had related.

On leaving the encampment, Mulready had followed one of the paths indicated by Paganel. He hastened, as much at least as the darkness of the night permitted him. According to his estimate, he had traveled a distance of about two miles, when several men—five, he thought—sprang to his horse's head. The animal reared. Mulready seized his revolver and fired. He thought that two of his assailants fell. By the flash of the report, he recognized Ben Joyce, but that was all. He had not time to fully discharge his weapon. A violent blow was struck upon his right side, which brought him to the ground. However, he had not yet lost consciousness. The assassins believed him dead. He felt them search him. Then a conversation ensued. "I have the letter," said one of them. "Give it to me," replied Ben Joyce; "and now the Duncan is ours!"

At this point in the story Glenarvan could not restrain a cry.

MacNabb continued:

A HOPELESS CHANCE.

"'Now, you others,' said Ben Joyce, 'catch the horse. In two days I shall be on board the Duncan, and in six at Twofold Bay. There is the place of meeting. The lord's party will be still fast in the marshes of the Snowy. Cross the river at Kemple Pier bridge, go to the coast, and wait for me. I will find means to bring you on board. With the crew once at sea, and a vessel like the Duncan, we shall be masters of the Indian Ocean.' 'Hurrah for Ben Joyce!' cried the convicts. Mulready's horse was then led up, and Ben Joyce disappeared at a gallop on the Lucknow road, while the band proceeded southeastward to the Snowy River. Mulready, although severely wounded, had strength to drag himself within two hundred paces of the encampment, where we picked him up almost dead. This," added MacNabb, "is Mulready's sad story. You understand now why the courageous sailor wished so much to speak."

This revelation terrified all.

"Pirates! pirates!" cried Glenarvan. "My crew massacred, my Duncan in the hands of these bandits!"

"Yes, for Ben Joyce will surprise the vessel," replied the major, "and then——"

"Well, we must reach the coast before these wretches," said Paganel.

"But how cross the Snowy?" asked Wilson.

"Like them," answered Glenarvan. "They will cross Kemple Pier bridge, and we will do the same."

"But what will become of Mulready?" inquired Lady Helena.

"We will take turns in carrying him. Shall I give up my defenceless crew to Ben Joyce's band?"

The plan of crossing Kemple Pier bridge was practicable, but perilous. The convicts might locate themselves at this point to defend it. It would be at least thirty against seven! But there are moments when we do not think of these things, when we must advance at all hazards.

"My lord," said Captain Mangles, at length, "before risking our last chance, before venturing towards the bridge, it is prudent to reconnoitre it first. I will undertake this."

"I will accompany you, captain," replied Paganel.

The animal reared. Mulready seized his revolver and fired.

THE BURNED BRIDGE.

This proposal was accepted, and the captain and Paganel prepared to start immediately. They were to follow along the bank of the river till they came to the place indicated by Ben Joyce, and keep out of sight of the convicts, who were probably lying in wait. These two courageous men accordingly, well furnished with arms and provisions, set out, and soon disappeared among the tall rushes of the river.

All day the little party waited for them. At evening they had not yet returned, and great fears were entertained. At last, about eleven o'clock, Wilson announced their approach. They arrived, worn out with the fatigues of a six-mile journey.

"The bridge? Is it there?" asked Glenarvan, rushing to meet them.

"Yes, a bridge of rushes," said Captain Mangles. "The convicts passed, it is true, but——"

"But what?" cried Glenarvan, who foresaw a new calamity.

"They burned it after their passage," replied Paganel.

CHAPTER XLIII

HELPLESS AND HOPELESS.

It was not the time to despair, but to act. If Kemple Pier bridge was destroyed, they must cross the Snowy at all events, and reach Twofold Bay before Ben Joyce's band. They lost no time, therefore, in vain words; but the next day Captain Mangles and Glenarvan went to examine the river, preparatory to a passage.

The tumultuous waters, swollen by the rains, had not subsided. They whirled along with indescribable fury. It was certain death to brave this torrent. Glenarvan, with folded arms and lowered head, stood motionless.

"Do you wish me to try to swim to the opposite bank?" asked Captain Mangles.

"No, John," replied Glenarvan, seizing the bold young man by the hand; "let us wait."

They both returned to the encampment. The day was passed in the most lively anxiety. Ten times did Glenarvan return to the river. He sought to contrive some bold plan of crossing it, but in vain. It would not have been more impassable if a torrent of lava had flowed between its banks.

During these long hours of delay, Lady Helena, with the major's assistance, bestowed upon Mulready the most skillful care. The sailor felt that he was returning to life. MacNabb ventured to affirm that no vital organ had been injured, the loss of blood sufficiently explained the patient's weakness. Thus, as soon as his wound was healed and the hemorrhage stopped, only time and rest were needed for his complete restoration. Lady Helena had insisted upon his occupying her end of the cart. Mulready felt greatly honored. His greatest anxiety was in the thought that his condition might delay Glenarvan, and he forced them to promise that they would leave him at the camp in charge of Wilson, as soon as the river became fordable.

Unfortunately, this was not possible, either that day or the next. At seeing himself thus detained, Glenarvan despaired. Lady Helena and the major tried in vain to pacify and exhort him to patience. Patience! when, at that moment perhaps, Ben Joyce was going on board the yacht, when the Duncan was weighing anchor and steaming towards that fatal coast, to which every hour brought her nearer!

ALMOST DESPAIRING.

Captain Mangles felt at heart all Glenarvan's anguish, and, as he wished to overcome the difficulty at all hazards, he constructed a canoe in the Australian fashion, with large pieces of the bark of the gum-trees. These slabs, which were very light, were held together by wooden cross-bars, and formed a very frail craft.

The captain and the sailor tried the canoe. All that skill, strength, or courage could do they did. But scarcely were they in the current, when they capsized and narrowly escaped with their lives. The boat was drawn into the eddies and disappeared. Captain Mangles and Wilson had not advanced ten yards into the river, which was swollen by the rains and melting snows till it was now a mile in breadth.

Two days were wasted in this way. The major and Glenarvan went five miles up stream without finding a practicable ford. Everywhere was the same impetuosity, the same tumultuous rush of water; all the southern slopes of the mountains had poured their liquid torrents into this single stream. They were forced, therefore, to give up any hope of saving the Duncan. Five days had passed since Ben Joyce's departure, the yacht was probably that very moment at the coast, in the hands of the convicts.

However, this state of things could not last long. Indeed, on the morning of the third day, Paganel perceived that the waters were beginning to subside. He reported to Glenarvan the result of his observations.

"What does it matter now?" replied Glenarvan; "it is too late!"

"That is no reason for prolonging our stay at the encampment," replied the major.

"Certainly not," said Captain Mangles; "to-morrow, perhaps, it will be possible to cross."

"But will that save my unfortunate crew?" cried Glenarvan.

"Listen to me, my lord," continued Captain Mangles. "I know Tom Austin. He was to execute your orders, and start as soon as his departure was possible. Who knows whether the Duncan was ready, or her injuries repaired, on the arrival of Ben Joyce at Melbourne? Supposing the yacht could not put to sea, and suffered one or two days of delay?"

"You are right, John," replied Glenarvan. "We must reach Twofold Bay. We are only thirty-five miles from Delegete."

"Yes," said Paganel, "and in that town we shall find rapid means of conveyance. Who knows whether we shall not arrive in time to prevent this calamity?"

"Let us start!" cried Glenarvan.

Captain Mangles and Wilson at once occupied themselves in constructing a raft of large dimensions. Experience had proved that pieces of bark could not resist the violence of the torrent. The captain cut down several gum-trees, of which he made a rude but substantial raft. It was a tedious task, and that day ended before the work was completed; but the next day it was finished.

The waters had now considerably subsided. The torrent had become a river again, with a rapid current. However, with proper management, the captain hoped to reach the opposite bank.

At noon they put on board as much provisions as each could carry for two days' travel. The rest was abandoned with the cart and the tent. Mulready was well enough to be moved; he was recovering rapidly.

Each took his place on the raft, which was moored to the bank. Captain Mangles had arranged on the starboard side, and confided to Wilson, a kind of oar to sustain the raft against the current, and prevent its drifting. As for himself, he stood at the stern, and steered by means of a clumsy rudder. Lady Helena and Mary Grant occupied the centre of the raft near Mulready. Glenarvan, the major, Paganel, and Robert surrounded them, ready to lend assistance.

"Are we ready, Wilson?" asked Captain Mangles.

"Yes, captain," replied the sailor, seizing his oar with a firm hand.

However, the raft was entangled in the midst of the river, half a mile below where they started.

"Attention, and bear up against the current."

Captain Mangles unmoored the raft, and with one push launched it into the current of the river. All went well for some time, and Wilson resisted the leeway. But soon the craft was drawn into the eddies, and turned round and round, so that neither oar nor rudder could keep it in a straight course. In spite of their efforts, they were soon placed in a position where it was impossible to use the oars.

They were forced to be passive; there was no means of preventing this gyratory motion. They were whirled about with a giddy rapidity, and sent out of their course. The captain, with pale face and set teeth, stood and gazed at the eddying water.

However, the raft was entangled in the midst of the river, half a mile below where they started. The current here was very strong, and, as it broke the eddies, it lessened the whirling motion. The captain and Wilson resumed their oars, and succeeded in propelling the craft in an oblique direction. In this way they approached nearer the left bank, and were only a few yards distant, when Wilson's oar broke. The raft, no longer sustained against the current, was carried down stream. The captain endeavored to prevent it, at the risk of breaking his rudder, and Wilson with bleeding hands assisted him.

At last they succeeded, and the raft, after a voyage of more than half an hour, ran upon the steeply-sloping bank. The shock was violent; the timbers were thrown apart, the ropes broken, and the foaming water came through. The travelers had only time to cling to the bushes that hung over the stream. They extricated Mulready and the two ladies, who were half drenched. In short, everybody was saved; but the greater part of the provisions and arms, except the major's rifle, were swept away with the fragments of the raft.

A WEARY PILGRIMAGE.

The river was crossed, but the little party were without resources, thirty-five miles from Delegete, in the midst of these untrodden deserts. They resolved to start without delay. Mulready saw that he would cause trouble, and desired to remain behind, even alone, and wait for aid from Delegete. But Glenarvan refused. He could not reach the town before three days. If the Duncan had left Melbourne several days before, what mattered a delay of a few hours?

"No, my friend," said he; "I will not abandon any one. We will make a litter, and take turns in carrying you."

The litter was made of branches covered with leaves, and upon this Mulready was placed. Glenarvan wished to be the first to bear the sailor, and, seizing one end of the litter and Wilson the other, they started.

What a sad sight! and how disastrously this journey, so well begun, had ended! They were no longer going in search of Captain Grant. This continent—where he was not, nor had ever been—threatened to be fatal to those who were seeking traces of him, and perhaps new discouragements still awaited them.

The first day passed silently and painfully. Every ten minutes they took turns in carrying the litter. All the sailor's companions uncomplainingly imposed upon themselves this duty, which was made still more arduous by the great heat.

At evening, after accomplishing only five miles, they encamped under a group of gum-trees. The rest of the provisions that had escaped the shipwreck furnished the evening meal. They must hereafter rely on the major's rifle; but he found no opportunity to fire a single shot. Fortunately, Robert found a nest of bustards, containing a dozen large eggs, which Olbinett cooked in the hot ashes. In addition to these embarrassments, their way became very difficult. The sandy plains were bristling with thorny plants that tore their garments and lacerated their limbs. The courageous ladies, however, did not complain, but valiantly advanced, setting the example, and encouraging each other by a word or a look.

On the third day Mulready traveled part of the way on foot. His wound had entirely healed. The town of Delegete was only ten miles distant, and at evening they encamped on the very frontiers of New South Wales.

A fine and penetrating rain had been falling for several hours, and all shelter would have failed, if Captain Mangles had not fortunately discovered a ruined and abandoned sawyer's hut. They were obliged to content themselves with this miserable hovel of branches and thatch. Wilson attempted to kindle a fire to prepare the food, and accordingly collected some dead wood that strewed the ground. But when he attempted to light the fuel he did not succeed; the great quantity of aluminous material that it contained prevented combustion. It was, therefore, necessary to dispense with fire and food, and sleep in wet garments, while the birds, hidden in the lofty branches, seemed to mock these unfortunate travelers.

However, Glenarvan and his friends were approaching the end of their sufferings; and it was time. The two ladies exerted themselves heroically, but their strength was failing every hour. They dragged themselves along, they no longer walked.

The next day they started at daybreak, and at eleven o'clock Delegete came in sight, fifty miles from Twofold Bay. Here means of conveyance were quickly obtained. Feeling himself so near the coast, hope returned to Glenarvan's heart; perhaps there had been some slight delay, and he would arrive before the Duncan! In twenty-four hours he would reach the bay!

At noon, after a comforting repast, all the travelers took their seats in a mail-coach, and left Delegete at the full speed of five strong horses. The postilions, stimulated by the promise of a large reward, drove them along at a rapid rate, over a well-kept road. No time was lost inchanging horses, and it seemed as if Glenarvan had inspired all with his own intense eagerness.

All day and all night they traveled with the same swiftness, and at sunrise the next morning a low murmur announced the proximity of the Indian Ocean. It was necessary, however, to pass around the bay to gain that part of the coast where Tom Austin was to meet the travelers.

The two ladies exerted themselves heroically, but their strength was failing every hour. They dragged themselves along, they no longer walked.

When the sea appeared, all eyes quickly surveyed the wide expanse. Was the Duncan there, by a miracle of Providence, as she had been discerned before by some of them on the Argentine coast? Nothing was seen; sky and water mingled in an unbroken horizon; not a sail brightened the vast extent of ocean.

One hope still remained. Perhaps Tom Austin had thought it best to cast anchor in Twofold Bay, as the sea was rough and a vessel could not be moored in safety near such shores.

"To Eden!" said Glenarvan.

The mail-coach at once took the road to the right, which ran along the edge of the bay, and proceeded towards the little town of Eden, only five miles distant. The postilions stopped not far from the light that guarded the entrance to the harbor. Several ships were anchored in the roadstead, but none displayed the flag of Malcolm Castle.

Glenarvan, Captain Mangles, and Paganel alighted immediately, and hastened to the custom-house. Here they questioned the employees, and consulted the latest arrivals. No vessel had entered the bay for a week.

"She may not have started!" cried Glenarvan, who would not despair. "Perhaps we have arrived before her!"

Captain Mangles shook his head. He knew Tom Austin; his mate would never have delayed so long to execute an order.

"I will know what this means," said Glenarvan. "Certainty is better than doubt."

THE LAST HOPE.

Fifteen minutes later a telegram was sent to the ship-brokers of Melbourne, and the travelers repaired to the Victoria Hotel. Not long after an answer was delivered to Lord Glenarvan. It read as follows:

"Lord Glenarvan,
Eden, Twofold Bay.
"Duncan started on the 18th instant for some unknown destination."

The dispatch fell from Glenarvan's hands. There was no more doubt! The honest Scotch yacht, in Ben Joyce's hands, had become a pirate-vessel!

Thus ended their search in Australia, begun under such favorable auspices. The traces of Captain Grant and his shipwrecked sailors seemed irrecoverably lost. This failure had cost the lives of an entire crew. Lord Glenarvan was crushed by the blow, and this courageous searcher, whom the leagued elements had failed to deter, was now baffled by the malice of men.

CHAPTER XLIV

A ROUGH CAPTAIN.

If ever the searchers for Captain Grant had reason to despair of seeing him again, was it not when every hope forsook them at once? To what part of the world should they venture a new expedition? how explore unknown countries? The Duncan was no longer in their possession, and they could not be immediately reconciled to their misfortune. The undertaking of these generous Scots had, therefore, failed. Failure! sad word, that finds no echo in a valiant soul; and yet, amid all the changes of destiny, Glenarvan was forced to acknowledge his powerlessness to pursue this work of mercy.

Mary Grant, in this situation, no longer had the courage to utter the name of her father. She suppressed her own anguish by thinking of the unfortunate crew. Controlling herself in the presence of her friend, it was she who consoled Lady Helena, from whom she had received so many consolations. The young girl was the first to speak of their return to Scotland. At seeing her so courageous and resigned, Captain Mangles admired her, and would have spoken a final word in favor of Captain Grant, if Mary had not stopped him with a look and then said:

"No, Mr. John; let us think of those who have sacrificed themselves. Lord Glenarvan must return to England."

"You are right, Miss Mary," replied he; "he must. The English authorities must also be informed of the fate of the Duncan. But do not give up all hope. The search that we have begun I would continue alone, rather than abandon. I will find Captain Grant, or succumb to the task!"

This was a solemn compact which John Mangles thus made. Mary accepted it, and gave her hand to the young captain, as if to ratify this treaty. On the part of the latter it was a devotion of his entire life; on the part of the former, an unchanging gratitude.

The time of their departure was now definitely decided. They resolved to proceed to Melbourne without delay. The next day Captain Mangles went to inquire about vessels that were upon the point of sailing. He expected to find frequent communication between Eden and Melbourne, but he was disappointed. The vessels were few; two or three anchored in Twofold Bay composed the entire fleet of the place. There were none for Melbourne, Sydney, or Point-de-Galle.

In this state of affairs, what was to be done? Wait for a ship? They might be delayed a long time, for Twofold Bay is little frequented. After some deliberation, Glenarvan was about to decide upon reaching Sydney by the coast, when Paganel made a proposal that was unexpected to every one.

The geographer had just returned from Twofold Bay. He knew that there were no means of transportation to Sydney or Melbourne; but, of the three vessels anchored in the roadstead, one was preparing to start for Auckland, the capital of Ika-na-Maoui, the northern island of New Zealand. Thither Paganel proposed to go by the bark in question, and from Auckland it would be easy to return to England by the steamers of the English company.

This proposition was taken into serious consideration, although Paganel did not enter into those extended arguments of which he was usually so lavish. He confined himself to stating the fact, and added that the voyage would not last more than five or six days.

Captain Mangles advocated Paganel's plan. He thought it should be adopted, since they could not wait for the uncertain arrival of other vessels. But, before deciding, he judged it advisable to visit the ship in question. Accordingly, he, with Glenarvan, the major, Paganel, and Robert, took a boat, and pulled out to where it was anchored.

It was a brig of two hundred and fifty tons, called the Macquarie, which traded between the different ports of Australia and New Zealand. The captain, or rather the "master," received his visitors very gruffly. They saw that they had to deal with an uneducated man, whose manners were not different from those of the five sailors of his crew. A coarse red face, big hands, a flat nose, a blinded eye, lips blackened by his pipe, and a specially brutish appearance, made Will Halley a very forbidding character. But they had no choice, and for a voyage of a few days there was no need to be very particular.

"What do you want?" asked Will Halley, as the strangers reached the deck of his vessel.

"The captain," replied Mangles.

A BUSINESS INTERVIEW.

"I am he," said Halley. "What then?"

"The Macquarie is loading for Auckland?"

"Yes. What of it?"

"What does she carry?"

"Anything that is bought or sold."

"When does she sail?"

"To-morrow, at the noon tide."

"Would she take passengers?"

"That depends upon the passengers, and whether they would be satisfied with the ship's mess."

"They would take their own provisions."

"Well, how many are there?"

"Nine,—two of them ladies."

"I have no cabins."

"We will arrange a place for their exclusive use."

"What then?"

"Do you accept?" asked Captain Mangles, who was not embarrassed by this curtness.

"I must see," replied the master of the Macquarie. He took a turn or two, striking the deck with his heavy, hobnailed boots; then, turning to Captain Mangles, said:

"What do you pay?"

"What do you ask?" was the reply.

"Fifty pounds."

Glenarvan nodded assent.

"Very well! Fifty pounds."

"But the passage in cash!" added Halley.

"In cash."

It was a brig of two hundred and fifty tons, called the Macquarie, which traded between the different ports of Australia and New Zealand.

"Food separate?"

"Separate."

"Agreed. Well?" said Will Halley, holding out his hand.

"What?"

"The advance-money."

"Here is half the fare,—twenty-five pounds," said Captain Mangles, counting out the sum, which the master pocketed without saying "thank you."

"Be on board to-morrow," said he. "Whether you are here or not, I shall weigh anchor."

"We will be here."

Thereupon Glenarvan, the major, Robert, Paganel, and Captain Mangles left the vessel, without Will Halley's having so much as touched the brim of his hat.

"What a stupid fellow!" was their first remark.

"Well, I like him," replied Paganel. "He is a real sea-wolf."

"A real bear!" remarked the major.

"And I imagine," added Captain Mangles, "that this bear has at some time traded in human flesh."

"What matter," replied Glenarvan, "so long as he commands the Macquarie, which goes to New Zealand? We shall see very little of him on the voyage."

Lady Helena and Mary Grant were very much pleased to know that they were to start the next day. Glenarvan observed, however, that the Macquarie could not equal the Duncan for comfort; but, after so many hardships, they were not likely to be overcome by trifles. Mr. Olbinett was requested to take charge of the provisions. The poor man, since the loss of the Duncan, had often lamented the unhappy fate of his wife, who had remained on board, and would be, consequently, the victim of the convicts' brutality. However, he fulfilled his duties as steward with his accustomed zeal, and their food might yet consist of dishes that were never seen on the ship's table.

In the mean time the major discounted at a money-changer's some drafts that Glenarvan had on the Union Bank of Melbourne. As for Paganel, he procured an excellent map of New Zealand.

Mulready was now quite well. He scarcely felt his wound, which had so nearly proved fatal. A few hours at sea would complete his recovery.

Wilson went on board first, charged with arranging the passengers' quarters. Under his vigorous use of the brush and broom the aspect of things was greatly changed. Will Halley shrugged his shoulders, but allowed the sailor to do as he pleased. As for Glenarvan and his friends, he scarcely noticed them; he did not even know their names, nor did he care to. This increase of cargo was worth fifty pounds to him, but he valued it less than the two hundred tons of tanned leather with which his hold was crowded,—the skins first, and the passengers next. He was a real trader; and by his nautical ability he passed for a good navigator of these seas, rendered so very dangerous by the coral reefs.

During the afternoon, Glenarvan wished to visit once more the supposed place of the shipwreck. Ayrton had certainly been the quartermaster of the Britannia, and the vessel might really have been lost on that part of the coast. And there, at all events, the Duncan had fallen into the hands of the convicts. Had there been a fight? Perhaps they would find on the beach traces of a struggle. If the crew had perished in the waves, would not the bodies have been cast ashore?

Glenarvan, accompanied by his faithful captain, undertook this examination. The landlord of Victoria Hotel furnished them with two horses, and they set out. But it was a sad journey. They rode in silence. The same thoughts, the same anxieties, tortured the mind of each. They gazed at the rocks worn by the sea. They had no need to question or answer; no sign of the Duncan could be found,—the whole coast was bare.

Captain Mangles, however, found on the margin of the shore evident signs of an encampment, the remains of fires recently kindled beneath the few trees. Had a wandering tribe of natives passed there within a few days? No, for an object struck Glenarvan's eye, which proved incontestably that the convicts had visited that part of the coast.

The landlord of Victoria Hotel furnished them with two horses, and they set out.

THE LAST NIGHT IN AUSTRALIA.

It was a gray and yellow jacket, worn and patched, left at the foot of a tree. It bore a number and badge of the Perth penitentiary. The convict was no longer there, but his cast-off garment betrayed him.

"You see, John," said Glenarvan, "the convicts have been here! And our poor comrades of the Duncan———"

"Yes," replied the captain, in a low voice, "they have certainly been landed, and have perished!"

"The wretches!" cried Glenarvan. "If they ever fall into my hands, I will avenge my crew!"

Grief and exposure had hardened Glenarvan's features. For several moments he gazed at the vast expanse of water, seeking perhaps to discern some ship in the dim distance. Then his eyes relaxed their fierceness, he regained his composure, and, without adding a word or making a sign, took the road to Eden.

Only one duty remained to be fulfilled,—to inform the constable of the events that had just transpired, which was done the same evening. The magistrate, Thomas Banks, could scarcely conceal his satisfaction at making out the official record. He was simply delighted at the departure of Ben Joyce and his band. The whole village shared his joy. The convicts had left Australia because of a new crime; but, at all events, they had gone. This important news was immediately telegraphed to the authorities of Melbourne and Sydney.

Having accomplished his object, Glenarvan returned to the Victoria Hotel. The travelers passed this last evening in Australia in sadness. Their thoughts wandered over this country, so fertile in misfortunes. They recalled the hopes they had reasonably conceived at Cape Bernouilli, now so cruelly disappointed at Twofold Bay.

Paganel was a prey to a feverish agitation. Captain Mangles, who had watched him since the incident at Snowy River, many times pressed him with questions which Paganel did not answer. But that evening, as he went with him to his chamber, the captain asked him why he was so nervous.

"My friend," replied Paganel evasively, "I am no more nervous than usual."

"Mr. Paganel, you have a secret that troubles you."

"Well, as you will," cried the geographer; "it is stronger than I."

"What is stronger than you?"

"My joy on the one hand, and my despair on the other."

"You are joyful and despairing at the same time?"

"Yes; joyful and despairing at visiting New Zealand."

"Have you any news?" asked Captain Mangles. "Have you discovered the lost trail?"

"No, friend. *People never return from New Zealand!* But yet—well, you know human nature. As long as we breathe we can hope; and my motto is '*dum spiro, spero,*' which is the best in the world."

CHAPTER XLV

THE WRECK OF THE MACQUARIE.

The next day the travelers were installed on board the Macquarie. Will Halley had not offered the ladies his cabin, which was not to be regretted, as the lair was only fit for the brute.

At noon they made ready to take the flood-tide. The anchor was weighed. A moderate breeze blew from the southwest. The sails were gradually set, but the five men worked slowly. At last, incited by the oaths of the skipper, they accomplished their task. But in spite of her spread of canvas the brig scarcely advanced. Yet, however poorly she sailed, in five or six days they hoped to reach the harbor of Auckland. At seven o'clock in the evening they lost sight of the shores of Australia, and the lighthouse at Eden. The sea was rough, and the vessel labored heavily in the trough of the waves. The passengers found their situation very uncomfortable; but, as they could not remain on deck, they were forced to submit to confinement.

But on the next day seven canoes of the islanders attacked it most violently and suddenly, causing it to capsize.

That evening conversation very naturally turned upon the land to which they were now sailing, its discovery and colonization; and just as naturally all turned to Paganel as to a bookcase, for some information thereon. It was very readily accessible, although evidently to the geographer's mind there was something of a painful character connected with the name, the impression, and the very thoughts of New Zealand and its Maori inhabitants.

"Monsieur Paganel," said Lady Helena, "have your friends, the English, been the only ones to search out this island?"

"By no means, madam," was the prompt reply. "On the contrary, they have come second, nay, third, in the race; only," and he looked half roguishly and half maliciously, "*they stayed when they came.*"

And then he told them of its first discovery by Abel Tasman, the Dutch navigator, in 1642; that, when first he landed, there seemed to be amicable feelings expressed by the islanders toward himself, a number of them coming back to his ship, and being apparently well pleased to cultivate intercourse. But on the next day, as he sent his boat to find good anchorage nearer to the shore, seven canoes of the islanders attacked it most violently and suddenly, causing it to capsize, and so vigorously assailing its occupants with their pikes that it was with difficulty any of them were able to swim back to their ship, leaving those of their companions who were not drowned to be butchered by the natives.

A SADDENING HISTORY.

Of course he did not forget to mention that a French navigator, Surville by name, was the next to visit the shores, and that his visit likewise was the cause of bloodshed and misery. But he gave them a more lengthy and extended narrative of Captain Cook's voyages, which were the most important in their results as well as the most interesting and tragic in many of their incidents. It was on the 6th of October, 1769, that this navigator first landed on the shores which he visited twice afterwards, and each time added greatly to the stock of previous knowledge concerning these islands, their productions, and their inhabitants. By him it was first ascertained that cannibalism was practiced by some, if not all, of the tribes at that time; and it was very evident, from the manner of Paganel's narration, that hereabout lay the extremely sensitive point of the worthy geographer's fears and forebodings. However, he was not deterred from rehearsing how one and another not merely visited, but began to settle, on the island, so that in the treaty of 1814 it was formally recognized as belonging to Great Britain, and twenty years after was important enough to have a separate official and governmental establishment.

Paganel also told, at great length, the tales of many of the sad incidents which from time to time have marked even the commercial intercourse between the European and the Maori; as, for instance, the sad tale of conflict and bloodshed connected with the death of Captain Marion, a French navigator, in 1772. He had landed near the spot where Surville had ill-treated some of the natives and traitorously seized a son of the chief, Takouri, who yet appeared to welcome this next French visitant, though remembering none the less the terrible duty of vengeance which is felt by the Maori to be so binding.

For a long time the cloak of friendship was worn by the natives, the more thoroughly to lull the suspicions of the whites, and to entice a larger number on shore; in which endeavor they succeeded only too well. The French ships being greatly out of repair, Marion was induced to fell timber at some distance in the interior, and to establish in this occupation a great number of his men, going frequently to them, and remaining with them and the apparently friendly chiefs.

On one of these occasions the Maoris fulfilled their revengeful project with a terrible satisfaction to themselves. Only one man, of all those in the interior, managed to escape, the commander himself falling a prey to their vengeance. They then endeavored to kill the second in command, who, with several others, was nearer to the shore. These, of course, at once started for their boats; breathless, they reached them, hotly pursued to the water's edge by the insatiate savages. Then, safe themselves, the French marksmen picked off the chief, and the previous exultation of the aborigines was, even in the hour of their triumph, turned to lamentation, coupled with wonder at the terrible power of the white man's fire-barrel.

*It was on the sixth of October, 1769, that this navigator (Captain Cook)
first landed on the shores.*

All this and much more did the geographer narrate; but it must be
confessed that he neither spoke, nor did they listen, with the
complacency evinced in his previous tales. Besides, their
surroundings were at the time uncomfortable, and the first
prognostications of a speedy passage were not likely to be verified.

Unfortunately, this painful voyage was prolonged. Six days after
her departure, the Macquarie had not descried the shores of
Auckland. The wind was fair, however, and still blew from the
southwest; but nevertheless the brig did not make much headway.

Safe themselves, the French marksmen picked off the chief.

The sea was rough, the rigging creaked, the ribs cracked, and the vessel rode the waves with difficulty.

Fortunately, Will Halley, like a man who was in no hurry, did not crowd on sail, or his masts would inevitably have snapped. Captain Mangles hoped, therefore, that this clumsy craft would reach its destination in safety; still, he was pained to see his companions on board in such miserable quarters.

PERSISTENT GRIEF.

But neither Lady Helena nor Mary Grant complained, although the continual rain kept them confined, and the want of air and rolling of the ship seriously incommoded them. Their friends sought to divert them, and Paganel strove to while the time with his stories, but did not succeed so well as previously.

Of all the passengers, the one most to be pitied was Lord Glenarvan. They rarely saw him below; he could not keep still. His nervous and excitable nature would not submit to an imprisonment between four wooden walls. Day and night, heedless of the torrents of rain and the dashing spray of the sea, he remained on deck, sometimes bending over the rail, sometimes pacing up and down with feverish agitation. His eyes gazed continually into space, and, during the brief lulls, his glass persistently surveyed the horizon. He seemed to question the mute waves; the mist that veiled the sky, the masses of vapor, he would have penetrated with a glance; he could not be resigned, and his countenance betokened an acute grief. The power and hopefulness of this man, hitherto so energetic and courageous, had suddenly failed.

Captain Mangles seldom left him, but at his side endured the severity of the storm. That day, Glenarvan, wherever there was an opening in the mist, scanned the horizon with the utmost persistency. The young captain approached him.

"Is your lordship looking for land?" he asked.

Glenarvan shook his head.

"It will yet be some time before we leave the brig. We ought to have sighted Auckland light thirty-six hours ago."

Glenarvan did not answer. He still gazed, and for a moment his glass was pointed towards the horizon to windward of the vessel.

"The land is not on that side," said Captain Mangles. "Your lordship should look towards the starboard."

"Why, John?" replied Glenarvan. "It is not the land that I am seeking."

"What is it, my lord?"

A COURAGEOUS CAPTAIN.

"My yacht, my Duncan! She must be here, in these regions, plowing these seas, in that dreadful employment of a pirate. She is here, I tell you, John, on this course between Australia and New Zealand! I have a presentiment that we shall meet her!"

"God preserve us from such a meeting, my lord!"

"Why, John?"

"Your lordship forgets our situation. What could we do on this brig, if the Duncan should give us chase? We could not escape."

"Escape, John?"

"Yes, my lord. We should try in vain. We should be captured, at the mercy of the wretches. Ben Joyce has shown that he does not hesitate at a crime. I should sell my life dearly. We would defend ourselves to the last extremity. Well! But, then, think of Lady Helena and Mary Grant!"

"Poor women!" murmured Glenarvan. "John, my heart is broken, and sometimes I feel as if despair had invaded it. It seems to me as if new calamities awaited us, as if Heaven had decreed against us! I am afraid!"

"You, my lord?"

"Not for myself, John, but for those whom I love, and whom you love also."

"Take courage, my lord," replied the young captain. "We need no longer fear. The Macquarie is a poor sailer, but still she sails. Will Halley is a brutish creature; but I am here, and if the approach to the land seems to me dangerous I shall take the ship to sea again. Therefore from this quarter there is little or no danger. But as for meeting the Duncan, God preserve us, and enable us to escape!"

Captain Mangles was right. To encounter the Duncan would be fatal to the Macquarie, and this misfortune was to be feared in these retired seas, where pirates could roam without danger. However, that day, at least, the Duncan did not appear, and the sixth night since their departure from Twofold Bay arrived without Captain Mangles's fears being realized.

But that night was destined to be one of terror. Darkness set in almost instantaneously towards evening; the sky was very threatening. Even Will Halley, whose sense of danger was superior to the brutishness of intoxication, was startled by these warning signs. He left his cabin, rubbing his eyes and shaking his great red head. Then he drew a long breath, and examined the masts. The wind was fresh, and was blowing strong towards the New Zealand coast.

Captain Halley summoned his men, with many oaths, and ordered them to reef the top-sails. Captain Mangles approved in silence. He had given up remonstrating with this coarse seaman; but neither he nor Glenarvan left the deck.

Two hours passed. The sea grew more tempestuous, and the vessel received such severe shocks that it seemed as if her keel were grating on the sand. There was no unusual roughness, but yet this clumsy craft labored heavily, and the deck was deluged by the huge waves. The boat that hung in the larboard davits was swept overboard by a rising billow.

Captain Mangles could not help being anxious. Any other vessel would have mocked these surges; but with this heavy hulk they might well fear foundering, for the deck was flooded with every plunge, and the masses of water, not finding sufficient outlet by the scuppers, might submerge the ship. It would have been wise, as a preparation for any emergency, to cut away the waistcloth to facilitate the egress of the water; but Will Halley refused to take this precaution.

Day and night, heedless of the torrents of rain and the dashing spray of the sea, he remained on deck.

A NAUTICAL COUP D'ETAT.

However, a greater danger threatened the Macquarie, and probably there was no longer time to prevent it. About half-past eleven Captain Mangles and Wilson, who were standing on the leeward side, were startled by an unusual sound. Their nautical instincts were roused, and the captain seized the sailor's hand.

"The surf!" said he.

"Yes," replied Wilson. "The sea is breaking on the reefs."

"Not more than two cable-lengths distant."

"Not more! The shore is here!"

Captain Mangles leaned over the railing, gazed at the dark waves, and cried:

"The sounding-lead, Wilson!"

The skipper, who was in the forecastle, did not seem to suspect his situation. Wilson grasped the sounding-line, which lay coiled in its pail, and rushed into the port-shrouds. He cast the lead; the rope slipped between his fingers; at the third knot it stopped.

"Three fathoms!" cried Wilson.

"We are on the breakers!" shouted the sober captain to the stupefied one.

Whether the former saw Halley shrug his shoulders or not is of little consequence. At all events, he rushed towards the wheel and crowded the helm hard alee, while Wilson, letting go the line, hauled upon the top-sail yard-arms to luff the ship. The sailor who was steering, and had been forcibly pushed aside, did not at all understand this sudden attack.

"To the port-yards! let loose the sails!" cried the young captain, managing so as to escape the reefs.

For half a minute, the starboard side of the brig grazed the rocks, and, in spite of the darkness, John perceived a roaring line of breakers that foamed a few yards from the ship.

VERY CRITICAL CIRCUMSTANCES.

At this moment Will Halley, becoming conscious of the imminent danger, lost his presence of mind. His sailors, who were scarcely sober, could not comprehend his orders. Moreover, his incoherent words and contradictory commands showed that this stupid drunkard's coolness had failed. He was surprised by the nearness of the land, which was only eight miles off, when he thought it thirty or forty. The currents had taken him unawares, and thrown him out of his ordinary course.

However, Captain Mangles's prompt management had rescued the brig from her peril; but he did not know his position. Perhaps he was inclosed by a chain of reefs. The wind blew fresh from the east, and at every pitch they might strike bottom.

The roar of the surf was soon redoubled, and it was necessary to luff still more. John crowded the helm down and braced farther to leeward. The breakers multiplied beneath the prow of the ship, and they were obliged to tack so as to put to sea. Would this manœuvre succeed with such an unsteady vessel, and under such reduced sail? It was uncertain, but as their only chance they must venture it.

"Hard alee!" cried Captain Mangles to Wilson.

The Macquarie began to approach the new line of reefs. Soon the water foamed above the submerged rocks. It was a moment of torturing suspense. The spray glittered on the crests of the waves. You would have thought a phosphorescent glow had suddenly illumined the water. Wilson and Mulready forced down the wheel with their whole weight.

Suddenly a shock was felt. The vessel had struck upon a rock. The bob-stays broke, and nearly overthrew the mainmast. Could they come about without any other injury? No; for all at once there was a calm, and the ship veered to windward again, and her movements suddenly ceased. A lofty wave seized and bore her forward towards the reefs, while she rolled heavily. The mainmast went by the board with all its rigging, the brig heaved twice and was motionless, leaning over to starboard. The pump-lights were shattered in pieces, and the passengers rushed to the deck; but the waves were sweeping it from one end to the other, and they could not remain without danger. Captain Mangles, knowing that the ship was firmly imbedded in the sand, besought them for their own sakes to go below again.

The sailor who was steering, and had been forcibly pushed aside, did not at all understand this sudden attack.

"The truth, John?" asked Glenarvan, faintly.

"The truth, my lord, is that we shall not founder. As for being destroyed by the sea, that is another question; but we have time to take counsel."

"Is it midnight?"

"Yes, my lord, and we must wait for daylight."

"Can we not put to sea in the boat?"

"In this storm and darkness it is impossible. And, moreover, where should we strike land?"

"Well, John, let us remain here till morning."

Meantime Will Halley was running about the deck like a madman. His sailors, who had recovered from their stupor, stove in a brandy-barrel and began to drink. Mangles foresaw that their drunkenness would lead to terrible scenes. The captain could not be relied upon to restrain them; the miserable man tore his hair and wrung his hands; he thought only of his cargo, which was not insured.

"I am ruined! I am lost!" cried he, running to and fro.

Captain Mangles scarcely thought of consoling him. He armed his companions, and all stood ready to repel the sailors, who were filling themselves with brandy, and cursing frightfully.

"The first of these wretches who approaches," said the major calmly, "I will shoot like a dog."

The sailors doubtless saw that the passengers were determined to keep them at bay, for, after a few attempts at plunder, they disappeared. Captain Mangles paid no more attention to these drunken men, but waited impatiently for day.

SLEEPING IN A SAND-CRADLE.

The ship was now absolutely immovable. The sea grew gradually calm, and the wind subsided. The hull could, therefore, hold out a few hours longer. At sunrise they would examine the shore. If it seemed easy to land, the yawl, now the only boat on board, would serve to transport the crew and passengers. It would require three trips, at least, to accomplish this, for there was room for only four persons. As for the gig, it had been swept overboard, during the storm, as before mentioned.

While reflecting on the dangers of his situation, the young captain, leaning against the binnacle, listened to the roar of the surf. He strove to pierce the dense darkness, and estimate how far he was from that desired yet dreaded coast. Breakers are frequently heard several leagues at sea. Could the frail cutter weather so long a voyage in her present shattered state?

While he was thinking thus, and longing for a little light in the gloomy sky, the ladies, relying upon his words, were reposing in their berths. The steadiness of the brig secured them several hours of rest. Glenarvan and the others, no longer hearing the cries of the drunken crew, refreshed themselves also by a hasty sleep, and, early in the morning, deep silence reigned on board this vessel, which had sunk to rest, as it were, upon her bed of sand.

About four o'clock the first light appeared in the east. The clouds were delicately tinged by the pale rays of the dawn. Captain Mangles came on deck. Along the horizon extended a curtain of mist. A few vague outlines floated in the vapors of the morning. A gentle swell still agitated the sea, and the outer waves were lost in the dense, motionless fog.

He waited. The light gradually brightened, and the horizon glowed with crimson hues. The misty curtain gradually enveloped the vast vault of the firmament. Black rocks emerged from the water. Then, a line was defined along a border of foam, and a luminous point kindled like a lighthouse at the summit of a peak against the still invisible disk of the rising sun.

"Land!" cried Captain Mangles.

His companions, awakened by his voice, rushed on deck, and gazed in silence at the coast that was seen on the horizon. Whether hospitable or fatal, it was to be their place of refuge.

"Where is that Halley?" asked Glenarvan.

"I do not know, my lord," replied Captain Mangles.

"And his sailors?"

"Disappeared, like himself."

"And like himself, doubtless, drunk," added MacNabb.

"Let us search for them," said Glenarvan; "we cannot abandon them on this vessel."

Mulready and Wilson went down to the bunks in the forecastle. The place was empty. They then visited between-decks, and the hold, but found neither Halley nor his sailors.

"What! nobody?" said Glenarvan.

"Have they fallen into the sea?" asked Paganel.

"Anything is possible," replied Captain Mangles, who cared little for their disappearance.

Then, turning towards the stern, he said,—

"To the boat!"

Wilson and Mulready followed, to assist in lowering it.

The yawl was gone!

The mainmast went by the board with all its rigging, the brig heaved twice and was motionless, leaning over to starboard.

As the Macquarie lay over on her starboard beams, her opposite side was raised, and the defective seams were out of water.

CHAPTER XLVI

VAIN EFFORTS.

Will Halley and his crew, taking advantage of the night and the passengers' sleep, had fled with the only boat left. They could not doubt it. This captain, who was in duty bound to be the last on board, had been the first to leave.

AN ADVANTAGEOUS LOSS.

"The rascals have fled," said Captain Mangles. "Well, so much the better, my lord. We are spared so many disagreeable scenes."

"I agree with you," replied Glenarvan. "Besides, there is a better captain on board, yourself, and courageous seamen, your companions. Command us; we are ready to obey you."

All endorsed Glenarvan's words, and, ranged along the deck, they stood ready for the young captain's orders.

"What is to be done?" asked Glenarvan.

John cast a glance over the ocean, looked at the shattered masts of the brig, and, after a few moments' reflection, said:

"We have two ways, my lord, of extricating ourselves from this situation: either to raise the vessel and put her to sea, or reach the coast on a raft, which can be easily constructed."

"If the vessel can be raised, let us raise it," replied Glenarvan. "That is the best plan, is it not?"

"Yes, my lord; for, once ashore, what would become of us without means of transport?"

"Let us avoid the coast," added Paganel. "We must beware of New Zealand."

"All the more so, as we have gone considerably astray," continued Captain Mangles. "Halley's carelessness has carried us to the south, that is evident. At noon I will take an observation; and if, as I presume, we are below Auckland, I will try to sail the Macquarie up along the coast."

"But the injuries of the brig?" inquired Lady Helena.

"I do not think they are serious, madam," replied Captain Mangles. "I shall rig a jury-mast at the bows; and we shall sail slowly, it is true, but still we shall go where we wish. If, unfortunately, the hull is stove in, or if the ship cannot be extricated, we must gain the coast, and travel by land to Auckland."

"Let us examine the state of the vessel, then," said the major. "This is of the first importance."

Glenarvan, the captain, and Mulready opened the main scuttle, and went down into the hold. About two hundred tons of tanned hides were there, very badly stowed away; but they could draw them aside without much difficulty, by means of the main-stay tackling, and they at once threw overboard part of this ballast so as to lighten the ship.

After three hours of hard labor, they could see the bottom timbers. Two seams in the larboard planking had sprung open as far up as the channel wales. As the Macquarie lay over on her starboard beams, her opposite side was raised, and the defective seams were out of water. Wilson hastened, therefore, to tighten the joints with oakum, over which he carefully nailed a copper plate. On sounding they found less than two feet of water in the hold, which the pumps could easily exhaust, and thus relieve the ship. After his examination of the hull, the captain perceived that it had been little injured in stranding. It was probable that a part of the false keel would remain in the sand, but they could pass over it.

Wilson, after inspecting the interior of the brig, dived, in order to determine her position on the reef. The Macquarie was turned towards the northwest, and lay on a very shelving, slimy sand-bar. The lower end of her prow and two-thirds of her keel were deeply imbedded in the sand. The rest, as far as the stern, floated where the water was five fathoms deep. The rudder was not, therefore, confined, but worked freely. The captain considered it useless to lighten her, as he hoped they would be ready to make use of her at the earliest opportunity. The tides of the Pacific are not very strong, but he relied upon their influence to float the brig, which had stranded an hour before high water. The only point was to extricate her, which would be a long and painful task.

LABOR FOR THE COMMON WEAL.

"To work!" cried the captain.

His improvised sailors were ready. He ordered them to reef the sails. The major, Robert, and Paganel, under Wilson's direction, climbed the maintop. The top-sail, swelled by the wind, would have prevented the extrication of the ship, and it was necessary to reef it, which was done as well as possible. At last, after much labor, severe to unaccustomed hands, the maintop-gallant was taken down. Young Robert, nimble as a cat, and bold as a cabin-boy, had rendered important services in this difficult operation.

It was now advisable to cast one anchor, perhaps two, at the stern of the vessel in the line of the keel. The effect of this would be to haul the Macquarie around into deep water. There is no difficulty in doing this when you have a boat, but here all the boats were gone, and something else must be supplied.

Glenarvan was familiar enough with the sea to understand the necessity of these arrangements. One anchor was to be cast to prevent the ship from stranding at low water.

"But what shall we do without a boat?" asked he of the captain.

"We will use the remains of the mizen-mast and the empty casks," was the reply. "It will be a difficult, but not impossible task, for the Macquarie's anchors are small. Once cast however, if they do not drag, I shall be encouraged."

"Very well, let us lose no time."

To accomplish their object, all were summoned on deck; each took part in the work. The rigging that still confined the mizen-mast was cut away, so that the maintop could be easily withdrawn. Out of this platform Captain Mangles designed to make a raft. He supported it by means of empty casks, and rendered it capable of carrying the anchors. A rudder was fastened to it, which enabled them to steer the concern.

This labor was half accomplished when the sun neared the meridian. The captain left Glenarvan to follow out his instructions, and turned his attention to determining his position, which was very important. Fortunately, he had found in Will Halley's cabin a Nautical Almanac and a sextant, with which he was able to take an observation. By consulting the map Paganel had bought at Eden, he saw that they had been wrecked at the mouth of Aotea Bay, above Cahua Point, on the shores of the province of Auckland. As the city was on the thirty-seventh parallel, the Macquarie had been carried a considerable distance out of her course. It was, therefore, necessary to sail northward to reach the capital of New Zealand.

"A journey of not more than twenty-five miles," said Glenarvan. "It is nothing."

"What is nothing at sea will be long and difficult on land," replied Paganel.

"Well, then," said Captain Mangles, "let us do all in our power to float the Macquarie."

This question being settled, their labors were resumed. It was high water, but they could not take advantage of it, since the anchors were not yet moored. Yet the captain watched the ship with some anxiety. Would she float with the tide? This point would soon be decided.

They waited. Several cracks were heard, caused either by a rising or starting of the keel. Great reliance had been placed upon the tide, but the brig did not stir.

The work was continued, and the raft was soon ready. The small anchor was put on board, and the captain and Wilson embarked, after mooring a small cable at the stern. The ebb-tide made them drift, and they therefore anchored, half a cable's length distant, in ten fathoms of water. The bottom afforded a firm hold.

A MIDNIGHT CONCLAVE.

The great anchor now remained. They lowered it with difficulty, transported it on the raft, and soon it was moored behind the other; the captain and his men returning to the vessel, and waiting for high water, which would be early in the morning. It was now six o'clock in the evening. The young captain complimented his sailors, and told Paganel that, with the aid of courage and good discipline, he might one day become quartermaster.

Meantime, Mr. Olbinett, after assisting in different operations, had returned to the kitchen, and prepared a very comforting and seasonable repast. The crew were tempted by a keen appetite, which was abundantly satisfied, and each felt himself invigorated for fresh exertions.

After dinner, Captain Mangles took a final precaution to insure the success of his experiment. He threw overboard a great part of the merchandise to lighten the brig; but the remainder of the ballast, the heavy spars, the spare yards, and a few tons of pig-iron, were carried to the stern, to aid by their weight in liberating the keel. Wilson and Mulready likewise rolled to the same place a number of casks filled with water. Midnight arrived before these labors were completed.

But at this hour the breeze subsided, and only a few capricious ripples stirred the surface of the water. Looking towards the horizon, the captain observed that the wind was changing from southwest to northwest. A sailor could not be mistaken in the peculiar arrangement and color of the clouds. He accordingly informed Glenarvan of these indications, and proposed to defer their work till the next day.

"A TIDE IN THE AFFAIRS OF MEN."

"And these are my reasons," said he. "First, we are very much fatigued, and all our strength is necessary to free the vessel. Then, when this is accomplished, how can we sail among the dangerous breakers, and in such profound darkness? Moreover, another reason induces me to wait. The wind promises to aid us, and I desire to profit by it, and am in hopes that it will drift the old hull out when the tide raises her. To-morrow, if I am not mistaken, the breeze will blow from the northwest. We will set the main-sails, and they will help to raise the brig."

These reasons were decisive. Glenarvan and Paganel, the most impatient on board, yielded, and the work was suspended.

The night passed favorably, and day appeared. Their captain's predictions were realized. The wind blew from the northwest, and continued to freshen. The crew were summoned. It was nine o'clock. Four hours were still to elapse before it would be high water, and that time was not lost. The laborers renewed their efforts with very good success.

Meantime the tide rose. The surface of the sea was agitated into ripples, and the points of the rocks gradually disappeared, like marine animals returning to their native element. The time for the final attempt approached. A feverish impatience thrilled all minds. No one spoke. Each gazed at the captain, and awaited his orders. He was leaning over the stern-railing, watching the water, and casting an uneasy glance towards the cables.

At last the tide reached its height. The experiment must now be made without delay. The main-sails were set, and the mast was bent with the force of the wind.

"To the windlass!" cried the captain.

Glenarvan, Mulready, and Robert on one side, and Paganel, the major, and Olbinett on the other, bore down upon the handles that moved the machine. At the same time the captain and Wilson added their efforts to those of their companions.

"Down! down!" cried the young captain; "all together!"

The cables were stretched taut under the powerful action of the windlass. The anchors held fast, and did not drag. But they must be quick, for high tide lasts only a few moments, and the water would not be long in lowering.

They therefore anchored, half a cable's length distant, in ten fathoms of water.

They redoubled their efforts. The wind blew violently, and forced the sails against the mast. A few tremors were felt in the hull, and the brig seemed on the point of rising. Perhaps a little more power would suffice to draw her from the sand.

"Helena! Mary!" cried Glenarvan.

The two ladies came and joined their efforts to those of their companions. A final crack was heard, but that was all! The experiment had failed. The tide was already beginning to ebb, and it was evident that, even with the aid of wind and tide, this insufficient crew could not float their ship.

As their first plan had failed, it was necessary to have recourse to the second without delay. It was plain that they could not raise the Macquarie, and that the only way was to abandon her. To wait on board for the uncertain arrival of assistance would have been folly and madness.

The captain therefore proposed to construct a raft strong enough to convey the passengers and a sufficient quantity of provisions to the New Zealand coast. It was not a time for discussion, but for action. The work was accordingly begun, and considerably advanced when night interrupted them.

In the evening, after supper, while Lady Helena and Mary Grant were reposing in their berths, Paganel and his friends conversed seriously as they paced the deck. The geographer had asked Captain Mangles whether the raft could not follow the coast as far as Auckland, instead of landing the passengers at once. The captain replied that it would be impossible with such a rude craft.

"And could we have done with the boat what we cannot do with the raft?"

"Yes, candidly speaking, we could," was the reply; "but with the necessity of sailing by day and anchoring by night."

A FRENCHMAN'S FOIBLE.

"Then these wretches, who have abandoned us——"

"Oh," said Captain Mangles, "they were drunk, and in the profound darkness I fear they have paid for their cowardly desertion with their lives."

"So much the worse for them," continued Paganel; "and for us, too, as this boat would have been useful."

The work was accordingly begun, and considerably advanced when night interrupted them.

"What do you mean, Paganel?" said Glenarvan. "The raft will take us ashore."

"That is precisely what I would avoid," replied the geographer.

"What! can a journey of not more than twenty miles terrify us, after what has been done on the Pampas and in Australia?"

Not long since, in the year 1864, one of these clergymen was seized by the chiefs and hung from the tree.

"My friends," resumed Paganel, "I do not doubt your courage, nor that of our fair companions. Twenty miles is nothing in any other country except New Zealand. Here, however, anything is better than venturing upon these treacherous shores."

"Anything is better than exposing yourself to certain death on a wrecked vessel," returned Captain Mangles.

"What have we to fear in New Zealand?" asked Glenarvan.

"The savages!" replied Paganel.

"The savages?" said Glenarvan. "Can we not avoid them by following the coast? Besides, an attack from a few wretches cannot intimidate ten well-armed and determined Europeans."

"It is not a question of wretches," rejoined Paganel. "The New Zealanders form terrible tribes that struggle against the English government, fight with invaders, frequently conquer them, and always eat them."

"Cannibals! cannibals!" cried Robert; and then he murmured, as though afraid to give full utterance to the words, "My sister! Lady Helena!"

"Never fear, my boy!" said Glenarvan; "our friend Paganel exaggerates."

"I do not exaggerate," replied Paganel. "With these New Zealanders war is what the sports of the chase are to civilized nations; and the game they hunt for they feast upon."

"Paganel," said the major, "this may be all very true, but have you forgotten the introduction of Christianity? has it not destroyed these anthropophagous habits?"

"No, it has not," was the prompt reply. "The records are yet fresh of ministers who have gone out to proclaim Christianity and have fallen victims to the murderous and cannibal instincts of those to whom they preached. Not long since, in the year 1864, one of these clergymen was seized by the chiefs, was hung to the tree, was tantalized and tortured to his last moments; and then, whilst some tore his body to pieces, others devoured the various members. No, the Maoris are still cannibals, and will remain so for some time to come."

But Paganel was on this point a pessimist, contrary to his usual characteristic.

CHAPTER XLVII

A DREADED COUNTRY.

What Paganel had stated was indisputable. The cruelty of the New Zealanders could not be doubted. There was, therefore, danger in landing. But if the danger had been a hundred times greater, it must have been faced. Captain Mangles felt the necessity of leaving this vessel, which would soon break up. Between two perils, one certain, the other only probable, there was no possible hesitation.

ANOTHER CHANGE OF RESIDENCE.

As for the chance of being picked up by some passing ship, they could not reasonably rely upon it, for the Macquarie was out of the course usually taken in going to New Zealand. The shipwreck had happened on the desert shores of Ika-Na-Maoui.

"When shall we start?" asked Glenarvan.

"To-morrow morning at ten o'clock," replied Captain Mangles. "The tide will begin to rise then, and will carry us ashore."

Early the next day the raft was finished. The captain had given his entire attention to its construction. They needed a steady and manageable craft, and one capable of resisting the waves for a voyage of nine miles. The masts of the brig could alone furnish the necessary materials.

The raft was at length completed. It could doubtless sustain the shock of the surges; but could it be steered, and the coast be reached, if the wind should veer? This was a question only to be decided by trial.

At nine o'clock the loading began. The provisions were first put on board in sufficient quantities to last until the arrival at Auckland, for there could be no reliance upon the products of this dreaded country. Olbinett furnished some preserved meats, the remains of the Macquarie's supplies. There was very little, however; and they were forced to depend upon the coarse fare of the mess, which consisted of very inferior ship-biscuits and two barrels of salt fish, greatly to the steward's regret.

These stores were inclosed in sealed cans and then secured to the foot of the mast. The arms and ammunition were put in a safe and dry place. Fortunately, the travelers were well supplied with rifles and revolvers.

A small anchor was taken on board, in case they should reach the shore at low tide and be forced to anchor in the offing. Flood-tide soon began, the breeze blew gently from the northwest, and a slight swell agitated the surface of the sea.

"Are we ready?" asked Captain Mangles.

"All is ready, captain," replied Wilson.

"Aboard, then!"

Lady Helena and Mary Grant descended the ship's side by a clumsy rope-ladder, and took their seats at the foot of the mast near the cases of provisions, their companions around them. Wilson took the helm, the captain stationed himself at the sail-tackling, and Mulready cut the cable that confined the raft to the brig. The sail was spread, and they began to move towards the shore under the combined influence of wind and tide.

The coast was only nine miles distant,—not a difficult voyage for a well-manned boat; but with the raft it was necessary to advance slowly. If the wind held out, they might perhaps reach land with this tide; but if there should be a calm, the ebb would carry them back, or they would be compelled to anchor and wait for the next tide.

However, Captain Mangles hoped to succeed. The wind freshened. As it had been flood now for some hours, they must either reach land soon, or anchor.

Fortune favored them. Gradually the black points of the rocks and the yellow sand of the bars disappeared beneath the waves; but great attention and extreme skill became necessary, in this dangerous neighborhood, to guide their unwieldy craft.

They were still five miles from shore. A clear sky enabled them to distinguish the principal features of the country. To the northeast rose a lofty mountain, whose outline was defined against the horizon in a very singular resemblance to the grinning profile of a monkey.

Paganel soon observed that all the sand-bars had disappeared.

"Except one," replied Lady Helena.

"Where?" asked Paganel.

"There," said Lady Helena, pointing to a black speck a mile ahead.

"That is true," answered Paganel. "Let us try to determine its position, that we may not run upon it when the tide covers it."

The yawl was drawn alongside.

"It is exactly at the northern projection of the mountain," said Captain Mangles. "Wilson, bear away towards the offing."

"Yes, captain," replied the sailor, bearing with all his weight upon the steering oar.

They approached nearer; but, strange to say, the black point still rose above the water. The captain gazed at it attentively, and, to see better, employed Paganel's telescope.

"It is not a rock," said he, after a moment's examination; "it is a floating object, that rises and falls with the swell."

"Is it not a piece of the Macquarie's mast?" asked Lady Helena.

"No," replied Glenarvan; "no fragment could have drifted so far from the ship."

"Wait!" cried Captain Mangles. "I recognize it. It is the boat."

"The brig's boat?" said Glenarvan.

"Yes, my lord, the brig's boat, bottom upwards."

"The unfortunate sailors!" exclaimed Lady Helena, "they have perished!"

"Yes, madam," continued the captain; "and they might have foreseen it; for in the midst of these breakers, on a stormy sea, and in such profound darkness, they fled to certain death."

"May Heaven have pity on them!" murmured Mary Grant.

For a few moments the passengers were silent. They gazed at this frail bark towards which they drew nearer and nearer. It had evidently capsized a considerable distance from land, and of those who embarked in it probably not one had survived.

"But this boat may be useful," said Glenarvan.

"Certainly," replied Captain Mangles. "Come about, Wilson."

REALITIES AND FANCIES.

The direction of the raft was changed, but the wind subsided gradually, and it cost them much time to reach the boat. Mulready, standing at the bow, warded off the shock, and the yawl was drawn alongside.

"Empty?" asked Captain Mangles.

"Yes, captain," replied the sailor, "the boat is empty, and her seams have started open. She is of no use to us."

"Can we not save any part?" asked MacNabb.

Night approached. Already the sun's disk was disappearing beneath the horizon.

"No," answered the captain. "She is only fit to burn."

"I am sorry," said Paganel, "for the yawl might have taken us to Auckland."

"We must be resigned, Mr. Paganel," rejoined the captain. "Moreover, on such a rough sea, I prefer our raft to that frail conveyance. A slight shock would dash it in pieces! Therefore, my lord, we have nothing more to stay here for."

"As you wish, John," said Glenarvan.

The ladies were carried in their companions' arms, and reached the shore without wetting a single fold of their garments.

"Forward, Wilson," continued the young captain, "straight for the coast!"

The tide would yet flow for about an hour, and in this time they could accomplish a considerable distance. But soon the breeze subsided almost entirely, and the raft was motionless. Soon it even began to drift towards the open sea under the influence of the ebb.

The captain did not hesitate a moment.

"Anchor!" cried he.

Mulready, who was in an instant ready to execute this order, let fall the anchor, and the raft drifted till the cable was taut. The sail was reefed, and arrangements were made for a long detention. Indeed, the tide would not turn till late in the evening; and, as they did not care to sail in the dark, they anchored for the night in sight of land.

Quite a heavy swell agitated the surface of the water, and seemed to set steadily towards the shore. Glenarvan, therefore, when he learned that the whole night would be passed on board, asked why they did not take advantage of this current to approach the coast.

"My lord," replied the young captain, "is deceived by an optical illusion. The apparent onward movement is only an oscillation of the water, nothing more. Throw a piece of wood into the water, and you will see that it will remain stationary, so long as the ebb is not felt. We must therefore have patience."

"And dinner," added the major.

Olbinett took out of a case of provisions some pieces of dried meat and a dozen biscuits, though reluctant to offer such meagre fare. It was accepted, however, with good grace, even by the ladies, whose appetites the fresh sea air greatly improved.

Night approached. Already the sun's disk, glowing with crimson, was disappearing beneath the horizon; and the waters glistened and sparkled like sheets of liquid silver under his last rays. Nothing could be seen but sky and water, except one sharply-defined object, the hull of the Macquarie, motionless on the reefs. The short twilight was rapidly followed by the darkness, and soon the land that bounded the horizon some miles away was lost in the gloom. In this perplexing situation these shipwrecked people lapsed into an uneasy and distressing drowsiness, and as the result at daybreak all were more exhausted than refreshed.

With the turn of the tide the wind rose. It was six o'clock in the morning, and time was precious. Preparations were made for getting under way, and the order was given to weigh anchor; but the flukes, by the strain of the cable, were so deeply imbedded in the sand that without the windlass even the tackling that Wilson arranged could not draw them out.

TERRA-FIRMA ONCE MORE.

Half an hour passed in useless efforts. The captain, impatient to set sail, cut the cable, and thus took away all possibility of anchoring, in case the tide should not enable them to reach the shore. The sail was unfurled, and they drifted slowly towards the land that rose in grayish masses against the background of the sky, illumined by the rising sun. The reefs were skillfully avoided, but, with the unsteady breeze, they did not seem to draw nearer the shore.

At last, however, land was less than a mile distant, craggy with rocks and very precipitous. It was necessary to find a practicable landing. The wind now moderated and soon subsided entirely, the sail flapping idly against the mast. The tide alone moved the raft; but they had to give up steering, and masses of sea-weed retarded their progress.

After awhile they gradually became stationary three cable-lengths from shore. But they had no anchor, and would they not be carried out to sea again by the ebb? With eager glance and anxious heart the captain looked towards the inaccessible shore.

Just at this moment a shock was felt. The raft stopped. They had stranded on a sand-bar, not far from the coast. Glenarvan, Robert, Wilson, and Mulready leaped into the water, and moored their bark firmly with cables on the adjoining reefs. The ladies were carried in their companions' arms, and reached the shore without wetting a single fold of their garments; and soon all, with arms and provisions, had set foot on the inhospitable shores of New Zealand.

While the fire served to dry their garments conversation beguiled the hours, as they lay or stood at ease.

Glenarvan, without losing an hour, would have followed the coast to Auckland; but since early morning the sky had been heavy with clouds, which, towards noon, descended in torrents of rain. Hence it was impossible to start on their journey, and advisable to seek a shelter.

Wilson discovered, fortunately, a cavern, hollowed out by the sea in the basaltic rocks of the shore, and here the travelers took refuge with their arms and provisions. There was an abundance of dry sea-weed, lately cast up by the waves. This formed a soft couch, of which they availed themselves. Several pieces of wood were piled up at the entrance and then kindled; and while the fire served to dry their garments conversation beguiled the hours, as they lay or stood at ease.

SEALS AND SIRENS.

Paganel, as usual, upon being appealed to, could tell them of the rise, extension, and consolidation of the British power upon the island; he informed them of the beginnings—and, to his belief, of the causes—of the strife which for years decimated the aborigines, and was very injurious to the colonists who had emigrated; then, in reply to Robert's questions, he went on to speak of those who on a narrower theatre had emulated by their heroism and patience the deeds of the world's great travelers and scientific explorers. He told them of Witcombe and Charlton Howitt, men known in their own circles and in connection with their own branch of the New Zealand government. At still greater length he detailed the adventures of Jacob Louper, who was the companion of Witcombe, and had gone as his assistant to discover a practicable route over the mountains in the north of the province of Canterbury. In those mountain wilds, which even the islanders rarely traverse, these two Europeans suffered greatly, but still worse was their fate when they descended to the water-level and essayed to cross the Taramakau near its mouth. Jacob Louper at length found two old and almost useless canoes, and by attaching the one to the other they hoped to accomplish the passage safely. Before they had reached the middle of the rapid current, however, both the tubs capsized. Louper, with difficulty, managed to support himself on one of them, and by clinging to it was at length carried to the river's bank, which his companion also reached; but when after a period of insensibility Louper returned to consciousness and found the body of Witcombe, it was lifeless. Though terribly bruised and still bleeding from his wounds,

Louper hollowed a grave for the remains, and then, after many more days of privation and danger, came to the huts of some of the Maoris, by whose assistance he at length reached the settled parts of the colony.

These facts and reminiscences, it must be confessed, were not of the most inspiriting character; but they were in the same key as most of Paganel's disquisitions and information concerning these islands, and they were before a late hour exchanged for peaceful though probably dreamy slumbers, by his hearers.

Early the next morning the signal for departure was given. The rain had ceased during the night, and the sky was covered with grayish clouds, which intercepted the rays of the sun, so that the temperature thus moderated enabled them to endure the fatigues of the journey.

By consulting the map, Paganel had calculated that they would have to travel eight days. But, instead of following the windings of the coast, he considered it best to proceed to the village of Ngarnavahia, at the junction of the Waikato and Waipa rivers. Here the overland mail-road passed, and it would thence be easy to reach Drury, and rest, after their hardships, in a comfortable hotel.

But before they left the shore their attention was drawn to the large number of seals, of a peculiar appearance and genus, which lay on the broad sands daily washed by the tidal water. These seals, with their rounded heads, their upturned look, their expressive eyes, presented an appearance, almost a physiognomy, that was mild and wellnigh tender, and served to recall to the traveler's memory the tales about the sirens of the olden and modern times, who served as the enchantresses to just such inhospitable shores as that seemed on which they had themselves been cast. These animals, which are very numerous on the coast of New Zealand, are hunted and killed for the sake of their oil and their skins, and Paganel was of course able to tell how much within the last few years they had been searched for by the traders and navigators on these seas.

Louper, with difficulty, managed to support himself on one of them.

Whilst speaking of these matters, Robert drew Paganel's attention to some curious amphibious creatures, resembling the seals, but larger, which were devouring with rapidity the large stones lying on the shore.

"Look," said he, "here are seals which feed on pebbles."

Paganel assured them that these sea-elephants were only weighting themselves preparatory to their descent into the water, and protested that if they would but wait for a time they might see them descend and subsequently return when they had unloaded themselves. The first part of this programme they saw accomplished; but, greatly to Paganel's grief, Glenarvan would not longer delay the party, and they soon began to see inland beauties and curiosities of another sort.

The district through which they had to walk this day and the next was one very thick with brush and under-wood, and there was no possibility of horse or vehicle passing or meeting them. They now regretted the absence of their Australian cart, for the height and frequency of the large ferns in the neighborhood prevented their making any rapid progress on foot.

THE LAST STAGE OF PERIPATETICS.

Here and there, however, Robert and Paganel would rejoice together over some choice bush or bird that they had met with. Notable among the latter was the New Zealand "kiwi," known to naturalists as the apteryx, and which is becoming very scarce, from the pursuit of its many enemies. Robert discovered in a nest on the ground a couple of these birds without tails or wings, but with four toes on the foot, and a long beak or bill like that of a woodcock, and small white feathers all over its body. Of this bird there was then an entire absence in the zoological collections of Europe, and Paganel indulged the hope that he might be able to be the proud contributor of such a valuable specimen to the "Jardin" of his own city. For the present, at least, the realization of his hopes had to be deferred; and at length, after some days of weariness and continued travel, the party reached the banks of the Waipa. The country was deserted. There was no sign of natives, no path that would indicate the presence of man in these regions. The waters of the river flowed between tall bushes, or glided over sandy shallows, while the range of vision extended to the hills that inclosed the valley on the east.

These seals, with rounded heads, upturned look, expressive eyes, presented an appearance, almost a physiognomy, that was mild and wellnigh tender.

At four o'clock in the afternoon nine miles had been valiantly accomplished. According to the map, which Paganel continually consulted, the junction of the Waikato and Waipa could not be more than five miles distant. The road to Auckland passed this point, and there they would encamp for the night. As for the fifty miles that would still separate them from the capital, two or three days would be sufficient for this, and even eight hours, if they should meet the mail-coach.

The New Zealand "kiwi," known to naturalists as the apteryx.

"Then," said Glenarvan, "we shall be compelled to encamp again to-night."

"Yes," replied Paganel; "but, as I hope, for the last time."

"So much the better; for these are severe hardships for Lady Helena and Mary Grant."

"And they endure them heroically," added Captain Mangles. "But, if I am not mistaken, Mr. Paganel, you have spoken of a village situated at the junction of the two rivers."

"Yes," answered the geographer; "here it is on the map. It is Ngarnavahia, about two miles below the junction."

"Well, could we not lodge there for the night? Lady Helena and Miss Grant would not hesitate to go two miles farther, if they could find a tolerable hotel."

"A hotel!" cried Paganel. "A hotel in a Maori village! There is not even a tavern. This village is only a collection of native huts; and, far from seeking shelter there, my advice is to avoid it most carefully."

"Always your fears, Paganel!" said Glenarvan.

"My dear lord, distrust is better than confidence among the Maoris. I do not know upon what terms they are with the English. Now, timidity aside, such as ourselves would be fine prizes, and I dislike to try New Zealand hospitality. I therefore think it wise to avoid this village, and likewise any meeting with the natives. Once at Drury, it will be different, and there our courageous ladies can refresh themselves at their ease for the fatigues of their journey."

The geographer's opinion prevailed. Lady Helena preferred to pass the last night in the open air rather than to expose her companions. Neither she nor Mary Grant required a halt, and they therefore continued to follow the banks of the river.

Two hours after, the first shadows of evening began to descend the mountains. The sun before disappearing below the western horizon had glinted a few rays through a rift in the clouds. The eastern peaks were crimsoned with the last beams of day.

Glenarvan and his friends hastened their pace. They knew the shortness of the twilight in this latitude, and how quickly night sets in. It was important to reach the junction of the two rivers before it became dark. But a dense fog rose from the earth, and made it very difficult to distinguish the way.

Fortunately, hearing availed in place of sight. Soon a distinct murmur of the waters indicated the union of the two streams in a common bed, and not long after the little party arrived at the point where the Waipa mingles with the Waikato in resounding cascades.

"Here is the Waikato," cried Paganel, "and the road to Auckland runs along its right bank."

"We shall see to-morrow," replied the major. "Let us encamp here. It seems to me as if those deeper shadows yonder proceeded from a little thicket of trees that has grown here expressly to shelter us. Let us eat and sleep."

A TRANSFORMATION SCENE.

"Eat," said Paganel, "but of biscuits and dried meat, without kindling a fire. We have arrived here unseen; let us try to go away in the same manner. Fortunately, this fog will render us invisible."

The group of trees was reached, and each conformed to the geographer's rigorous regulations. The cold supper was noiselessly eaten, and soon a profound sleep overcame the weary travelers.

CHAPTER XLVIII

INTRODUCTION TO THE CANNIBALS.

The next morning at break of day a dense fog was spreading heavily over the river, but the rays of the sun were not long in piercing the mist, which rapidly disappeared under the influence of the radiant orb. The banks of the stream were released from their shroud, and the course of the Waikato appeared in all its morning beauty.

A narrow tongue of land bristling with shrubbery ran out to a point at the junction of the two rivers. The waters of the Waipa, which flowed more swiftly, drove back those of the Waikato for a quarter of a mile before they mingled; but the calm power of the one soon overcame the boisterous impetuosity of the other, and both glided peacefully together to the broad bosom of the Pacific.

As the mist rose, a boat might have been seen ascending the Waikato. It was a canoe seventy feet long and five broad. The lofty prow resembled that of a Venetian gondola, and the whole had been fashioned out of the trunk of a pine. A bed of dry fern covered the bottom. Eight oars at the bow propelled it up the river, while a man at the stern guided it by means of a movable paddle.

This man was a native, of tall form, about forty-five years old, with broad breast and powerful limbs. His protruding and deeply furrowed brow, his fierce look and his sinister countenance, showed him to be a formidable individual.

He was a Maori chief of high rank, as could be seen by the delicate and compact tattooing that striped his face and body. Two black spirals, starting from the nostrils of his aquiline nose, circled his tawny eyes, met on his forehead, and were lost in his abundant hair. His mouth, with its shining teeth, and his chin, were hidden beneath a net-work of varied colors, while graceful lines wound down to his sinewy breast.

There was no doubt as to his rank. The sharp albatross bone, used by Maori tattooers, had furrowed his face five times, in close and deep lines. That he had reached his fifth promotion was evident from his haughty bearing. A large flaxen mat, ornamented with dog-skins, enveloped his person; while a girdle, bloody with his recent conflicts, encircled his waist. From his ears dangled earrings of green jade, and around his neck hung necklaces of "pounamous," sacred stones to which the New Zealanders attribute miraculous properties. At his side lay a gun of English manufacture, and a "patou-patou," a kind of double-edged hatchet.

Near him nine warriors, of lower rank, armed and of ferocious aspect, some still suffering from recent wounds, stood in perfect immobility, enveloped in their flaxen mantles. Three dogs of wild appearance were stretched at their feet. The eight rowers seemed to be servants or slaves of the chief. They worked vigorously, and the boat ascended the current of the Waikato with remarkable swiftness.

In the centre of this long canoe, with feet tied, but hands free, were ten European prisoners clinging closely to each other. They were Lord Glenarvan and his companions.

A TESTING TIME.

The evening before, the little party, led astray by the dense fog, had encamped in the midst of a numerous tribe of natives. About midnight, the travelers, surprised in their sleep, were made prisoners and carried on board the canoe. They had not yet been maltreated, but had tried in vain to resist. Their arms and ammunition were in the hands of the savages, and their own bullets would have quickly stretched them on the earth had they attempted to escape.

They were not long in learning, by the aid of a few English words which the natives used, that, being driven back by the British troops, they were returning, vanquished and weakened, to the regions of the upper Waikato. Their chief, after an obstinate resistance, in which he lost his principal warriors, was now on his way to rouse again the river tribes. He was called Kai-Koumou, a terrible name, which signified in the native language "he who eats the limbs of his enemy." He was brave and bold, but his cruelty equaled his bravery. No pity could be expected from him. His name was well known to the English soldiers, and a price had been set upon his head by the governor of New Zealand.

This terrible catastrophe had come upon Glenarvan just as he was about reaching the long-desired harbor of Auckland, whence he would have returned to his native country. Yet, looking at his calm and passionless countenance, you could not have divined the depth of his anguish, for in his present critical situation he did not betray the extent of his misfortunes. He felt that he ought to set an example of fortitude to his wife and his companions, as being the husband and chief. Moreover, he was ready to die first for the common safety, if circumstances should require it.

CHIEFS, CIVILIZED AND UNCIVILIZED.

His companions were worthy of him; they shared his noble thoughts, and their calm and haughty appearance would scarcely have intimated that they were being carried away to captivity and suffering. By common consent, at Glenarvan's suggestion, they had resolved to feign a proud indifference in the presence of the savages. It was the only way of influencing those fierce natures.

Since leaving the encampment, the natives, taciturn like all savages, had scarcely spoken to each other. However, from a few words exchanged, Glenarvan perceived that they were acquainted with the English language. He therefore resolved to question the chief in regard to the fate that was in store for them. Addressing Kai-Koumou, he said, in a fearless tone:

"Where are you taking us, chief?"

Kai-Koumou gazed at him coldly without answering.

"Say, what do you expect to do with us?" continued Glenarvan.

The chief's eyes blazed with a sudden light, and in a stern voice he replied:

"To exchange you, if your friends will ransom you; to kill you, if they refuse."

Glenarvan asked no more, but hope returned to his heart. Doubtless, some chiefs of the Maori tribe had fallen into the hands of the English, and the natives would attempt to recover them by way of exchange; their situation, therefore, was not one for despair.

Meantime the canoe rapidly ascended the river. Paganel, whose changeable disposition carried him from one extreme to another, had regained his hopefulness. He believed that the Maoris were sparing them the fatigue of their journey to the English settlements, and that they were certain to arrive at their destination. He was, therefore, quite resigned to his lot, and traced on his map the course of the Waikato across the plains and valleys of the province. Lady Helena and Mary Grant, suppressing their terror, conversed in low tones with Glenarvan, and the most skillful physiognomist could not have detected on their faces the anxiety of their hearts.

The Waikato River is worshiped by the natives, as Paganel knew, and English and German naturalists have never ascended beyond its junction with the Waipa. Whither did Kai-Koumou intend to take his captives? The geographer could not have guessed if the word "Taupo," frequently repeated, had not attracted his attention. By consulting his map, he saw that this name was applied to a celebrated lake in the most mountainous part of the island, and that from it the Waikato flows.

Paganel, addressing Captain Mangles in French, so as not to be understood by the savages, asked him how fast the canoe was going. The captain thought about three miles an hour.

"Then," replied the geographer, "if we do not travel during the night, our voyage to the lake will last about four days."

"But whereabouts are the English garrisons?" asked Glenarvan.

"It is difficult to say," replied Paganel. "At all events, the war must have reached the province of Taranaki, and probably the troops are collected beyond the mountains, on the side of the lake where the habitations of the savages are concentrated."

"God grant it!" said Lady Helena.

Glenarvan cast a sorrowful glance at his young wife and Mary Grant, exposed to the mercy of these fierce natives, and captives in a wild country, far from all human assistance. But he saw that he was watched by Kai-Koumou, and, not wishing to show that one of the captives was his wife, he prudently kept his thoughts to himself, and gazed at the banks of the river with apparent indifference.

ACCESSIONS, AND PROGRESS.

The sun was just sinking below the horizon as the canoe ran upon a bank of pumice-stones, which the Waikato carries with it from its source in the volcanic mountains. Several trees grew here, as if designed to shelter an encampment. Kai-Koumou landed his prisoners.

The men had their hands tied, the ladies were free. All were placed in the centre of the encampment, around which large fires formed an impassable barrier.

Before Kai-Koumou had informed his captives of his intention to exchange them, Glenarvan and Captain Mangles had discussed various methods of recovering their liberty. What they could not venture in the boat they hoped to attempt on land, at the hour for encamping, under cover of the night.

But since Glenarvan's conversation with the chief, it seemed wise to abandon this design. They must be patient. It was the most prudent plan. The exchange offered chances that neither an open attack nor a flight across these unknown regions could afford. Many circumstances might indeed arise that would delay, and even prevent, such a transaction; but still it was better to await the result. What, moreover, could ten defenceless men do against thirty well-armed savages? Besides, Glenarvan thought it likely that Kai-Koumou's tribe had lost some chief of high rank whom they were particularly anxious to recover; and he was not mistaken.

A boat might have been seen ascending the Waikato. It was a canoe seventy feet long and five broad.

The next day the canoe ascended the river with increased swiftness. It stopped for a moment at the junction of a small river which wound across the plains on the right bank. Here another canoe, with ten natives on board, joined Kai-Koumou. The warriors merely exchanged salutations, and then continued their course. The new-comers had recently fought against the English troops, as could be seen by their tattered garments, their gory weapons, and the wounds that still bled beneath their rags. They were gloomy and taciturn, and, with the indifference common to all savage races, paid no attention to the captives.

Towards evening Kai-Koumou landed at the foot of the mountains, whose nearer ridges reached precipitously to the river-bank. Here twenty natives, who had disembarked from their canoes, were making preparations for the night. Fires blazed beneath the trees. A chief, equal in rank to Kai-Koumou, advanced with measured pace, and, rubbing his nose against that of the latter, saluted him cordially. The prisoners were stationed in the centre of the encampment, and guarded with extreme vigilance.

The next morning the ascent of the Waikato was resumed. Other boats came from various affluents of the river. Sixty warriors, evidently fugitives from the last insurrection, had now assembled, and were returning, more or less wounded in the fray, to the mountain districts. Sometimes a song arose from the canoes, as they advanced in single file. One native struck up the patriotic ode of the mysterious "Pihé," the national hymn that calls the Maoris to battle. The full and sonorous voice of the singer waked the echoes of the mountains; and after each stanza his comrades struck their breasts, and sang the warlike verses in chorus. Then they seized their oars again, and the canoes were headed up stream.

During the day a singular sight enlivened the voyage. About four o'clock the canoe, without lessening its speed, guided by the steady hand of the chief, dashed through a narrow gorge. Eddies broke violently against numerous small islands, which rendered navigation exceeding dangerous. Never could it be more hazardous to capsize, for the banks afforded no refuge, and whoever had set foot on the porous crust of the shore would probably have perished. At this point the river flowed between warm springs, oxide of iron colored the muddy ground a brilliant red, and not a yard of firm earth could be seen. The air was heavy with a penetrating sulphureous odor. The natives did not regard it, but the captives were seriously annoyed by the noxious vapors exhaled from the fissures of the soil and the bubbles that burst and discharged their gaseous contents. Yet, however disagreeable these emanations were, the eye could not but admire this magnificent spectacle.

The canoes soon after entered a dense cloud of white smoke, whose wreaths rose in gradually decreasing circles above the river. On the shores a hundred geysers, some shooting forth masses of vapor, and others overflowing in liquid columns, varied their effects, like the jets and cascades of a fountain. It seemed as though some engineer was directing at his pleasure the outflowings of these springs, as the waters and vapor, mingling in the air, formed rainbows in the sunbeams.

For two miles the canoes glided within this vapory atmosphere, enveloped in its warm waves that rolled along the surface of the water. Then the sulphureous smoke disappeared, and a pure swift current of fresh air refreshed the panting voyagers. The region of the springs was passed. Before the close of the day two more rapids were ascended, and at evening Kai-Koumou encamped a hundred miles above the junction of the two streams. The river now turned towards the east, and then again flowed southward into Lake Taupo.

The next morning Jacques Paganel consulted his map and discovered on the right bank Mount Taubara, which rises to the height of three thousand feet. At noon the whole fleet of boats entered Lake Taupo, and the natives hailed with frantic gestures a shred of cloth that waved in the wind from the roof of a hut. It was the national flag.

At this point the river flowed between warm springs, and not a yard of firm earth could be seen.

CHAPTER XLIX

A MOMENTOUS INTERVIEW.

NEW ZEALAND TOPOGRAPHY.

Long before historic times, an abyss, twenty-five miles long and twenty wide, must at some period have been formed by a subsidence of subterranean caverns in the volcanic district forming the centre of the island. The waters of the surrounding country have rushed down and filled this enormous cavity, and the abyss has become a lake, whose depth no one has yet been able to measure.

Such is this strange Lake Taupo, elevated eleven hundred and fifty feet above the level of the sea, and surrounded by lofty mountains. On the west of the prisoners towered precipitous rocks of imposing form; on the north rose several distant ridges, crowned with small forests; on the east spread a broad plain furrowed by a trail and covered with pumice-stones that glittered beneath a net-work of bushes; and on the north, behind a stretch of woodland, volcanic peaks majestically encircled this vast extent of water, the fury of whose tempests equaled that of the ocean cyclones.

But Paganel was scarcely disposed to enlarge his account of these wonders, nor were his friends in a mood to listen. They gazed in silence towards the northeast shore of the lake, whither the canoe was bringing them.

The mission established at Pukawa, on the western shores, no longer existed. The missionary had been driven by the war far from the principal dwellings of the insurrectionists. The prisoners were helpless, abandoned to the mercy of the vengeful Maoris, and in that wild part of the island to which Christianity has never penetrated. Kai-Koumou, leaving the waters of the Waikato, passed through the little creek which served as an outlet to the river, doubled a sharp promontory, and landed on the eastern border of the lake, at the base of the first slopes of Mount Manga.

A quarter of a mile distant, on a buttress of the mountain, appeared a "pah," a Maori fortification, situated in an impregnable position. The prisoners were taken ashore, with their hands and feet free, and conducted thither by the warriors. After quite a long détour, Glenarvan and his companions reached the pah.

This fortress was defended by an outer rampart of strong palisades, fifteen feet high. A second line of stakes, and then a fence of osiers, pierced with loop-holes, inclosed the inner space, the court-yard of the pah, in which stood several Maori tents, and forty huts which were symmetrically arranged.

On their arrival, the captives were terribly impressed at sight of the heads that ornamented the stakes of the second inclosure. Lady Helena and Mary Grant turned away their eyes with more of disgust than terror. These heads had most of them belonged to hostile chiefs, fallen in battle, whose bodies had served as food for the conquerors. The geographer knew them to be such by their hollow and eyeless sockets!

In Kai-Koumou's pah only the heads of his enemies formed this frightful museum; and here, doubtless, more than one English skull had served to increase the size of the chief's collection.

His hut, among those belonging to warriors of lower rank, stood at the rear of the pah, in front of a large open terrace. This structure was built of stakes, interlaced with branches, and lined inside with flax matting.

Only one opening gave access to the dwelling. A thick curtain, made of a vegetable tissue, served as a door. The roof projected so as to form a water-shed. Several faces, carved at the ends of the rafters, adorned the hut, and the curtain was covered with various imitations of foliage, symbolical figures, monsters, and graceful sculpturing, a curious piece of work, fashioned by the scissors of the native decorators.

FEMININE ORATORY.

Inside of the habitation the floor was made of hard-trodden earth, and raised six inches above the ground. Several rush screens and some mattresses, covered with woven matting of long leaves and twigs, served as beds. In the middle of the room a hole in a stone formed the fireplace, and another in the roof answered for a chimney.

The smoke, when it became sufficiently thick, perforce escaped at this outlet, but it of course blackened the walls of the house.

On one side of the hut were storehouses, containing the chief's provisions, his harvest of flax, potatoes, and edible ferns, and the ovens where the various articles of food were cooked by contact with heated stones. Farther off, in small pens, pigs and goats were confined, and dogs ran about seeking their scanty sustenance. They were rather poorly kept, for animals that formed the Maori daily food.

Glenarvan and his companions had taken in the whole at a glance. They awaited beside an empty hut the good pleasure of the chief, exposed to the insults of a crowd of old women, who surrounded them like harpies, and threatened them with their fists, crying and howling. Several English words that passed their lips clearly indicated that they were demanding immediate vengeance.

In the midst of these cries and threats, Lady Helena affected a calmness that she could not feel in her heart. This courageous woman, in order that her husband's coolness might not forsake him, heroically controlled her emotions. Poor Mary Grant felt herself growing weak, and Captain Mangles supported her, ready to die in her defence. The others endured this torrent of invectives in various ways, either indifferent like the major, or increasingly annoyed like Paganel.

Glenarvan, wishing to relieve Lady Helena from the assaults of these shrews, boldly approached Kai-Koumou, and, pointing to the hideous throng, said:

"Drive them away!"

The Maori chief gazed steadily at his prisoner without replying. Then with a gesture he silenced the noisy horde. Glenarvan bowed in token of thanks, and slowly resumed his place among his friends.

Kai-Koumou, fearing an insurrection of the fanatics of his tribe, now led his captives to a sacred place, situated at the other end of the pah, on the edge of a precipice. This hut rested against a rock that rose a hundred feet above it and was a steep boundary to this side of the fortification. In this consecrated temple the priests, or "arikis," instruct the New Zealanders. The building was spacious and tightly closed, and contained the holy and chosen food of the god.

On their arrival, the captives were terribly impressed at sight of the heads that ornamented the stakes of the second inclosure.

Here the prisoners, temporarily sheltered from the fury of the natives, stretched themselves on the flax mats. Lady Helena, her strength exhausted and her energy overcome, sank into her husband's arms. Glenarvan pressed her to his breast, and said:

"Courage, my dear Helena; Heaven will not forsake us!"

At noon the whole fleet of boats entered Lake Taupo.

Robert was scarcely within the hut before he climbed on Wilson's shoulders, and succeeded in thrusting his head through an opening between the roof and the wall, where strings of pipes were hanging. From this point his view commanded the whole extent of the pah, as far as Kai-Koumou's hut.

"They have gathered around the chief," said he, in a low voice. "They are waving their arms, and howling. Kai-Koumou is going to speak."

The boy was silent for a few moments, then continued:

"Kai-Koumou is speaking. The savages grow calm; they listen."

"This chief," said the major, "has evidently a personal interest in protecting us. He wishes to exchange his prisoners for some chiefs of his tribe. But will his warriors consent?"

"Yes, they are listening to him," continued Robert. "They are dispersing; some return to their huts,—others leave the fortification."

"Is it really so?" cried the major.

"Yes, Mr. MacNabb," replied Robert. "Kai-Koumou remains alone with the warriors that were in the canoe. Ha! one of them is coming towards us!"

"Get down, Robert," said Glenarvan.

At this moment Lady Helena, who had risen, seized her husband's arm.

"Edward," said she, in a firm voice, "neither Mary Grant nor I shall fall alive into the hands of those savages!"

And, so saying, she presented to her husband a loaded revolver.

"A weapon!" exclaimed Glenarvan, whose eyes suddenly brightened.

"Yes. The Maoris do not search their female prisoners; but this weapon is for us, Edward, not for them."

"Glenarvan," said MacNabb quickly, "hide the revolver. It is not time yet."

The weapon was immediately concealed in his clothes. The mat that closed the entrance of the hut was raised. A native appeared. He made a sign to the captives to follow him. Glenarvan and his companions passed through the pah, and stopped before Kai-Koumou.

Robert was scarcely within the hut before he climbed on Wilson's shoulders, and succeeded in thrusting his head through an opening.

Around him were assembled the principal warriors of his tribe, among whom was seen the chief whose canoe had first joined Kai-Koumou on the river. He was a man of about forty, robust, and of fierce and cruel aspect. His name was Kara-Tété, which means in the native language "The Irascible." Kai-Koumou treated him with some respect, and from the delicacy of his tattooing it was evident that he occupied a high rank in his tribe. An observer, however, would have detected a rivalry between the two chiefs. The major, indeed, perceived that Kara-Tété's influence surpassed that of Kai-

Koumou. They both ruled the powerful tribes of the Waikato with equal rank; and, during this interview, although Kai-Koumou smiled, his eyes betrayed a deep hostility.

He now questioned Glenarvan.

"You are English?" said he.

"Yes," replied Glenarvan, without hesitation, for this nationality would probably facilitate an exchange.

THE RATE OF BARTER.

"And your companions?" asked Kai-Koumou.

"My companions are also English. We are shipwrecked travelers, and, if you care to know, we have taken no part in the war."

"No matter," replied Kara-Tété, brutally. "Every Englishman is our enemy. Your people have invaded our island. They have stolen away our fields; they have burned our villages."

"They have done wrong," said Glenarvan, in a grave tone. "I say so because I think so, and not because I am in your power."

"Listen," continued Kai-Koumou. "Tohonga, the high-priest of Nouï-Atoua, has fallen into the hands of your brothers. He is prisoner of the Pakekas (Europeans). Our god commands us to ransom his life. I would have torn out your heart, I would have hung your companions' heads and yours forever to the stakes of this palisade. But Nouï-Atoua has spoken."

So saying, Kai-Koumou, who had hitherto controlled himself, trembled with rage, and his countenance was flushed with a fierce exultation. Then, after a few moments, he resumed, more coolly:

"Do you think the English will give us our Tohonga in exchange for you?"

Glenarvan hesitated, and watched the Maori chief very attentively.

"I do not know," said he, after a moment's silence.

"Speak," continued Kai-Koumou. "Is your life worth that of our Tohonga?"

"No," answered Glenarvan. "I am neither a chief nor a priest among my people."

Paganel was astounded at this reply, and gazed at Glenarvan in profound wonder. Kai-Koumou seemed equally surprised.

"Then you doubt it?" said he.

"I do not know," repeated Glenarvan.

"Will not your people accept you in exchange for our Tohonga?"

"Not me alone," replied Glenarvan; "but perhaps all of us."

"Among the Maoris," said Kai-Koumou, "it is one for one."

"Offer these ladies first in exchange for your priest," answered Glenarvan, pointing to Lady Helena and Mary Grant. Lady Helena would have rushed towards her husband, but the major restrained her.

"These two ladies," continued Glenarvan, turning respectfully towards them, "hold a high rank in their country."

The warrior glanced coldly at his prisoner. A malicious smile passed over his face; but he almost instantly repressed it, and replied, in a voice which he could scarcely control:

"Do you hope, then, to deceive Kai-Koumou by false words, cursed European? Do you think that Kai-Koumou's eyes cannot read your heart?"

Then, pointing to Lady Helena, he said:

"That is your wife!"

"No, mine!" cried Kara-Tété.

At last his voice rose above the tumult. "Taboo! taboo!" cried he.

Then, pushing back the prisoners, the chief laid his hand on Lady Helena's shoulder, who grew pale at the touch.

"Edward!" cried the unfortunate woman, in terror.

Glenarvan, without uttering a word, raised his arm. A report resounded. Kara-Tété fell dead.

At this sound a crowd of natives issued from the huts. The pah was filled in an instant. A hundred arms were raised against the captives. Glenarvan's revolver was snatched from his hand.

Kai-Koumou cast a strange look at Glenarvan, and then, guarding with one hand the person of him who had fired, he controlled with the other the throng that was rushing upon the Europeans.

At last his voice rose above the tumult.

"Taboo! taboo!" cried he.

At this word the crowd fell back before Glenarvan and his companions, thus temporarily preserved by a supernatural power. A few moments after they were led back to the temple that served as their prison; but Robert Grant and Paganel were no longer with them.

CHAPTER L

THE CHIEF'S FUNERAL.

Kai-Koumou, according to a custom quite ordinary in New Zealand, joined the rank of priest to that of chief, and could, therefore, extend to persons or objects the superstitious protection of the taboo.

The taboo, which is common to the tribes of Polynesia, has the power to prohibit at once all connection with the object or person tabooed. According to the Maori religion, whoever should lay his sacrilegious hand on what is declared taboo would be punished with death by the offended god; and in case the divinity should delay to avenge his own insult, the priests would not fail to excite his anger.

As for the prisoners confined in the temple, the taboo had rescued them from the fury of the tribe. Some of the natives, the friends and partisans of Kai-Koumou, had stopped suddenly at the command of their chief, and had protected the captives.

THE TORTURES OF SUSPENSE.

Glenarvan, however, was not blind to the fate that was reserved for him. Only his death could atone for the murder of a chief. Among savage races death is always preceded by a protracted torture. He therefore expected to cruelly expiate the righteous indignation that had nerved his arm, but hoped that Kai-Koumou's rage would fall only on himself.

What a night he and his companions passed! Who could depict their anguish, or measure their sufferings? Neither poor Robert nor brave Paganel had reappeared. But how could they doubt their fate? Were they not the first victims of the natives' vengeance? All hope had vanished even from the heart of the major, who did not easily despair. John Mangles felt himself growing mad at sight of the sad dejection of Mary Grant, thus separated from her brother. Glenarvan thought of that terrible request of Lady Helena, who, rather than yield to torture or slavery, preferred to die by his hand. Could he summon this fearful courage? As for an escape, that was plainly impossible. Ten warriors, armed to the teeth, guarded the entrance of the temple.

Morning came at last. There had been no communication between the natives and the prisoners. The hut contained a considerable quantity of food, which the unfortunates scarcely touched. Hunger gave place to grief. The day passed without bringing a change or a hope. Doubtless the hour for the dead chief's funeral and their torture would be the same.

However, although Glenarvan concluded that Kai-Koumou must have abandoned all idea of exchange, the major on this point retained a gleam of hope.

"Who knows," said he, reminding Glenarvan of the effect produced upon the chief by the death of Kara-Tété,—"who knows but that Kai-Koumou in reality feels obliged to you?"

But, in spite of these observations, Glenarvan would no longer hope. The next day also passed away without the preparations for torture being made. The reason of the delay was this.

The Maoris believe that the soul, for three days after death, inhabits the body of the deceased, and therefore during this time the corpse remains unburied. This custom was rigorously observed, and for two days the pah was deserted. Captain Mangles frequently stood on Wilson's shoulders and surveyed the fortification. No native was seen; only the sentinels guarded in turn at the door of their prison.

But on the third day the huts were opened. The savages, men, women, and children, to the number of several hundreds, assembled in the pah, silent and calm. Kai-Koumou came out of his house, and, surrounded by the principal warriors of his tribe, took his place on a mound several feet high in the centre of the fortification. The crowd of natives formed a semicircle around him, and the whole assembly preserved absolute silence.

At a sign from the chief, a warrior advanced towards the temple.

"Remember!" said Lady Helena to her husband.

Glenarvan clasped his wife to his heart. At this moment Mary Grant approached John Mangles.

"Lord and Lady Glenarvan," said she, "I think that, if a wife can die by the hand of her husband to escape a degrading existence, a maiden can likewise die by the hand of her lover. John (for I may tell you at this critical moment), have I not long been your betrothed in the depths of your heart? May I rely upon you, dear John, as Lady Helena does upon Lord Glenarvan?"

"Mary!" cried the young captain, in terror. "Ah! dear Mary——"

He could not finish: the mat was raised, and the captives were dragged towards Kai-Koumou. The two women were resigned to their fate, while the men concealed their anguish beneath a calmness that showed superhuman self-control. They came before the chief, who did not delay sentence.

"You killed Kara-Tété!" said he to Glenarvan.

"I did."

THE BEGINNING OF THE END.

"You shall die to-morrow at sunrise."

"Alone?" inquired Glenarvan, whose heart beat quickly.

"What! as if our Tohonga's life were not more precious than yours!" cried Kai-Koumou, whose eyes expressed a fierce regret.

At this moment a commotion took place among the natives. Glenarvan cast a rapid glance around him. The crowd opened, and a warrior, dripping with sweat and overcome with fatigue, appeared.

As soon as Kai-Koumou perceived him, he said in English, evidently that he might be understood by the captives:

"You come from the camp of the pale-faces?"

"Yes," replied the Maori.

"You saw the prisoner, our Tohonga?"

"I did."

"Is he living?"

"He is dead! The English have shot him."

The fate of Glenarvan and his companions was settled.

"You shall all die to-morrow at daybreak!" cried Kai-Koumou.

The unfortunates were therefore to suffer a common death. Lady Helena and Mary Grant raised towards heaven a look of thankfulness.

A terrible scene of cannibalism, which followed in all its horrible details.

The captives were not taken back to the temple. They were to attend that day the funeral of the dead chief, and the bloody ceremonies connected therewith. A party of natives conducted them to the foot of an enormous koudi, where these guardians remained without losing sight of their prisoners. The rest of the tribe, absorbed in their official mourning, seemed to have forgotten them.

The customary three days had elapsed since the death of Kara-Tété. The soul of the deceased had therefore forever abandoned its mortal abode. The sacred rites began.

The body was carried to a small mound in the centre of the fortification, clothed in splendid costume, and enveloped in a magnificent flaxen mat. The head was adorned with plumes, and wore a crown of green leaves. The face, arms, and breast had been rubbed with oil, and therefore showed no mortification.

The parents and friends of the deceased came to the foot of the mound, and all at once, as if some director were beating time to a funeral dirge, a great concert of cries, groans, and sobs arose on the air. They mourned the dead in plaintive and modulated cadences. His relations struck their heads together; his kinswomen lacerated their faces with their nails, and showed themselves more lavish of blood than of tears. These unfortunate females conscientiously fulfilled their barbarous duty.

But these demonstrations were not enough to appease the soul of the deceased, whose wrath would doubtless have smitten the survivors of his tribe; and his warriors, as they could not recall him to life, wished that he should have no cause to regret in the other world the happiness of this.

Kara-Tété's wife was not to forsake her husband in the tomb. Moreover, the unfortunate woman would not have been allowed to survive him; it was the custom, in accordance with duty, and examples of such sacrifices are not wanting in New Zealand history. The woman appeared. She was still young. Her hair floated in disorder over her shoulders. Vague words, lamentations, and broken phrases, in which she celebrated the virtues of the dead, interrupted her groans; and, in a final paroxysm of grief, she stretched herself at the foot of the mound, beating the ground with her head.

At this moment Kai-Koumou approached her. Suddenly the unfortunate victim rose; but a violent blow with the "méré," a formidable club, wielded by the hand of the chief, struck her lifeless to the earth.

The corpses, folded together, in a sitting posture, and tied in their clothes by a girdle of withes, were placed on this primitive bier.

POOR HUMANITY!

Frightful cries at once broke forth. A hundred arms threatened the captives, who trembled at the horrible sight. But no one stirred, for the funeral ceremonies were not ended.

Kara-Tété's wife had joined her husband in the other world. Both bodies lay side by side. But for the eternal life his faithful spouse could not alone suffice the deceased. Who would serve them in presence of Nouï-Atoua, if their slaves did not follow them?

Six unfortunates were brought before the corpse of their master and mistress. They were servants, whom the pitiless laws of war had reduced to slavery. During the life of the chief they had undergone the severest privations, suffered a thousand abuses, had been scantily fed, and compelled constantly to labor like beasts; and now, according to the Maori belief, they were to continue their existence of servitude for eternity.

They appeared to be resigned to their fate, and were not astonished at a sacrifice they had long anticipated. Their freedom from all bonds showed that they would meet death unresistingly. Moreover, this death was rapid, protracted sufferings were spared them. These were reserved for the captives who stood trembling not twenty paces distant. Six blows of the méré, given by six stalwart warriors, stretched the victims on the ground in a pool of blood. It was the signal for a terrible scene of cannibalism, which followed in all its horrible details.

Glenarvan and his companions, breathless with fright, strove to hide this awful scene from the eyes of the two unhappy ladies. They now understood what awaited them at sunrise the next day, and what cruel tortures would doubtless precede such a death. They were dumb with horror.

The funeral dance now began. Strong spirits, extracted from an indigenous plant, maddened the savages till they seemed no longer human. Would they not forget the taboo of the chief, and throw themselves in their final outbreaks upon the prisoners who trembled at their frenzy?

But Kai-Koumou had preserved his reason in the midst of the general intoxication. He allowed this bloody orgy an hour to reach its utmost intensity. The last act of the funeral was played with the usual rites.

The bodies of Kara-Tété and his wife were taken up, and their limbs bent and gathered against the stomach, according to the New Zealand custom. The place for the tomb had been chosen outside of the fortification, about two miles distant, on the summit of a small mountain, called Maunganamu, situated on the right shore of the lake.

Thither the bodies were to be carried. Two very rude palanquins, or rather litters, were brought to the foot of the mound. The corpses, folded together, in a sitting posture, and tied in their clothes by a girdle of withes, were placed on this primitive bier. Four warriors bore it between them, and the entire tribe, chanting the funeral hymn, followed them in procession to the place of burial.

The captives, who were always watched, saw them leave the inner inclosure of the pah, and then the songs and cries gradually died away. For about half an hour this funeral escort continued in sight, in the depths of the valley. Finally they perceived it again winding along the mountain paths. The distance gave a fantastic appearance to the undulating movements of the long, sinuous column.

The tribe stopped at the summit of the mountain, which was eight hundred feet high, at the place prepared for Kara-Tété's interment. A common Maori would have had only a hole and a heap of stones for a grave; but for a powerful and dreaded chief, destined doubtless for a speedy deification, a tomb worthy of his exploits was reserved.

THE LAST NIGHT.

The sepulchre had been surrounded by palisades, while stakes, ornamented with faces reddened with ochre, stood beside the grave where the bodies were to lie. The relatives had not forgotten that the "waidoua" (the spirit of the dead) feeds on substantial nourishment like the body during this perishable life. Food had therefore been deposited in the inclosure, together with the weapons and clothes of the deceased.

Nothing was wanting for the comfort of the tomb. Husband and wife were laid side by side, and then covered with earth and grass after a series of renewed lamentations. Then the procession silently descended the mountain, and now no one could ascend it under penalty of death, for it was tabooed.

CHAPTER LI

STRANGELY LIBERATED.

Just as the sun was disappearing behind Lake Taupo, the captives were led back to their prison. They were not to leave it again until the summit of the Wahiti mountains should kindle with the first beams of the day. One night remained to prepare for death. In spite of the faintness, in spite of the horror with which they were seized, they shared their repast in common.

"We shall need all the strength possible to face death," said Glenarvan. "We must show these barbarians how Europeans and Christians can die."

The meal being finished, Lady Helena repeated the evening prayer aloud, while all her companions, with uncovered heads, joined her. Having fulfilled this duty, and enjoyed this privilege, the prisoners embraced each other. Lady Helena and Mary Grant then retired to one corner of the hut, and stretched themselves upon a mat. Sleep, which soothes all woes, soon closed their eyes, and they slumbered in each other's arms, overcome by fatigue and long wakefulness.

Glenarvan, taking his friends aside, said:

"My dear companions, our lives and those of these poor ladies are in God's hands. If Heaven has decreed that we shall die to-morrow, we can, I am sure, die like brave people, like Christians, ready to appear fearlessly before the final Judge. God, who does read the secrets of the soul, knows that we are fulfilling a noble mission. If death awaits us instead of success, it is his will. However severe his decree may be, I shall not murmur against it. But this is not death alone; it is torture, disgrace; and here are two women——"

Glenarvan's voice, hitherto firm, now faltered. He paused to control his emotion. After a moment's silence, he said to the young captain:

"John, you have promised Mary Grant what I have promised Lady Helena. What have you resolved?"

"This promise," replied John Mangles, "I believe I have the right in the sight of God to fulfill."

"Yes, John; but we have no weapons."

"Here is one," answered John, displaying a poniard. "I snatched it from Kara-Tété's hands when he fell at your feet. My lord, he of us who survives the other shall fulfill this vow."

At these words a profound silence reigned in the hut. At last the major interrupted it by saying:

"My friends, reserve this extreme measure till the last moment. I am no advocate of what is irremediable."

"I do not speak for ourselves," replied Glenarvan. "We can brave death, whatever it may be. Ah, if we were alone! Twenty times already would I have urged you to make a sally and attack those wretches. But *they*——"

THE APPROACH OF DAY.

At this moment Captain Mangles raised the mat and counted twenty-five natives, who were watching at the door of their prison. A great fire had been kindled, which cast a dismal light over the irregular outlines of the pah. Some of these savages were stretched around the fire; and others, standing and motionless, were darkly defined against the bright curtain of flame.

It is said that, between the jailer who watches and the prisoner who wishes to escape, the chances are on the side of the latter. Indeed, the design of one is stronger than that of the other, for the first may forget that he is guarding, but the second cannot forget that he is guarded; the captive thinks oftener of escaping than his guardian thinks of preventing his escape. But here it was hate and vengeance that watched the prisoners, and not an indifferent jailer. They had not been bound, for bonds were useless where twenty-five men guarded the only outlet of the prison.

This hut was built against the rock that terminated the fortification, and was only accessible by a narrow passage that connected it with the front of the pah. The other two sides of the building were flanked by towering precipices, and stood on the verge of an abyss a hundred feet deep. A descent this way was therefore impossible. There was no chance of escaping in the rear, which was guarded by the enormous rock. The only exit was the door of the temple, and the Maoris defended the narrow passage that connected it with the pah. All escape was therefore out of the question; and Glenarvan, after examining the walls of his prison, was forced to acknowledge this disheartening fact.

Meantime, the hours of this night of anguish were passing away. Dense darkness had covered the mountain. Neither moon nor stars illumined the deep shades. A few gusts of wind swept along the side of the pah. The stakes of the hut groaned, the fire of the natives suddenly revived at this passing draught, and the flames cast rapid flashes into the temple, illumining for a moment the group of prisoners. These poor people were absorbed with their last thoughts; a deathly silence reigned in the hut.

It must have been about four o'clock in the morning, when the major's attention was attracted by a slight sound that seemed to come from behind the rear stakes, in the back wall that lay towards the rock. At first he was indifferent to the noise, but finding that it continued, he listened. At last, puzzled by its persistence, he put his ear close to the ground to hear better. It seemed as if some one was scraping and digging outside.

When he was certain of this fact, he passed quietly towards Glenarvan and the captain, and led them to the rear of the hut.

"Listen," said he, in a low voice, motioning to them to bend down.

The scrapings became more and more audible. They could hear the little stones grate under the pressure of a sharp instrument and fall down outside.

"Some creature in its burrow," said Captain Mangles.

Glenarvan, with bewildered gaze, stood astonished.

"Who knows," said he, "but that it is a man?"

"Man or animal," replied the major, "I will know what is going on."

Wilson and Olbinett joined their companions, and all began to dig in the wall, the captain with his poniard, the others with stones pulled out of the ground, or with their nails, while Mulready, stretched on the earth, watched the group of natives through the loop-hole of the mat. But they were motionless around the fire, and did not suspect what was transpiring twenty paces from them.

The soil was loose and crumbling, and lay upon a bed of clay, so that, in spite of the want of tools, the hole rapidly enlarged. It was soon evident that somebody, clinging to the sides of the pah, was making a passage in its outer wall. What could be the object? Did he know of the existence of the prisoners, or could a mere chance attempt at escape explain the work that seemed nearly completed?

HEAVENLY HELP FROM AN EARTHLY HAND.

The captives redoubled their efforts. Their lacerated fingers bled, but still they dug on. After half an hour's labor, the hole they were drilling had reached a depth of three feet. They could perceive by the sounds, which were now more distinct, that only a thin layer of earth prevented immediate communication.

A few moments more elapsed, when suddenly the major drew back his hand, which was cut by a sharp blade. He suppressed a cry that was about to escape him. Captain Mangles, holding out his poniard, avoided the knife that was moving out of the ground, but seized the hand that held it. It was the hand of a woman or a youth, a European hand. Not a word had been uttered on either side. There was plainly an object in keeping silent.

"Is it Robert?" murmured Glenarvan.

But, though only whispering this name, Mary Grant, awakened by the movement that was taking place in the hut, glided towards Glenarvan, and, seizing this hand all soiled with mud, covered it with kisses.

"It is you! it is you!" cried the young girl, who could not be mistaken, "you, my Robert!"

"Yes, little sister," replied Robert, "I am here to save you all! But silence!"

"Brave lad!" repeated Glenarvan.

"Keep watch of the savages outside," continued Robert.

Mulready, whose attention had been diverted for a moment by the appearance of the hand, resumed his post of observation.

"All is well," said he. "Only four warriors are watching now. The others have fallen asleep."

"Courage!" replied Wilson.

In an instant the hole was widened, and Robert passed from the arms of his sister into those of Lady Helena. Around his body was wound a rope of flax.

"My boy! my boy!" murmured Lady Helena; "these savages did not kill you?"

"No, madam," replied Robert. "Somehow, during the uproar, I succeeded in escaping their vigilance. I crossed the yard. For two days I kept hidden behind the bushes. At night I wandered about, longing to see you again. While the tribe were occupied with the funeral of the chief, I came and examined this side of the fortification, where the prison stands, and saw that I could reach you. I stole this knife and rope in a deserted hut. The tufts of grass and the bushes helped me to climb. By chance I found a kind of grotto hollowed out in the very rock against which this hut rests. I had only a few feet to dig in the soft earth, and here I am."

Twenty silent kisses were his only answer.

"Let us start," said he, in a decided tone.

"Is Paganel below?" inquired Glenarvan.

"Mr. Paganel?" repeated the boy, surprised apparently at the question.

"Yes; is he waiting for us?"

"No, my lord. What! is he not here?"

"He is not, Robert," replied Mary Grant.

"What! have you not seen him?" exclaimed Glenarvan. "Did you not meet each other in the confusion? Did you not escape together?"

"No, my lord," answered Robert, at a loss to understand the disappearance of his friend Paganel.

First her husband, and then she, slid down the rope to the point where the perpendicular wall met the summit of the slope.

"Let us start," said the major; "there is not a moment to lose. Wherever Paganel may be, his situation cannot be worse than ours here. Let us go."

Indeed, the moments were precious. It was high time to start. The escape presented no great difficulties, but for the almost perpendicular wall of rock outside of the grotto, twenty feet high. The declivity then sloped quite gently to the base of the mountain, from which point the captives could quickly gain the lower valleys, while the Maoris, if they chanced to discover their flight, would be forced to make a very long détour, since they were not aware of the passage that had been dug in the mountain.

They now prepared to escape, and every precaution was taken to insure their success. The captives crawled one by one through the narrow passage, and found themselves in the grotto. Captain Mangles, before leaving the hut, concealed all traces of their work, and glided in his turn through the opening, which he closed with the mats. Their outlet was therefore entirely hidden.

The object now was to descend the perpendicular wall of rock, which would have been impossible if Robert had not brought the flax rope. It was unwound, fastened to a point of rock, and thrown over the declivity.

Before allowing his friends to trust their weight to these flaxen fibres, Captain Mangles tested them. They seemed to be quite strong, but it would not answer to venture rashly, for a fall might be fatal.

"This rope," said he, "can only bear the weight of two bodies, and we must therefore act accordingly. Let Lord and Lady Glenarvan slide down first. When they have reached the bottom, three shakes at the rope will be the signal to follow them."

"I will go first," replied Robert. "I have discovered at the base of the slope a sort of deep excavation, where those who descend first can wait for the others in safety."

"Go then, my boy," said Glenarvan, clasping the boy's hand.

Robert disappeared through the opening of the grotto. A moment after, three shakes of the rope informed them that he had accomplished his descent successfully.

Glenarvan and Lady Helena now ventured out of the grotto. The darkness below was still profound, but the gray light of dawn was already tinging the top of the mountain. The keen cold of the morning reanimated the young wife; she felt stronger, and commenced her perilous escape.

A PRECIPITATE DESCENT.

First her husband, and then she, slid down the rope to the point where the perpendicular wall met the summit of the slope. Then Glenarvan, going before his wife and assisting her, began to descend the declivity of the mountain backwards. He sought for tufts of grass and bushes that offered a point of support, and tried them before placing Lady Helena's feet upon them. Several birds, suddenly awakened, flew away with shrill cries, and the fugitives shuddered when a large stone rolled noisily to the base of the mountain.

They had accomplished half the distance when a voice was heard at the opening of the grotto.

"Stop!" whispered Captain Mangles.

Glenarvan, clinging with one hand to a tuft of grass and holding his wife with the other, waited, scarcely breathing.

Wilson had taken alarm. Hearing some noise outside, he had returned to the hut, and, raising the mat, watched the Maoris. At a sign from him the captain had stopped Glenarvan.

In truth, one of the warriors, startled by some unaccustomed sound, had risen and approached the prison. Standing two paces from the hut, he listened with lowered head. He remained in this attitude for a moment, that seemed an hour, with ear intent and eye on the alert. Then, shaking his head as a man who is mistaken, he returned to his companions, took an armful of dead wood and threw it on the half-extinct fire, whose flames revived. His face, brightly illumined by the blaze, betrayed no more anxiety, and, after gazing at the first glimmers of dawn that tinged the horizon, he stretched himself beside the fire to warm his cold limbs.

"All right!" said Wilson.

The captain made a sign to Glenarvan to continue his descent. The latter, accordingly, slid gently down the slope, and soon Lady Helena and he stood on the narrow path where Robert was waiting for them. The rope was shaken three times, and next Captain Mangles, followed by Mary Grant, took the same perilous course. They were successful, and joined Lord and Lady Glenarvan.

Five minutes later all the fugitives, after their fortunate escape from the hut, left this temporary retreat, and, avoiding the inhabited shores of the lake, made their way by narrow paths farther down the mountain. They advanced rapidly, seeking to avoid all points where they might be seen. They did not speak, but glided like shadows through the bushes. Where were they going? At random, it is true, but they were free.

About five o'clock day began to break. Purple tints colored the lofty banks of clouds. The mountain peaks emerged from the mists of the morning. The orb of day would not be long in appearing, and instead of being the signal for torture, was to betray the flight of the condemned.

Before this dreaded moment arrived it was important that the fugitives should be beyond the reach of the savages. But they could not advance quickly, for the paths were steep. Lady Helena scaled the declivities, supported and even carried by Glenarvan, while Mary Grant leaned upon the arm of her betrothed. Robert, happy and triumphant, whose heart was full of joy at his success, took the lead, followed by the two sailors.

For half an hour the fugitives wandered at a venture. Paganel was not there to guide them,—Paganel, the object of their fears, whose absence cast a dark shadow over their happiness. However, they proceeded towards the east as well as possible, in the face of a magnificent dawn. They had soon reached an elevation of five hundred feet above Lake Taupo, and the morning air at this altitude was keen and cold. Hills and mountains rose one above another in indistinct outlines; but Glenarvan only wished to conceal himself and his companions. Afterwards they would see about issuing from this winding labyrinth.

They saw, but were also seen.

At last the sun appeared and flashed his first rays into the faces of the fugitives. Suddenly a terrible yelling, the concentrated union of a hundred voices, broke forth upon the air. It rose from the pah, whose exact position Glenarvan did not now know. Moreover, a thick curtain of mist stretched at their feet, and prevented them from distinguishing the valleys below.

But the fugitives could not doubt that their escape had been discovered. Could they elude the pursuit of the natives? Had they been perceived? Would their tracks betray them?

At this moment the lower strata of vapor rose, enveloping them for an instant in a moist cloud, and they discerned, three hundred feet below them, the frantic crowd of savages.

They saw, but were also seen. Renewed yells resounded, mingled with barks; and the whole tribe, after vainly endeavoring to climb the rock, rushed out of the inclosure and hastened by the shortest paths in pursuit of the prisoners, who fled in terror from their vengeance.

CHAPTER LII

THE SACRED MOUNTAIN.

The summit of the mountain was a hundred feet higher. It was important for the fugitives to reach it, that they might conceal themselves from the sight of the Maoris, on the opposite slope. They hoped that some practicable ridge would then enable them to gain the neighboring peaks. The ascent was, therefore, hastened, as the threatening cries came nearer and nearer. The pursuers had reached the foot of the mountain.

"Courage, courage, my friends!" cried Glenarvan, urging his companions with word and gesture.

A SCENE OF ENCHANTMENT.

In less than five minutes they reached the top of the mountain. Here they turned around to consider their situation, and take some route by which they might evade the Maoris.

From this height the prospect commanded Lake Taupo, which extended towards the west in its picturesque frame of hills. To the north rose the peaks of Pirongia; to the south the flaming crater of Tongariro. But towards the east the view was limited by a barrier of peaks and ridges.

Glenarvan cast an anxious glance around him. The mist had dissolved under the rays of the sun, and his eye could clearly distinguish the least depressions of the earth. No movement of the Maoris could escape his sight.

The natives were not five hundred feet distant, when they reached the plateau upon which the solitary peak rested. Glenarvan could not, for ever so short a time, delay longer. At all hazards they must fly, at the risk of being hemmed in on all sides.

"Let us go down," cried he, "before our only way of escape is blocked up."

But just as the ladies rose by a final effort, MacNabb stopped them, and said:

"It is useless, Glenarvan. Look!"

And all saw, indeed, that an inexplicable change had taken place in the movements of the Maoris. Their pursuit had been suddenly interrupted. Their ascent of the mountain had ceased, as if by an imperious interdict. The crowd of natives had checked their swiftness, and halted, like the waves of the sea before an impassable rock.

All the savages, thirsting for blood, were now ranged along the foot of the mountain, yelling, gesticulating, and brandishing guns and hatchets; but they did not advance a single foot. Their dogs, like themselves, as though chained to earth, howled with rage.

What was the difficulty? What invisible power restrained the natives? The fugitives gazed without comprehending, fearing that the charm that enchained Kai-Koumou's tribe would dissolve.

"Be seated, my dear lord; breakfast is awaiting you."

Suddenly Captain Mangles uttered a cry that caused his companions to turn. He pointed to a little fortress at the summit of the peak.

"The tomb of the chief Kara-Tété!" cried Robert.

"Are you in earnest?" asked Glenarvan.

"Yes, my lord, it is the tomb; I recognize it."

Robert was right. Fifty feet above, at the extreme point of the mountain, stood a small palisaded inclosure of freshly-painted stakes. Glenarvan, likewise, recognized the sepulchre of the Maori chief. In their wanderings they had come to the top of the Maunganamu, where Kara-Tété had been buried.

Followed by his companions, he climbed the sides of the peak, to the very foot of the tomb. A large opening, covered with mats, formed the entrance. Glenarvan was about to enter, when, all at once, he started back suddenly.

"A savage!" said he.

"A savage in this tomb?" inquired the major.

"Yes, MacNabb."

"What matter? Let us enter."

Glenarvan, the major, Robert, and Captain Mangles passed into the inclosure. A Maori was there, clad in a great flax mantle. The darkness of the sepulchre did not permit them to distinguish his features. He appeared very calm, and was eating his breakfast with the most perfect indifference.

Glenarvan was about to address him, when the native, anticipating him, said, in an amiable tone, and in excellent English:

"Be seated, my dear lord; breakfast is awaiting you."

It was Paganel. At his voice all rushed into the tomb, and gazed with wonder at the worthy geographer. Paganel was found! The common safety was represented in him. They were going to question him: they wished to know how and why he was on the top of the mountain; but Glenarvan checked this unseasonable curiosity.

"The savages!" said he.

"The savages," replied Paganel, shrugging his shoulders, "are individuals whom I supremely despise."

"But can they not——?"

"They! the imbeciles! Come and see them."

Each followed Paganel, who issued from the tomb. The Maoris were in the same place, surrounding the foot of the peak, and uttering terrible cries.

"Cry and howl till you are tired, miserable creatures!" said Paganel. "I defy you to climb this mountain!"

"And why?" asked Glenarvan.

"Because the chief is buried here; this tomb protects us, and the mountain is tabooed."

"Tabooed?"

"Yes, my friends; and that is why I took refuge here, as in one of those asylums of the Middle Ages, open to unfortunates."

Indeed, the mountain was tabooed, and by this consecration had become inaccessible by the superstitious savages.

The safety of the fugitives was not yet certain, but there was a salutary respite, of which they strove to take advantage. Glenarvan, a prey to unspeakable emotion, did not venture a word; while the major nodded his head with an air of genuine satisfaction.

"And now, my friends," said Paganel, "if these brutes expect us to test their patience they are mistaken. In two days we shall be beyond the reach of these rascals."

"We will escape!" said Glenarvan; "but how?"

"I do not know," replied Paganel, "but we will do so all the same."

All now wished to hear the geographer's adventures. Strangely enough, in the case of a man loquacious usually, it was necessary to draw, as it were, the words from his mouth. He, who was so fond of telling stories, replied only in an evasive way to the questions of his friends.

"Paganel has changed," thought MacNabb.

THE WORTH OF SPECTACLES.

Indeed, the countenance of the geographer was no longer the same. He wrapped himself gloomily in his great flaxen mantle, and seemed to shun too inquisitive looks. However, when they were all seated around him at the foot of the tomb, he related his experiences.

After the death of Kara-Tété, Paganel had taken advantage, like Robert, of the confusion of the natives, and escaped from the pah. But less fortunate than young Grant, he had fallen upon an encampment of Maoris, who were commanded by a chief of fine form and intelligent appearance, who was evidently superior to all the warriors of his tribe. This chief spoke English accurately, and bade him welcome by rubbing his nose against that of the geographer. Paganel wondered whether he should consider himself a prisoner; but seeing that he could not take a step without being graciously accompanied by the chief, he soon knew how matters stood on this point.

The chief, whose name was "Hihy" (sunbeam), was not a bad man. The spectacles and telescope gave him a high opinion of Paganel, whom he attached carefully to his person, not only by his benefits, but by strong flaxen ropes, especially at night.

This novel situation lasted three long days. Was he well or badly treated? Both, as he stated without further explanation. In short, he was a prisoner, and, except for the prospect of immediate torture, his condition did not seem more enviable than that of his unfortunate friends.

Fortunately, last night he succeeded in biting asunder his ropes and escaping. He had witnessed at a distance the burial of the chief, knew that he had been interred on the summit of Maunganamu mountain, and that it was tabooed in consequence. He therefore resolved to take refuge there, not wishing to leave the place where his companions were held captives. He succeeded in his undertaking, arrived at Kara-Tété's tomb, and waited in hope that Providence would in some way deliver his friends.

Such was Paganel's story. Did he omit designedly any circumstance of his stay among the natives? More than once his embarrassment led them to suspect so. However that might be, he received unanimous congratulations; and as the past was now known, they returned to the present.

Their situation was still exceedingly critical. The natives, if they did not venture to climb the mountain, expected that hunger and thirst would force their prisoners to surrender. It was only a matter of time, and the savages had great patience. Glenarvan did not disregard the difficulties of his position, but waited for the favorable issue which Providence seemed to promise.

And first he wished to examine this improvised fortress; not to defend it, for an attack was not to be feared, but that he might find a way of escaping. The major and the captain, Robert, Paganel, and himself, took the exact bearings of the mountain. They observed the direction of the paths, their branches and declivities. A ridge a mile in length united the Maunganamu to the Wahiti range, and then declined to the plain. Its narrow and winding summit presented the only practicable route, in case escape should become possible. If the fugitives could pass this point unperceived, under cover of the night, perhaps they might succeed in reaching the deep valleys and outwitting the Maoris.

But this course offered more than one danger, as they would have to pass below within gun-shot. The bullets of the natives on the lower ramparts of the pah might intercept them, and form a barrier that no one could safely cross.

Glenarvan and his friends, as soon as they ventured on the dangerous part of the ridge, were saluted with a volley of shots; but only a few wads, borne by the wind, reached them. They were made of printed paper. Paganel picked them up out of curiosity, but it was difficult to decipher them.

A STRANGE COLPORTEUR.

"Why!" said he, "do you know, my friends, what these creatures use for wads in their guns?"

"No," replied Glenarvan.

"Leaves of the Bible! If this is the use they make of the sacred writings, I pity the missionaries. They will have difficulty in founding Maori libraries."

"And what passage of the Scriptures have these natives fired at us?" asked Glenarvan.

"A mighty promise of God," replied Captain Mangles, who had also read the paper. "It bids us hope in Him," added the young captain, with the unshaken conviction of his Scottish faith.

"Read, John," said Glenarvan.

He read this line, which had so strangely reached them:

"Because he hath set his love upon Me, therefore will I deliver him:" Psalm xci. I.

"My friends," said Glenarvan, "we must make known the words of hope to our brave and dear ladies. Here is something to reanimate their hearts."

Glenarvan and his companions ascended the steep paths of the peak, and proceeded towards the tomb, which they wished to examine. On the way they were astonished to feel, at short intervals, a certain trembling of the ground. It was not an irregular agitation, but that continued vibration which the sides of a boiler undergo when it is fully charged. Steam, in large quantities, generated by the action of subterranean fires, seemed to be working beneath the crust of the mountain.

This peculiarity could not astonish people who had passed between the warm springs of the Waikato. They knew that this region of Ika-Na-Maoui is volcanic. It is like a sieve, from the holes of which ever issue the vapors of subterranean laboratories.

Paganel, who had already observed this, called the attention of his friends to the circumstance. The Maunganamu is only one of those numerous cones that cover the central portion of the island. The least mechanical action could provoke the formation of a crater in the clayey soil.

"And yet," said Glenarvan, "we seem to be in no more danger here than beside the boiler of the Duncan. This crust is firm."

"Certainly," replied the major; "but a boiler, however strong it may be, will always burst at last after too long use."

"MacNabb," said Paganel, "I do not desire to remain on this peak. Let Heaven show me a way of escape, and I will leave it instantly."

Lady Helena, who perceived Lord Glenarvan, now approached.

"My dear Edward," said she, "you have considered our position! Are we to hope or fear?"

"Hope, my dear Helena," replied Glenarvan. "The natives will never come to the top of the mountain, and we shall have abundant time to form a plan of escape."

"Moreover, madam," said Captain Mangles, "God himself encourages us to hope."

So saying, he gave her the text of the Bible which had been sent to them. She and Mary Grant, whose confiding soul was always open to the ministrations of Heaven, saw, in the words of the Holy Book, an infallible pledge of safety.

"Now to the tomb!" cried Paganel, gayly. "This is our fortress, our castle, our dining-room, and our workshop. No one is to disarrange it. Ladies, permit me to do the honors of this charming dwelling."

All followed the good-natured Paganel. When the savages saw the fugitives desecrate anew this tabooed sepulchre, they fired numerous volleys, and uttered yells no less terrible. But fortunately their bullets could not reach as far as their cries, for they only came half-way, while their vociferations were lost in empty air.

BOARD AND LODGING.

Lady Helena, Mary Grant, and their companions, quite reassured at seeing that the superstition of the Maoris was still stronger than their rage, entered the tomb. It was a palisade of red painted stakes. Symbolical faces, a real tattooing on wood, described the nobleness and exploits of the deceased. Strings of pipes, shells, and carved stones extended from one stake to another. Inside, the earth was hidden beneath a carpet of green leaves. In the centre a slight protuberance marked the freshly-made grave. Here reposed the weapons of the chief, his guns loaded and primed, his lance, his splendid hatchet of green jade, with a supply of powder and balls sufficient for the hunts of the other world.

"Here is a whole arsenal," said Paganel, "of which we will make a better use than the deceased. It is a good idea of these savages to carry their weapons to heaven with them."

"But these are English guns!" said the major.

"Doubtless," replied Glenarvan; "it is a very foolish custom to make presents of fire-arms to the savages, who then use them against the invaders, and with reason. At all events, these guns will be useful to us."

"But still more useful," said Paganel, "will be the provisions and water intended for Kara-Tété."

The parents and friends of the dead had, indeed, faithfully fulfilled their duties. The amount of food testified their esteem for the virtues of the chief. There were provisions enough to last ten persons fifteen days, or rather the deceased for eternity. They consisted of ferns, sweet yams, and potatoes, which were introduced some time before by the Europeans. Tall vases of fresh water stood near, and a dozen baskets, artistically woven, contained numerous tablets of green gum.

The fugitives were, therefore, fortified for several days against hunger and thirst, and they needed no urging to take their first meal at the chief's expense. Glenarvan directed Mr. Olbinett's attention to the food necessary for his companions; but he, with his usual exactness, even in critical situations, thought the bill of fare rather scanty. Moreover, he did not know how to prepare the roots, and there was no fire.

But Paganel solved the difficulty, and advised him to simply bury his ferns and potatoes in the ground itself, for the heat of the upper strata was very great. Olbinett, however, narrowly escaped a serious scalding, for, just as he had dug a hole to put his roots in, a stream of watery vapor burst forth, and rose to the height of several feet. The steward started back in terror.

"Close the hole!" cried the major, who, with the aid of the two sailors, covered the orifice with fragments of pumice-stone, while Paganel murmured these words:

"Well! well! ha! ha! very natural!"

"You are not scalded?" inquired MacNabb of Olbinett.

"No, Mr. MacNabb," replied the steward; "but I scarcely expected——"

"So many blessings," added Paganel, in a mirthful tone. "Consider Kara-Tété's water and provisions, and the fire of the earth! This mountain is a paradise! I propose that we found a colony here, cultivate the soil, and settle for the rest of our days. We will be Robinson Crusoes of Maunganamu. Indeed, I look in vain for any deficiency on this comfortable peak."

"Nothing is wanting if the earth is firm," replied Captain Mangles.

The steward started back in terror.

"Well, it was not created yesterday," said Paganel. "It has long resisted the action of internal fires, and will easily hold out till our departure."

"Breakfast is ready," announced Mr. Olbinett, as gravely as if he had been performing his duties at Malcolm Castle.

The fugitives at once sat down near the palisade, and enjoyed the repast that Providence had so opportunely furnished to them in this critical situation. No one appeared particular about the choice of food, but there was a diversity of opinion concerning the edible ferns. Some found them sweet and pleasant, and others mucilaginous, insipid, and acrid. The sweet potatoes, cooked in the hot earth, were excellent.

Their hunger being satiated, Glenarvan proposed that they should, without delay, arrange a plan of escape.

"So soon!" said Paganel, in a truly piteous tone. "What! are you thinking already of leaving this delightful place?"

"I think, first of all," replied Glenarvan, "that we ought to attempt an escape before we are forced to it by hunger. We have strength enough yet, and must take advantage of it. To-night let us try to gain the eastern valleys, and cross the circle of natives under cover of the darkness."

"Exactly," answered Paganel; "if the Maoris will let us pass."

"And if they prevent us?" asked Captain Mangles.

"Then we will employ the great expedients," said Paganel.

"You have great expedients, then?" inquired the major.

"More than I know what to do with," rejoined Paganel, without further explanation.

They could now do nothing but wait for night to attempt crossing the line of savages, who had not left their position. Their ranks even seemed increased by stragglers from the tribe. Here and there freshly-kindled fires formed a flaming girdle around the base of the peak. When darkness had invaded the surrounding valleys, the Maunganamu seemed to rise from a vast conflagration, while its summit was lost in a dense shade. Six hundred feet below were heard the tumult and cries of the enemy's camp.

At nine o'clock it was very dark, and Glenarvan and Captain Mangles resolved to make an exploration before taking their companions on this perilous journey. They noiselessly descended the declivity some distance, and reached the narrow ridge that crossed the line of natives fifty feet above the encampment.

ANOTHER SUNRISE.

All went well so far. The Maoris, stretched beside their fires, did not seem to perceive the two fugitives, who advanced a few paces farther. But suddenly, to the left and right of the ridge, a double volley resounded.

"Back!" cried Glenarvan; "these bandits have eyes like a cat, and the guns of riflemen!"

Captain Mangles and he reascended at once the precipitous slopes of the mountain, and speedily assured their terrified friends of their safety. Glenarvan's hat had been pierced by two bullets. It was, therefore, dangerous to venture on the ridge between these two lines of marksmen.

"Wait till to-morrow," said Paganel; "and since we cannot deceive the vigilance of these natives, permit me to give them a dose in my own way."

The temperature was quite cold. Fortunately, Kara-Tété wore in the tomb his best night-robes, warm, flaxen coverings, in which each one wrapped himself without hesitation; and soon the fugitives, protected by the native superstition, slept peacefully in the shelter of the palisades, on the earth that seemed to quake with the internal commotion.

CHAPTER LIII

A BOLD STRATAGEM.

The rising sun awakened with his first rays the sleepers on the Maunganamu. The Maoris for some time had been moving to and fro at the foot of the peak without wandering from their post of observation. Furious cries saluted the appearance of the Europeans as they issued from the desecrated tomb.

Each cast a longing glance towards the surrounding mountains, the deep valleys, still veiled in mist, and the surface of Lake Taupo, gently rippling beneath the morning wind. Then all, eager to know Paganel's new project, gathered around him with questioning looks; while the geographer at once satisfied the restless curiosity of his companions.

"My friends," said he, "my project has this advantage, that if it does not produce the result that I expect, or even fails, our situation will not be impaired. But it ought to and will succeed."

"And this project?" asked the major.

"This is it," replied Paganel. "The superstition of the natives has made this mountain a place of refuge, and this superstition must help us to escape. If I succeed in convincing Kai-Koumou that we have become the victims of our sacrilege, that the wrath of Heaven has fallen upon us, in short, that we have met a terrible death, do you think that he will abandon the mountain and return to his village?"

"Probably," said Glenarvan.

"And with what horrible death do you threaten us?" inquired Lady Helena.

"The death of the sacrilegious, my friends," continued Paganel. "The avenging flames are under our feet. Let us open a way for them."

"What! you would make a volcano?" cried Captain Mangles.

"Yes, a factitious, an improvised one, whose fury we will control. There is quite a supply of vapors and subterranean fires that only ask for an outlet. Let us arrange an artificial eruption for our own advantage."

"The idea is good," said the major, "and well conceived, Paganel."

"You understand," resumed the geographer, "that we are to feign being consumed by the flames of Pluto, and shall disappear spiritually in the tomb of Kara-Tété."

A VOLCANO IN MINIATURE.

"Where we shall remain three, four, or five days, if necessary, till the savages are convinced of our death, and abandon the siege."

"But if they think of making sure of our destruction," said Miss Grant, "and climb the mountain?"

"No, my dear Mary," replied Paganel, "they will not do that. The mountain is tabooed, and if it shall itself devour its profaners the taboo will be still more rigorous."

"This plan is really well conceived," remarked Glenarvan. "There is only one chance against it, and that is, that the savages may persist in remaining at the foot of the mountain till the provisions fail us. But this is scarcely probable, especially if we play our part skillfully."

"And when shall we make this last venture?" asked Lady Helena.

"This very evening," answered Paganel, "at the hour of the greatest darkness."

"Agreed," said MacNabb. "Paganel, you are a man of genius; and although from habit I am scarcely ever enthusiastic, I will answer for your success. Ha! these rascals! we shall perform a little miracle for them that will delay their conversion a good century. May the missionaries pardon us!"

Paganel's plan was therefore adopted, and really, with the superstitious notions of the Maoris, it might and ought to succeed. It only remained to execute it. The idea was good, but in practice difficult. Might not this volcano consume the audacious ones who should dig the crater? Could they control and direct this eruption when the vapors, flames, and lava should be let loose? Would it not engulf the entire peak in a flood of fire? They were tampering with those phenomena whose absolute control is reserved for forces higher than theirs.

Paganel had foreseen these difficulties, but he expected to act prudently, and not to venture to extremes. An illusion was enough to deceive the Maoris, without the awful reality of a large eruption.

How long that day seemed! Each one counted the interminable hours. Everything was prepared for flight. The provisions of the tomb had been divided, and made into convenient bundles. Several mats, and the fire-arms, which had been found in the tomb of the chief, formed light baggage. Of course these preparations were made within the palisaded inclosure and unknown to the savages.

At six o'clock the steward served a farewell feast. Where and when they should eat in the valleys no one could foretell.

Twilight came on. The sun disappeared behind a bank of dense clouds of threatening aspect. A few flashes illumined the horizon, and a distant peal of thunder rumbled along the vault of the sky. Paganel welcomed the storm that came to the aid of his design.

At eight o'clock the summit of the mountain was hidden by a foreboding darkness, while the sky looked terribly black, as if for a background to the flaming outbreak that Paganel was about to inaugurate. The Maoris could no longer see their prisoners. The time for action had come. Rapidity was necessary, and Glenarvan, Paganel, MacNabb, Robert, the steward, and the two sailors at once set to work vigorously.

The place for the crater was chosen thirty paces from Kara-Tété's tomb. It was important that this structure should be spared by the eruption, for otherwise the taboo would become ineffective. Paganel had observed an enormous block of stone, around which the vapors seemed to pour forth with considerable force. This rocky mass covered a small natural crater in the peak, and only by its weight prevented the escape of the subterranean flames. If they could succeed in overturning it, the smoke and lava would immediately issue through the unobstructed opening.

VULCANS AT WORK.

The fugitives made themselves levers out of the stakes of the tomb, and with these they vigorously attacked the ponderous mass. Under their united efforts the rock was not long in moving. They dug a sort of groove for it down the side of the mountain, that it might slide on an inclined plane.

As their action increased, the trembling of the earth became more violent. Hollow rumblings and hissings sounded under the thin crust. But the bold experimenters, like real Vulcans, governing the underground fires, worked on in silence. Several cracks and a few gusts of hot smoke warned them that their position was becoming dangerous. But a final effort detached the block, which glided down the slope of the mountain and disappeared.

The thin covering at once yielded. An incandescent column poured forth towards the sky with loud explosions, while streams of boiling water and lava rolled towards the encampment of the natives and the valleys below. The whole peak trembled, and you might almost have thought that it was disappearing in a general conflagration.

Glenarvan and his companions had scarcely time to escape the shock of the eruption. They fled to the inclosure of the tomb, but not without receiving a few scalding drops of the water, which bubbled and exhaled a strong sulphureous odor.

Then mud, lava, and volcanic fragments mingled in the scene of devastation. Torrents of flame furrowed the sides of the Maunganamu. The adjoining mountains glowed in the light of the eruption, and the deep valleys were illumined with a vivid brightness.

The savages were soon aroused, both by the noise and the heat of the lava that flowed in a scalding tide through the midst of their encampment. Those whom the fiery flood had not reached fled, and ascended the surrounding hills, turning and gazing back at this terrific phenomenon, with which their god, in his wrath, had overwhelmed the desecrators of the sacred mountain; while at certain moments they were heard howling their consecratory cry:

"Taboo! taboo! taboo!"

The fugitives made themselves levers out of the stakes of the tomb.

Meantime an enormous quantity of vapor, melted stones, and lava had escaped from the crater. It was no longer a simple geyser. All this volcanic effervescence had hitherto been confined beneath the crust of the peak, since the outlets of Tangariro sufficed for its expansion; but as a new opening had been made, it had rushed forth with extreme violence.

All night long, during the storm that raged above and below, the peak was shaken with a commotion that could not but alarm Glenarvan. The prisoners, concealed behind the palisade of the tomb, watched the fearful progress of the outbreak.

An incandescent column poured forth towards the sky with loud explosions, while streams of boiling water and lava rolled towards the encampment of the natives.

Morning came. The fury of the volcano had not moderated. Thick, yellowish vapors mingled with the flames, and torrents of lava poured in every direction. Glenarvan, with eye alert and beating heart, glanced between the interstices of the inclosure, and surveyed the camp of the Maoris.

The natives had fled to the neighboring plateaus, beyond the reach of the volcano. Several corpses, lying at the foot of the peak, had been charred by the fire. Farther on, towards the pah, the lava had consumed a number of huts, that were still smoking. The savages, in scattered groups, were gazing at the vapory summit of Maunganamu with religious awe.

Kai-Koumou came into the midst of his warriors, and Glenarvan recognized him. The chief advanced to the base of the peak, on the side spared by the eruption, but did not cross the first slopes. Here, with outstretched arms, like a sorcerer exorcising, he made a few grimaces, the meaning of which did not escape the prisoners. As Paganel had foreseen, Kai-Koumou was invoking upon the mountain a more rigorous taboo.

Soon after, the natives descended, in single file, the winding paths that led towards the pah.

A WEARY WAITING.

"They are going!" cried Glenarvan. "They are abandoning their post! God be thanked! Our scheme has succeeded! My dear Helena, my brave companions, we are now dead and buried; but this evening we will revive, we will leave our tomb, and flee from these barbarous tribes!"

It would be difficult to describe the joy that reigned within the palisade. Hope had reanimated all hearts. These courageous travelers forgot their past trials, dreaded not the future, and only rejoiced in their present deliverance; although very little reflection would show how difficult was the task of reaching an European settlement from their present position. But if Kai-Koumou was outwitted, they believed themselves safe from all the savages of New Zealand.

A whole day must pass before the decisive attempt could be made, and they employed their time in arranging a plan of escape. Paganel had preserved his map of New Zealand, and could therefore search out the safest routes.

After some discussion, the fugitives resolved to proceed eastward towards the Bay of Plenty. This course would lead them through districts that were very rarely visited. The travelers, who were already accustomed to overcoming natural difficulties, only feared meeting the Maoris. They therefore determined to avoid them at all hazards, and gain the eastern coast, where the missionaries have founded several establishments. Moreover, this portion of the island had hitherto escaped the ravages of the war and the depredations of the natives. As for the distance that separated Lake Taupo from the Bay of Plenty, it could not be more than one hundred miles. Ten days would suffice for the journey. The missions once reached, they could rest there, and wait for some favorable opportunity of gaining Auckland, their destination.

These points being settled, they continued to watch the savages till evening. Not one of them remained at the foot of the mountain, and when darkness invaded the valleys of the lake, no fire betokened the presence of the Maoris at the base of the peak. The coast was clear.

At nine o'clock it was dark night, and Glenarvan gave the signal for departure. His companions and he, armed and equipped at Kara-Tété's expense, began to cautiously descend the slopes of the Maunganamu. Captain Mangles and Wilson led the way, with eyes and ears on the alert. They stopped at the least sound,—they examined the faintest light; each slid down the declivity, the better to elude detection.

Two hundred feet below the summit, Captain Mangles and his sailor reached the dangerous ridge that had been so obstinately guarded by the natives. If, unfortunately, the Maoris, more crafty than the fugitives, had feigned a retreat to entice them within reach, if they had not been deceived by the eruption, their presence would be discovered at this point. Glenarvan, in spite of his confidence and Paganel's pleasantries, could not help trembling. The safety of his friends was at stake during the few moments necessary to cross the ridge. He felt Lady Helena's heart beat as she clung to his arm.

But neither he nor Captain Mangles thought of retreating. The young captain, followed by the others, and favored by the dense obscurity, crawled along the narrow path, only stopping when some detached stone rolled to the base of the mountain. If the savages were still in ambush, these unusual sounds would provoke from each side a formidable volley.

However, in gliding like serpents along this inclined crest, the fugitives could not advance rapidly. When Captain Mangles had gained the lowest part, scarcely twenty-five feet separated him from the plain where the natives had encamped the night before. Here the ridge ascended quite steeply towards a coppice about a quarter of a mile distant.

TABOOED NO LONGER.

The travelers crossed this place without accident, and began the ascent in silence. The thicket was invisible, but they knew where it was, and, provided no ambuscade was laid there, Glenarvan hoped to find a secure refuge. However, he remembered that they were now no longer protected by the taboo. The ascending ridge did not belong to the sacred mountain, but to a chain that ran along the eastern shores of Lake Taupo. Therefore not only the shots of the savages, but also a hand-to-hand conflict, were to be feared.

For a short time the little party slowly mounted towards the upper elevations. The captain could not yet discern the dark coppice, but it could not be more than two hundred feet distant.

Suddenly he stopped, and almost recoiled. He thought he heard some sound in the darkness. His hesitation arrested the advance of his companions.

He stood motionless long enough to alarm those who followed him. With what agonizing suspense they waited could not be described. Would they be forced to return to the summit of the mountain?

But, finding that the noise was not repeated, their leader continued his ascent along the narrow path. The coppice was soon dimly defined in the gloom. In a few moments it was reached, and the fugitives were crouching beneath the thick foliage of the trees.

CHAPTER LIV

FROM PERIL TO SAFETY.

Darkness favored the escape; and making the greatest possible progress, they left the fatal regions of Lake Taupo. Paganel assumed the guidance of the little party, and his marvelous instinct as a traveler was displayed anew during this perilous journey. He managed with surprising dexterity in the thick gloom, chose unhesitatingly the almost invisible paths, and kept constantly an undeviating course.

At nine o'clock in the morning they had accomplished a considerable distance, and could not reasonably require more of the courageous ladies. Besides, the place seemed suitable for an encampment. The fugitives had reached the ravine that separates the Kaimanawa and Wahiti ranges. The road on the right ran southward to Oberland. Paganel, with his map in his hand, made a turn to the northeast, and at ten o'clock the little party had reached a sort of steep buttress, formed by a spur of the mountain.

The provisions were taken from the sacks, and all did ample justice to them. Mary Grant and the major, who had not hitherto been very well satisfied with the edible ferns, made this time a hearty meal of them. They rested here till two o'clock in the afternoon, then the journey towards the east was resumed, and at evening the travelers encamped eight miles from the mountains. They needed no urging to sleep in the open air.

The next day very serious difficulties were encountered. They were forced to pass through a curious region of volcanic lakes and geysers that extends eastward from the Wahiti ranges. It was pleasing to the eye, but fatiguing to the limbs. Every quarter of a mile there were obstacles, turns, and windings, far too many for rapid progress; but what strange appearances and what infinite variety does nature give to her grand scenes!

ALMOST TIRED OUT!

Over this expanse of twenty square miles the overflow of subterranean forces was displayed in every form. Salt springs, of a singular transparency, teeming with myriads of insects, issued from the porous ground. They exhaled a penetrating odor, and deposited on the earth a white coating like dazzling snow. Their waters, though clear, were at the boiling-point, while other neighboring springs poured forth ice-cold streams. On every side water-spouts, with spiral rings of vapor, spirted from the ground like the jets of a fountain, some continuous, others intermittent, as if controlled by some capricious sprite. They rose like an amphitheatre, in natural terraces one above another, their vapors gradually mingling in wreaths of white smoke; and flowing down the semi-transparent steps of these gigantic staircases, they fed the lakes with their boiling cascades.

It will be needless to dilate upon the incidents of the journey, which were neither numerous nor important. Their way led through forests and over plains. The captain took his bearings by the sun and stars. The sky, which was quite clear, was sparing of heat and rain. Still, an increasing weariness delayed the travelers, already so cruelly tried, and they had to make great efforts to reach their destination.

However, they still conversed together, but no longer in common. The little party was divided into groups, not by any narrow prejudice or ill feeling, but to some extent from sadness. Often Glenarvan was alone, thinking, as he approached the coast, of the Duncan and her crew. He forgot the dangers that still threatened him, in his grief for his lost sailors and the terrible visions that continually haunted his mind.

They no longer spoke of Harry Grant. And why should they, since they could do nothing for him? If the captain's name was ever pronounced, it was in the conversations of his daughter and her betrothed. The young captain had not reminded her of what she had said to him on the last night of their captivity on the mountain. His magnanimity would not take advantage of words uttered in a moment of supreme despair.

ACCOMPLISHING THE LAST STAGE.

When he did speak of Captain Grant, he began to lay plans for a further search. He declared to Mary that Lord Glenarvan would resume this undertaking, hitherto so unsuccessful.

He maintained that the authenticity of the document could not be doubted. Her father must, therefore, be somewhere; and though it were necessary to search the whole world, they were sure to find him. The young girl was cheered by these words; and both, bound by the same thoughts, now sympathized in the same hope. Lady Helena often took part in the conversation, and was very careful not to discourage the young people with any sad forebodings.

On every side water-spouts, with spiral rings of vapor, spirted from the ground like the jets of a fountain.

Glenarvan and his companions, after many vicissitudes, reached the foot of Mount Ikirangi, whose peak towered five thousand feet aloft. They had now traveled almost one hundred miles since leaving the Maunganamu, and the coast was still thirty miles distant. Captain Mangles had hoped to make the journey in ten days, but he was ignorant then of the difficulties of the way. There were still two good days of travel before they could gain the ocean, and renewed activity and extreme vigilance became necessary, for they were entering a region frequented by the natives. However, each conquered the fatigue, and the little party continued their course.

Between Mount Ikirangi, some distance on their right, and Mount Hardy, whose summit rose to the left, was a large plain, thickly overspread with twining plants and underbrush. Progress here was tedious and difficult in the extreme; for the pliant tendrils wound a score of folds about their bodies like serpents. Hunting was impossible; the provisions were nearly exhausted, and could not be renewed, and water failed, so that they could not allay their thirst, rendered doubly acute by their fatigue. The sufferings of Glenarvan and his friends were terrible, and for the first time their moral energy now almost forsook them.

At last, dragging themselves along, wearied to the utmost degree in body, almost despairing in mind, they reached Lottin Point, on the shores of the Pacific.

At this place several deserted huts were seen, the ruins of a village recently devastated by the war; around them were abandoned fields, and everywhere the traces of plunder and conflagration. But here fate had reserved a new and fearful test for the unfortunate travelers.

They were walking along the coast, when, at no great distance, a number of natives appeared, who rushed towards the little party, brandishing their weapons. Glenarvan, shut in by the sea, saw that escape was impossible, and, summoning all his strength, was about to make preparations for battle, when Captain Mangles cried:

"A canoe! a canoe!"

And truly, twenty paces distant, a canoe, with six oars, was lying on the beach. To rush to it, set it afloat, and fly from this dangerous place was the work of an instant; the whole party seemed to receive at once a fresh accession of bodily strength and mental vigor.

In ten minutes the boat was at a considerable distance. The sea was calm. The captain, however, not wishing to wander too far from the coast, was about to give the order to cruise along the shore, when he suddenly ceased rowing. He had observed three canoes starting from Lottin Point, with the evident intention of overtaking and capturing the unfortunate fugitives.

"To sea! to sea!" cried he; "better perish in the waves than be captured!"

The canoe, under the strokes of its four oarsmen, at once put to sea, and for some time kept its distance. But the strength of the weakened fugitives soon grew less, and their pursuers gradually gained upon them. The boats were now scarcely a mile apart. There was therefore no possibility of avoiding the attack of the natives, who, armed with their long guns, were already preparing to fire.

DEATH ON EVERY HAND.

What was Glenarvan doing? Standing at the stern of the canoe, he looked around as if for some expected aid. What did he expect? What did he wish? Had he a presentiment?

All at once his face brightened, his hand was stretched towards an indistinct object.

"A ship!" cried he; "my friends, a ship! Row, row!"

Not one of the four oarsmen turned to see this unexpected vessel, for they must not lose a stroke. Only Paganel, rising, directed his telescope towards the place indicated.

"Yes," said he, "a ship, a steamer, under full headway, coming towards us! Courage, captain!"

The fugitives displayed new energy, and for several moments longer they kept their distance. The steamer grew more and more distinct. They could clearly discern her masts, and the thick clouds of black smoke that issued from her smoke-stack. Glenarvan, giving the helm to Robert, had seized the geographer's glass, and did not lose a single movement of the vessel.

But what were Captain Mangles and his companions to think when they saw the expression of his features change, his face grow pale, and the instrument fall from his hands. A single word explained this sudden emotion.

"The Duncan!" cried Glenarvan,—"the Duncan and the convicts!"

"The Duncan?" repeated the captain, dropping his oar and rising.

"Yes, death on all sides!" moaned Glenarvan, overcome by so many calamities.

It was indeed the yacht—without a doubt,—the yacht, with her crew of bandits! The major could not repress a malediction. This was too much.

Meantime the canoe was floating at random. Whither should they guide it, whither flee? Was it possible to choose between the savages and the convicts?

A MYSTERIOUS PRESERVATION.

Just then a shot came from the native boat, that had approached nearer. The bullet struck Wilson's oar; but his companions still propelled the canoe towards the Duncan. The yacht was advancing at full speed, and was only half a mile distant. Captain Mangles, beset on all sides, no longer knew how to act, or in what direction to escape. The two poor ladies were on their knees, praying in their despair.

A second ball whistled over their heads, and demolished the nearest of the three canoes.

The savages were now firing a continued volley, and the bullets rained around the canoe. Just then a sharp report sounded, and a ball from the yacht's cannon passed over the heads of the fugitives, who remained motionless between the fire of the Duncan and the natives.

Captain Mangles, frantic with despair, seized his hatchet. He was on the point of sinking their own canoe, with his unfortunate companions, when a cry from Robert stopped him.

"Tom Austin! Tom Austin!" said the child. "He is on board! I see him! He has recognized us! He is waving his hat!"

The hatchet was suspended in mid-air. A second ball whistled over their heads, and demolished the nearest of the three canoes, while a loud hurrah was heard on board the Duncan. The savages fled in terror towards the coast.

"Help, help, Tom!" cried Captain Mangles, in a piercing voice. And a few moments afterwards the ten fugitives, without knowing how, or scarcely comprehending this unexpected good fortune, were all in safety on board the Duncan.

CHAPTER LV

WHY THE DUNCAN WENT TO NEW ZEALAND.

The feelings of Glenarvan and his friends, when the songs of old Scotland resounded in their ears, it is impossible to describe. As soon as they set foot on deck the bagpiper struck up a well remembered air, while hearty hurrahs welcomed the owner's return on board. Glenarvan, John Mangles, Paganel, Robert, and even the major, wept and embraced each other. Their emotions rose from joy to ecstasy. The geographer was fairly wild, skipping about and watching with his inseparable telescope the canoes returning to shore.

But at sight of Glenarvan and his companions, with tattered garments, emaciated features, and the traces of extreme suffering, the crew ceased their lively demonstrations. These were spectres, not the bold and dashing travelers whom, three months before, hope had stimulated to a search for the shipwrecked captain. Chance alone had led them back to this vessel that they had ceased to regard as theirs, and in what a sad state of exhaustion and feebleness!

However, before thinking of fatigue, or the imperative calls of hunger and thirst, Glenarvan questioned Tom Austin concerning his presence in these waters. Why was the Duncan on the eastern coast of New Zealand? Why was she not in the hands of Ben Joyce? By what providential working had God restored her to the fugitives? These were the questions that were hurriedly addressed to Tom Austin. The old sailor did not know which to answer first. He therefore concluded to listen only to Lord Glenarvan, and reply to him.

"But the convicts?" inquired Glenarvan. "What have you done with the convicts?"

"The convicts!" replied Tom Austin, like a man who is at a loss to understand a question.

"Yes; the wretches who attacked the yacht."

"What yacht, my lord? The Duncan?"

"Of course. Did not Ben Joyce come on board?"

"I do not know Ben Joyce; I have never seen him."

"Never?" cried Glenarvan, amazed at the answers of the old sailor. "Then will you tell me why the Duncan is now on the shores of New Zealand?"

MYSTERY MORE MYSTERIOUS!

Although Glenarvan and his friends did not at all understand Austin's astonishment, what was their surprise when he replied, in a calm voice:

"The Duncan is here by your lordship's orders."

"By my orders?" cried Glenarvan.

"Yes, my lord. I only conformed to the instructions contained in your letter."

"My letter?" exclaimed Glenarvan.

The ten travelers at once surrounded Tom Austin, and gazed at him in eager curiosity. The letter written at the Snowy River had reached the Duncan.

"Well," continued Glenarvan, "let us have an explanation; for I almost think I am dreaming. You received a letter, Tom?"

"Yes; a letter from your lordship."

"At Melbourne?"

"At Melbourne; just as I had finished the repair of the ship."

"And this letter?"

"It was not written by you; but it was signed by you, my lord."

"Exactly; it was sent by a convict, Ben Joyce."

"No; by the sailor called Ayrton, quartermaster of the Britannia."

"Yes, Ayrton or Ben Joyce; it is the same person. Well, what did the letter say?"

"It ordered me to leave Melbourne without delay, and come to the eastern shores of——"

"Australia!" cried Glenarvan, with an impetuosity that disconcerted the old sailor.

"Australia?" repeated Tom, opening his eyes. "No, indeed; New Zealand!"

"Australia, Tom! Australia!" replied Glenarvan's companions, with one voice.

As soon as they set foot on deck the bagpiper struck up a well remembered air, while hearty hurrahs welcomed the owner's return on board.

Austin was now bewildered. Glenarvan spoke with such assurance, that he feared he had made a mistake in reading the letter. Could he, faithful and accurate sailor that he was, have committed such a blunder? He began to feel troubled.

"Be easy, Tom," said Lady Helena. "Providence has decreed——"

"No, madam, pardon me," returned the sailor; "no, it is not possible! I am not mistaken. Ayrton also read the letter, and he, on the contrary, wished to go to Australia."

This sally finished the poor geographer.

"Ayrton?" cried Glenarvan.

"The very one. He maintained that it was a mistake, and that you had appointed Twofold Bay as the place of meeting."

"Have you the letter, Tom?" asked the major, greatly puzzled.

"Yes, Mr. MacNabb," replied Austin. "I will soon bring it."

He accordingly repaired to his own cabin. While he was gone, they gazed at each other in silence, except the major, who, with his eye fixed upon Paganel, said, as he folded his arms:

"Indeed, I must confess, Paganel, that this is a little too much."

At this moment Austin returned. He held in his hand the letter written by Paganel, and signed by Glenarvan.

"Read it, my lord," said the old sailor.

Glenarvan took the letter, and read:

"Order for Tom Austin to put to sea, and bring the Duncan to the eastern coast of New Zealand."

"New Zealand?" cried Paganel, starting.

He snatched the letter from Glenarvan's hands, rubbed his eyes, adjusted his spectacles to his nose, and read in his turn.

"New Zealand!" repeated he, in an indescribable tone, while the letter slipped from his fingers.

Just then he felt a hand fall upon his shoulder. He turned, and found himself face to face with the major.

PAGANEL IN THE WITNESS-BOX.

"Well, my good Paganel," said MacNabb, in a grave tone, "it is fortunate that you did not send the Duncan to Cochin-China."

This sally finished the poor geographer. A fit of laughter seized the whole crew. Paganel, as if mad, ran to and fro, holding his head in his hands, and tearing his hair. However, when he had recovered from his frenzy, there was still another unavoidable question to answer.

"Now, Paganel," said Glenarvan, "be candid. I acknowledge that your absent-mindedness has been providential. To be sure, without you the Duncan would have fallen into the hands of the convicts; without you we should have been recaptured by the Maoris. But do tell me, what strange association of ideas, what unnatural aberration, induced you to write New Zealand instead of Australia?"

"Very well," said Paganel. "It was——"

But at that moment his eyes fell upon Robert and Mary Grant, and he stopped short, finally replying:

"Never mind, my dear Glenarvan. I am a madman, a fool, an incorrigible being, and shall die a most famous blunderer!"

The affair was no longer discussed. The mystery of the Duncan's presence there was solved; and the travelers, so miraculously saved, thought only of revisiting their comfortable cabins and partaking of a good breakfast.

However, leaving Lady Helena, Mary Grant, the major, Paganel, and Robert to enter the saloon, Glenarvan and Captain Mangles retained Tom Austin with them. They wished to question him further.

"Now, Tom," said Glenarvan, "let me know: did not this order to sail for the coast of New Zealand seem strange to you?"

"Yes, my lord," replied Austin. "I was very much surprised; but, as I am not in the habit of discussing the orders I receive, I obeyed. Could I act otherwise? If any accident had happened from not following your instructions should I not have been to blame? Would you have done differently, captain?"

"No, Tom," answered Captain Mangles.

"But what did you think?" asked Glenarvan.

"I thought, my lord, that, in the cause of Captain Grant, it was necessary to go wherever you directed me; that by some combination of circumstances another vessel would take you to New Zealand, and that I was to wait for you on the eastern coast of the island. Moreover, on leaving Melbourne, I kept my destination secret, and the crew did not know it till we were out at sea and the shores of Australia had disappeared from sight. But then an incident occurred that perplexed me very much."

"What do you mean, Tom?" inquired Glenarvan.

"I mean," he replied, "that when the quartermaster, Ayrton, learned, the day after our departure, the Duncan's destination——"

"Ayrton!" cried Glenarvan. "Is he on board?"

"Yes, my lord."

"Ayrton here!" repeated Glenarvan, glancing at Captain Mangles.

"Wonderful indeed!" said the young captain.

In an instant, with the swiftness of lightning, Ayrton's conduct, his long-contrived treachery, Glenarvan's wound, the attack upon Mulready, their sufferings in the marshes of the Snowy, all the wretch's deeds, flashed upon the minds of the two men. And now, by a strange fatality, the convict was in their power.

"Where is he?" asked Glenarvan quickly.

"In a cabin in the forecastle," replied Tom Austin, "closely guarded."

"Why this confinement?"

AN UNOFFICIAL TRIBUNAL.

"Because, when Ayrton saw that the yacht was sailing for New Zealand, he flew into a passion; because he attempted to force me to change the ship's course; because he threatened me; and, finally, because he urged my men to a mutiny. I saw that he was a dangerous person, and was compelled, therefore, to take precautions against him."

"And since that time?"

"Since that time he has been in his cabin, without offering to come out."

"Good!"

At this moment Glenarvan and Captain Mangles were summoned to the saloon. Breakfast, which they so much needed, was ready. They took seats at the table, but did not speak of Ayrton.

However, when the meal was ended, and the passengers had assembled on deck, Glenarvan informed them of the quartermaster's presence on board. At the same time he declared his intention of sending for him.

"Can I be released from attending this tribunal?" asked Lady Helena. "I confess to you, my dear Edward, that the sight of this unfortunate would be very painful to me."

"It is only to confront him, Helena," replied Glenarvan. "Remain, if you can. Ben Joyce should see himself face to face with all his intended victims."

Lady Helena yielded to this request, and Mary Grant and she took their places beside him, while around them stood the major, Paganel, Captain Mangles, Robert, Wilson, Mulready, and Olbinett, all who had suffered so severely by the convict's treason. The crew of the yacht, who did not yet understand the seriousness of these proceedings, maintained a profound silence.

"Call Ayrton!" said Glenarvan.

CHAPTER LVI

AYRTON'S OBSTINACY.

Ayrton soon made his appearance. He crossed the deck with a confident step, and ascended the poop-stairs. His eyes had a sullen look, his teeth were set, and his fists clinched convulsively. His bearing displayed neither exultation nor humility. As soon as he was in Lord Glenarvan's presence, he folded his arms, and calmly and silently waited to be questioned:

"Ayrton," said Glenarvan, "here we all are, as you see, on board the Duncan, that you would have surrendered to Ben Joyce's accomplices."

At these words the lips of the quartermaster slightly trembled. A quick blush colored his hard features,—not the sign of remorse, but the shame of defeat. He was prisoner on this yacht that he had meant to command as master, and his fate was soon to be decided.

However, he made no reply. Glenarvan waited patiently, but Ayrton still persisted in maintaining an obstinate silence.

"Speak, Ayrton; what have you to say?" continued Glenarvan.

The convict hesitated, and the lines of his forehead were strongly contracted. At last he said, in a calm voice:

"I have nothing to say, my lord. I was foolish enough to let myself be taken. Do what you please."

A DUMB PRISONER.

Having given his answer, the quartermaster turned his eyes toward the coast that extended along the west, and affected a profound indifference for all that was passing around him. You would have thought, to look at him, that he was a stranger to this serious affair.

But Glenarvan had resolved to be patient. A powerful motive urged him to ascertain certain circumstances of Ayrton's mysterious life, especially as regarded Harry Grant and the Britannia. He therefore resumed his inquiries, speaking with extreme mildness, and imposing the most perfect calmness upon the violent agitation of his heart.

"I hope, Ayrton," continued he, "that you will not refuse to answer certain questions that I desire to ask you. And, first, am I to call you Ayrton or Ben Joyce? Are you the quartermaster of the Britannia?"

Ayrton remained unmoved, watching the coast, deaf to every question. Glenarvan, whose eye flashed with some inward emotion, continued to question him.

"Will you tell me how you left the Britannia, and why you were in Australia?"

There was the same silence, the same obstinacy.

"Listen to me, Ayrton," resumed Glenarvan. "It is for your interest to speak. We may reward a frank confession, which is your only resort. For the last time, will you answer my questions?"

Ayrton turned his head towards Glenarvan, and looked him full in the face.

"My lord," said he, "I have nothing to answer. It is for justice to prove against me."

"The proofs will be easy," replied Glenarvan.

USELESS APPEALS.

"Easy, my lord?" continued the quartermaster, in a sneering tone. "Your lordship seems to me very hasty. I declare that the best judge in Westminster Hall would be puzzled to establish my identity. Who can say why I came to Australia, since Captain Grant is no longer here to inform you? Who can prove that I am that Ben Joyce described by the police, since they have never laid hands upon me, and my companions are at liberty? Who, except you, can charge me, not to say with a crime, but even with a culpable action?"

Ayrton had grown animated while speaking, but soon relapsed into his former indifference. He doubtless imagined that this declaration would end the examination: but Glenarvan resumed, and said:

"Ayrton, I am not a judge charged with trying you. This is not my business. It is important that our respective positions should be clearly defined. I ask nothing that can implicate you, for that is the part of justice. But you know what search I am pursuing, and, with a word, you can put me on the track I have lost. Will you speak?"

Ayrton shook his head, like a man determined to keep silent.

"Will you tell me where Captain Grant is?" asked Glenarvan.

"No, my lord."

"Will you point out where the Britannia was wrecked?"

Ayrton soon made his appearance. He crossed the deck with a confident step,
and ascended the poop-stairs.

"Certainly not."

"Ayrton," said Glenarvan, in almost a suppliant tone, "will you, at least, if you know where Captain Grant is, tell his poor children, who are only waiting for a word from your lips?"

The quartermaster hesitated; his features quivered; but, in a low voice, he muttered:

"I cannot, my lord."

Then, as if he reproached himself for a moment's weakness, he added, angrily:

"No, I will not speak! Hang me if you will!"

"Hang, then!" cried Glenarvan, overcome by a sudden feeling of indignation.

But finally controlling himself, he said, in a grave voice:

"There are neither judges nor hangmen here. At the first landing-place you shall be put into the hands of the English authorities."

"Just what I desire," replied the quartermaster.

Thereupon he was taken back to the cabin that served as his prison, and two sailors were stationed at the door, with orders to watch all his movements. The witnesses of this scene retired indignant and in despair.

Since Glenarvan had failed to overcome Ayrton's obstinacy, what was to be done? Evidently to follow the plan formed at Eden, of returning to England, and resuming hereafter this unsuccessful enterprise, for all traces of the Britannia now seemed irrevocably lost. The document admitted of no new interpretation. There was no other country on the line of the thirty-seventh parallel, and the only way was to sail for home.

He consulted his friends, and more especially Captain Mangles, on the subject of return. The captain examined his store-rooms. The supply of coal would not last more than fifteen days. It was, therefore, necessary to replenish the fuel at the first port. He accordingly proposed to Glenarvan to sail for Talcahuana Bay, where the Duncan had already procured supplies before undertaking her voyage. This was a direct passage. Then the yacht, with ample provisions, could double Cape Horn, and reach Scotland by way of the Atlantic.

This plan being adopted, the engineer was ordered to force on steam. Half an hour afterwards the yacht was headed towards Talcahuana, and at six o'clock in the evening the mountains of New Zealand had disappeared beneath the mists of the horizon.

WOMANLY INFLUENCE.

It was a sad return for these brave searchers, who had left the shores of Scotland with such hope and confidence. To the joyous cries that had saluted Glenarvan on his return succeeded profound dejection. Each confined himself to the solitude of his cabin, and rarely appeared on deck. All, even the loquacious Paganel, were mournful and silent. If Glenarvan spoke of beginning his search again, the geographer shook his head like a man who has no more hope, for he seemed convinced as to the fate of the shipwrecked sailors. Yet there was one man on board who could have informed them about this catastrophe, but whose silence was still prolonged. There was no doubt that the rascally Ayrton knew, if not the actual situation of the captain, at least the place of the shipwreck. Probably Harry Grant, if found, would be a witness against him; hence he persisted in his silence, and was greatly enraged, especially towards the sailors who would accuse him of an evil design.

Several times Glenarvan renewed his attempts with the quartermaster. Promises and threats were useless. Ayrton's obstinacy was carried so far, and was so inexplicable, that the major came to the belief that he knew nothing; which opinion was shared by the geographer and corroborated his own ideas in regard to Captain Grant.

But if Ayrton knew nothing, why did he not plead his ignorance? It could not turn against him, while his silence increased the difficulty of forming a new plan. Ought they to infer the presence of Harry Grant in Australia from meeting the quartermaster on that continent? At all events, they must induce Ayrton to explain on this subject.

Lady Helena, seeing her husband's failures, now suggested an attempt, in her turn, to persuade the quartermaster. Where a man had failed, perhaps a woman could succeed by her gentle entreaty. Glenarvan, knowing the tact of his young wife, gave his hearty approval. Ayrton was, accordingly, brought to Lady Helena's boudoir. Mary Grant was to be present at the interview, for the young girl's influence might also be great, and Lady Helena would not neglect any chance of success.

For an hour the two ladies were closeted with the quartermaster, but nothing resulted from this conference. What they said, the arguments they used to draw out the convict's secret, all the details of this examination, remained unknown. Moreover, when Ayrton left them they did not appear to have succeeded, and their faces betokened real despair.

When the quartermaster was taken back to his cabin, therefore, the sailors saluted his appearance with violent threats. But he contented himself with shrugging his shoulders, which so increased the rage of the crew, that nothing less than the intervention of the captain and his lordship could restrain them.

But Lady Helena did not consider herself defeated. She wished to struggle to the last with this heartless man, and the next day she went herself to Ayrton's cabin, to avoid the scene that his appearance on deck occasioned.

For two long hours this kind and gentle Scotch lady remained alone face to face with the chief of the convicts. Glenarvan, a prey to nervous agitation, lingered near the cabin, now determined to thoroughly exhaust the chances of success, and now upon the point of drawing his wife away from this painful and prolonged interview.

For an hour the two ladies were closeted with the quartermaster, but nothing resulted from this conference.

But this time, when Lady Helena reappeared, her features inspired confidence. Had she, then, brought this secret to light, and stirred the dormant feeling of pity in the heart of this poor creature?

MacNabb, who saw her first, could not repress a very natural feeling of incredulity. However, the rumor soon spread among the crew that the quartermaster had at length yielded to Lady Helena's entreaties. All the sailors assembled on deck more quickly than if Tom Austin's whistle had summoned them.

He contented himself with shrugging his shoulders, which so increased the rage of the crew, that nothing less than the intervention of the captain and his lordship could restrain them.

"Has he spoken?" asked Lord Glenarvan of his wife.

"No," replied Lady Helena; "but in compliance with my entreaties he desires to see you."

"Ah, dear Helena, you have succeeded!"

"I hope so, Edward."

"Have you made any promise that I am to sanction?"

"Only one: that you will use all your influence to moderate the fate in store for him."

VERY BUSINESS-LIKE.

"Certainly, my dear Helena. Let him come to me immediately."

Lady Helena retired to her cabin, accompanied by Mary Grant, and the quartermaster was taken to the saloon where Glenarvan awaited him.

Chapter LVII

A DISCOURAGING CONFESSION.

As soon as the quartermaster was in Lord Glenarvan's presence his custodians retired.

"You desired to speak to me, Ayrton?" said Glenarvan.

"Yes, my lord," replied he.

"To me alone?"

"Yes; but I think that if Major MacNabb and Mr. Paganel were present at the interview it would be better."

"For whom?"

"For me."

Ayrton spoke calmly. Glenarvan gazed at him steadily, and then sent word to MacNabb and Paganel, who at once obeyed his summons.

"We are ready for you," said Glenarvan, as soon as his two friends were seated at the cabin-table.

Ayrton reflected for a few moments, and then said:

"My lord, it is customary for witnesses to be present at every contract or negotiation between two parties. That is why I requested the presence of Mr. Paganel and Major MacNabb; for, properly speaking, this is a matter of business that I am going to propose to you."

Glenarvan, who was accustomed to Ayrton's manners, betrayed no surprise, although a matter of business between this man and himself seemed strange.

BARGAINING FOR TERMS.

"What is this business?" said he.

"This is it," replied Ayrton. "You desire to know from me certain circumstances which may be useful to you. I desire to obtain from you certain advantages which will be valuable to me. Now, I will make an exchange, my lord. Do you agree or not?"

"What are these circumstances?" asked Paganel, quickly.

"No," corrected Glenarvan: "what are these advantages?"

Ayrton bowed, showing that he understood the distinction.

"These," said he, "are the advantages for which I petition. You still intend, my lord, to deliver me into the hands of the English authorities?"

"Yes, Ayrton; it is only justice."

"I do not deny it," replied the quartermaster. "You would not consent, then, to set me at liberty?"

"Do you agree or not?"

Glenarvan hesitated before answering a question so plainly asked. Perhaps the fate of Harry Grant depended upon what he was about to say. However, the feeling of duty towards humanity prevailed, and he said:

"No, Ayrton, I cannot set you at liberty."

"I do not ask it," replied the quartermaster, proudly.

"What do you wish, then?"

"An intermediate fate, my lord, between that which you think awaits me and the liberty that you cannot grant me."

"And that is———?"

"To abandon me on one of the desert islands of the Pacific, with the principal necessaries of life. I will manage as I can, and repent, if I have time."

Glenarvan, who was little prepared for this proposal, glanced at his two friends, who remained silent. After a few moments of reflection, he replied:

"Ayrton, if I grant your request, will you tell me all that it is for my interest to know?"

"Yes, my lord; that is to say, all that I know concerning Captain Grant and the Britannia."

"The whole truth?"

"The whole."

"But who will warrant———?"

"Oh, I see what troubles you, my lord. You do not like to trust to me,—to the word of a malefactor! That is right. But what can you do? The situation is thus. You have only to accept or refuse."

"I will trust you, Ayrton," said Glenarvan, simply.

"And you will be right, my lord. Moreover, if I deceive you, you will always have the power to revenge yourself."

"How?"

"By recapturing me on this island, from which I shall not be able to escape."

Ayrton had a reply for everything. He met all difficulties, and produced unanswerable arguments against himself. As was seen, he strove to treat in his business with good faith. It was impossible for a person to surrender with more perfect confidence, and yet he found means to advance still further in this disinterested course.

"My lord and gentlemen," added he, "I desire that you should be convinced that I am honorable. I do not seek to deceive you, but am going to give you a new proof of my sincerity in this affair. I act frankly, because I rely upon your loyalty."

"Go on, Ayrton," replied Glenarvan.

"My lord, I have not yet your promise to agree to my proposition, and still I do not hesitate to tell you that I know little concerning Harry Grant."

"Little!" cried Glenarvan.

"Yes, my lord; the circumstances that I am able to communicate to you are relative to myself. They are personal experiences, and will scarcely tend to put you on the track you have lost."

REVELATIONS AND DISCLOSURES.

A keen disappointment was manifest on the features of Glenarvan and the major. They had believed the quartermaster to possess an important secret, and yet he now confessed that his disclosures would be almost useless.

However that may be, this avowal of Ayrton, who surrendered himself without security, singularly affected his hearers, especially when he added, in conclusion:

"Thus you are forewarned, my lord, that the business will be less advantageous for you than for me."

"No matter," replied Glenarvan; "I accept your proposal, Ayrton. You have my word that you shall be landed at one of the islands of the Pacific."

"Very well, my lord," said he.

Was this strange man pleased with this decision? You might have doubted it, for his impassive countenance betrayed no emotion. He seemed as if acting for another more than for himself.

"I am ready to answer," continued he.

"We have no questions to ask you," rejoined Glenarvan. "Tell us what you know, Ayrton, and, in the first place, who you are."

"Gentlemen," replied he, "I am really Tom Ayrton, quartermaster of the Britannia. I left Glasgow in Captain Grant's ship on the 12th of March, 1861. For fourteen months we traversed together the Pacific, seeking some favorable place to found a Scottish colony. Harry Grant was a man capable of performing great deeds, but frequently serious disputes arose between us. His character did not harmonize with mine. I could not yield; but with Harry Grant, when his resolution is taken, all resistance is impossible. He is like iron towards himself and others. However, I dared to mutiny, and attempted to involve the crew and gain possession of the vessel. Whether I did right or wrong is of little importance. However it may be, Captain Grant did not hesitate to land me, April 8, 1862, on the west coast of Australia."

"Australia!" exclaimed the major, interrupting Ayrton's story. "Then you left the Britannia before her arrival at Callao, where the last news of her was dated?"

"Yes," replied the quartermaster; "for the Britannia never stopped at Callao while I was on board. If I spoke of Callao at O'Moore's farm, it was your story that gave me this information."

"Go on, Ayrton," said Glenarvan.

MORE BLANKS THAN PRIZES.

"I found myself, therefore, abandoned on an almost desert coast, but only twenty miles from the penitentiary of Perth, the capital of Western Australia. Wandering along the shore, I met a band of convicts who had just escaped. I joined them. You will spare me, my lord, the account of my life for two years and a half. It is enough to know that I became chief of the runaways, under the name of Ben Joyce. In the month of September, 1864, I made my appearance at the Irishman's farm, and was received as a servant under my true name of Ayrton. Here I waited till an opportunity should be offered to gain possession of a vessel. This was my great object. Two months later the Duncan arrived. During your visit at the farm you related, my lord, the whole story of Captain Grant. I then learned what I had not known, the Britannia's stoppage at Callao, the last news of her, dated June, 1862, two months after my abandonment, the finding of the document, the shipwreck of the vessel, and finally the important reasons you had for seeking Captain Grant in Australia. I did not hesitate, but resolved to appropriate the Duncan,—a marvelous ship, that would have distanced the best of the British navy. However, there were serious injuries to be repaired. I therefore let her start for Melbourne, and offered myself to you in my real character of quartermaster, volunteering to guide you to the scene of the shipwreck, which I falsely located on the eastern coast of Australia. Thus followed at a distance and sometimes preceded by my band of convicts, I conducted your party across the province of Victoria. My companions committed a useless crime at Camden Bridge, since the Duncan, once at Twofold Bay, could not have escaped me, and with it I should have been master of the ocean. I brought you thus unsuspectingly as far as the Snowy River. The horses and oxen fell dead one by one, poisoned by the gastrolobium. I entangled the cart in the marshes. At my suggestion——but you know the rest, my lord, and can be certain that, except for Mr. Paganel's absent-mindedness, I should now be commander on board the Duncan. Such is my story, gentlemen. My disclosures, unfortunately, cannot set you on the track of Captain Grant, and you see that in dealing with me you have made a bad bargain."

The quartermaster ceased, crossed his arms, according to his custom, and waited. Glenarvan and his friends were silent. They felt that this strange criminal had told the entire truth. The capture of the Duncan had only failed through a cause altogether beyond his control. His accomplices had reached Twofold Bay, as the convict's blouse, found by Glenarvan, proved. There, faithful to the orders of their chief, they had lain in wait for the yacht, and at last, tired of watching, they had doubtless resumed their occupation of plunder and burning in the fields of New South Wales.

The major was the first to resume the examination, in order to determine the dates relative to the Britannia.

"It was the 8th of April, 1862, then, that you were landed on the west coast of Australia?" he asked of the quartermaster.

"Exactly," replied Ayrton.

"And do you know what Captain Grant's plans were then?"

"Vaguely."

"Continue, Ayrton," said Glenarvan. "The least sign may set us on the track."

"What I can say is this, my lord. Captain Grant intended to visit New Zealand. But this part of his programme was not carried out while I was on board. The Britannia might, therefore, after leaving Callao, have gained the shores of New Zealand. This would agree with the date, June 27, 1862, given in the document as the time of the shipwreck."

"Evidently," remarked Paganel.

"But," added Glenarvan, "there is nothing in these half-obliterated portions of the document which can apply to New Zealand."

"That I cannot answer," said the quartermaster.

"Well, Ayrton," continued Glenarvan, "you have kept your word, and I will keep mine. We will decide on what island of the Pacific you shall be abandoned."

"Oh, it matters little to me," answered Ayrton.

"Return to your cabin now, and await our decision."

The quartermaster retired, under guard of the two sailors.

"This villain might have been a great man," observed the major.

"Yes," replied Glenarvan. "He has a strong and self-reliant character. Why must his abilities be devoted to crime?"

"But Harry Grant?"

"I fear that he is forever lost! Poor children! who could tell them where their father is?"

"I!" cried Paganel.

As we have remarked, the geographer, although so loquacious and excitable usually, had scarcely spoken during Ayrton's examination. He had listened in total silence. But this last word that he had uttered was worth more than all the others, and startled Glenarvan at once.

"You, Paganel!" he exclaimed; "do you know where Captain Grant is?"

"As well as can be known," answered the geographer.

"And how do you know?"

"By that everlasting document."

A GEOGRAPHER'S REMINISCENCES.

"Ah!" said the major, in a tone of the most thorough incredulity.

"Listen first, MacNabb, and shrug your shoulders afterwards. I did not speak before, because you would not have believed me. Besides, it was useless. But if I speak to-day, it is because Ayrton's opinion corroborates mine."

"Then New Zealand——?" asked Glenarvan.

"Hear and judge," replied Paganel. "I did not commit the blunder that saved us, without reason. Just as I was writing that letter at Glenarvan's dictation, the word Zealand was troubling my brain.

You remember that we were in the cart. MacNabb had just told Lady Helena the story of the convicts, and had handed her the copy of the *Australian and New Zealand Gazette* that gave an account of the accident at Camden Bridge. As I was writing, the paper lay on the ground, folded so that only two syllables of its title could be seen, and these were *aland*. What a light broke in upon my mind! 'Aland' was one of the very words in the English document,—a word that we had hitherto translated *ashore*, but which was the termination of the proper name Zealand."

"Ha!" cried Glenarvan.

"Yes," continued Paganel, with profound conviction, "this interpretation had escaped me, and do you know why? Because my examinations were naturally confined more particularly to the French document, where this important word was wanting."

"Ho! ho!" laughed the major, "that is too much imagination, Paganel. You forget your previous conclusions rather easily."

"Well, major, I am ready to answer you."

"Then what becomes of your word *austral?*"

"It is what it was at first. It simply means the southern (*australes*) countries."

"Very well. But that word *indi*, that was first the root of Indians (*indiens*), and then of natives (*indigènes*)?"

"The third and last time, it shall be the first two syllables of the word *indigence* (destitution)."

"And *contin!*" cried MacNabb; "does it still signify *continent?*"

"No, since New Zealand is only an island."

"Then?" inquired Glenarvan.

"My dear lord," replied Paganel, "I will translate the document for you, according to my third interpretation, and you shall judge. I only make two suggestions. First, forget as far as possible the previous interpretations; and next, although certain passages will seem to you forced, and I may translate them wrongly, still, remember that they have no special importance. Moreover, the French document serves as the basis of my interpretation, and you must consider that it was written by an Englishman who could not have been perfectly familiar with the idioms of our language."

So saying, Paganel, slowly pronouncing each syllable, read the following:

"On the 27th of June, 1862, the brig Britannia, of Glasgow, foundered, after a long struggle (*agonie*), in the South (*australes*) Seas, on the coasts of New Ze*aland*. Two sailors and Captain Grant succeeded in landing (*abor*der). Here, continually (*contin*uellement) a prey (*pr*oie) to a cruel (*crue*Λe) destitution (*indi*gence), they cast this document into the sea, at longitude —— and latitude 37° 11'. Come to their assistance, or they are lost."

Paganel stopped. His interpretation was admissible. But, although it appeared as probable as the other, still it might be as false. Glenarvan and the major therefore no longer attempted to dispute it. However, since the traces of the Britannia had not been encountered on the coasts of Patagonia or Australia, the chances were in favor of New Zealand.

"Now, Paganel," said Glenarvan, "will you tell me why, for about two months, you kept this interpretation secret?"

UNANIMITY IN DESPAIR.

"Because I did not wish to give you vain hopes. Besides, we were going to Auckland, which is on the very latitude of the document."

"But afterwards, when we were taken out of our course, why did you not speak?"

"Because, however just this interpretation may be, it cannot contribute to the captain's rescue."

"Why, Paganel?"

"Because, admitting that Captain Grant was wrecked on the coast of New Zealand, as long as he has not made his appearance for two years since the disaster, he must have fallen a victim to the sea or the savages."

"Then your opinion is———?" asked Glenarvan.

"That we might perhaps find some traces of the shipwreck, but that the seamen of the Britannia have perished."

"Keep all this silent, my friends," replied Glenarvan, "and leave me to choose the time for telling this sad news to the children of Captain Grant."

CHAPTER LVIII

A CRY IN THE NIGHT.

The crew soon learned that Ayrton's disclosures had not thrown light upon the situation of Captain Grant. The despair on board was profound, for they had relied on the quartermaster, who, however, knew nothing that could put the Duncan on the track of the Britannia. The yacht therefore continued on the same course, and the only question now was to choose the island on which to leave Ayrton.

Paganel and Captain Mangles consulted the maps on board. Exactly on the thirty-seventh parallel was an island, generally known by the name of Maria Theresa, a lone rock in the midst of the Pacific, three thousand five hundred miles from the American coast, and one thousand five hundred miles from New Zealand. No ship ever came within hail of this solitary isle; no tidings from the world ever reached it. Only the storm-birds rested here during their long flights, and many maps do not even indicate its position.

If anywhere absolute isolation was to be found on earth, it was here, afar from the ocean's traveled highways. Its situation was made known to Ayrton, who consented to live there; and the vessel was accordingly headed towards the island. Two days later the lookout hailed land on the horizon. It was Maria Theresa, low, long, and scarcely emerging from the waves, appearing like some enormous sea-monster. Thirty miles still lay between it and the yacht, whose prow cut the waves with such speed that soon the island grew distinct. The sun, now sinking towards the west, defined its outlines in glowing light. Several slight elevations were tinged with the last rays of the day.

At five o'clock Captain Mangles thought he distinguished a faint smoke rising towards the sky.

"Is that a volcano?" he inquired of Paganel, who, with his telescope, was examining the land.

"I do not know what to think," replied the geographer. "Maria Theresa is a point little known. However, I should not be surprised if its origin was due to some volcanic upheaval."

"But then," said Glenarvan, "if an eruption created it, may we not fear that the same agency will destroy it?"

"That is scarcely probable," answered Paganel. "Its existence has been known for several centuries; and this seems a guarantee for its continuance."

"Well," continued Glenarvan, "do you think, captain, that we can land before night?"

ANOTHER ARTIFICIAL VOLCANO.

"No, certainly not. I ought not to endanger the Duncan in the darkness, on a coast that is not familiar to me. I will keep a short distance from land, and to-morrow at daybreak we will send a boat ashore."

At eight o'clock Maria Theresa, although only five miles to windward, appeared like a lengthened shadow, scarcely visible. An hour later, quite a bright light, like a fire, blazed in the darkness. It was motionless and stationary.

"That would seem to indicate a volcano," said Paganel, watching it attentively.

"However," replied Captain Mangles, "at this distance we ought to hear the commotion that always accompanies an eruption, and yet the wind brings no sound to our ears."

"Indeed," observed Paganel, "this volcano glows, but does not speak. You might say that it throws out intermittent flashes like a lighthouse."

"You are right," continued Captain Mangles; "and yet we are not on the illuminated side. Ha!" cried he, "another fire! On the shore this time! See! it moves, it changes its place!"

He was not mistaken. A new light had appeared, that sometimes seemed to go out, and then all at once flash forth again.

"Is the island inhabited?" asked Glenarvan.

"Evidently, by savages," replied Paganel.

"Then we cannot abandon the quartermaster here."

"No," said the major; "that would be giving even savages too dangerous a present."

"We will seek some other deserted island," resumed Glenarvan, who could not help smiling at MacNabb's delicacy. "I promised Ayrton his life, and I will keep my promise."

"At all events, let us beware," added Paganel. "The New Zealanders have the barbarous custom of misleading ships by moving fires. The natives of Maria Theresa may understand this deception."

"Bear away a point," cried the captain to the sailor at the helm. "To-morrow, at sunrise, we shall know what is to be done."

At eleven o'clock the passengers and the captain retired to their cabins. At the bow the first watch was pacing the deck, while at the stern the helmsman was alone at his post.

In the stillness Mary and Robert Grant came on deck. The two children, leaning upon the railing, gazed sadly at the phosphorescent sea and the luminous wake of the yacht. Mary thought of Robert's future; Robert thought of his sister's; both thought of their father. Was that beloved parent still living? Yet must they give him up? But no, what would life be without him? What would become of them without his protection? What would have become of them already, except for the magnanimity of Lord and Lady Glenarvan?

The boy, taught by misfortune, divined the thoughts that were agitating his sister. He took her hand in his.

"Mary," said he, "we must never despair. Remember the lessons our father taught us. 'Courage compensates for everything in this world,' he said. Let us have that indomitable courage that overcomes all obstacles. Hitherto you have labored for me, my sister, but now I shall labor for you."

"Dear Robert!" replied the young girl.

"I must tell you one thing," continued he. "You will not be sorry, Mary?"

"Why should I be sorry, my child?"

"And you will let me do as I wish?"

"What do you mean?" asked she, anxiously.

"My sister, I shall be a sailor——!"

"And leave me?" cried the young girl, clasping her brother's hand.

EULOGY AND THRENODY.

"Yes, sister, I shall be a sailor, like my father, and like Captain John. Mary, my dear Mary, he has not lost all hope! You will have, like me, confidence in his devotion. He has promised that he will make me a thorough and efficient sailor, and we shall seek our father together. Say that you are willing, sister. What our father would have done for us it is our duty, or mine at least, to do for him. My life has but one object, to which it is wholly devoted,—to search always for him who would never have abandoned either of us. Dear Mary, how good our father was!"

"And so noble, so generous!" added Mary. "Do you know, Robert, that he was already one of the glories of our country, and would have ranked among its great men if fate had not arrested his course?"

"How well I know it!" answered Robert.

Mary pressed her brother to her heart, and the child felt tears dropping upon his forehead.

"Mary! Mary!" cried he, "it is in vain for them to speak, or to keep silent. I hope still, and shall always do so. A man like our father does not die till he has accomplished his purpose!"

Mary Grant could not reply; sobs choked her utterance. A thousand emotions agitated her soul at the thought that new attempts would be made to find her father, and that the young captain's devotion was boundless.

"Does Mr. John still hope?" asked she.

"Yes," replied Robert. "He is a brother who will never forsake us. I shall be a sailor, shall I not, sister,—a sailor to seek my father with him? Are you willing?"

"Yes," said Mary. "But must we be separated?"

"You will not be alone, Mary, I know. John has told me so. Lady Helena will not permit you to leave her. You are a woman, and can and ought to accept her benefits. To refuse them would be ungrateful. But a man, as my father has told me a hundred times, ought to make his own fortune."

"But what will become of our house at Dundee, so full of associations?"

"We will keep it, my sister. All that has been well arranged by our friend John and Lord Glenarvan, who will keep you at Malcolm Castle like a daughter. He said so to John, who told me. You will be at home there, and wait till John and I bring back our father. Ah, what a joyful day that will be!" cried Robert, whose face was radiant with enthusiasm.

"My brother, my child!" exclaimed Mary, "how happy our father would be if he could hear you! How much you resemble him, dear Robert! When you are a man you will be quite like him!"

"God grant it, Mary!" said Robert, glowing with holy and filial pride.

"But how shall we pay our debt to Lord and Lady Glenarvan?" continued Mary.

"Oh, that will not be difficult," answered Robert, with his boyish impulsiveness. "We will tell them how much we love and respect them, and we will show it to them by our actions."

"That is all we can do!" added the young girl, covering her brother's face with kisses; "and all that they will like, too!"

Then, relapsing into reveries, the two children of the captain gazed silently into the shadowy obscurity of the night. However, in fancy they still conversed, questioned, and answered each other. The sea rocked the ship in silence, and the phosphorescent waters glistened in the darkness.

But now a strange, a seemingly supernatural event took place. The brother and sister, by one of those magnetic attractions that mysteriously draw the souls of friends together, experienced at the same instant the same curious hallucination.

"METHOUGHT, THE BILLOWS SPOKE!"

From the midst of these alternately brightening and darkening waves, they thought they heard a voice issue, whose depth of sadness stirred every fibre of their hearts.

"Help! help!" cried the voice.

"Mary," said Robert, "did you hear?"

And, raising their heads above the bulwarks, they both gazed searchingly into the misty shadows of the night. Yet there was nothing but the darkness stretching blankly before them.

"Robert," said Mary, pale with emotion, "I thought—yes, I thought like you."

At this moment another cry reached them, and this time the illusion was such that these words broke simultaneously from both their hearts:

"My father! my father!"

This was too much for Mary Grant. Overcome by emotion, she sank senseless into her brother's arms.

"Help!" cried Robert. "My sister! my father! help!"

The man at the helm hastened to Miss Grant's assistance, and after him the sailors of the watch, Captain Mangles, Lady Helena, and Lord Glenarvan, who had been suddenly awakened.

"My sister is dying, and my father is yonder!" exclaimed Robert, pointing to the waves.

No one understood his words.

"Yes," repeated he, "my father is yonder! I heard his voice, and Mary did too!"

Just then Mary Grant recovered consciousness, and, looking wildly around, cried:

"My father, my father is yonder!"

The unfortunate girl arose, and, leaning over the bulwark, would have thrown herself into the sea.

"My lord! Madam!" repeated she, clasping her hands, "I tell you my father is there! I declare to you that I heard his voice issue from the waves like a despairing wail, like a last adieu!"

THE POSITIVENESS OF DISBELIEF.

Then her feelings overcame the poor girl, and she became insensible. They carried her to her cabin, and Lady Helena followed, to minister to her wants, while Robert kept repeating:

"My father! my father is there! I am sure of it, my lord!"

The witnesses of this sorrowful scene perceived at last that the two children had been the sport of an hallucination. But how undeceive their senses, which had been so strongly impressed? Glenarvan, however, attempted it, and taking Robert by the hand, said:

"You heard your father's voice, my dear boy?"

"Yes, my lord. Yonder, in the midst of the waves, he cried, 'Help! help!'"

"And you recognized the voice?"

"Did I recognize it? Oh, yes, I assure you! My sister heard and recognized it, too. How could both of us be deceived? My lord, let us go to his rescue. A boat! a boat!"

Glenarvan saw plainly that he could not undeceive the poor child. Still, he made a last attempt, and called the helmsman.

The unfortunate girl arose, and, leaning over the bulwark, would have thrown herself into the sea.

"Hawkins," asked he, "you were at the wheel when Miss Grant was so singularly affected?"

"Yes, my lord," replied Hawkins.

"And you did not see or hear anything?"

"Nothing."

"You see how it is, Robert."

"If it had been *his* father," answered the lad, with irrepressible energy, "he would not say so. It was *my* father, my lord! my father, my father——!"

Robert's voice was choked by a sob. Pale and speechless, he, too, like his sister, lost consciousness. Glenarvan had him carried to his bed, and the child, overcome by emotion, sank into a profound slumber.

"Poor orphans!" said Captain Mangles; "God tries them in a terrible way!"

"Yes," replied Glenarvan, "excessive grief has produced upon both at the same moment a similar effect."

"Upon both!" murmured Paganel. "That is strange!"

Then, leaning forward, after making a sign to keep still, he listened attentively. The silence was profound everywhere. Paganel called in a loud voice, but there was no answer.

"It is strange!" repeated the geographer, returning to his cabin; "an intimate sympathy of thought and grief does not suffice to explain this mystery."

Early the next morning the passengers (and among them were Robert and Mary, for it was impossible to restrain them) were assembled on deck. All wished to examine this land, which had been scarcely distinguishable the night before. The principal points of the island were eagerly scanned. The yacht coasted along about a mile from the shore, and the unassisted eye could easily discern the larger objects.

Suddenly Robert uttered a cry. He maintained that he saw two men running and gesticulating, while a third was waving a flag.

"Yes: the flag of England!" cried Captain Mangles, when he had used his glass.

"It is true!" said Paganel, turning quickly towards Robert.

"My lord!" exclaimed the boy, trembling with excitement,—"my lord, if you do not wish me to swim to the island, you will lower a boat! Ah, my lord, if you please, I do wish to be the first to land!"

A COMPENSATION FOR ALL.

No one knew what to say. Were there three men, shipwrecked sailors, Englishmen, on that island? All recalled the events of the night before, and thought of the voice heard by Robert and Mary. Perhaps, after all, they were not mistaken. A voice might have reached them. But could this voice be that of their father? No, alas, no! And each, thinking of the terrible disappointment that was probably in store, trembled lest this new trial would exceed their strength. But how restrain them? Lord Glenarvan had not the courage.

"Lower the boat!" cried he.

In a moment this was done; the two children, Glenarvan, Captain Mangles, and Paganel stepped into it, and six earnest and skilled oarsmen sped away towards the shore.

At ten yards therefrom, Mary uttered again the heart-rending cry:

"My father!"

A man was standing on the beach between two others. His form was tall and stout, while his weather-beaten yet pleasant countenance betrayed a strong resemblance to the features of Mary and Robert Grant. It was, indeed, the man whom the children had so often described. Their hearts had not deceived them. It was their father, it was Captain Grant!

He heard his daughter's cry, he opened his arms, and supported her fainting form.

Chapter LIX

CAPTAIN GRANT'S STORY.

Joy does not kill, for the long lost father and his recovered children were soon rejoicing together and preparing to return to the yacht. But how can we depict that scene, so little looked for by any? Words are powerless.

THE JOYS OF REUNION.

As soon as he gained the deck, Harry Grant sank upon his knees. The pious Scotchman, on touching what was to him the soil of his country, wished, first of all, to thank God for his deliverance. Then, turning towards Lady Helena; Lord Glenarvan, and their companions, he thanked them in a voice broken by emotion. While on their way to the yacht, his children had briefly told him the story of the Duncan.

A man was standing on the beach between two others. His form was tall and stout.

How great a debt of gratitude did he feel that he owed this noble woman and her companions! From Lord Glenarvan down to the lowest sailor, had not all struggled and suffered for him? Harry Grant expressed the feelings of thankfulness that overflowed his heart with so much simplicity and nobleness, and his manly countenance was illumined by so pure and sincere a sentiment, that all felt themselves repaid for the trials they had undergone. Even the imperturbable major's eye was wet with a tear that he could not repress. As for Paganel, he wept like a child who does not think of hiding his emotion.

Captain Grant could not cease gazing at his daughter. He found her beautiful and charming, and told her so again and again, appealing to Lady Helena as if to be assured that his fatherly love was not mistaken. Then, turning to his son, he cried rapturously:

"How he has grown! He is a man!"

He lavished upon these two beings, so dearly loved, the thousand expressions of love that had been unuttered during long years of absence. Robert introduced him successively to all his friends. All had alike proved their kindness and good wishes towards the two orphans. When Captain Mangles came to be introduced, he blushed like a young girl, and his voice trembled as he saluted Mary's father.

Lady Helena then told the story of the voyage, and made the captain proud of his son and daughter. He learned the exploits of the young hero, and how the boy had already repaid part of his obligation to Lord Glenarvan at the peril of his life. Captain Mangles' language to Mary and concerning her was so truly loving, that Harry Grant, who had been already informed on this point by Lady Helena, placed the hand of his daughter in that of the noble young captain, and, turning towards Lord and Lady Glenarvan, said:

"My lord and lady, join with me to bless our children!"

It was not long before Glenarvan related Ayrton's story to the captain, who confirmed the quartermaster's declaration in regard to his having been abandoned on the Australian coast.

"He is a shrewd and courageous man," added he; "but his passions have ruined him. May meditation and repentance lead him to better feelings!"

But before Ayrton was transferred to Tabor Island, Harry Grant wished to show his new friends the bounds of his habitation. He invited them to visit his house, and sit for once at his table. Glenarvan and his companions cordially accepted the invitation, and Robert and Mary were not a little desirous to see those haunts where their father had doubtless at times bewailed his fate. A boat was manned, and the whole party soon disembarked on the shores of the island.

A few hours sufficed to traverse Captain Grant's domain. It was in reality the summit of a submarine mountain, covered with basaltic rocks and volcanic fragments. When the shipwrecked seamen of the Britannia took refuge here, the hand of man began to control the development of nature's resources, and in two years and a half the captain and his companions had completely metamorphosed their island home.

The visitors at last reached the house, shaded by verdant gum-trees, while before its windows stretched the glorious sea, glittering in the rays of the sun. Harry Grant set his table in the shade, and all took seats around it. Some cold roast meat, some of the produce of the breadfruit-tree, several bowls of milk, two or three bunches of wild chicory, and pure, fresh water, formed the elements of the simple but healthful repast. Paganel was in ecstasies. It recalled his old idea of Robinson Crusoe.

THE RULING PASSION STILL STRONG.

"That rascal Ayrton will have no cause to complain," cried he in his enthusiasm. "The island is a paradise!"

"Yes," replied Harry Grant, "a paradise for three poor sailors whom Heaven sheltered here. But I regret that Maria Theresa is not a large and fertile island, with a river instead of a rivulet, and a harbor instead of a coast so exposed to the force of the waves."

"And why, captain?" asked Glenarvan.

Harry Grant set his table in the shade, and all took seats around it.

"Because I would have laid here the foundation of that colony that I wish to present to Scotland."

"Ah!" said Glenarvan. "Then you have not abandoned the idea that has made you so popular in your native land?"

"No, my lord; and God has saved me, through your instrumentality, only to permit me to accomplish it. Our poor brothers of old Caledonia shall yet have another Scotland in the New World. Our dear country must possess in these seas a colony of her own, where she can find that independence and prosperity that are wanting in many European empires."

"That is well said, captain," replied Lady Helena. "It is a noble project, and worthy of a great heart. But this island——?"

"No, madam, it is a rock, only large enough to support a few colonists; while we need a vast territory, rich in all primitive treasures."

"Well, captain," cried Glenarvan, "the future is before us! Let us seek this land together!"

The hands of both men met in a warm clasp, as if to ratify this promise. All now wished to hear the story of the shipwrecked sailors of the Britannia during those two long years of solitude. Harry Grant accordingly hastened to satisfy the desires of his new friends, and began as follows:

A TALE OF INDUSTRY.

"It was on the night of the 26th of June, 1862, that the Britannia, disabled by a six days' tempest, was wrecked on the rock of Maria Theresa. The sea was so high that to save anything was impossible, and all the crew perished except my two sailors, Bob Learce and Joe Bell, and myself; and we succeeded in reaching the coast after many struggles. The land that we thus reached was only a desert island, two miles wide and five long, with a few trees in the interior, some meadow land, and a spring of fresh water that, fortunately, has never ceased to flow. Alone with my two sailors, in this quarter of the globe, I did not despair, but, placing my confidence in God, engaged in a resolute struggle. Bob and Joe, my companions and friends in misfortune, energetically aided my efforts. We began, like Robinson Crusoe, by collecting the fragments of the vessel, some tools, a little powder, several weapons, and a bag of precious seeds. The first weeks were very toilsome, but soon hunting and fishing furnished us subsistence, for wild goats swarmed in the interior of the island, and marine animals abounded on its coast. Gradually our daily routine was regularly organized. I determined our exact situation by my instruments, which I had saved from the shipwreck. We were out of the regular course of ships, and could not be rescued except by a providential interposition. Although thinking of those who were dear to me, and whom I never expected to see again, still I accepted this trial with fortitude, and my most earnest prayers were for my two children. Meantime we labored resolutely. Much of the land was sown with the seeds taken from the Britannia; and potatoes, chicory, sorrel, and other vegetables improved and varied our daily food. We caught several goats, which were easily kept, and had milk and butter. The breadfruit-tree, which grew in the dry creeks, furnished us with a sort of nourishing bread, and the wants of life no longer gave us any alarm. We built a house out of the fragments of the Britannia, covered it with sails, carefully tarred, and under this shelter the rainy season was comfortably passed. Here many plans were discussed, and many dreams enjoyed, the best of which has just been realized! At first I thought of braving the sea in a boat made of the wreck of the vessel; but a vast distance separated us from the nearest land. No boat could have endured so long a voyage. I therefore abandoned my design, and no longer expected deliverance, except through a Divine interposition. Ah, my poor children, how many times, on the rocks of the coast, have we waited for ships at sea! During the entire period of our exile only two or three sails appeared on the horizon, and these soon to disappear again. Two years and a half passed thus. We no longer hoped, but still did not wholly despair. At last, yesterday afternoon, I had mounted the highest summit of the island, when I perceived a faint smoke in the west, which grew clearer, and I soon distinctly discerned a vessel that seemed to be coming towards us. But would she not avoid this island, which offered no landing-place? Ah, what a day of anguish, and how my heart throbbed! My companions kindled a fire on one of the peaks. Night came, but the ship gave no signal for approach. Deliverance was there, and should we see it vanish? I hesitated no longer. The darkness increased. The vessel might double the island during the night. I threw myself into the sea, to swim to her. Hope increased my strength. I beat the waves with almost superhuman energy, and approached the yacht. Scarcely thirty yards separated me, when she tacked. Then I uttered those despairing cries which my two children alone heard, for they were no illusion. I returned to the shore, exhausted and overcome by fatigue and emotion. It was a terrible night, this last one on the island. We believed ourselves forever abandoned, when, at daybreak, I perceived the yacht slowly coasting along the shores. Your boat was then lowered,—we were saved, and, thanks to the Divine goodness of Heaven, my dear children were there to stretch out their arms to me!"

THE DOCUMENT ONCE MORE!

Harry Grant's story was finished amid a fresh shower of kisses and caresses from Robert and Mary. The captain learned now, for the first time, that he owed his deliverance to that hieroglyphic document that, eight days after his shipwreck, he had inclosed in a bottle and confided to the mercy of the waves.

But what did Jacques Paganel think during this recital? The worthy geographer revolved the words of the document a thousand ways in his brain. He reviewed his three interpretations, which were all false. How had this island been indicated in these damaged papers? He could no longer restrain himself, but, seizing Harry Grant's hand, cried:

"Captain, will you tell me what your undecipherable document contained?"

At this request curiosity was general, for the long-sought clew to the mystery would now be given.

"Well, captain," said Paganel, "do you remember the exact words of the document?"

The passengers could see the quartermaster, with folded arms, standing motionless as a statue, on a rock, and gazing at the vessel.

"Perfectly," replied Harry Grant; "and scarcely a day has passed but memory has recalled those words upon which our only hope hung."

"And what are they, captain?" inquired Glenarvan. "Tell us, for our curiosity is great."

"I am ready to satisfy you," continued Harry Grant; "but you know that, to increase the chances of success, I inclosed in the bottle three documents, written in three languages. Which one do you wish to hear?"

"They are not identical, then?" cried Paganel.

"Yes, almost to a word."

"Well, give us the French document," said Glenarvan. "This one was spared the most by the waves, and has served as the principal basis for our search."

"This is it, my lord, word for word," answered Harry Grant.

"'On the 27th June, 1862, the brig Britannia, of Glasgow, was lost 1500 leagues from Patagonia, in the southern hemisphere. Carried by the waves, two sailors and Captain Grant reached Tabor Island——'"

"Ha!" interrupted Paganel.

"'Here,'" resumed Harry Grant, "'continually a prey to a cruel destitution, they cast this document into the sea at longitude 153° and latitude 37° 11'. Come to their aid, or they are lost.'"

At the word "Tabor," Paganel had suddenly risen, and then, controlling himself no longer, he cried:

"How Tabor Island? It is Maria Theresa."

"Certainly, Mr. Paganel," replied Harry Grant; "Maria Theresa on the English and German, but Tabor on the French maps."

At this moment a vigorous blow descended upon Paganel's shoulder. Truth compels us to say that it was from the major, who now failed in his strict habits of propriety.

"A fine geographer you are!" said MacNabb, in a tone of badinage. "But no matter, since we have succeeded."

"No matter?" cried Paganel; "I ought never to have forgotten that twofold appellation! It is an unpardonable mistake, unworthy of the secretary of a Geographical Society. I am disgraced!"

When the meal was finished, Harry Grant put everything in order in his house. He took nothing away, for he was willing that the guilty convict should inherit his possessions.

They returned to the vessel; and, as he expected to sail the same day, Glenarvan gave orders for the quartermaster's landing. Ayrton was brought on deck, and found himself in the presence of Harry Grant.

"It is I, Ayrton," said he.

"Yes, captain," replied Ayrton, without betraying any astonishment at Harry Grant's appearance. "Well, I am not sorry to see you again in good health."

"It seems, Ayrton, that I made a mistake in landing you on an inhabited coast."

"It seems so, captain."

"You will take my place on this desert island. May Heaven lead you to repentance!"

"May it be so," rejoined Ayrton, in a calm tone.

Then Glenarvan, addressing the quartermaster, said:

"Do you still adhere, Ayrton, to this determination to be abandoned?"

"Yes, my lord."

"Does Tabor Island suit you?"

"Perfectly."

"Now listen to my last words. You will be far removed from every land, and deprived of all communication with your fellow-men. Miracles are rare, and you will not probably remove from this island, where we leave you. You will be alone, under the eye of

God, who reads the uttermost depths of all hearts; but you will not be lost, as was Captain Grant. However unworthy you may be of the remembrance of men, still they will remember you. I know where you are, and will never forget you."

"Thank you, my lord!" replied Ayrton, simply.

Such were the last words exchanged between Glenarvan and the quartermaster. The boat was ready, and Ayrton embarked. Captain Mangles had previously sent to the island several cases of preserved food, some clothes, tools, weapons, and a supply of powder and shot. The abandoned man could therefore employ his time to advantage. Nothing was wanting, not even books, foremost among which was a Bible.

The hour for separation had come. The crew and passengers stood on deck. More than one felt the heart strangely moved. Lady Helena and Mary Grant could not repress their emotion.

"Must it then be so?" inquired the young wife of her husband. "Must this unfortunate be abandoned?"

"FAREWELL! A LONG FAREWELL!"

"He must, Helena," answered Glenarvan. "It is his punishment."

At this moment the boat, commanded by Captain Mangles, started. Ayrton raised his hat and gave a grave salute. Glenarvan and the crew returned this last farewell, as if to a man about to die, as he departed, in a profound silence.

On reaching the shore, Ayrton leaped upon the sand, and the boat returned. It was then four o'clock in the afternoon, and from the upper deck the passengers could see the quartermaster, with folded arms, standing motionless as a statue, on a rock, and gazing at the vessel.

"Shall we start, my lord?" asked Captain Mangles.

"Yes, John," replied Glenarvan, quickly, with more emotion than he wished to manifest.

"All right!" cried the captain to the engineer.

The steam hissed, the screw beat the waves, and at eight o'clock the last summits of Tabor Island disappeared in the shadows of the night.

Chapter LX

PAGANEL'S LAST ENTANGLEMENT.

Eleven days after leaving Tabor Island the Duncan came in sight of the American coast, and anchored in Talcahuana Bay. Five months had elapsed since her departure from this port, during which time the travelers had made the circuit of the world on this thirty-seventh parallel. Their efforts had not been in vain, for they had found the shipwrecked survivors of the Britannia.

The Duncan, having taken in her necessary stores, skirted the coasts of Patagonia, doubled Cape Horn, and steamed across the Atlantic. The voyage was very uneventful. The yacht carried a full complement of happy people; there seemed to be no secrets on board.

A mystery, however, still perplexed MacNabb. Why did Paganel always keep hermetically incased in his clothes, and wear a comforter over his ears? The major longed to know the motive for this singular fancy. But in spite of his questions, hints, and suspicions, Paganel did not unbutton his coat.

Early in the afternoon the travelers reached Malcolm Castle, amidst the hurrahs of their tenantry and friends.

At last, fifty-three days after leaving Talcahuana, Captain Mangles descried the lighthouse of Cape Clear. The vessel entered St. George's Channel, crossed the Irish Sea, and passed into the Frith of Clyde. At eleven o'clock they anchored at Dumbarton, and early in the afternoon the travelers reached Malcolm Castle, amidst the hurrahs of their tenantry and friends.

Thus it was that Harry Grant and his two companions were rescued, and that John Mangles married Mary Grant in the old cathedral of St. Mungo, where the Rev. Mr. Morton, who nine months before had prayed for the rescue of the father, now blessed the union of the daughter with one of his deliverers. It was arranged that Robert should be a sailor, like his father and brother-in-law, and that he should continue the contemplated project of the former, under the munificent patronage of Lord Glenarvan.

But was Jacques Paganel to die a bachelor? Certainly not; for, after his heroic exploits, the worthy geographer could not escape celebrity. His eccentricities (and his abilities) made him much talked of in Scotland. People seemed as though they could not show him enough attention.

Just at this time an amiable lady of thirty, none other than the major's cousin, a little eccentric herself, but still agreeable and charming, fell in love with the geographer's peculiarities. Paganel was far from being insensible to Miss Arabella's attractions, yet did not dare to declare his sentiments.

The major accordingly undertook the part of Cupid's messenger between these two congenial hearts, and even told Paganel that marriage was "the last blunder" that he could commit. But the geographer was very much embarrassed, and, strangely enough, could not summon courage to speak for himself.

"Does not Miss Arabella please you?" MacNabb would say to him.

"Oh, major, she is charming!" cried Paganel,—"a thousand times too charming for me; and, if I must tell you, would please me better if she were less so. I should like to find a defect."

"Be easy," answered the major; "she has more than one. The most perfect woman always has her share. Well, then, Paganel, are you decided?"

"I do not dare."

Fifteen weeks after a marriage was celebrated with great pomp in the chapel of Malcolm Castle.

"But, my learned friend, why do you hesitate?"

"I am unworthy of her!" was the geographer's invariable reply.

At last, one day, driven desperate by the irrepressible major, Paganel confessed to him, under the pledge of secrecy, a peculiarity that would facilitate his identification, if the police should ever be on his track!

"Bah!" exclaimed the major.

"It is as I tell you," persisted Paganel.

"What matter, my worthy friend?"

"Is that your opinion?"

"On the contrary, you are only more remarkable. This adds to your personal advantages. It makes you the inimitable individual of whom Arabella has dreamed."

And the major, preserving an imperturbable gravity, left Paganel a prey to the most acute anxiety.

A short interview took place between MacNabb and the lady, and fifteen weeks after a marriage was celebrated with great pomp in the chapel of Malcolm Castle.

The geographer's secret would doubtless have remained forever buried in the abysses of the unknown if the major had not told it to Glenarvan, who did not conceal it from Lady Helena, who communicated it to Mrs. Mangles. In short, it reached the ear of Mrs. Olbinett, and spread.

Jacques Paganel, during his three days' captivity among the Maoris, had been tattooed from head to foot, and bore on his breast the picture of an heraldic kiwi with outstretched wings, in the act of biting at his heart.

This was the only adventure of his great voyage for which Paganel could never be consoled or pardon the New Zealanders. In spite of the representations of his friends, he dared not go back to France, for fear of exposing the whole Geographical Society in his person to the jests and railleries of the caricaturists.

The return of Captain Grant to Scotland was welcomed as a cause for national rejoicing, and he became the popular man of old

Caledonia. His son Robert has become a sailor like himself, and, under the patronage of Lord Glenarvan, has undertaken the plan of founding a Scottish colony on the shores washed by the Pacific Ocean.

THE END.

ABOUT JULES VERNE

Jules Verne, a 19th century French author, is famed for such revolutionary science-fiction novels as 'Around the World in Eighty Days' and 'Twenty Thousand Leagues Under the Sea.'

Born in Nantes, France, in 1828, Jules Verne pursued a writing career after finishing law school. He hit his stride after meeting publisher Pierre-Jules Hetzel, who nurtured many of the works that would comprise the author's Voyages Extraordinaires. Often referred to as the "Father of Science Fiction," Verne wrote books about a variety of innovations and technological advancements years before they were practical realities. Although he died in 1905, his works continued to be published well after his death, and he became the second most translated author in the world.

Jules Verne was born on February 8, 1828, in Nantes, France, a busy maritime port city. There, Verne was exposed to vessels departing and arriving, sparking his imagination for travel and adventure. While attending boarding school, he began to write short stories and poetry. Afterward, his father, a lawyer, sent his oldest son to Paris to study law.

While he tended to his studies, Jules Verne found himself attracted to literature and the theater. He began frequenting Paris' famed literary salons, and befriended a group of artists and writers that included Alexandre Dumas and his son. After earning his law degree in 1849, Verne remained in Paris to indulge his artistic leanings. The following year, his one-act play Broken Straws (Les Pailles rompues) was performed.

Verne continued to write despite pressure from his father to resume his law career, and the tension came to a head in 1852, when Verne refused his father's offer to open a law practice in Nantes. The aspiring writer instead took a meager-paying job as secretary of the Théâtre-Lyrique, giving him the platform to produce Blind Man's Bluff (Le Colin-maillard) and The Companions of the Marjolaine (Les Compagnons de la Marjolaine).

In 1856, Verne met and fell in love with Honorine de Viane, a young widow with two daughters. They married in 1857, and, realizing he needed a stronger financial foundation, Verne began working as a stockbroker. However, he refused to abandon his writing career, and that year he also published his first book, The 1857 Salon (Le Salon de 1857).

In 1859, Verne and his wife embarked on the first of approximately 20 trips to the British Isles. The journey made a strong impression on Verne, inspiring him to pen Backwards to Britain (Voyage en Angleterre et en Écosse), although the novel wouldn't be published until well after his death. In 1861, the couple's only child, Michel Jean Pierre Verne, was born.

Verne's literary career had failed to gain traction to that point, but his luck would change with his introduction to editor and publisher Pierre-Jules Hetzel in 1862. Verne was working on a novel that imbued a heavy dose of scientific research into an adventure narrative, and in Hetzel he found a champion for his developing style. In 1863, Hertzel published Five Weeks in a Balloon (Cinq semaines en ballon), the first of a series of adventure novels by Verne that would comprise his Voyages Extraordinaires. Verne subsequently signed a contract in which he would submit new works every year to the publisher, most of which would be serialized in Hetzel's Magasin d'Éducation et de Récréation.

In 1864, Hetzel published The Adventures of Captain Hatteras (Voyages et aventures du capitaine Hatteras) and Journey to the Center of the Earth (Voyage au centre de la Terre). That same year, Paris in the Twentieth Century (Paris au XXe siècle) was rejected for publication, but in 1865 Verne was back in print with From the Earth to the Moon (De la Terre à la Lune) and In Search of the Castaways (Les Enfants du capitaine Grant).

Inspired by his love of travel and adventure, Verne soon bought a ship, and he and his wife spent a good deal of time sailing the seas. Verne's own adventures sailing to various ports, from the British Isles to the Mediterranean, provided plentiful fodder for his short stories and novels. In 1867, Hetzel published Verne's Illustrated Geography of France and Her Colonies (Géographie illustrée de la France et de ses colonies), and that year Verne also traveled with his brother to the United States. He only stayed a week — managing a trip up the Hudson River to Albany, then on to Niagara Falls — but his visit to America made a lasting impact and was reflected in later works.

In 1869 and 1870, Hetzel published Verne's Twenty Thousand Leagues under the Sea (Vingt mille lieues sous les mers), Around the Moon (Autour de la Lune) and Discovery of the Earth (Découverte de la Terre). By this point, Verne's works were being translated into English, and he could comfortably live on his writing.

Beginning in late 1872, the serialized version of Verne's famed Around the World in Eighty Days (Le Tour du monde en quatre-vingts jours) first appeared in print. The story of Phileas Fogg and Jean Passepartout takes readers on an adventurous global tour at a time when travel was becoming easier and alluring. In the century plus since its original debut, the work has been adapted for the theater, radio, television and film, including the classic 1956 version starring David Niven.

Verne remained prolific throughout the decade, penning The Mysterious Island (L'Île mystérieuse), The Survivors of the Chancellor (Le Chancellor), Michael Strogoff (Michel Strogoff), and Dick Sand: A Captain at Fifteen (Un Capitaine de quinze ans), among other works.

Although he was enjoying immense professional success by the 1870s, Jules Verne began experiencing more strife in his personal life. He sent his rebellious son to a reformatory in 1876, and a few years later Michel caused more trouble through his relations with a minor. In 1886, Verne was shot in the leg by his nephew Gaston, leaving him with a limp for the rest of his life. His longtime publisher and collaborator Hetzel died a week later, and the following year his mother passed away as well.

Verne did, however, continue to travel and write, churning out Eight Hundred Leagues on the Amazon (La Jangada) and Robur the Conqueror (Robur-le-conquérant) during this period. His writing soon became noted for a darker tone, with books like The Purchase of the North Pole (Sans dessus dessous), Propeller Island (L'Île à hélice) and Master of the World (Maître du monde) warning of dangers wrought by technology.

Having established his residence in the northern French city of Amiens, Verne began serving on its city council in 1888. Stricken with diabetes, he died at home on March 24, 1905.

However, his literary output didn't end there, as Michel assumed control of his father's uncompleted manuscripts. Over the following decade, The Lighthouse at the End of the World (Le Phare du bout du monde), The Golden Volcano (Le Volcan d'or) and The Chase of the Golden Meteor (La Chasse au météore) were all published following extensive revisions by Michel.

Additional works surfaced decades later. Backwards to Britain finally was printed in 1989, 130 years after it was written, and Paris in the Twentieth Century, originally considered too far-fetched with its depictions of skyscrapers, gas-fueled cars and mass transit systems, followed in 1994.

Printed in Great Britain
by Amazon

35215191R00374